# STOLEN MOUNTAIN

A Trowbridge Vermont Novel

## A Novel by
## I. M. AIKEN

**LITERARY FICTION**
**CRIME/THRILLER**

Published by Flare Books,
an imprint of Catalyst Press, El Paso, Texas

Copyright © 2025 by I.M. Aiken

All rights reserved. No part of this book may be reproduced in any form or by any electronic or mechanical means, including information storage and retrieval systems, without permission in writing from the publisher, except by a reviewer who may quote brief passages in a review.

9781963511284 paperback $21.95
9781963511291 ebook $12.95

For further information, write info@catalystpress.org
In North America, this book is distributed by
Consortium Book Sales & Distribution, a division of Ingram.
Phone: 612/746-2600
cbsdinfo@ingramcontent.com
www.cbsd.com

In South Africa, Namibia, and Botswana,
this book is distributed by Protea Distribution.
For information, email orders@proteadistribution.co.za.

Library of Congress Control Number: 2025936329

To
All of those who walk, or run, towards danger

# STOLEN MOUNTAIN

A Trowbridge Vermont Novel

## A Novel by
## I. M. AIKEN

LITERARY FICTION
CRIME/THRILLER

# 1 | You Belong Here

I am looking at someone else's dream.

I turn my head to watch it roll past. A fabulous image of a solo skier executing a perfect turn, on a perfect white slope, below a perfect blue sky.

"You Belong Here."

Once I read that I belong there, I cannot stop seeing this image in my mind. I do assume the "You Belong Here" refers to the skier carving down the slope and not to the city bus transporting the image. I've got nothing against the M22, a blue and green clean-energy bus. I am walking east on Chambers Street, and it, the M22, travels west. Although I do not recognize that photo, that hill, that skier, I think I know that mountain. It is a rare day when we see skies that blue at home. A bit of photo editing in the spirit of marketing. Grecian blue skies over the Green Mountains are stunning.

The next poster I spy has been installed around a trash can near City Hall at Centre Street. "You Belong Here." This time, it is a stunning image of a golden-brown fire built for a lord in his manor. I scan the QR code to discover The Branston Club.

The website is the dude version of my own vision of home. The dude version is painted richly with colors of warm chestnut, heated maple syrup, October beech leaves, and leather. I can nearly smell the single malt and humidor not shown. I am clearly supposed to want to be there, not in the trash can, but on that mountain. Odd place to advertise, I think. The only people using these trash cans are the tourists. Wouldn't it be better to buy ad space in the back seat of a black car service? Or maybe Joe Branston Club did, and I've just not seen the ads yet. Not that I use black-car services too often. I like walking.

I like black-car services, too. And I have ridden the M22, thank you very much.

Just don't think that I live in a palatial manor house on a grand hill in a small town in Vermont, I don't. Well, I do, but not like that. I have herbs hanging to dry from the beams in the kitchen. And we have wooden drying racks that I can lower from the ceiling. Clothing and towels dry quickly near a brick fireplace in the kitchen. And yes, it does have a 200-year-old bread oven built into the structure, and an iron kettle rack. Given I eschew plastics, my kitchen is dominated by ceramics, fiber-based products, wooden tools, and metal. Some busybody might say that my kitchen resembles a witch's lair. Of course, I am not a witch. The house is a 200-year-old home standing proudly on the shoulder of a gorgeous hill in Trowbridge, Vermont. We do watch the morning fog lift from the village below us.

I know you can picture both versions of Vermont—the dude version with cut crystal, amber-colored booze, cordovan leather, and sumptuous oak. In my non-dude version, I've hung lavender and sage from hooks in the ceilings, cotton towels drying near the stove. A visitor smells freshly baked bread and spies woolly sheep grazing out the window. Can't you? You've seen that photo. In the olden days, it was a postcard you bought at that cute general store. You picked it from a rack standing between maple candy and the Missus Fuzzy's gingham-dressed raspberry jelly. In the modern days, it is the money shot on social media.

What you can't tell from most selfies in our village is that the church spire is about five degrees off from the vertical and the spine of that roof has the sway of a twenty-year-old mare. The fire station sits over the road from the single church that we have in town. That fire station, built by volunteer hands nearly sixty years ago, does have vertical sides and square corners. That's good. The fact remains that the building is ugly. What you want is a striking brick firehouse with a tall, square, imposing hose tower, but you get this cinderblock rectangle finished with cheap T1-11 siding tucked into irregularly shaped gaps, such as the triangle space below the roof peak.

Opposite the firehouse stands a 150-year-old grange building. It is classically beautiful, honoring the best ideas of the Georgian period. Except it has been neglected since World War II.

# 1 | YOU BELONG HERE

Nobody takes selfies in our village.

Ok, the ironic tourist might. The tourist looking for the rich luxury of The Branston Club would regard Trowbridge with impatience and intolerance. They would recognize themselves as lost, out of place, and maybe slipped out of time. Who knows what they think? I only hear them yell at me, but that is for later.

The normal tourist visits Trowbridge for three reasons. First, someone showed them a shortcut to the ski hills of Southern Vermont, and they don't even know they went through the corner of Trowbridge. Second, they got lost after falling off the two-lane state highway—a punishment for arguing with the GPS mapping on a mobile phone. Then, after having fallen from the grid, they cannot get their map to refresh because there is no signal. Or three, they venture from their resort, or country BnB, desiring an adventure in the wilds of "the other" Vermont. Y'know, the Vermont not on social media. The Vermont with trailer homes, gray plywood shacks, and trees growing through abandoned schoolhouses that are rotting in the forest next to neglected roads. Cue the banjos.

This guy, Joe Branston Club guy, sells luxury. He sells exclusivity. He sells premier spa trips and the world's best black truffles, curated by a dog named Pierre in France. The jamón ibérico and European raw milk cheese await your arrival. I expect the bathrobes to be plush, warm, and yet made from something exotic, such as the downy wool of Tibetan yaks, harvested by gorgeous women in stunning colorful outfits combing the beasts, with alpenglow fading on the glaciated Himalayas.

I shouldn't be too critical. I am wearing a handmade suit from London. I tried domestic. The local guys I tried in New York told me I was wrong. "This is the way it is done," they said to me. "Your skirts need to be A-line and not much below the knee." I did get a suit made by them, although I returned twice with complaints about the fit of the skirt over my thighs, the tension of the buttons over my breasts, and the tightness of the shirts at my shoulders and upper arms. Instead, I flew to London a few times. Yeah, I got to hear, "Sure, gladly ma'am," in an East London accent.

Fine, now you know that about me, too. I hang herbs and laundry in my kitchen, and I fly to London for a fitting. And I have chickens, and I have sheep. And I am wearing a bespoke woolen suit with a full skirt that comes to my ankles. My vest has a lot of buttons, and my blazer has a mildly Victorian flare at the hips. It is bloody comfortable, and warm, and allows me amazing freedom to move. Have you tried to climb up into a truck or SUV with an A-line skirt and an ill-fitting blazer? I have. I was always tugging at things to keep bits covered, untangled, or loose.

I understand the allure of Vermont.

There are not many businesswomen in lower Manhattan wearing long skirts on their way to a conference room. I just don't fit well in jeans and trousers. Of course, I have skads of them. Jeans fit too tightly in the wrong places, and seem a bit low over my backside. I don't know. Seems un-American to say such a thing. Who am I to dish on Levi's? I am a lady walking Centre Street in a custom business suit that pays homage to the shape of a Victorian woman. I am ok with that. Are you?

Maybe we should pause for a minute before I open the next door. Maybe you don't want to join me. That's fine. Walk away now. My name is Brighid Doran. My wife calls me Brie, like the cheese. I call her Sam. Our marriage is still a secret marriage because Sam is better known to the U.S. Army as Major Sarah Ann Musgrave. She has earned the Bronze Star Medal with the "V" device, two Purple Hearts, and a combat action badge. Her class A uniform includes five rows of ribbons. I am pretty sure that her boss, Colonel Darius Jackson, knows he cannot ask the world's most stupid question of her. The army still cares. If Sam were to be outed, she would join the three to five thousand people kicked out of the military each year for being outed. Why are we married, you ask? Because Sam has this bad habit of flying off to Iraq and Afghanistan to undertake missions on behalf of our government and the citizens of this nation. She's a perfect soldier. She's a great military leader. Regardless, if Uncle learns of our love, our marriage, our shared home, Sam loses everything except me and our home. I love her and she loves me. It has been that

## 1 | YOU BELONG HERE

way since before she enlisted. It has been that way since my first week on campus as a freshman.

The law does not permit me to be an army wife, but I am legally allowed to be an army widow. Ironic, no? Idiots.

In my leather satchel, I touch my laptop, a paper notebook, and turn my phone off with my thumb. I open the door. Honestly, I could have briefed this team via phone or video conference, but I wanted an excuse to spend time in Manhattan. Sam has deployed again. I pull my luggage trolley through the door, to the reception desk. The folks I am meeting are lawyers. They like paper. Me, I could have done with a thumb drive or SD card with the data on it. Those would have fit into my shoulder bag. They want the evidence and my handwritten notes.

I get escorted into an empty conference room. I lift the boxes from my trolley, fold my trolley, wrap the bungee cords around it. When the first two enter the room, they discover me looking out the window. I again imagine the appeal of a rustic lodge with perfect snow, deluxe appointments. The lodge staff will be immaculately trained and deferential in their rustic livery. I struggle to imagine any of my neighbors playing the role of trained and deferential staff, silently accepting orders from rich, arrogant incomers.

"Brighid, glad you came."

"Happy to be invited." I shake hands.

"You know you didn't have to drive down."

"I know. But it is New York in October. And you needed to see me in person anyway." I wave my hand dismissively.

"Isn't it a long drive?"

"Three hours and twenty minutes. I stopped the clock at the parking garage on Chambers Street."

"I know where you live. That's every bit of four hours from here."

"I don't get pulled over much. There is not a lot of traffic at that time of the morning. Anyway, I left early. I had to have; I am standing here at 9 o'clock in the morning"

"I see boxes."

"You see evidence. I carried the boxes, they are all yours now."

I direct their attention to the white banker's boxes on the floor. I sit opposite Benica Lopez. She goes by "Special Agent" if you don't know her and Benny if you do. Special Agent Louis Larocque—and before you pronounce it wrong and push a hidden button on that FBI agent, he pronounces his own name the French way, Louie, like old song "Louie Louie" written by Richard Berry.

I ask, "Anyone else joining us?"

"Nope, we're it," Lopez says.

"Start anytime," adds Larocque.

"Got a projector? Or a screen I can cast to?"

"Sure." Lopez retrieves an HDMI cable from under the table, then uses a remote to turn on a wall-mounted monitor.

I pull my laptop from the satchel. I do the geek thing while keeping the banter going. Then, with an image up, I start. I set context. I skip over all of the ridiculous stories of trying to make contact with the FBI about a major fraud case involving FEMA funds. It is not like calling 911 where you describe what you need, and someone supposedly comes to help—maybe. I called the FBI in DC. Apparently, they get a lot of calls and 99.99% of them are junk. Like any receptionist, or help desk person, the operator's goal involved getting me off the phone as fast as possible. That human told me to call the Department of Homeland Security Office of Inspector General. An OIG person listened and explained that while FEMA funds were involved, the crimes I discussed were solidly within the FBI's jurisdiction. Back to the FBI then. Because the case involved the Florida panhandle, I got routed to District 22 in North Florida. When they learned I was calling from Southern Vermont, they told me to call the Boston district office. The person answering the phone for District 7 informed me that I was talking to the New England District Office of the FBI. I started my story with, "My name is Brighid Doran, and I am from Trowbridge, Vermont."

"Oh, Vermont. That is in District 1, you'll need to call New York." I guess the FBI doesn't think Vermont is in New England. Odd.

By the time I called the New York FBI office, I focused on the key words describing financial fraud, y'know, Wall Street. Oh, it wasn't

## 1 | YOU BELONG HERE

a Wall Street crime, but adjacent. I got connected to Special Agent Lopez.

In the conference room, I skip that story. I survived the screening process. I am here with boxes of stuff. Before getting here, I had to win over Special Agent Lopez. Over the phone, I presented the key elements of the case to her. She demonstrated interest and provided me with her email address. Weeks later, I stand in a modest conference room at One Federal Plaza a few hours from my hilltop home.

On the monitor with a series of slides, I attempt to untangle the "murder board" we created in our office: photographs, notes, names, red yarn, pins, and a map of the Florida panhandle.

The thing about a well-executed fraud case, and even a good con, is that they are intrinsically understated. Murder? You've got tears, a life full of potential cut short, a community missing a pillar. Major heists? That's earned a spot as a Hollywood genre. You've got comedy heists, rom-com heists, real-crime heists, fantastical heists beyond the reach of plausible. Then there is garden variety fraud. Yawn.

Fraud is like watching a winter ice fishing derby back home. Ever watched an ice fishing derby? People sit in a little ice shack with a small fire going. A shack big enough for one seat. Fishers enter, close the door, light their fire, drop a line through a hole in the ice. Hours later, they step out with a fish. You saw nothing. More boring than golf. There is nothing to see. Why are heist movies a thing? Because of the storytelling. They tend to show it to you twice. Here's the heist going perfectly, as planned. Nothing happened. Then here's the heist as it happened with Inspector Knobhead arriving too early, or too late. Some movies show it once as seen from the unsuspecting eyes of the camera and the watchers. Then they show it again with the hidden movements. Done masterfully, the trick isn't even revealed. I guess you could jazz up ice fishing by filming it from the fish's point of view. "Damn, it's cold. I can't breathe. The end." Ok, still not super interesting.

Fraudsters don't want you to study them. They do not want to be seen. Even after the victims find themselves cold, dry, and unable to breathe in a bucket slowly freezing on the ice.

That was my challenge. A client from Florida presented me with hints of fraud. He and his colleagues looked around and said, "Hey, where did all the government money go?" Forgive the shift in metaphors. The client's story conveyed the behavior of separate venomous snakes popping up in the region. My client thought it was not separate snakes but the multiheaded hydra leveraged by many skilled fraudsters. Snakes, in Florida? Shocker. Petty crime and FEMA fraud in Florida, ho-hum. Just like watching ice fishing on a northern lake, the trick is to see the unseen.

I probably should not tell you this story. Aren't I supposed to change the names to protect the innocent and all of that? It is possible that one of the people in my list of bad guys could have been swept up with the other debris. I don't believe any of the idiots that I researched met the simplest definition of "innocent." I invested weeks in my research and undertook one failed trip to Florida. Without subpoenas, I could not see the unseen. Whilst I got closer to the story, what was hidden remained hidden.

When starting the investigation, I listened to my new client. He vented like a member of the tinfoil hat brigade. "They are all out to get me." He found that he, his business, and his family had been surrounded by a variety of snakes, each coming at him from different sides, each looking for new targets. Of course, he unfolded the story chronologically. Gator—yes, that is the client's name—had a clue that all of the snakes were of the same family. Frankly, he didn't know that his photo was the key to unlocking the mystery to his own bad luck.

I observed the members and behavior of a large extended family. I start my slideshow to the FBI with the central character, the deputy chief of the State of Florida's disaster response agency. This guy and his agency are the intermediate between FEMA disaster funds and the communities that use those funds to clean up then rebuild. A guy in the state government interacting with a federal funding agency must be held to standards of integrity and honesty.

But no, I have photos of him satiating his belly with beer, prawns, crawdads, and corn at a family gathering. Who's there?

## 1 | YOU BELONG HERE

This cousin runs the largest and most visible FEMA consulting firm in the region. If you are a municipal government, county government, nonprofit, or something similar, then you hire these guys to do your FEMA paperwork. They promise good results. "We'll get you your FEMA money quickly."

This other cousin runs the now-largest debris removal company in the region. His business grew so fast, he bought the last three local competitors. Surprisingly, the competitors were not winning a lot of bids. Hmm? Who guided the local governments through that procurement and evaluation process? That was the above-mentioned cousin who owns an independent and trusted FEMA consultancy in the region.

The story expands.

FEMA has had a long-standing distrust of debris haulers. FEMA pays them by the ton, by the miles driven, or the hours worked. The debris haulers pick up trees, parts of houses, sand, dirt, or whatever a storm brings in. They learned years ago that they can increase their revenue by hauling more debris, driving more miles, and making more trips. After debris haulers learned to ballast their trucks, FEMA required scales at the dump sites. The scales required monitors. The debris haulers doctored the miles driven to generate more revenue. FEMA required more monitors to confirm mileage. Debris haulers learned to run smaller loads to get more trips. FEMA required monitors in the field, as a check and balance. FEMA and the debris haulers locked themselves into a classic predator-prey relationship.

Not a surprise—another cousin owned the largest and most successful debris monitoring company.

And another cousin owned a restaurant that got all of the county contracts for providing food to the Emergency Operations Center and catering at emergency scenes: work that once rotated among restaurant owners near the EOC.

Photo after photo shows how my red yarn connected these elements. It isn't much of a surprise. All of the elements attended the same family gatherings.

I talk. I advance through my slides. I keep making eye contact with the mannequin-like humans in the conference room. I ask myself, "Is this what my Sam looks like during a professional briefing?" I've seen her go full statue on me just like these two.

The storyteller in me wants to start at the beginning and slowly reveal each clue as they unfold. My job in this conference room is not to build suspense and write a novel. It is to brief two FBI agents on a series of crimes involving federal funds.

Yeah so, you have Joe Consultant guy handing his paperwork off to his cousin Barney the State Agency boss. Sketchy. Cousin Fred, with his debris hauling company, is carefully monitored by Cousin Dino, and his debris monitoring company.

Why did my client Gator care? Because he was pissed off that the county's emergency operations center stopped ordering food, snacks, and coffee from his restaurant, one of those restaurants that used to provide food to the EOC. As noted, the county emergency operations center once rotated their food orders among the local restaurants in an effort to be fair. FEMA money that paid for staff meals and coffee used to be shared among the local business owners. Then sharing tapered away to nothing. Months went by without delivering coffee and donuts, or anything, on training days. A year went by without a dinner order for long running shifts. All drink and meal orders went to one restaurant, and that restaurant was miles further from the EOC.

Gator, when he found me, identified his motive as revenge. He wanted a piece of the county contract, again. He wanted the unfair practice of giving all food orders to a single business to end.

The next slide contains a photograph of parked cars. I annotated each car with the owner's name, each a member of this clan. *There*, I point to the photos, *is the body of the hydra*.

In front of the FBI, I tell the story of linking humans. But I could not break through the barriers needed to prove financial dealings. Isn't that the great dream in Florida? Find the buried or sunken treasure. I wanted to find the ill-gotten booty.

That required travel. I flew to Florida to find original data and perform my own analysis. I cannot hide my northernness. I am a yankee. I sound it. I dress it. Well, given the struggles Florida faces with

# 1 | YOU BELONG HERE

cultural issues, I felt a bit unwelcome down there. I tried. I seriously tried to blend in.

Failing that, I gave people options. These records, by law, are public. The funding is public. Florida has sunshine laws that guarantee public access to records. I explained to two clerks that public is public.

When I asked municipal and county governments for their public records, they said no.

You know this conversation. You go to the counter. You know the public records law. You know how to file a Freedom of Information Act request. The person on the other side of the counter says no. We've all had conversations with idiots like this. They win because they have a counter, a locking door, and because they run a police department. They win because I am a nobody and they have police.

What does right count for?

I stand now before two FBI agents with boxes of evidence tied neatly with a figurative bow like a birthday present.

At noon thirty, I pause. The wax mannequins never asked a question. They never needed a bio-break. They barely moved.

"Guys, I am talked out. How about I buy you lunch?"

I lock my laptop and close the lid.

Lopez immediately says, "Well, I am sorry, we're not allowed to accept lunch from you."

Rude.

"Yeah, yeah, Lopez, I know the law as well as you do. It is a segue. I am tired and hungry, and I want lunch. You are my hosts, and according to the rules my mother taught me, I need to wait for you to invite me to stop for lunch. I flipped the script with a polite and common turn-of-phrase. Of course, I won't actually pay for your lunch, but I'd enjoy your company if you are game." I try to be funny and patient, but miss—sometimes.

I mean...

I had just been telling them about how meals and money can influence poor decision making in government officials. Hadn't I just linked a ham-and-cheese sandwich with debris-hauling dump trucks, unscrupulous consultants, and the deputy chief of a state agency?

With the right view on the fraud, you could say that a ham-and-cheese sandwich bought a family a lot of new cars. I get it. Fraud is fraud. The ham-and-cheese sandwich teeters over a slippery slope.

"Come on, guys, nobody is going to miss us for an hour. I got up at three to drive here. Furthermore, look at my stunning evidence."

I know, they both know, that the evidence I brought will never be seen in a courtroom. These two, or FBI agents in Florida, will go do what I did, but for themselves, as FBI agents. Instead of encountering stubborn and obstructive clerks who do not hand over data, these agents start with federal warrants. I drove two boxes of evidence that they will treat as probable cause. I am not employed by a professional law enforcement service. I did not go to federal law enforcement school, or even law school. That makes me an amateur sleuth.

I am a sleuth. And I get paid for it.

I call myself a data analyst and a researcher. Normally, I perform due diligence reports for corporations during mergers and acquisitions. I find criminal histories and sometimes I find ongoing or recent crimes. Not a gumshoe or a creepy guy driving a crappy old car with a telephoto lens snapping pics of extramarital shenanigans. I sit at home in a modern Scandinavian-inspired office that Sam and I share. The massive windows look south down the slope to the village. To our left is Nidoba Hill, a lovely, rounded hill that has been in Sam's family since before the founding of Vermont.

I stand with my satchel. I leave the laptop. Why not leave it? I am working in a secure conference room on a floor dedicated to the Federal Bureau of Investigation in the Jacob K. Javits Federal Building at 26 Federal Plaza, which hosts federal agencies. Ought to be safe from basic crimes, don't you think?

I had to turn in my temporary ID at the lobby. Rules trump logic.

Out on Centre Street, we three walk to a restaurant.

Social banter with two FBI agents in dark suits feels awkward. I too am wearing a dark wool suit, but I am easy to talk with. The waiter asks, "Three checks?" after scanning the table.

They won't talk about their private lives and families. I can't or shouldn't discuss Sam and her career, nor admit that we live in a

# 1 | YOU BELONG HERE

loving relationship. While DOD policy is beyond the FBI's scope, who's to say what the next set of rules, laws, or politicians will bring? In a moment of blandness, I ask them about their past duty stations. Both young agents admit that New York is their first assignment. I try asking about recent cases. Stonewalled by the ever-present need to protect sources, information, and the confidentiality of ongoing activities. Strike.

They try for conversation too. They really do.

After my fish and chips arrive, I watch a man sitting near us. Both FBI agents sense my alert. Lopez can see my target without turning her head. Larocque glances once, assessing his own threat level. Then he turns towards Lopez. Both stop eating. Why? Because my body and my face communicated something.

"Be right back." I stand.

From the inside pocket of my blazer, I pull out my leather badge wallet. I flash it at the guy, then hang my badge around my neck. "My name is Brighid, and I am an Advanced EMT and captain of a rescue service. Can I help you?"

I register utter surprise from the fellow's face.

"I am going to take your pulse. Is that ok?" I use a special handshake that Alex Flynn, my chief back home, taught me. My head bobs with the beat of his heart. Faster than a dance beat, which puts it over 140 beats per minute. The pulse does not pound under my fingers. It is weak, likely indicating that his blood pressure is low.

"Sir, I am going to touch your neck. I've got you." At the carotid, I feel the pulse better. It is a bigger artery, and also confirms that his blood pressure is not great. My decision, for I do have one to make, is to identify if this pulse is regular or irregular. My head bobs. Every bob of my head matches the pulse in his neck. An EKG is the only real diagnostic tool for what I am trying to find out. You run a strip, fold it, then hold it to the light. If the peaks and valleys on the graph align, then the rate is regular. If they don't, the rate is irregular. I zero in on super ventricular tachycardia, believing I feel a regular rate.

I look at Lopez, who never takes her eyes off of me. "911, ambulance, Cardiac. Forthwith."

Larocque has pivoted his chair to watch me and watch the door, too.

"Sir," I say to my patient, "I am pretty sure that you are having a run of SVT or Super Ventricular Tachycardia. Have you ever heard those terms before?"

The guy looks like a white-tailed deer that has been trapped too tightly against a fence. His eyes bulge in fear.

"I'll get you through this. And we have an ambulance coming. I am going to have you try something. Are you up for it? It could stop this episode and return your heart to normal. You game?"

He nods.

"Ever get your ears blocked on an airplane or go scuba diving? This is going to look really stupid, but it works. You are going to stick your thumb in your mouth and try to blow your hand up like a balloon. Keep your mouth sealed around your thumb. Then you are going to blow and blow hard. It will hurt and your ears will pop. Ready?"

He nods.

"Thumb in. My hand will be on your neck. You start blowing on my three." I had already made several circular movements on his right carotid sinus. "Ok, blow. Push hard. Try to push air into your thumb." He does. A vertical vein on his forehead presents, his face turns red. I count to twenty. "Ok, relax."

The forehead vein drops, his color fades. His heart rate drops to about one hundred. The relief appears on every face in the restaurant.

I stand. The diners applaud. I grab a spare chair, sitting next to my patient. I hold my patient's hand.

"What is your name?" I ask. He answers.

"And your age?" He answers.

"And your birthday?" Again, he answers, although I have no idea what the correct answer ought to be. "And can you tell me your office address? Or the address where you are working today?" Again, I got a full answer as the anxiety drains from my guy.

"You'll be alright, sir. You had a cardiac event where your heart sped up. You'll spend time in an ER today. Then they'll schedule you

## 1 | YOU BELONG HERE

a follow-up with a cardiac specialist who will order a cardiac monitor that you'll wear for days or weeks. All very manageable. Have some water, and you might think of finishing your lunch before the ambulance comes. You'll not see food that good for the rest of the day."

He touches my hand and touches my badge. It is small like an FBI badge, except differently shaped and silver. The State of Vermont seal sits in the middle with Trowbridge EMS and EMT-I in the ring. Embossed in the metal is my call sign, 14RC5. That Alex and the crew elected me captain thrilled the shit out of me.

"Thank you, Captain. You saved my life."

Maybe I did. Maybe I did not. SVT is a funny beast. It can disappear as quickly as it comes on. Or it can kill. Both are true.

The ambulance stops and two EMTs enter the restaurant.

I brief them with the familiar jargon of a professional. They both glance at my badge. They transfer the patient to a folding stair chair for the short ride to the ambulance. I kept my mouth firmly shut about the carotid massage. I may have been trained on this technique, but it is not in our protocols, and I do not know New York protocols. Rules. When breaking them, keep your gob shut. Carotid massage, like so many medical treatments, can save a life or kill. Rub an artery loaded with plaque, you may dislodge a bit, then you've given your patient an obstructive stroke by putting a big sticky booger in a too-small artery, thus starving tissue of oxygen and glucose. Oopsie.

I return to my two FBI agents and my food. I start eating immediately as my fish has cooled. I dip my French fries into the tartar sauce, which makes Lopez's lip curl. I sip water and eat. The FBI agents watch me.

"That's what I do back home," I say as I remove my badge from my neck. I neaten the neck chain and return it to the leather pouch. These two wear their tiny badges discreetly on their belts and they have neck lanyards with their FBI credentials. Those creds open doors, unlock elevators, and let them move through their building with ease. With my badge, I have no special privileges or rights. Except for the knowledge of how to save lives.

I finish my fish and chips, placing my fork on the plate. I probably should have washed my hands after helping that guy. Instead, I return to eating fish and fries with bare fingers. Too much time on a small farm, I guess.

The waiter comes over.

"That table has offered to buy your lunch." He addresses all three of us. "I told them that management will comp your lunch today instead. We all know that the FBI office is a few blocks away, but I never thought…" He didn't finish the sentence.

"Sorry to say, my friend, those two will make a show out of declining your offer as they are real FBI agents. Me, I am just a rescue captain from rural Vermont. I am happy to have a free meal. And I thank you. By the way, the fish was excellent. I'd be back here in a heartbeat."

Lopez and Larocque execute in accordance with their script, declining a free meal.

The waiter returns with three leatherette folders. Larocque and Lopez each place credit cards in theirs. I open mine. I find a voucher for a free dinner plus a bottle of wine. I substitute a twenty-dollar bill for the voucher. So, I tipped heavily. I don't mind.

The afternoon flows with greater ease. I finish presenting my evidence in the conference room. I sign the evidence logs and other official documents. My two new friends give me a brief tour of the building. I enter their tactical operations unit under escort. I meet the special agent in charge. To my surprise, she has already heard of our lunchtime adventure. In her handshake, she presents me with an FBI coin.

"You represented today." It is what she says. Not like she can say much else. Should I expect her to say, "Welcome to the tiny badge team?" No.

"I'd like you to have my business card. Should you ever need anything, please call on either of these two or me."

Sam has a huge coin collection. She enlisted in the army before leaving college in 2001. She earned coins from her units and time as a military police officer, then as a military intelligence officer. Her adventures have resulted in global encounters and interactions with all sorts of federal agencies and foreign armies. Behind each of her coins hides a story.

I just earned my first coin ever. And a story.

Lopez and Larocque escort me out of Federal Plaza. I walk Chambers Street back to my car where I grab my overnight bag. I shuffle off to my hotel at a New Yorker's pace.

I arrive at the same restaurant in the same outfit I wore at lunch. At the table, I retrieve my coin, placing it on the white linens. I photograph it, sending it to Sam via our own private email system.

I cross into Vermont from New York State on Vermont Route 1. The green sign welcomes me to the Green Mountain State. With that I say aloud, to no one, "You belong here."

And I do.

I've got it pretty good.

I belong here, or so I think.

# 2 | Choices

After crossing half of the skinny end of Vermont on Route 1, I turn right. The pavement disappears from under my wheels.

The house will be empty and cold. The chickens and sheep won't notice when I roll in. As long as they have water and feed, they don't care about me.

Ever had hot dog fried rice? Crispy disks of hot dog add something to the ol' egg-and-rice dish. I'd rather make something, anything else, and I would if Sam were home. Hot dog fried rice is a dish I have never made for anyone but me. It is my bachelor food. My too-lazy food. My Sam's-gone meal. Actually, it isn't bad. I like it. I've gone entire deployments with eggs (which are free), rice, cheese, stir-fry, and bits of lamb (also free-ish).

I carry new wood in. I light three fireplaces, adding wood until the masonry that rises through the core of the house warms.

The bedroom will be empty and cold. I did make the bed before leaving. Little Miss Army and I differ on that. I may have once said that the bounce-a-quarter trick belongs in barracks and not at home. I am the pull-the-sheet-and-blanket-up sort. My bed looks more like a cumulonimbus than a professionally folded gift box.

"How can you stand it? The seam is sideways!"

"My toes are covered."

"No, your toes are freezing, then you put them on my calves."

"I can move them further north."

"Don't you dare."

When she is gone, I do pivot the house 'round right. What if she does come home? Every day, I have that thought, "What if she comes home today?" The toothpaste is in the drawer, barrettes are all clipped neatly to a satin ribbon and not just tossed in the windowsill. I do, honestly, make the bed, pulling each layer tight. How does she

## 2 | CHOICES

know? She's not here to see the results of my effort. I even close the butter-door in the fridge when she is gone. She always blames me for the butter-bomb that drops when you pull open the refrigerator. It never happens when I am home, alone. But she never sees that. She doesn't believe me, and never will.

When alone, I wake, having slept diagonally with my face on her pillow and my chilly toes on my side of the bed.

I tug at this and push at that with her voice in my head. The linens tight, the blankets square, forming a parade ground. I stand the pillows at attention with each toe on the yellow line, their hands in loose fists at their thighs. I can hear those pillows, in unison, responding: "Yes, ma'am." Damn right. "Ten-hut!"

Know what else is different when she is gone? I put her picture on the bed stand, on her side. She's found it there a few times when a mission ends early. I sneak it away later, not that I can sneak anything past a woman who spent part of her career as an MP then the rest as a military intelligence officer. Love doesn't have to resemble a Hallmark movie, does it?

The moment I hear her car trip the driveway alarm, I regret the fights I picked. I excel at finding justifications for an immature dust-up. She did not tell me of a plan, she shifted the plan, the army shifted the plan, she won't tell me where she is going, I bought something special, and she won't be here, laundry, clothes, firewood not chopped, firewood stacked wrong, my mud boots standing with left and right reversed, barn coat has chicken shit on the sleeve. It is all her fault thus, therefore, I make the declarative imperative.

I yell.

I should never admit that I have hit her with girly fists against the bit of chest above her breasts. When she pulls me in, we hug. I don't cry, no.

We both know I am no different than anyone else who says "see ya" to a soldier who they love. Every time she goes, I wonder if the last words I said are the best words for her to carry onto the battlefield. I'll never know which day is the day I will have to say goodbye. I can't fucking say goodbye. We both know and believe in her mission.

I support that, until the day before she leaves. Then there is no forgiveness for her leaving me. I refuse to watch her go out of sight. That's the worst luck. I must always turn away first.

Know what it's like to fly to Germany and walk into the army hospital at Landstuhl? Me. Also, I get to say, "Better than Dover." What an ass I am to prop myself up at the expense of another soldier's misfortune. Those landing at Dover have flags over their caskets. These are my choices. I have four. One, I can wait patiently for her to return healthy. Two, I can get a call from the unit's family support group informing me that she has been flown on a medevac jet to Germany, again. Three, Colonel Jackson or someone he designates arrives at my door with the Dover news. Four, I leave her. Yeah, so I have only three options. I am not leaving her. It is too good 99.99% of the time.

Bumping over our driveway, I recognize what a shit I am, what a shit I always am when she prepares to deploy. Am I supposed to give over a hug, share a kiss, kick my ankle skyward saying, "Have fun storming the castle, honey? I'll have a nice supper for you when you get back. Love ya."

I get angry.

I get angry at her. Then I get angry at me. Then I cry. I try like hell not to cry in front of her. Thus, therefore, hitherto her departure, I too flee. This time, I drove to Manhattan for no reason.

I return to our home stained with stale tears, cold, damp fireplaces, and a candid photo of Sarah next to her pillow, a pillow which stands at attention.

It has been a decade. Not all of it at this house. We moved here after she left active duty. That seems like a stupid statement. She enlisted before graduating. She excelled at everything; got selected for Green to Gold. The army paid for her degree, commissioned her, and never missed an opportunity to send her overseas. Her first trip to Iraq was in 2003 as a sergeant. Yeah, she expected to be sent to Afghanistan. She deployed as a platoon leader in 2005. As a captain in 2009. After a decade of uniform service, Captain Musgrave requested a transfer to the U.S. Army Reserves. She then immediately deployed

## 2 | CHOICES

to Afghanistan with a new unit. She has spent more than a third of her career deployed overseas. Her time at home involved ramping down from a year overseas or training for yet another year overseas.

Her reserve unit is in Ayer, Massachusetts. Her new dream recalls the old ads: one weekend per month, and two weeks per year. She promised she'd get a nice local job like with the county sheriff, execute her occasional duty in Massachusetts with this new battalion, and enjoy the second half of her military career.

At least she doesn't deploy for year-long chunks of time, anymore. This is tougher. The cycles remain short, tight, targeted, and iterative. She's still a full-time soldier. I don't know what to say. She'd argue with me. "I am not full time." Then she flies off, emailing me hints of one square meter of someone else's country.

I find it easy to get fussed off at her again as I open the front door to our empty home.

I love the smell of rosemary and sage. I should have gotten the compost out. I forgive me, it was three o'clock in the blessed a.m. That's my own fault. I can't blame that on Sarah, not this time. She was already gone before I forgot to carry the kitchen scraps to the hens. Oops.

I return from our bedroom in farm clothes ready to haul firewood, check on chickens, harvest eggs, feed the woolies, turn the lights on in our office.

To the chickens I am the gold giver, or rather the food giver. They demonstrate enthusiasm for seeing me when I have kitchen scraps or when I am filling their feeder or waterer. When I mess about in the coop, I toss several handfuls of freeze-dried mealworms into their run. They love those. Freeze-dried mealworms are often called "chicken crack" at our farmer's co-op. I count the hens as they crash through their small door. Eleven. I freshen their bedding, clean and fluff their nest boxes, and check the health of the coop. The sheep too recognize me as the bringer of food. They gather around me. I evaluate their gaits for tender feet and their faces and eyes for other health issues.

Sam and I have a plan here. I know it. We do talk about it. I do my research and analyst thing in our office. She does similar army stuff or helps me while sitting at a desk opposite. We will grow our little company together. She does her army weekends and two weeks at adult-summer-camp with other part-time soldiers. She retires when she's done her twenty years. Ooh, lá lá. Hello, Italy? Paris? Damn, even just a weekend in Boston or New York would be nice. We're still in the phase of life where a trip requires that she carry her five-day army bag, just in case.

Well, I put my EMS pager and radio on just in case, too.

Want my recipe for hot dog fried rice? Slice hot dogs in the round about as thick as your finger. Pan fry them. Fry old, cooked rice after the hot dog gets color, beat an egg in, add a bag of frozen veg from the freezer, the more freezer burnt the better. Season. Eat.

Except I don't eat. The Trowbridge Rescue tones drop.

Alex Flynn, our fearless chief, points me toward the patient. I get the patient free of the red BMW that this fellow drove off of the road. Alex would tell me to never say "drunk" and not write the word "drunk" in our official documentation. Depositions suck. This fellow is a particular friend of Bacchus. I'd guess he would have enjoyed the ancient festival of Saturnalia. The local version involves him sitting and drinking at a titty bar in Massachusetts all afternoon. He imbibed with the impunity of a skilled celebrant. No doubt he shared his dollar bills whilst enjoying the shoes on the stage (for shoes are the only required element of a dancer's wardrobe). He drove back into Vermont. The trip proved challenging when the road took a turn and a birch tree bloomed where his engine once sat. Clambering down to him was tough. The steep climb made difficult by early, crusty snow. The patient seems alert, oriented, conversational, and drunk. I take a few pictures of the inside of his vehicle and the patient in situ. I then stumble around the car, opening the passenger side door. I discreetly photograph a forty-five-caliber semi-automatic pistol. I photograph two bottles of prescription narcotics. I roll them with my gloved hand to catch the full label of each. I photograph a mostly empty bottle of Lot 40 Canadian Rye.

"Sir, I am not part of the show. The show is over." Handsy idiot. I sit him on the tailgate of my truck. Seriously, no injuries. He drove twenty, thirty meters through brush, parking at least twenty feet below the level of the road.

I listen to the Vermont State Police sergeant dress Alex down.

"You parked on critical evidence," he barks.

"In fact, I did not, Sergeant. Those tire tracks are perfectly preserved." Alex points to the dirt.

"Look how close you parked."

"I did park close," Alex answers. "I also have photographs for you as backup. And you know me."

The cop and our chief both look at apparent evidence that the BMW drove off the road and down the embankment without braking. Had the driver applied the brakes or even turned, then the tracks would show that. These tracks begged the question: Did the operator intend to drive off the road in a suicidal effort? Or was the driver asleep? That's the cop's problem, not mine.

I have nothing to do for this patient. The seat belts did their job perfectly. The airbags did the rest. The car's crumple zones crumpled. I step through the standard efforts as described in our protocols. Name, date of birth, chief complaint, history, mechanism of injury (what injury?), the history of his day (sitting at a bar drinking while watching mostly-naked women dance), what legal and prescribed medications he takes. I take vitals signs. Then I stand around as his non-custodial attendant.

When the Trent Valley ambulance arrives, I walk the guy to the side door. I brief the crew and step back. I talk with my chief while the Vermont State Police sergeant does his evidence-gathering routine. The patient's pistol gets placed in a white cardboard evidence box. The bottles of pills get sealed into plastic evidence bags.

The driver of the ambulance honks to get my attention. "We're heading south into Mass."

"Uh, oh. Hold on." I shuffle to the ambulance.

"He's asking to go to Mass," the driver says.

"Well, I don't think he can."

"It is his right and the protocols say 'nearest appropriate facility.'"

Oops, I need to remember who I am talking to.

"True. I'll have a chat." I open the door without waiting for an invitation. I hear the ambulance click back into park.

"Hey." I touch the patient on the shoulder. "Listen, my friend. You've got a choice. You can pick letter A or letter B. Here's option A for you. You can go to the hospital over the line in Massachusetts." I pull out my phone, unlock it, then queue up the photos.

"We have your driver's license, your car registration, and your insurance card. The state police know where you live. That's easy. In Mass, you'll have to tell the story of your afternoon. Your phone and your BMW both have the GPS waypoints of your trip from the bar to that birch tree where you parked the car." I flip through the pictures one at a time, including the birch tree rising from his red car.

"If you go to Massachusetts, then your phone and car can be used as evidence. Suddenly, you'll face a weapons charge for carrying a firearm without a permit. That's a felony with sentencing minimums in Mass. It is legal in Vermont." I show the picture of the pistol, then I advance to the picture of the pill vials. "These narcotics are in someone else's name. Some Mass cop might count them, weigh them, then decide you are carrying felony weight or try for a distribution charge. And have you noticed how Mass state cops dress? They look like the bad guys in World War II movies."

I continue, "Option B involves working with the Vermont state troopers. They dress like park rangers. The pistol is legal here. And as everyone knows, Vermont is a catch-and-release state. No time in jail awaiting hearings and such. Mass? You'll spend time sitting in someone's jail. In Vermont, you'll get a ticket to appear. You'll hire a lawyer and buy a new BMW for yourself. No weapons charge. That's it. You get to choose A or B? A—you stay in Vermont, get a ticket to appear from the nice park-ranger looking guy, or B—you go to Mass and face felony weapons charges and sleep in a jail cell until a hearing."

I leave the ambulance before he answers. What do I honestly care? He already made several bad decisions and wrecked an expensive car.

"Dispatch 15A1," I hear the driver of the ambulance call out. After dispatch answers, she says, "15A1 en route Winchester Memorial with one." Gee, what a surprise, the patient decided to stay in

## 2 | CHOICES

Vermont. I have no training as a cop. Sarah does. She went to the Vermont Police Academy as a part-time employee of the Winchester County Sheriff's department. That's a job that gets very little of her attention. No doubt the sheriff's department are disappointed, but the department can't fight back. She is protected by federal law as a member of the U.S. military reserve forces. My legal expertise comes from TV shows. I studied law under Dick Wolf.

Without my intervention, the police sergeant would have had to make a decision. If he arrests the patient, then he has to escort the patient to the hospital. That requires leaving the car wreck cum crime scene. The crime scene has evidence including a pistol, illegal narcotics, and an open container of alcohol. The sergeant has to maintain proper chain of custody of the evidence, meaning he can't just hand the crime scene to Alex and run to the ER in the back of an ambulance. As a solo cop, he can maintain the crime scene or have a drunk driver in custody, but not both. Not alone.

Major Sarah Musgrave would have looked at the fellow, "Sit, please. You're done. You're heading to Winchester Memorial..." She's got the look. Years in and out of combat as an enlisted soldier, an officer, and a boss. The look. The this-ain't-a-discussion look. The people-say-yes-ma'am look.

I type fast, wear loose skirts and blousy shirts made from all natural fabrics. I have longish hair. There are chicken pellets and wood shavings that I use as animal bedding in the back of my truck. I often smell like lanolin and have a red hen feather stuck to my barn coat. I don't have the look. Major Musgrave has the look. That big VSP sergeant has the look. Let's admit, based on what I just said, the sergeant's look didn't work just now on Alex. EMS Chief Alex Flynn had barked back at the armed cop. That's Alex though. Alex, he has the look.

With my not-yet-arrested patient traveling to the hospital, and the scene still blocking most traffic on the state highway, I wander towards Robby at the north end.

"Hey," I say in greeting.

He says into his radio, "Got five, last is a small white pickup.

- 25 -

Sending now." He looks at me. "I heard you went to New York City."

"Yeah, quick trip."

"Do anything fun?"

"Quick rescue at a restaurant and four hours of meetings with two FBI agents. No Broadway musicals, and no shopping." I had fun. Like the church spire in our village, I admit that I am a little off plumb.

"Too bad." He turns the slow/stop paddle telling traffic to wait. "Hey, I got a friend who might want to talk with you. I still don't know what you actually do, but it might be a good fit."

"Yeah, sure. Give him my number. Have him text me."

"Duke."

"Duke?"

"His name is Duke Hazen. He owns a construction firm called Great Pines."

"Cool." I've got so many questions, but Robby won't know the answers. "Anyway, I came up to help. Need a break or anything?"

"Nah, I'm good."

I lean on Harry's tailgate in silence. Harry's red-and-white emergency lights alert the oncoming cars to slow down—or so we prefer to believe, anyway.

Silence is an accepted form of communication with my neighbors. Handshakes, less so.

On the third round of traffic, I pick up the paddle to stand there with a sign that reads: Stop. The old rule is two-in and two-out. If that works for interior firefighting, then it is good practice for any of these easy duties. Directing traffic is more dangerous than fighting fire. It is more likely that Robby and I die on the hood of a car next to a highway than anything else including fires, shit falling on us, or people shooting us. It is like drivers all over the U.S. look at emergency personnel with confusion. Should I go through or around? My exit strategy, as it often does, involves running towards the vehicle while cutting sideways, then diving over the embankment. I'll likely land badly on a beech sapling but live. Don't run in the same direction as the car. They'll chase you down.

Leaning against Harry's truck with its light rhythmically dancing on the bare trees around us, Robby doesn't speak. We take turns holding traffic, then lean against a friend's truck.

"Trowbridge Command, north traffic."

"Yeah, go."

"Tow truck is here."

"Send it and hold the traffic on both ends."

Driving home, thinking of cold hot dog fried rice with rubbery egg that seems as unappealing as another night sleeping diagonally in our bed, alone, touching Sarah's photo with affection before Beethoven's violin concerto rocks me to an empty sleep.

Duke parks his clean white truck. When in our mudroom, he performs the boots-on/boots-off dance. I endeavor to say, "Leave 'em on," as he pulls laces from the top three inches.

"I know your wife, Brenda, I think?" I offer. "She cut my hair a couple of times back when she worked at that salon in town. I haven't seen her in a while." I had seen Duke around the community over the years.

Smiling, Duke says, "I built her a studio off the garage." He's still unlacing his tall work boots.

"Ooh, can I get a number or email? I'll see her in a second. She's super sweet, too. Tea? Still warm from breakfast? It's all I've got. No coffee, sorry."

Confused by tea, Duke accepts the mug.

"Cream? From Allen's parlor, only yesterday." He holds the mug out for fresh cream.

"You're on the fire department with Allen, right?" he asks me, using only the family name, y'know Allen, as in Ethan Allen. History book Allen, a real person. The family still lives here over two centuries later.

"Lots of them…two cousins and a couple of sons-in-law."

The conversation explores the people and families of the town for a bit. Some here have big, bushy family trees, the roots tangling with hundreds of other families—a part of the forests covering these hills, one can never see how the family trees and their roots communicate and weave together below our feet.

I am treated as an outsider in Trowbridge. Sam, while raised here, has a family tree that gets drawn with diagonal lines. Regardless of her family's heritage, she is treated as neither local nor flatlander but still "other" for some reason.

The lull comes as the tea mugs empty. Duke looks down. We both wait for the conversation to turn. Steering the topic doesn't come easily to him. I study the man. Something is a bit off. My first thought is that he has cancer. The collar of his white Oxford button-down shirt is too big for his neck. His eyes have shrunk some. His beard looks shabby and ill-groomed. Over the years, I have seen him change his look, but within normal variations. He'll do the perpetual three-day beard thing for a while. Then he'll let his red beard grow, but he trains it with geometrically precise lines. Today, the beard hair lengths vary, and there is a hollow shadow under both cheeks. The brown hair on his head looks ill-kept as well.

There is a pair of folds under his leather belt. Either his jeans grew, or a few inches dropped from Duke's waist.

"I've heard you...," then an uncomfortable pause, "that you sometimes help people recover money and help with research. Are you a private investigator?"

"Not really a private investigator, but sort of, close enough sometimes."

"My firm is building the base lodge up at that new ski area."

"That will be gorgeous when it is done." I add, "But I did chuckle when the article described it as timber frame and showed steel I-beams." I follow the construction and the massive project in the local papers. I read the stories, no matter how poorly written, and how unclear the stories end.

"Ernie hasn't paid me for over a year. I took loans out to carry the materials and staffing through for the summer. He's full of promises and big ideas, and cash for everyone else."

"Ernie?"

"Ernie von Eberbach, the new owner of the ski hill. We're building the timber-frame building as the new base lodge for the place."

"Oh." With a near whisper, I ask, "How much?"

"Over half a million, probably close to 600K with interest and some wintertime costs and equipment leasing costs."

I ask, "Where did you get to on the project last summer?"

"Foundations are dug. We've gotten most of the steel up and the first floor is poured."

I add, "Eberbach claims the building to be worth twenty million and is timber frame. Wasn't that the quote in the *Trent Valley Viewer*? 'The most elegant and luxurious building in the region,' or some such? Spas and movie theater and game rooms and multiple restaurants—that's what I keep reading in the papers."

"He does make those claims." Duke pauses, then continues, getting warmed up. "Ernie started calling me to plan the spring and summer. He tells the papers that he has sold something like 1,500 memberships. He told some of the politicians around here that his project will yield over five million in taxes annually to Haworth and Carlton. Me, I got a down payment for the summer. I've invoiced him for over five-hundred-thousand dollars. I am sitting on another 100Ks' worth of invoices not yet sent. And now he wants me to start planning for the summer." Duke breathes again. "He wants to start selecting wood and tiles. He insists that it is time to order materials for next summer. I've told him I need to be paid. Linda, at the bank, started calling me over a month ago."

"And?"

"I am holding the bank back. If it weren't for the press that the project gets, I am certain that the bank would be a lot tougher. When I talk with Ernie, he goes into sales mode. He recaps the sales for the winter, the excitement for the project, the importance of the project for the local economy. He'll be hiring a hundred people in the twenty to twenty-four age range, all that noise. I have employees I can no longer pay. I have paid every vendor, every supplier, every subcontractor, and everyone that works for me, but at Christmas, I will have to furlough everyone. Everyone. And no one will get Christmas bonuses. I'll pay for my family's winter with my personal credit cards. As it is, I am paying credit-card level interest to put food on the kids' plates."

Duke's face shows more than frustration. He communicates fear and regret.

"I've got my regular guys texting, wanting work for the summer. I don't know what to say to them. If I don't hire them, the others will. I've even thought of shopping myself out or subbing to someone. I don't want to lie, and I don't want to lose them."

I interject: "I've got two questions and an offer for you. What do you owe? And what does Ernie owe you?"

"The bank note, line of credit, has been pushed to four-hundred-and-fifty-seven thousand. That goes up several grand every month. I've invoiced Ernie over six fifty and I am still sitting on some invoices, maybe 700K."

I make an offer to a neighbor and friend of a friend. "We won't charge you anything for the first five hundred thousand. Please invoice him everything and send him statements with all associated late fees for the past due invoices. Start sending them monthly. We will charge a percent of anything above the first five hundred. Email me the invoices, the statements, the contracts, and if you have copies of the checks he's used in the past, send me those too. Maybe your bank has a copy."

"That one check came almost a year ago. I was so naïve, so excited then. This was to be our biggest job ever. I'll try to get you that check."

Wanting to refocus and calm him down, I add: "Duke, we've got you."

"Is there a contract or something you need me to sign?"

"Nah, not just yet."

I pull a piece of printer paper from the kitchen drawer. I write, "Sam and Brighid will help Great Pines Construction recover past invoices from The Branston Club at a rate of five percent after the first 500K."

I put the date on it and sign it. I slide it to him. He signs it. I snap a picture with my phone, then text it to him. In case you think that I am profiting from the misfortunes of a neighbor, my rate, our rate, is less than the interest he is currently paying on credit cards and on bank loans. Without me and Sam, the banks lose. Duke loses.

Duke's family loses. Who knows what the next step down will bring? Divorce, anger, violence, suicide?

"When I started on my own, I did renovations on ski and vacation condos. It paid the bills, but I wanted something more, something substantial. Imagine being one of the guys who built the Empire State or the new World Trade Center in New York. You look at that with pride. You show your kids. Your kids show their kids. I am a fucking idiot for thinking that Ernie von Asshole would be my legacy project. You know what it's like to get handed such an opportunity? What I missed is that three bigger firms walked away before me. I'd be proud of a ski lodge built here at home. I saw the dollar signs, my first million-dollar project, and its promise to be worth multiple millions. I'd look at that and say, 'I did that.'"

Oh, Duke. I don't say, "You're contacting me on the wrong side of the project." He doesn't understand that companies employ our firm to avoid these problems. We crawl through the real and virtual garbage of companies and their officers. I write a report, such as, "This guy has four wives in four states with alimony to two other women." Sure, it's not about Ernie von Asshole. But with a minute of digging, I'll bet that there is a long list of vendors who pinned dreams of famous projects and big paychecks only to discover that Ernie's paperwork already forced them into arbitration in Delaware or North Dakota while preventing them from disclosing the conflict due to a tangle of non-disclosure and confidentiality agreements. I have no evidence. Maybe Ernie is a good guy plodding through his own miseries. Isn't it possible that Ernie is at the core honest?

This man breathes the sigh of the weary.

The conversation ends. Duke stands. I stand. Duke steps to the kitchen door.

"Ok."

I ignore Duke as he fusses at his boots in our mudroom.

Through the kitchen window, his truck tells me the same story the man did. He won a big contract. He bought the right sized truck for a boss, had it customized with lettering and a few lights. He washes the Vermont dust from the doors, likely daily. He keeps the Great

Pines Construction logo immaculate. And yet, I'll bet he would give anything to use his December truck payment to buy gifts for his kids.

# 3 | Barred Owls and Predators

The barred owl, a predator and threat to any critter under the snow, deceives. Perched on a favorite branch of a maple tree, the owl remains hidden—except to me, watching her from our office window. I saw her land. She flies silently, another deception. The owl's face works like a surveillance mic, listening to sounds from the unseen. Camouflage, stealth, and stillness generate an illusion of royalty.

Deception becomes the hunter.

Wither prey breathe, a hunter watches. Like my barred owl neighbor, the hunter disappears into the grays and blacks of the winter forest, the golden browns of grasslands, the deep greens of the canopy, the blue-white of a snowy field.

She twitches, spinning her head rapidly.

The driveway alarm dings a second later.

I looked for my friend Sister Owl in the maple. She has disappeared.

I ought to put a wireless camera facing the drive. But it is good for me to get up and see the propane truck, UPS truck, FedEx truck, or whomever. I know it isn't one of the guys on the squad or Alex. They always text first.

At the door, I glimpse the rear of Sam's car.

How did I not feel her cross the state line into Vermont?

How did I not know it was she who shooed our owl?

That's why I make the bed when she is gone, and put the toothpaste away every morning, and fold the towels neatly, and pick my clothes from the floor, placing them in the hamper. I am free to run to the car with no apologies to anyone.

She looks at me, hopelessly tired.

I help her from the car and lift her five-day bag from the backseat. She takes her backpack and a small hard case.

Of course, we kiss. And of course, I babble incomprehensibly.

But that is why I get pissed off after all of these years. The army returns an empty shell of a human to me. When she stands, I play the child's game: What is the difference between these two pictures? We all played this on the placemat at a local diner. You can picture it. Is it an extra rung on a cartoon chair, a second cat near the flowerpot, and a tree standing outside the window? With Sarah, it's wounds, the color of the skin around her eyes, the weight she's lost, the condition of her hair. I send her off intact, healthy, pink, strong, and alert.

She walks tired.

She moves tired.

Her limp is more pronounced.

And her face. That's my clue, but the uniform covers her from the soles of her desert combat boots up through every inch of her combat uniform, down her long sleeves to her gloved hands. Her head is covered in a cap.

We drop the bags in the mudroom at the washer and dryer.

I am still talking.

She is still walking. Yes, she kissed me back and hugged me and did all of the right things. Why wouldn't she? She loves me.

She unlaces her boots in the kitchen. I immediately take them to the mudroom. The odor inspires me to put them outside on the porch. I set them neatly. Step away, then pivot. They need some air and whatever that odor is, it doesn't belong trapped in our mudroom for days. Outside they go, next to my barn boots. I don't think she changed her boots or even socks during this mission.

When I am back, I see what I see.

My wife stands in the army's birth-control panties and a black sports bra. The calf is an old injury, but I can see that the hollow area is puffy with inflammation. There is a new line of sutures on her neck right across the trapezius. Seven stitches? Like Duke, her eyes are dark and sunken. Her hair is all but gone. It is never very long. She keeps her thick black hair cropped short during deployments. "Less fuss." This time it appears that someone shaved her head, and recently. Her scalp is as white as the sands of a Grecian beach. I surmise that something happened there.

We hug properly and I feel the warmth of her skin. I kiss her on her neck, opposite the latest wound. I want to ask, "Did you get another Purple Heart?" Know what? It doesn't matter. Ten toes, ten fingers, two legs, two arms, an intact torso, lungs that move air, and a heart that beats blood.

The rest we can fix.

She showers to get clean and wash the faraway lands from her body. I join her in the warm and steamy shower.

Today, she may not have been able to complete a 10K march with full packs, but she had enough energy for me. I like the feeling of oxytocin and vasopressin coursing through my blood, and Sam's hands on my body.

At midnight, when I pee, I hide her photo in a drawer. I prefer her exhausted, hurt, warm flesh in our bed to a goofy photo taken years ago, shortly after we met.

Sister Owl returns. This time, she sits on a T-shaped perch we built on a fence post. This centers her in our office window. Whilst I see her, most might not. She blends with the winter scape, the white-and-gray clouds. The mice below the snow never hear her and never see her. I do. I see the alert.

This alert results in the hyperfocus of a predator listening to her prey. The owl tracks tiny movements with her head, then a swoop and a strike. Some might want to turn away from an owl tearing a mouse part. I don't. I watch her lift the mouse from the snow, returning to her maple tree. With her beak, she pulls the mouse apart while holding the carcass in her talons.

I love Sister Owl for being an owl. She is glorious.

My Sam hunts.

Unlike the tiny mouse, Sam's prey often fights back. Sure, the little mouse struggled and did his mouse-best to fight the talons and beak of an owl. That's not a fair fight. Sam's M4 rifle and Glock pistol are an even match against a Kalashnikov and fighting military-aged combatants. Sam's got the stealth of an owl and shares the determination. Let's admit I am a little taller than she and my shoulders are just a bit wider—not so much that I can't wear one of her shirts when she is deployed.

In the windowsill is an arrangement of found objects. I have two whole owl pellets and one partially dissected. I once teased it apart to identify bits of mouse arm bones, and jawbone, and brown fur that closely resembles my own hair color. To be fair to the mouse, it had a nice uniform coat. My hair has about five colors in it, more like a calico barn cat with the occasional dark brown, blonde, red, and black hairs. I am not a mouse. Next to the owl pellets is a bird's nest I saved after trimming a wild rose bush that had grown crazy.

As three in the afternoon approaches, so does evening.

Sam can disappear into anything: an empty field, a crowd, or a street. She folds light around her. She falls transparently into the soundscape. Like Sister Owl, she watches. She is lethal. When true sleep does come to her, she becomes as still as the leather sofa. Silence folds around her. I love to finally see her let go.

I know every other type of night she endures.

No, that is not true. There are two types of nights that I do not know but can see in my mind's eye. First, is the night with no sleep, a day so long that it stretches yesterday's dawn past tomorrow's sunset. Fighting micro-naps with hands ready to grab weapons. Second, are those field nights where the crew each sleep for two hours in a kitty hole hollowed out of the dirt. A sleep so bad that your hand never releases from your pistol's grip. I also don't know the feeling of flying away from a mission in the back of a cargo aircraft. Four engines roar, your ass in a fabric sling-seat with your back against the round hull of the plane.

I understand the other nights.

She sleeps now because her body insists.

She sleeps now because she is safe.

She can sleep because I am with her.

In five days, she will climb from our shared bed, pull on flannel pajamas and sit in the living room before a quiet fire. I don't like to see her sleeping in that chair. But I understand it. This chair-sleep comes in a few flavors—all of them bitter. There are the mornings I find a

## 3 | BARRED OWLS AND PREDATORS

pistol next to her. What does that say to me? She's not feeling safe. I mean, that is the best message, isn't it? It isn't the only explanation I am willing to believe. You can read into that if you want to. I have also found a bottle of booze next to her. Which is worse?

We've been lucky so far. The booze sounds bad, but I see that she had one, maybe two, drinks. Isn't that the top of a slippery slope? Even with a bit missing, I worry. Private, sergeant, second lieutenant, first lieutenant, captain, major, and working towards a promotion to lieutenant colonel. Let's hope it doesn't get worse. I don't know how to help with these types of nights. I can't see what she sees.

Where do we go from here? The army gives her education, a career, medals, health care, retirement, and post-retirement health care. But does the army see this? Maybe they do. There isn't a combat soldier who doesn't know these nights, and so it has been for millennia.

I read a clip from the local newspaper, the *Trent Valley Viewer*.

> The Branston Club will hire approximately 100 employees in the 20 to 24 age group. Eberbach echoes goals he identified in the valley's economic development platform. The club offers year-round entertainment and various corporate events. Businesses in Vermont, Connecticut, New Jersey, New York, Massachusetts, and Rhode Island are being targeted for corporate memberships. Eberbach says: "We can rent out the mountain for a day. They'll fill up the inns in the valley."
>
> "The value of the new base lodge is $20 million. It will serve 1,500 members." Eberbach continues:
>
> "There's a lot going on here. During the day, we'll have a really nice restaurant with high-end service, where people can order food. Then at night, it turns into a single-plated dining experience with a more family style. Downstairs, there will be a movie theater room, teen recreation center, arcade and a video editing room. The editing room will offer guests the opportunity to edit and post videos online that were taken during the day.

*"Also, in the lower area of the lodge, there will be a hair salon, a spa with 14 treatment rooms, a workout facility and Pilates and yoga studios. A nursery and ski development program are among the planned operations."*

Reading on, I see that Ernie says, "The marketing budget is almost three-quarters of a million." So roughly what he owes Duke. I wonder silently if they have been paid. Or maybe that is why the posters I saw in lower Manhattan were mounted on trash cans.

The fire/EMS tones alert me. Both my radio and my hip pager go off. The Spotted Dog application on my phone vibrates. "Man down near a snow blower, not conscious, not breathing." I step to my door chair where I keep a uniform and a set of fire pants—turn-out gear. Sam stirs only enough for me to know she heard the tones. I know two things while changing into my uniform and safety clothing. One, the unconscious guy not breathing while lying near his snow blower will never get up. Two, Ernie von Eberbach is a predator, one who sees his fellow humans as prey.

Ernie's numbers are just big enough to impress yet scaled down to match Vermont's economy. Some of his numbers measure larger than most of municipal budgets in Vermont. Figures that perpetually seem out of reach, yet shimmer with reality.

I head towards an emergency that is not an emergency to anyone except the living person waiting for us to arrive. Once there, one of us will say the obvious, repeat worn phrases of condolence. We will wait an hour or more for the state police to arrive. Until then we manage a crime scene devoid of any crime. In Vermont, and most places in the United States, we treat a dead body as the de facto evidence of a crime. Sometimes they are, often they are not.

Sam knows hours will pass before I return home.

I push through Trowbridge with two hands on the wheel looking for pathways through the mud. I travel as fast as possible, as slow as necessary. The words of the dispatcher echo in my head: "Unconscious and not breathing."

Sometimes, we hear: "Unconscious but breathing." The squad

## 3 | BARRED OWLS AND PREDATORS

calls this butt-breathing, as in, breathing through one's butt. We pinch our cheeks into a fish-face with hands in pantomime of a butt breathing in and breathing out. Unconscious and not breathing will be reported shortly as an "untimely", the politest term for "dead" in our vocabulary.

In contrast to radio terminology protocols, we're trained to tell loved ones that Fred is dead—clear, definitive, unambiguous. On the radio, courtesy dictates we state: "This is an untimely."

I pull into the driveway, regretting that I am the first one here. I will touch the body then say the words to the family or whoever is there waiting. I will say other words to dispatch seventy-five miles away in New Hampshire. Parking as to prevent anyone from passing my truck, I remember an older call, "one-hundred-and-one-year-old man, likely untimely." Untimely huh? How can the death of a one-hundred-and-one-year-old man be untimely? Was he late to meet his maker or early?

On scene, there is one person standing. That one living person looks at me expectantly. I shuffle quickly down the remaining parts of the drive. Am I expected to run with kit bouncing, then dive into CPR? Walk with slow dignity? My quick shuffle splits the difference.

My remaining task involves aligning the facts as they present themselves with any hopeful expectations of what I could do. I draft the sentence as I scan the scene, looking for hazards, for signs of trouble. The sentence will go like this: "I am very sorry to tell you this fellow is dead." I won't add "and has been dead for a goodly while." Hopefully, I'll get his name before I speak the sentence and insert it in place of "this fellow."

Arriving, I learn his name. Leaning over my patient, I shout his name, shake the stiffening body, do a quick examination looking for the most reportable and clearest indication of death—stiff jaw, dependent lividity, stiff finger. I make my statement to the neighbor-lady watching my efforts, inform her of my next actions, then return to my truck with my unneeded medical bag.

I think the neighbor knew as well as I did that little could be done. Anxiety clearly passes through her as she lets go unstated thoughts of her own inactivity, and her own doubts. My practiced sentence unveils relief on her part. She did nothing to help save this guy's life. She did not kneel in the snow to do CPR or breathe for him. Now, she has been unhooked from that responsibility. She did nothing wrong. Then I witness her wave of grief and her sense of relief.

On the radio, I finish the other half of the duty: "Dispatch, Trowbridge rescue confirming this is an untimely. Please return the ambulance to quarters then dispatch state police." Robby Stark parks on the road and joins me without a formal greeting.

I initiate my own paperwork with arrival time, observations, attestations and demonstrations of death, name of the physician at the emergency department who confirmed my diagnosis. A few quick photos of the scene. Discreet photo of the neighbor who called 911, a photo of her driver's license, a narrative statement from her.

I encourage the neighbor towards her home. Under the strictest of rules, I ought to keep her at the scene as a witness. Second best is that I sit her in my truck. Instead, I state that a trooper will likely knock at her door for a chat. I drive my truck to the end of the drive sitting at the edge of the public road. Then I, too, wait with Robby—actively controlling a crime scene in a town with twenty people per square mile, in a town made nearly impassible with mud. Actively controlling a crime scene requires that we sit watching a dead body not move. I silently hope that Robby and I do not have to shoo away canids, or a recently woken bear.

I'll brief the trooper, then we three will wait another hour for two detectives and a call from the associate medical examiner. Eventually, hours from now, I'll return home. After I hand over my documentation, give my statements, and get recorded, yet again, as a person of interest at another Vermont crime scene.

Not once did Robby inquire after Duke, Great Pines Construction, or the nature of that interaction. He probably already knows and likely knows more than I do. I appreciate Robby for staying with me: two-in/two-out is a good rule always. So much of what goes on in this town travels through unseen networks. While waiting, we barely talk. We pass time in comfortable silence, broken with occasional

## 3 | BARRED OWLS AND PREDATORS

stories of people who pass by in their trucks. "She's getting divorced."
"Who's that?"
"Frannie."
I wrinkle my face.
"She just drove by in the red truck. That's Donnie's truck. He's partying a bit too much and steppin' out on Frannie."
"Oh, the roofing guy?"
"Been putting the company profits up his nose, she's saying."
"Damn, cocaine, here? I haven't seen cocaine in years, not since college time."
"I know, but it is here."
"Seems like a city drug, a rich man's drug. All I ever see is weed and opiates. Aren't we lucky that the worst of the meth skipped by this region?"
"Maybe." We both know that dozens have died from opiates. "It all kills." The populations of the towns near us range between 500 and 2,000. Dozens of overdoses represent a significant problem.
"Sure, but we never got the clandestine labs. Imagine dealing with that here as well? That would suck. Rolling up to a scene and facing that shit?"
"Frannie said that the office manager for the roofing company embezzled 20K."
"Sure, or the money went up Donnie's nose and he's blaming the office lady."
"One way or another, they've laid folks off too."
I asked the dumb question, "How do you get coke here?"
"Likely the same way you get everything else?"
"Well, I keep finding the same doctor's name on pill bottles at these ODs."
Robby pauses, "Yeah, and he took over from a doc who was a drug addict."
"Oh, I didn't know that. Who?"
"Before your time. Fox."
"I know the name, seen it. Isn't there a plaque or something to him? A memorial?"

"Maybe. He was pretty much the first full-time doctor up here. A hero to some, I guess."

That's telling. I cuss more than Robby and maybe I shouldn't. He tends to treat people gently with his words, even when they don't deserve gentility.

"Remember that poster that DHS was trying to distribute? The telltale signs of a meth lab, or terrorist bomber? It was light blue."

"Kinda."

"It lists half of the stuff we have in our barn and found in most barns around here. Solvents, fertilizer, batteries, and then mason jars, allergy meds."

"There probably were labs here, I don't doubt. But yeah, meth never really caught on here."

"Why make meth when you can get pills cheaper and easier?"

"I guess. Just as dead."

"Think the guy over there is going to get an autopsy?"

"It costs the state money, and they have to transport him three hours north to cut him open."

Leaving that question open.

We wait, scanning the terrain. We wait for the state police.

When Robby does see them, he points. I flip on my flashing red and white emergency lights, pulling out of the driveway. I park on the road, flipping my lights off. Just enough to affirmatively mark the site. The trooper also parks on the road, leaving the drive open.

The trooper's small SUV has been bathed in mud from the mirrors down. We know him, he knows us. It is our neighbor Richie from Langford. We do not give the trooper grief about the ninety minutes we waited. And he does not give us grief about the mud. We radio to dispatch, informing them that the Vermont State Troopers have arrived and report the release of command to the same VSP. Richie smiles, saying, "I don't want command."

"Sorry, it's all yours—the dead guy, the snow blower, the empty house. We're just witnesses now." We can't leave, though. And we three know the routine. There is nothing for us to do after the brief and a careful tour of the not-quite-a-crime scene. We behave as if it is.

## 3 | BARRED OWLS AND PREDATORS

Robby and I clear the scene ninety minutes later, after we present our brief for the two detectives who arrive from the new barracks further north.

# 4 | A New Firetruck

The sun remains obscured by the crest of Nidoba hill to the east. Hard to know if Harry will call before that first flash of orange or wait until sun-up.

I answer my phone, imitating Hermionie Grainger, "'ello 'arry." Sam smiles at me. She looks so much better. Her hair has filled in. She almost needs to comb it occasionally. The bruising appeared, then faded from purples to blues to yellow, then back to her normal skin tone.

"No, I haven't any idea why people should not swim in Paris," I say to the assistant chief of Trowbridge EMS. But that's a conversation with Harry. A random joke, an observation, or some other odd news of the town. In truth, he wants the scoop on the call from the prior day.

"I know you are always listening. Yes, I know I can call. I know I am never alone when you are around," I answer. Sam watches the conversation, hearing only my side.

"It is a long drive from your place. Of course, I had it under control. Robby came by after a while."

I tell him of the call. Every detail…the position of the body, my guess as to cause of death, which doc I called at the hospital, which trooper came. Then we race each other for the *Law and Order* Lenny-line that is often delivered over a TV corpse. "Snowflakes win again."

Harry cares for me deeply. It feels like the kind of love one gets from the best uncle or an older brother. Certainly, he is interested in the call and likes to be in the know. Harry gets me laughing and I end up saying things to him that I would not normally tell Sam.

It is a parity issue, isn't it? She comes home from combat missions and can't or won't tell me all of the details. Partially, because she can't talk about operational activities. Partially, because she is deep in the world of military intelligence. Partially, because she doesn't want me worrying about the stuff that happens in and around a battlefield. Therefore, I don't tell her about my missions either.

Except, I do, don't I? I tell Harry while Sam listens.

And who am I kidding. Sam reads me and knows me. I can't keep secrets from her.

Before wrapping up the call, we talk of the weather, the spring, and Harry's upcoming travels.

"No, you didn't need to come over. With the mud and the distance, I had it. You take care of your side of town, and I've got the stuff over here. Zone defense, remember, that was your idea, I think."

"No, I would never say such a thing. That was Alex."

When I hang up, Sam asks, "Alright…why should you never swim in Paris?"

"According to Harry, because people will think you are *in Seine*."

The joke falls flat. I laugh again saying: "It is one of his stupider jokes," and seeing my blank face, "the river, in Paris, *in Seine, insane*?" Dad jokes and bad puns. He's my friend and becoming dear to me.

Thus, giving further proof to Harry's character.

I bound downstairs for breakfast, saying, "Rockingham got a call." I hear the fire radio downstairs, recognizing the two-note tones that precede each new emergency call out of a fire or rescue squad in the region.

The murder board, my name for the display of names, networks, and timeline that I build for our cases. It shows the "Big Plans" for the ski area. "Big Plans" is the name of a news article dated from last August, months before I met with Duke. As I reread the article, I acknowledge that no journalism interfered with the writing of the article. The paper reprinted a poorly written press release under their own byline.

"We bought the mountain and the next day, we were out selling memberships," reads a quote from Ernie von Eberbach. He states that he will be spending $31 million on projects and that the towns will earn $5.5 million in tax revenue. The base lodge, Duke's project, sounds like a European-style spa, or something lifted from the choicest resorts in the U.S., including an expansion of the tiny local airport. Eberbach promises routine commercial flights to Teterboro, New Jersey and Westchester, New York from an airport with weeds growing from the asphalt cracks. There is no control tower. We have lake-effect snow through most of the winter. What lake, you ask? The Great Lakes, four hundred and fifty miles away. Odd, huh? Blame the mountains. They scrape the underbelly of the clouds passing by. We also get clear sky snow. Therefore, this guy is going to enhance a neglected regional airstrip and convert it to a commercial airport to be used by regional jets, and the private aircraft of billionaires, ex-presidents, and famous people. To fulfill his insane promises, you need billionaires, ex-presidents, and famous people to flock to a tiny ski hill in Southern Vermont instead of going to Vail, Alaska, or Europe. This hill is different because it is private, it is exclusive. "Ski the East." But to have that happen, he needs a tarted-up airport, a fence, a jazzed-up building, and a car rental lot stocked with good-looking, mud-free, fancy cars—the very sort that can't drive through Trowbridge six months out of the year.

We do have a few billionaires and a smattering of famous people. They discreetly buy homes on large properties. Their neighbors get to know them and forget that they are famous, until it is time to raise funds for the fire company, the community club, and the kids' after-school activities. Let's admit that the famous and super rich don't want their Vermont estate in Vail or Saint Moritz. For whatever reason, they bought in a tiny town founded before the Revolution. During mud season, these folks either run away or drive high-clearance vehicles with mud-smeared paint like the rest of us.

There is a famous lady actor that bought a place two towns away. She was in a few big movies in the 1970s and 1980s. Still fabulous looking. We had that one lady from a daytime talk show buy a place in Snellend. It is a huge property that Harry once managed as a full-time farming job. They seem like the sort that would side with locals to keep Vermont off the map.

By the way, Vermont does fall off the map, or parts of it do. Not in the old days when maps were paper and kept in dad's glove box.

## 4 | A NEW FIRETRUCK

Today, when driving or hiking, sections of the maps disappear because you lost signal and didn't previously download and save the map of where you are now. You stand there, a dot on a gray background. There's no map anymore. And nobody, except a few first responder nerds, keeps Dad's paper maps in a car.

What do you do when you fall off the map? Option one: go forward, hoping for a mobile phone signal or a useful road sign that points to something you know. Option two: go a different direction, picked at random hoping for mobile phone signal or a useful road sign that points to something you know. Option three: yell at the first responders who are blocking the road. Tell them emphatically that you must go through and follow this road. Once you've done that, tell those first responders how important you are and that you know the way, and tell them loudly you'll be just fine, thank you. Then when that fails, ask the same question three times. As if answers two and three will magically transform answer one into, "Oh, sure, just go through." Eventually, you'll just start yelling at us because you weren't prepared for a very rural environment with dirt roads, steep hills, short sightlines, and mobile phone masts that are always just one hill too far away to be reached.

One way that Vermont accidentally avoids being on the digital landscape is by keeping their public records private. Legally public, of course. They play by the rules, unlike the clerks I encountered in Florida. To get access to any records, you have to drive to the town clerk's office. In Haworth, a focal town in this unfolding story, their town office is adjacent to a traffic light. Listen, I get it. In most of America, nearly everything is adjacent to a traffic light. Bennington, Brattleboro, Rutland, Starkville, and Warrenton all have traffic lights. There is that clusterfuck of lights in Brattleboro that attempts to regulate the flow of traffic at a six-way intersection that resembles an asterisk. Except, one of the roads heads immediately to the only railroad track.

If the Vermonter is heading north, you wait until the three passengers get off and one gets on. If the Vermonter is heading south, then you wait for six people to board for the slowest possible trip to Penn Station in New York City. If a large tractor trailer turned down that road and avoided the train, then he, the tractor trailer, must wait for all of the little cars and farm trucks to clear from the bridge that spans the Connecticut River. The bridge is too narrow for full-sized trucks to cross if there is any other traffic. The traffic backs up on the New Hampshire side, leaving a gap for the truck. Oh, then there are the pedestrians. On every cycle of the lights, someone decided to grant rights to folks walking. Everyone waits for them to limp, slide, and shuffle over the road. If there is no train hauling goods, and no tractor trailer trucks, and no slow walkers, and no illegal turns, and no asshole from New York jumping the light, then that intersection works perfectly well, given that it is called Dysfunction Junction.

Here in the southern hills, we have one traffic light that escaped these towns. It cropped up on Route 1 like a marijuana stalk that nobody planted. During ski season, during leaf peeping season, during holiday weekends, drivers often wait several cycles to edge forward. If your target is east, or west, or north, or south, then you wait patiently in Haworth to travel east, or west, or north, or south. Every tourist region has this problem including our Green Mountains.

I sit in the traffic knowing that my destination is the traffic light and I need to park. The town office has three parking spaces. One of them has a "No Parking" sign. The tiny public lot is south of the intersection. The maybe-parking-spot is on the north edge of the road. Half of the blinkers indicate north, which is a right turn. I slowly approach the town office during the peak of ski season. The blessed cop car is parked in the real parking space leaving the cop-car-only space with the No Parking sign empty. What, am I going to park under the "No Parking" sign just behind the cop? That's his job. He parks under the "No Parking" sign like a good cop. Citizens then park in the legal spot.

I am on the right side of the road. As established, the one legal parking space is occupied. I can't turn left from the right lane, therefore I must flow north onto Route 100. I make that turn because I am trapped. Facing north, I stop my truck. I now need to cross the two-lane state highway to make a U-turn. All cars behind me stop. I cause a jam at the light. The cars heading south are impatient because they sense a green light coming. You get the point. After my U-ey, I wait two cycles for the light and park at the now-abandoned pizza place built in a 100-year-old cabin. Then I walk through that same intersection. By the way, this is not called Dysfunction Junction. It is just a wayward traffic light that escaped the bounds of the more urban towns and set itself up here.

Oh, and don't try to fix it. If you do, you'll run into three problems. The first is terrain. There is a river eroding the edges of the east-west highway, good ol' Route 1. The traffic light marks the confluence of that river and a fast-moving mountain stream that floods with every heavy rainstorm. The second problem is that this town was placed here a hundred years ago. These old buildings were moved up the hill from the original town center. Some somebody in Massachusetts wanted cool, fresh mountain water to drink in their stinky industrial town, so they built a drinking water reservoir in Vermont. They moved the po' mountain folks out of their gorgeous sprawling valley and pushed the town up the side of a mountain. One just might ask, "What could possibly go wrong with that idea?" But no one did, not in the late 19[TH] century. Oxen and steam engines dragged the commercial buildings up the hillside. The private homes and two churches remain drowned. The things you can do in a valley, you can't do while gripping the edge of the oldest mountain range on the planet. It is eroding. These mountains once looked like the Himalayas. They don't anymore and it isn't our fault—for once. It isn't carbon's fault, not this time. Just geological time. And ol' geological time doesn't think a bustling tourist town and its one traffic light is worth keeping. Your third problem is the local attitude. One way or another, everyone here now depends on these cars to buy t-shirts, books, stuffed bears, hand-knitted hats, local maple syrup, and farm-to-table meals at restaurants.

For about the ninth time, I wait for the lights at Route 1 and Route 100 to change again. Of course, I crossed against the light once because the road that goes south from the intersection is very, very, very short. Except the road dead-ends at the new reservoir. The dead-end part of the road loses a foot or so per decade as the soil washes downstream, then to the Trent River, then the Cold River, then the Connecticut River, then to Long Island Sound right near where Katherine Hepburn lived (she is a hero of mine).

About the use of the word "new" here. It has two definitions. Most commonly, it refers to pretty much anything built after the Civil War. Our house is not "new" because the construction finished in 1810. It isn't old either because it is well kept and not from the Revolutionary War times. The other definition of "new" is used when the wood is still blonde and you see it for the first time. It is ok to call that new, too. Old, here, tends to mean neglected and in need of love. Just like the three buildings opposite the town offices. Those buildings are old. Some poor ox dragged them up the hill. They got used for a few decades, then sometime after World War II someone stopped using them

I had all the time in the world to tell you this story because that is what it takes to get to the Haworth Town Office to gain access to their public records. Six red lights, a faux right, a real right, stop traffic for U-turn, then wait for two red lights to make my way south to the municipal lot where I then jaywalk and wait just one more red light before crossing to the town office. And the cop car is gone. A black Tahoe with blue Connecticut plates has just now parked at the only spot reserved for the town office, the one abandoned by the town's cop car. I enter the office as the tourist family wanders off to buy whatever they buy.

"Hey, my name is Brighid Doran." I introduce myself to the town clerk. "I came to do a bit of research on property records."

"You a lawyer?"

"Nope."

"Been here before?"

"Nope."

"Well, come around and I'll show you what to do. We close at two. Except today. I have a PT appointment, so I am closing at one."

He walks me into the town vault, which is a room of its own. Honestly, it is bigger than one found at any nearby bank. It has a worktable and two chairs. Every manner of document storage is present. Handwritten ledgers from the 1700s and 1800s. You can tell the difference from the penmanship. The documents from World War II and on are typed. The more modern stuff is printed from laser printers. Paper lasts a thousand years, and digital records last about a decade.

I brought a modern map with the target properties with me. The clerk showed me the official town map which serves as the Rosetta Stone between what we see mapped on the internet and how this room is organized. Every parcel has an identifier. The pattern is easy. The first few letters represent the street name. And no, they don't change often. Then a dot, then the numeric designation for the property address. As I learned from Chief Alex, the house numbering system in Southern Vermont is based on the mile travelled from the start of the road. He showed me that house number 500 is one-half of a mile from the start of the road. And for the Canadians and Europeans driving these roads, number 621 is one kilometer from that same starting point. Sorry, you have to push buttons on your dashboard and phone, ditch the cool modern and logical metric system for the archaic nonsense that the British king left us with. Miles are tolerable. The Romans were happy with them. Two thousand plus years of history right there. If it was good enough for the Roman legions in England, then it is good enough for modern Vermont and America.

Regrettably, Vermont describes the width of roads in terms of rods. Did you miss that day of math class where the teacher taught you about rods? Probably not. We stopped teaching that measure a long time ago. Still commonly used here, certainly more common than the Smoot. To catch you up on what you never needed to know about the rod: most of the roads in Trowbridge are three-rod roads meaning that they are three times the 16½ feet or three times 5½ yards or, even more awkwardly, $1/320^{TH}$ of a mile. Blame the Romans who invaded Britannia in 43 BCE. It was their mile and their rod that the English brought here to New England. And then some red-bearded pirate stole the authentic and calibrated metric standards during the voyage from France after their Revolution. We might have been excited to adopt those standards in our young country. But the letter to France asking for new stuff got lost or something. Then we forgot. It has only screwed us all up a couple of times such as the oopsie with the Hubble Telescope where the American team worked in Imperial measures and the European team worked in metric. We had to send the space shuttle up to fix that. For those still following, a rod is about five meters, but don't say that around here. They'll think you are a communist or a socialist or European.

Regarding the Smoot. First, it is real. Second, you're on your own. Worry not, it is both a safe word to search for and a linear measure invented here in New England.

Obscurity matters in a Vermont town vault. In some cases, I had to measure the distance, in miles, from the start of the road. In other cases, I had to estimate the distance between other properties. Where is 621 Merriam Street, Haworth? As said, it is about six-tenths of a mile from the start on the road. Where does the road start? Often at the village center. Odd, huh. It happens this way. You drive out of Trowbridge on Old Stagecoach Road that connects Trowbridge to the east. The house numbers start at one, right there in the village. It goes to 3598. Then, if you are very observant, you might see a rusty speed limit sign leaning on an elm tree. On this side is a large pad of road fill where the Trowbridge town trucks turn around. On the other side of that elm tree is another turnaround spot for the Town of Dilham. Then, for a while, the house numbers descend. Why? Because you crossed the town line and the numbering starts in their town center, not ours. If you are walking or riding a slow horse, this system works great. How far did I get? Oh, here's Brown Boulders farm with a house number. Boom, you've got a mile marking. Then we invented GPS and cars and the United States Post Service shut down all the little post offices in the villages and gave the entire region one postal code. Therefore 621 Post Road is one kilometer or a half-ish mile from Trowbridge, but 964 Post Road is six miles further because the number goes up to 3598, then gradually counts down again.

As I said, it is useful for walking.

And tolerable for running to a 911 call in the middle of the night. You watch your odometer.

## 4 | A NEW FIRETRUCK

Know what is less helpful? When Joe Connecticut calls in a car accident at 964 Post Road in Trowbridge. We run to the town line, call dispatch, and ask them to tone Dilham's fire and rescue crew. Because 964 Post Road is in Dilham. Also, let's admit that the UPS and FedEx drivers who have arrived from faraway places get rather confused. Seriously, one postal code for a region the size of a county? Every one of them has a Stark Road and a Putnam Road and an Allan Road. And roads that share the same name don't touch. Oh, and we love changing road names at town lines. Langford Road goes from Trowbridge to Langford. Trowbridge Road goes from Langford village towards Trowbridge. At the rusty speed limit sign where each town has their truck-turnaround spots, the road name changes. The intersection of Trowbridge Road in Langford and Langford Road in Trowbridge is a straight line. Langford put up a green street sign that reads, "Trowbridge Rd." The importance of the color is that our tree leaves are green. Green signs buried in green trees are not very visible. And nobody expects that a straight road would just up and randomly change names at a rusty speed limit sign. Why read a sign you cannot see and would not even think to look for? Trowbridge reciprocated two years later, putting up a street sign on our side that reads, "Langford Rd." Yay. Everyone is compliant with the new road sign rules.

I admit to still getting confused by the signs. I am not confused by the names or the transition, just the stupid signs.

There was one night early with my time on Trowbridge Rescue. I didn't want to let Alex down. I was pushing hard at three in the morning on a dark night. No moon, nothing. I came to a stone marker with "VT" carved into the granite.

"Shit, I fell into Massachusetts." I did the stinky anxiety sweat thing that I just know Alex Flynn will smell. And my EMS chief is expecting me. I drove faster to find a landmark I knew. Snow, darkness, etc. The lands and the properties became less and less familiar. I turned around. I came back to the granite marker. This time it was marked "MASS."

Know what my problem was? I read a 200-year-old stone road marker. Back then, they put the "VT" on the Vermont side of the stone and "MASS" on the Massachusetts side of the stone. It makes perfect sense if you are walking or on a horse. This side of the stone is in Vermont, therefore it says VT. Why not. It was good enough for the Romans. In fact, it was such a good process that that English brought that advanced tech here. How does the old hymn go? "If it's good enough for the old Romans, it's good enough for me." Maybe?

The Romans never actually invaded Vermont. Yet here is their legacy.

Us modern people, we write "Welcome to Mass" on the Vermont side and "Welcome to Vermont" on the Mass side. You must have seen those big white signs Massachusetts uses each time you cross a town line. It looks like a book unfolding. "WELCOME TO FLORIDA." Yeah, they have one. I guess they ran out of English town names and Algonquin place names. Florida, Massachusetts is an odd place. It is known for a mountain that has a bronze elk standing at an overlook. Florida is a Spanish word for garden. Likely the only Spanish place name in New England. And the elk is equally out of place. We've got moose, deer, bobcat, lynx, mountain lions, and bear but no elk. Just to save you from looking it up, Florida, Massachusetts was incorporated forty years before Florida was accepted into the union—which it promptly left twenty-one years later in rebellion. Florida, Massachusetts sits on a snowy mountain with an ersatz elk and a proud history of not rebelling against the United States government.

I get why someone would name a town Florida. We already have five Manchesters within two hours of each other. And there are at least five Marlboros within that same circle. Marlboro, Vermont; Marlborough, New Hampshire; Marlborough, Massachusetts; Marlborough, Connecticut; and even the former village of Marlboro, Maine. Every New England state seems to have a Lincoln, too. We also love Worcester, Gloucester, Bolton, Boston, and Essex.

We do have a Colrain nearby in Massachusetts. Not super remarkable, a name borrowed from a town in Northern Ireland just up the A37 from Derry/Londonderry. The challenge I face driving through Colrain, Mass, is that they spell the name three different ways. Colerain, Colrain, and Colraine, just to cover all of the bases.

## 4 | A NEW FIRETRUCK

Each of the spellings are historically correct.

My own family is part of the problem. Two brothers or cousins (the historical records disagree about their relationship) hired a ship to sail from Londonderry, Ireland. I just stepped into a political quagmire over Derry and Londonderry. My uncles won't let me continue without correcting my use of the city's name. But I am telling you a story from the 1720s, so back then the name was a bit less problematic. This story only works if you let me say Londonderry, leaving the pedantic corrections to my uncles. In 1720, these ancestors sailed over the Atlantic, landed in New Hampshire and founded a new town. They named it, well, Londonderry. The next generation, feeling cramped and such, moved west across the Connecticut River. They settled a new town. They called it? Yeah, Londonderry. Want to find my ancestor's graves? Go look in a town named Londonderry. Or Manchester because of lot of them migrated to Manchester, too. Just don't ask me which one. I mean, which Manchester? My family likely buried their bones in more than one Manchester. We weren't exclusive about dying in towns that we founded.

That puts me in a rural Vermont town office leafing through property records. I had already done what I could from a computer in our office. But our designated bad buy, Ernie von Shithead, put every property into a separate LLC and registered them with a local registered agent. Super brilliant names. Names intended to confuse and obfuscate his actions. I mean, worse than New England town names and Vermont road signs. 1-2-3 Main Street, LLC owns the properties located at number 1, number 2, and number 3 Main Street in Haworth. These are the three old buildings at the traffic light that oxen dragged up from the valley floor a hundred years ago.

The Vermont Secretary of State has an easy-to-use website. You might think that researching a bunch of LLCs named for properties would make the research difficult. Ernie kept his name off of the public documents. There is Bjorn Frederickson's name stamped on dozens of them. This Viking name proved to be the linker between the LLCs.

If you want to obscure a family name in these hills, pick any

- 55 -

member of the Green Mountain Boys from the Revolution, 1775 through 1783, and you'll find a family still living and breeding in these hills: Allen, Baker, Fay, Lyon, Robinson, Rowley, Warner. Toss in some local war heroes from that time such as John and Molly Stark, or Jeffery Amherst, and you've got the old family names covered. Except for Musgrave. Sorry, Sam. Sam has a little secret hidden deep in her Musgrave lineage.

Bjorn Frederickson stands boldly on paperwork that is filled with Shippee, Hamilton, Smith, Thatcher, and the like.

Now I am doing the search the other way around.

I start with the known addresses and my map, then I identify each abutting property. Then I research the owner's name and family. Like the board game *Risk*, I could measure Eberbach's gradual accumulation of properties. He purchased every property touching the municipal airport. Every purchase under a different LLC name.

Know what that does in Vermont law?

It makes him an abutter to his own property and projects. There is a law in Vermont called Act 250 that gives abutters special rights to object to development projects. They are designated as "interested parties" by the law. They can make demands of the state, and Vermont's environment court. If you are your own abutter and you buy all of the abutting property, then you have eliminated the legal standing of neighbors, to some degree. I rather doubt that EVE Capital Funding, LLC is going to make demands of Trent Valley Holdings, LLC, two LLCs connected to Bjorn Frederickson.

I had already linked either Ernie von Eberbach or Bjorn the Viking to twenty-three company names, LLCs, or limited liability companies. I searched Branston Club, then Branston, then every associated address, then associated zip code, associated town names, and any registered agent associated with a hit on the list.

A pattern appears in these data. A brief list includes:
Branston Club, LLC
Branston Club Real Estate Holding Company
Branston Club Real Estate, LLC
Trent Valley Holdings, LLC

EVE Capital Funding, LLC
Fox Leap Facility Maintenance, LLC
EVE Investment, LLC
Trent Lands, LLC
28 High Street, LLC
1-2-3 Main Street, LLC

If I find a property in the target zone owned by someone named George and Martha Fussbottom, then I expect one of two things. One, Ernie is trying to buy them out. Or two, they already said no. I suppose there is a third option, the complex paperwork option, in which Ernie does a reverse mortgage and acquires the property when they die or totter off to the care homes located near the Connecticut River or west near the New York border. Apparently, we forgot to build care homes here. Which is ok, given there is no hospital here either.

I thumb through each deed. I photograph them, convert them to a PDF, and inventory the owner's names and addresses—which are not always the address of the properties. Then move to the next.

Deep in my rhythm, the clerk returns, announcing that he is closing in fifteen minutes.

I cross against the red light because…traffic happened.

I escape Haworth because I do a right turn on red and happily find myself on Route 1, heading east and uphill towards, well, another Vermont mountain. I turn right before the climb gets steep and drop back to my version of Vermont with dirt roads and dirty pickup trucks and no ski hill.

By supper time, I have taped and tiled standard printer paper to create a large format map on cardboard. During the week, I annotate properties with owners, color coding then drawing boundaries of Eberbach's fake empire.

On Thursday, the *Trent Valley Viewer* informs us of changes to two properties on Main Street. I read the article, then reread it. I hand it to Sarah, saying "Two separate inns undergoing development and zoning board review. The two inns seem to be owned by two different LLCs, but there is only one application and one applicant for both properties. I could not be more confused."

I pick it apart with a pad of paper, scribbling notes:

Two inns but three addresses: Stark House; 25 Main Street; 1, 2, and 3 Main St.

Development Review Board (DRB), hosts a hearing.

One applicant: Branston Club Real Estate Holding Company; Trent Valley, LLC; ET Stark House, LLC. The paper stated that there was one applicant then listed three separate companies. Ah, modern local journalism. Listen, *Trent Valley Viewer*, if I am confused by your facts, then maybe you should dig more. One isn't three and three isn't one. You can't write a sentence that says one applicant and list three companies. That is against the rules. And it confuses me.

Ok, to the newspaper's credit, this badly written nonsense came from the Eberbach publicity engine. Of course, everything on the page related to The Branston Club, and Bjorn Frederickson's name got mentioned a lot. Let's admit that when I was a kid, I got very confused by my grandmother's explanation of the holy trinity: three is one and one is three. *In nomine patris, et filii, et spiritus sancti.* That's another day's worry. I wonder about this guy Ernie. Is he brilliant? Or stupid? Is he strategically inconsistent? Or can't walk a straight line from one thought to another?

Looking at my notes and to Sam, I say slowly, "I count three LLCs, five addresses, one representative. Do you think that Stark House is the same as one of the addresses? Did it say that one of the inns won't serve food but that it is a bar now?" The article just muddled me further.

Please, world, let's promote literacy, especially in journalism. One thing is to distract with razzle-dazzle during a magic trick, a long con, or during a fraud. It is another when you have a few inches of ink in a local newspaper. What is the lead? Local ski area buys and renovates properties in downtown Haworth? Or maybe that isn't the story. All I see is the razzle-dazzle.

Sam responds by reading a line aloud: "Most of the renovations will be interior except changes needed to the exterior to meet fire code…but look, then it goes on to describe a crumbling foundation

## 4 | A NEW FIRETRUCK

and rotted board and handicap access to an ancient building. This just isn't possible." Sam pauses, then continues, "But look, it has the full support of Alec Ballou, the executive director of Discover Trent Valley. Alec even petitioned the Haworth Selectboard asking the board to accept Discover Trent Valley as an interested party to the hearings. I don't know Alec Ballou, do you?"

"Sure, I've heard of the family name. Lots of fingers, lots of pies..."

"This is more razzle-dazzle stuff. Distraction and confusion as a strategy."

"So, what are they hiding?" I ask.

"What are they hiding! Look, the Haworth Fire Chief is angling for something. He's concerned about access to buildings. All of the buildings are standing now and have been for 150 years."

I say, "Not a new concern," then realize, "He wants something."

Ernie von Eberbach is playing *Risk* in Southern Vermont. Got it. And he communicates as if playing *Clue*. There is something there, but I just can't see it yet.

"Eberbach slings the promise of money around, and the fire chief wants his slice."

Haworth is larger than Trowbridge.

Haworth has a traffic light, as established.

Haworth sits at the intersection of an east-west highway and the key north-south highway that bisects Vermont like a zipper down the Appalachians or Green Mountains.

Haworth has a real police car and a few police officers.

Haworth has retail business, several fuel stations, restaurants, inns, BnBs, and paved roads.

Haworth has a town-owned fire station, the fire chief is on the town's payroll, and the fire service is a department within town government.

I should not have to explain the town as if it were new or different or unusual. As a general rule, if a town has a traffic light, it likely employs a few police officers and likely owns at least one police cruiser. And hopefully better than the Vermont State Police's rear-wheel drive sedans. If a town has a cop then they also likely have a fire chief. If they have a fire chief, then they likely own a fire station.

When you remove the traffic light from the equation, the rest of the formula falls apart like Jenga. Ok, Vermont nights get long especially when it starts getting dark at three in the afternoon. Sam and I can make sex last for an hour. That's fun. What are the options during long, dark evenings? Keep going to bed earlier and earlier, chasing the sun? I like sex at five a.m., too. You're all cozy and warm. The juices flow. No cold feet. But eventually, your choices are food, sex, work, TV, and kitchen table games with your tiny family. Vermont is the third snowiest state in the nation and one of the most northern. Alaska tops both of those lists, obviously. You can while away the evenings with TV or table games. Sam and I are flexible. Games, sex, TV are all options. We take them separately or together. It is our house. And it is cold out.

Tiny hill towns like Trowbridge forgot to evolve from the Revolutionary War days two-and-a-half centuries ago. Back then, the local boys grabbed muskets, a small pack, their horse, and a skin of homebrew cider and ran towards trouble. Vermont was invaded by New York once. And we had a lovely war with the French and Indians and Canada where we fought on the side of the British and other Native American tribes. But we used the same model for fighting fires. Once per month, the Starks, Putnams, Allans, Hamiltons, and others shot tree stumps with their lead musket balls, drank more cider, and elected officers.

And that is why Trowbridge Fire is officially named Trowbridge Volunteer Fire Company, Inc. The town government has no legal oversight, and the fire company is not a department of the town government. The fire chief reports to no one except the men of the company who elected him. It is a civic boy's club. The configuration worked acceptably well before workers' compensation, insurance bills, liability claims, and OSHA. In the 1950s, when the fire whistle blew, men dashed to the station to grab what they could. In the 1960s, when the present Trowbridge fire chief joined as a young man, safety gear involved a long coat, tall boots, and a leather helmet. Today, he laments the loss of those days. The only safety gear that he will wear

# 4 | A NEW FIRETRUCK

to a call is his coat and white helmet. He's served the community as chief for over fifty years.

My fire gear, when it was issued, smelled of mold. On the back of the tan coat, reflective letters spelled "P.F.D." a reference to the fire department that deemed this gear too old to use and below legal minimum standards. The name stitched across the bottom is "BROWN." My name is Brighid Doran. My name is not Brown, unless of course if you asked my fire coat. Then I guess I am Brown. The turnout pants were black and my coat was brown. It was the color brown with the family name "BROWN" stitched in reflective letters that had long ago chipped away their own reflectiveness.

The Haworth fire chief, Chief Wegman, is unlike our own local fire chief, Thomas Reed. Chief Reed seeks nothing except donations and the least expensive fire apparatus. Not one truck in our firehouse has been built after 1991. Our chief requires manual transmissions and mechanical water pumps that are fully accessible while lying on the ground. "Oh, I remember back in the winter of..." then pick some year "—we had a helluva fire, but the pump kept freezin' up. So, I'd roll under and tap it with a hammer. I kept that ol' pump runnin' all night long." Chief Reed loves the old days and the old ways.

I believe that Thomas Reed laid at least half of the cement block for the firehouse. Our firehouse has doors that are too short and too narrow for modern fire apparatus. The firehouse's meeting room includes a men's toilet, a dirty kitchen, hand-me-down sofas, and once-plush chairs. The women's toilet has become a storage closet. The toilet water is deep brown with iron staining from the unfiltered water drawn from the station's shallow well. The room smells musty like an old, wet basement. The walls of the fire station have dark patches from the massive farts of diesel smoke ejected from the ass of starting trucks.

Given our fire station is not town owned, it cannot be a town problem. Instead of the safety of the building and volunteers falling within the jurisdiction of the town, the responsibility goes to a tiny nonprofit corporation with no income except donations. Twenty unpaid volunteers, responding to incidents at eight hundred properties scattered over forty square miles, using equipment that has been scrounged from the trash of departments funded by tax dollars. Reed abhors taxes, doesn't want to pay them, won't support collecting them. Legally he can. The chief engineer of a fire district is authorized by Vermont law to hold a district meeting, akin to a town meeting, and raise taxes. In case you are confused by "chief engineer," that was some old-timey phrase for the fire chief. Maybe it was the term the Romans used. Who knows. Who cares. Vermont laws are filled with arcane ideas and language. We still have a law that prohibits dogs from worrying livestock. The modern reader would need to translate that verb "worrying" to mean "harassing" or "injuring." The legislature just struck the law from the books. On the modern tongue, the sentence "my dog worries sheep" fails to convey a comprehensive and clear message. Vermont law and Merriam Webster diverged in a snowy wood long, long ago.

Maybe that is the problem with our local newspaper. They learned their craft with old-timey English. Who knows?

I worry about Ernie von Eberbach.

Ernie von Eberbach worries his neighbors. And like a bad dog in a field of sheep, he harasses and herds his neighbors into his own design. That's English for you. A lot of words borrowed from a lot of other languages and a millennia of misuse.

Sam hates the entire process of volunteer public safety: fire and EMS and even our elected constable. She hates the resulting mess. She hates the complete lack of training. I hate the lack of professional leadership. I hate the complete lack of funding.

On the other hand, Haworth, Vermont decided decades ago to get modern. They pay for a full-time fire chief. They pay for the fire apparatus. They own the fire department buildings. As a result, Chief Wegman of Haworth is a full-time paid town employee. Not bad for a guy already retired from a professional department in Connecticut where the laws required continuous training and certifications. He is the only paid member of that department. Everybody else is an unpaid volunteer. But their turnout gear meets safety standards and has their own name on the coats.

I think they even have modern accountability tags over there in Haworth.

Chief Thomas Reed, when learning that firefighter accountability at a scene was a thing to do, solved the problem his own way. He headed to the farmer's co-op and bought cattle ear tags. Plastic ones. Each firefighter was issued a pair of yellow, tear-drop shaped plastic disks. I am number 79. I am supposed to hand the plastic ear tag to the accountability officer before entering a scene, then I am to wear my "79" plastic ear tag on my fire coat. It might work, if we actually had an accountability officer. And plastic…fire…heat…. you get the picture. Therefore, we skip the cattle ear tag cum accountability tags process. All too modern for Chief Reed.

When the tones announce a call over the regional fire radio network, volunteers put down what they are doing to rush off. The tones are two notes—one high, one low. Each town has its own pair of tones. The tones are then followed by verbal instructions describing the nature of the call and location, as best as it is known.

I receive a text message from Robby Stark.

"Brie, Wegman wants a new ladder truck. But a ladder truck won't fit in their current station from the 1970s, so he's pushing for a new station closer to the condo developments and ski hills."

I thumb a message back to Robby.

The game of *Risk* now includes the local fire department too. Somehow Chief Wegman thinks he can outdo Ernie von Eberbach and get a new modern fire station that meets NFPA, OSHA, VOSHA, and U.S. building codes. And in this bonanza, he can get a new ladder truck thrown in.

Who is playing whom?

Come on, Chief Wegman, don't you see it?

Ernie von Eberbach accidentally snared a new group to victimize with this racket. Standard rural engines and trucks prove to be a mildly effective defense again one- and two-story structure fires. Ski condos tend to go vertical and are made of wood. The increased development will require more apparatus including those that can fight fires in taller buildings. And this will require more training from the firefighters. This will require more firefighters. This will require larger stations. The ski area developments will push fire departments and fire companies towards a professional force, resulting in tax increases on people struggling to keep taxes low. You need a ladder truck to reach up into the five- and six-story condo buildings.

What a surprise, Eberbach promises $5.5 million in additional tax growth. That will be enough to buy a firehouse, new apparatus, new safety gear, to enhance training, and to give Chief Wegman what he needs to increase the quality and value of his department.

Fraudsters fraud.

They just can't help it, can they? Offer to buy the fire department, and you have endeared yourself to every firefighter and EMT in the region. That is a powerful voting bloc.

# 5 | Taxes

A lady near the door hands Sam a clipboard.

"Sign in, please."

Sam neatly writes "Sarah Doran," using my family name. She then hands me the clipboard. I write my own name: "Brighid Doran."

I hear the grumbling deep in Sam's mind. She's thinking that they have no right to require your name and address at a public meeting. It is a public selectboard meeting, part of the public record. Fine, and it does no harm to sign in either. Except Sam lied when she signed in. And why not?

When Sam grumbles in her mind, she doesn't show it. I do. Sam has a trained stoicism. People cannot read her. I know what she is going to say. She's said it before, and she'll say it again when we get into the car. She'll also point out that there is no penalty for lying either. Sam's internal dialog will conclude with, "Are they going to send the police after us?" We don't have this conversation out loud. No need. We've had it before. I know what she is thinking all too well, thank you.

I drag her to the meeting because the Haworth Selectboard stated that they would be discussing the annual property tax rate. In normal Vermont fashion, the members of the selectboard do not introduce themselves, nor do they have nameplates. I didn't know anyone at the selectboard table. At precisely seven p.m., the board starts talking to each other in normal dinner-table voices, voices soft enough that I can't understand them in row five.

Papers shuffle from one member to the next down the table. More mumbling and the papers travel back the other way. Sam refuses to go to selectboard meetings without a strong reason, and I normally fail to find one. I drag her here as part of our investigation into Eberbach.

Now, the guy in the middle of the table reads aloud from a form.

"I've got a report here from the listers stating that the town's grand list has increased from seven thousand, two-hundred and thirty-four properties to seven-thousand, three-hundred and twenty-five properties. Each of the ninety-one properties has an appraised value higher than town's median property value for residential sites." He speaks to the paper, reading each word with precision, whilst not caring if anyone understands him. "The combination of property sales and the prior year's taxes resulted in a surplus of six-hundred and fourteen thousand dollars."

He looks around the room for a response. I think the news was known to most here. The audience doesn't move or speak. The town has surplus cash. Whoo-hoo. Ok, that would be my approach.

The guy continues, "I make a motion that we reduce the tax rate by three and a quarter cents."

The woman next to him mutters, "Second."

The guy looks at the two people at the table dramatically "Any discussion on the motion?" Clearly, the guy wishes to communicate only to the board and not the audience.

The board members remain silent.

"Any public comments?" The guy, I'm guessing the selectboard chair, looks to the audience.

Nobody moves or says anything.

"All those in favor of reducing the property tax rate for this year by three and a quarter cents indicated by saying aye."

Three selectboard members mumble "aye," including the chair.

"Opposed?" The lady at the table head operates the voice recorder and writes notes. She does not speak, nor vote.

"Motion carried unanimously." The chair gently taps the little gavel on the table.

Half of the audience stir in their chairs, shifting to pick up bags. Their noise and movement communicates, "It is time to go." Then they leave. Nearly everyone in the room stands to let these people escape. In the town clerk's office beyond the doorway, I witness several clusters of people whispering to each other. Some leave the building, some stay to chat in the outer room which doubles as the clerk's office. They came to hear the news that their taxes will drop next year.

The board, ignoring the buzz from the next room, continue with their agenda, starting with the town's road department. The road boss wends his way through a report that even the board fails to listen to.

The chair then states, "We'll hear from visitors now before continuing with the agenda."

Sam does groan at this moment, just soft enough for me to hear it and feel her shoulders sag. I look around the room.

The room remains quiet.

We sit through the animal control officer's report about dogs and two escaped pigs.

"Alec, do you have a report?" I saw Discover Trent Valley, a regional economic advocacy group, on the agenda before I begged Sam to come. I am curious about Alec.

Alec Ballou stands, introducing himself for the public record, a courtesy no one else had offered.

"Alec Ballou, executive director Discover Trent Valley. We have some exciting news for the valley. Six local projects have been selected by the governor to share in 2.4 million dollars' worth of tax incentives. We believe that these tax incentives will jumpstart transformation in our community and reward businesses that have brought jobs, businesses, and housing to downtowns and villages. This is a reflection of the ongoing and increasing growth in town. We have many downtown businesses that were purchased and are being renovated now. They are going to open shortly."

Alec speaks with the expectation that people will actually listen to him—unlike the selectboard, or as the rest of America calls the board, "the town council." From that I learn: he thinks himself to be an important man.

"There will be a ceremony in Burlington on Monday hosted by the governor. It is really an amazing opportunity for people here but there is still a lot to do. These approved tax credits show the foresight of those involved in forming the downtown district.

"It shows that long-term planning can really bring resources to the town that would not have otherwise existed. It is nice to have one more tool that will encourage property owners to leap into investing in their building. The 2.4 million invested by the state helps further nearly $78 million worth of projects around the state."

Sam records this on her phone. I take written notes.

Alec continues, "The Stark house is currently under renovation and will become a new hotel. It used to be a tavern and inn that is over one-hundred and fifty years old. The construction costs are nine-hundred and thirty-five thousand, one-hundred and ninety-eight dollars. That project will receive seventy-four thousand, five hundred and twenty-four dollars in tax credits. That project is also getting discounts on materials from local vendors."

I love numbers and yet these numbers wash over me as meaningless. Nice strategy. Big numbers are big. Good.

"The owners of the properties at 1, 2, and 3 Main St have put one million, forty-two hundred thousand and forty-six dollars towards building retail space, a needed coffee bar, and an elevator. The state is providing one-hundred and twenty-five thousand in tax credits to this project.

"The former steak restaurant will be rehabilitated for commercial retail and office use. It has been vacant, as many of these facilities have, for years. The project will cost four-hundred and twelve thousand three hundred and seventy dollars. That project will get seventy-five thousand four hundred and twenty-two dollars in tax credits.

"These properties are owned by several different LLCs based here in Haworth."

You lying fuck. All of the LLCs are owned by one guy, and you know it.

"We are excited that these businesses will provide year-round jobs and greater economic stabilization to the region. Additionally, the new hotel rooms will be subject to the one-percent local option tax revenue."

Alec pauses.

The chair, seeing an opportunity, asks "Do you have a written report?" So, except for what got recorded by the selectboard secretary and on Sam's phone, the good news was a blur of good news, as if the breaking-news crawl at the bottom of the screen zipped by too fast. Good stuff is happening. Good here and good there. And look, we've already reduced your own property tax. Hey, Rocky, watch me pull a rabbit out of my hat.

"Sorry, Jeff, just my notes. I'll be sure to get this to you. I only just learned about the governor's ceremony and the approval of these tax credits. I probably should not even be giving these details publicly yet, but it seems pretty locked-in."

Bullshit.

Alec's statement confirms the name of the selectboard chair: Jeff Rowley. Hey, I know that last name, don't I? Other than he is our state representative, I think. His Xth times grandfather was the "bard of the Green Mountains." His great work goes thus:

> West of the Mountains Green
> Lies Rutland Fair
> The best that ever was seen
> For land and air…
> We value not New York
> With all her Powers
> Here we'll stay and Work
> The land is Ours…
> This is the noble land by conquest won
> Took from a savage band by sword and gun
> We drove them to the west, they could not stand the test

Thomas Rowley wrote that in the 1760s.

Oh, Vermont, you've changed so little over the centuries.

Alec continues to describe two other projects. He stated that "a dilapidated apartment will be rehabilitated to provide housing for local residents." The last property on the list is owned by a housing trust, and that will be converted to provide affordable housing.

"There is a lot of financing built into that project from various state sources," Alec says. "This is just one piece of the puzzle to get the projects done."

The regional economic wizard and self-appointed local hero sits.

Jeff Rowley, the chair, now using a proper outdoor voice, says, "Thank you, Alec, for your hard work on these matters. It has been a long time coming. You and your team have been tireless in your efforts and advocacy for our neighbors." Who is kissing whose whatsit? Seems like mutual smooching to me.

Sam and I slip out of the nearly empty room.

"Eberbach?" I ask in an excited whisper as we walk to my red pickup truck.

"Oh, yeah. Razzle."

"Dazzle."

"I think I need to dig a little on those two: Alec Ballou and Jeff Rowley. They demonstrated some mutual admiration. Ooh lá lá. Oh, give me more big numbers, baby."

"Did you notice his precision with the numbers? Down to the dollar."

"All we were supposed to hear was 'big' and 'number' and 'bigger' and 'number.' I tried keeping a running tally, but lost track of the commas and the thousands." Which likely was the point.

The following morning, I read the *Trent Valley Viewer* online edition. I'm looking at an article written by Brian Stuart. The big banner headline reads: "Haworth Reduces Taxes".

Hey, great headline, Brian.

In the first paragraph, Brian provides context we did not have during the selectboard meeting. He has a quote from the town manager that dampens any excitement over the property tax reduction. The town manager stated that taxes will be going up. "Haworth taxpayers will continue to see increases in their property tax bills. Unfortunately, as every Vermonter knows, the majority of their tax bill goes to the state education fund, which more than offsets the modest reduction in the town rate."

In the second paragraph, the story reverses itself again. The drop in taxes is attributed to the sale of properties at Upton Mountain. The town had previously acquired 650 undeveloped properties at the Upton Mountain development or village. Upton Mountain, as Sam

## 5 | TAXES

and I know, is the former name of The Branston Club property. Therefore Brian Stuart, stalwart reporter, left The Branston Club and Ernie von Eberbach out the article.

Let's observe how the first paragraph and the second paragraph diametrically oppose each other. Fact one in graph one, taxes will go up. Fact two in graph two, taxes went down because the town sold a big chunk of land it never wanted to own anyway.

Reporter Brian then provides a detailed inventory of the tax incentive package, retelling the information we heard during the selectboard meeting. Seeing the numbers written out, I calculate that Eberbach is getting just about nine percent in tax credits on the three million he's announced he is spending on buildings in Haworth Village.

The article starts with a bold headline about tax rates going down, then describes taxes going up, then justifies the reduction in taxes by the sale of hundreds of empty lots. The article then closes with details about hundreds of thousands of dollars in tax credits provided by the state.

Brian Stuart, political reporter for the *Trent Valley Viewer,* does not mention that the tax credits do not go to the town or the town's people. The tax credits offset the taxes for one individual, our guy Ernest von Eberbach. It sure felt like the town was getting tax credits from the State of Vermont.

Brian, you did an amazing job muddling the message. Taxes down, taxes up, taxes down. People watch the bouncing ball bounce. Up and down and so much movement. So, so very much like watching three-card Monte, razzle and dazzle. All accomplished without Eberbach's name in the paper.

Eberbach, the humble. Eberbach, the giver of gold.

"Should we go take some pictures? I am up for it," I ask.

"Of what?"

"Of the numerous projects under construction, right? I am really curious. The paper says that they are under construction right now. Let's see if they are!"

We take Sam's Volvo instead of my fire-red pickup truck. We load in cameras and a tripod into the back, then we drive north towards Haworth. We park in the same spot we used for the selectboard meeting. When in the village, we leave the fancy cameras behind in the car, opting to use our phones.

1, 2, and 3 Main Street shows that someone had removed materials from the interior of the building. The walls are gone. The buildings seem to be empty shells. The ongoing construction appears to be limited to the gutting of an old building. We see no evidence of current work. Click, click, click. We press our phones to the windows for pictures as well. The windows are single-pane with a traditional wavey look of century-old glass. Certainly not modern multi-pane insulated glass.

Number 2 Main Street is called the Professional Building. The cement foundation of Number 2 has full-thickness cracks running vertically from the ground level up to the sill plate. Some of the concrete cracks reveal a block or stone foundation that cannot be more than one hundred years old. An older foundation would be made of stone that is either dry laid or mortared in place. Who cares. It was pulled up a mountainside by a team of oxen. It is possible someone may need to jack up the building to re-do the foundation. Been done before. I'll bet that when this building sat in the valley, the valley now covered by drinking water for Massachusetts residents, it had a strong foundation. Someone cut corners after they moved it.

I struggle to understand how that $1.8 million will fully habilitate all three of these structures to modern code. This second building needs to be lifted and have a new foundation built.

I think we'll all learn that that budget is a lie, or that our friend Ernie will run out of funds to finish. Let me offer this: I'd bet 1.8 million bucks that the town gets this building back in a few years in worse condition than it is now. I don't have $1.8 million to lose. But somebody will lose and somebody else will walk away with that cash. Poof!

There are three buildings on this block.

The next building we investigate in Haworth has a mansard roof that likely dates from the late 19th century. It is three stories tall.

While mansard roofs hint at French influences, the window and door details say classical. In significant need of painting, and with danger signs and obviously rotted wood on the porch, we take pictures from a distance. The ground-floor windows have all been boarded up.

We struggle to find the third building. The third building is a baby sister to the first building we studied. We first identified it as a small garage. It is so small it should not count as a building. Oh well. It is bigger than an outhouse and outhouses are buildings. I guess this little thing counts as a "building" too.

I don't have Duke's experience at estimating costs, so I should ask him.

Together, Sam and I walked through the village along the main road to the Stark House, an impressive three-story building with a Greek Revival façade. This building, unlike the others, looks ready for a Hollywood film set. Put a few rocking chairs on the porch, turn on the lighting, call the scene to "action." You pick the scene. Is it two army buddies saving their commanding general's inn? Or city people running a country inn? We photograph this building from across the street, then follow an alley around back. The front looks significantly better than the back. We did find two pickup trucks and a construction trailer in the back, hinting at the presence of a crew working inside. It will take two guys months and months to burn through the million-dollar budget for the Stark Inn. To earn the tax credit, the million would have to be spent between now and some deadline set by the State of Vermont.

While I understand that spending a million dollars is easy, this inn is not that much larger than the house that Sam inherited from The Aunts. A million dollars would not replace our house. That's the thing about old houses. One rotted sill plate, one boo-boo in the chimney and an ancient, uninsulated basement with a dirt floor and dry-laid stone is only the beginning of costs. Dirt basements with dry-laid stone don't meet modern building code. Lift the building, dig out and pour a modern American foundation, then you can start the rest of the project.

Eberbach announced he will spend three million dollars on three humble buildings in a Southern Vermont village that presently has a few crumble-down places on the main street, ratty apartment buildings from a century ago, boarded-up store fronts, often impossible parking, and the longest traffic jams in the region. During leaf peeper season, summer weekends, and winter holiday weekends, the traffic can back up a mile or more. One mile going back to the east. One mile coming down from the north, and often one mile coming in from the west.

After returning to our car, we drive up to see Duke's timber-frame lodge, the timber-frame lodge made from steel I-Beams. Once there, I set up a tripod to take photos. This helps me stabilize the heavy telephoto lens and helps me frame images taken from wider angles. With the tripod up, I snap pictures of and into any building I can see.

Sam and I approach the construction site with only our phones to take pictures. We see Duke at an improvised table made of scrap plywood. Duke is comfortable in his element.

We wander aimlessly around the bottom of the ski area. Although the grasses remain brown, hints of spring green just peek through. The ski lift equipment seems dated to the 1970s, a bit rusty, a bit old-fashioned. With that observation, I note that ski areas look at their worst at this moment of late spring. Within weeks, grasses will green and colorful wildflowers will pop. Right now, the only plants blooming are the spring ephemerals such as trillium and trout lilies seeking their moment of sunlight before spending the rest of their year trapped below the dark canopy of a New England forest. During these weeks, you feel summer pushing spring out of the way.

We loop back towards the construction site, finishing the circumnavigation of the open terrain at the bottom of the ski hill. We then walk to the car.

My phone buzzes with a text when I sit down next to Sam.

It reads: "I see you."

I reply to Duke: "All good here. Just got nosy and wanted to get out for a bit. Project looks amazing." I then add, "No news yet, still researching."

"Thanks."

"Bye!" I text as I wave my outstretched arm through the open window.

Sam asks, "Duke?"

"Yeah, he wrote: 'I see you.'"

Sam drives through twisty paved roads within The Branston Club housing development. We observe dozens of foundations and homes in various states of construction. Trucks and work trailers are everywhere. "For Sale" signs stand in front of finished homes and nearly finished homes. Where no home exists, the signs read: "Build to Suit." The "For Sale" signs advertise a realtor from New York named Auremweld Properties. I take photos through the passenger side window to augment those that Sam took weeks ago when icy, dirty snow still covered parts of these construction sites.

The sound of saws and hammers and generator motors buzz continuously as we drive.

I ask, "How many of these guys are going to have to sue Eberbach to get paid?"

"And they don't know it yet, do they? Promises of big money. And maybe they'll get something when a lot sells."

Leaving the housing development, we both spot a Haworth police cruiser at the side of the road. The road carries us towards the state highway. From the cruiser's spot, he can see traffic on the highway while remaining out of sight. At the stop sign, Sam stops and mutters, "Uno, dos, tres, vamanos," and with her turn signal on, she turns right onto the two-lane highway. Within a few meters, we both spot the blue lights then hear the burp of the siren. Again, with her turn signal, Sam indicates she is pulling right before she pulls to the shoulder of the road.

Sam is a part-time deputy with the Winchester County Sheriffs. During the early part of her Army career, she served as a military police soldier and officer. With both hands on the wheel and the window down, she looks straight ahead. Her license and the Volvo's registration are pinched between two fingers in her left hand.

The cop steps just to the door but behind Sam's eyeline—in compliance with current training standards.

"Do you know why I pulled you over?"

I have several answers in my head for that stupid question, but like Sam, I face forward with my mouth shut.

"I do not, sir." She knows the rules. Never answer that dumb question. The cop requires probable cause to pull a car over. That is the cop's job, not the driver's, to provide the justification. But cops love letting drivers talk their way into trouble.

"I pulled you over for several reasons. First, we had a report of a stolen Volvo XC90 from the area. Second, you failed to come to a complete stop before entering the highway. Third, you failed to use your turn signal for the right turn. And fourth, when you entered the highway, your turn swung wide, crossing the yellow line."

From my seat, I can see no real yellow line. One may have been painted there last summer, but a winter's worth of road plowing and road sanding abraded the color to a mere hint.

Sam, in her flat tone, says: "I understand your probable cause statement. A vehicle similar to mine was stolen nearby. You've stated that I failed to stop for the stop sign and failed to indicate my turn. My driver's license and registration are in my left hand. With your permission, I will move my left hand to the window so you can take the documents."

From the cop's safe position, he can see hands and shoulders and assess threats. We remain stationary, affirmatively proving that we offer no threat, although there are at least two pistols in this car, including the one on Sam's right hip.

He takes Sam's documents, flipping through them, then he adds, "I'll need your insurance card as well."

Sam says, "I will have to reach into the glove box for that. Will that be a problem?"

"Go ahead."

Sam hands the packet to the officer. He says, "Do you mind removing the paper from the plastic case?" Sam complies as the cop steps forward. Sam keeps her hands high and near the steering wheel. The cop looks at me then says, "Why don't I get your license, too?"

Sam repeats that request: "You are asking for the passenger's

## 5 | TAXES

identification cards. We will comply."

The cop bends down slightly now to see the inside of the Volvo better. I dig out my driver's license then hand it to the cop while reaching across Sam's face. Her hands return to the ten-and-two position on the steering wheel.

The cop does not register the dashboard camera mounted next to the rearview mirror. Either he did not see it or did not understand the importance of the recordings.

After the cop returns to his cruiser, we wait. Sam does not even show impatience. My brain is full of babbling thoughts and words. I don't get pulled over in my red truck. First, it is a local's truck. The cops tend to leave me alone. Second, it has visible emergency lights and a tall whip antenna for my fire/EMS radio. Third, my Trowbridge Fire & Rescue placard is mounted above my front license plate. Fourth, I am your run-of-the-mill Vermont lady driving. I just don't expect to get pulled over. Most of the cops know me and they should know Sam too, given she is a very part-time deputy with the sheriff's department. That's the problem with the cops around here. If the cops continue to pull over foreigners and flatlanders, then the claims of profiling stick to them with super glue. These guys certainly do a fair share of profiling. Granted, they do pop some locals for drunk driving and speeding. But during normal business hours, the cops display a basic human curiosity about foreigners. I think they just want to know, "Who are you? And where are you going?"

Nearly fifteen years ago, Sam and I got pulled over when were still students. We'd been driving her ragtop Jeep down to a cousin's place in central Tennessee. We called my cousin from the courthouse square, parked the Jeep, then laid down on the courthouse lawn. My eyes had been closed for a few minutes when I felt and heard the rush of activity around us.

Two cop cars sped to the Jeep then blocked it in. Their described cars described a V-shape. An unmarked car parked aggressively on our side of the courthouse square. We sat up. Their guns were all drawn, pointing at us. The asshole cop from the unmarked car seemed stereotypical with mirrored aviator sunglasses and a button-down shirt that showed just too much chest hair for my pleasure.

I put my hands up. Sam planted her hands down on the grass.

The cops stood us up and patted us down. The uniform cops rummaged our wallets, then tossed the wallets to the lawn after grabbing our licenses.

"What are y'all doing here?"

"Waiting for my cousin, sir." I tripped over sir. I just don't say that word. Well, I didn't. I've learned to use it with limited comfort after years with Sam. Back then, I never said "sir" to anyone.

"We got a report of a stolen Jeep in the area."

Sam retorted aloud before thinking, "Oh, yeah, with Vermont plates, is that right?"

Fuck.

They cuffed Sam, then plopped her on the ground to sit. I remained standing, then asked: "Do you want me to sit?"

"Yes, over here," a cop motioned. "Sit here and put your hands under yourself. Sit on your hands and don't move."

I ticked through our offenses: northerners; two women traveling together; two women laying on the grass together; foreigners. We heard the message: You are not really welcome here. The cops interviewed us separately, asking me about my travel time on the road, which highways did we take, did we stop for anything, what were we carrying, did we have weapons with us, and on. One cop removed our bags from the Jeep, searching everything thoroughly.

Then it was over.

The event hung sourly over our visit in Tennessee.

That was Tennessee. Today, we are in Haworth, Vermont, one town north of Trowbridge.

Back in Tennessee, Sam was eruptive, untamed, and occasionally uncontrollable. Outgunned, outflanked, outmaneuvered, Sam demonstrated minimally needed patience to let events step through their natural course. We both knew that other people died in this type of situation. Other people got imprisoned in such encounters. She maintained the arrogance that as bad as this was, at least she would, probably, live through it. In the years since our trip to Tennessee,

## 5 | TAXES

she has endured thousands of hours of training and years in conflict zones. She is not the same Sam of our college days.

Here in Vermont, Sam bides her time and her temper. She knows she is in complete control. Like a spider in a web, she is the actual predator in this scenario. I know she wants this asshole cop to present her with tickets for every offense. If this cop chooses to continue…If he decides to write citations for Sam's driving, he'll have to tangle with Sam's evidence. It is an unfair fight. The cop's words will fail when faced with the digital evidence Sam already has. Additionally, she'll require the release of the cruiser's video recordings.

I don't flash back to hundreds of stories of cops arriving to help me at various scenes. I probably should. Instead, I remember the one painful incident from Tennessee when we were students.

During my years with fire and rescue, Vermont State Police troopers have become real people to me. They are men and women with families who live in the area, having stories of their own. We've shared horrors and sadness together at crime scenes, scenes of deep tragedy, scenes of routine sadness, scenes involving stupid decisions going badly for decent people. Those cops are people with names, people I respect. Those cops, I recognize them now by their license plate numbers and radio call signs: 538 and 513. Cops that I can recognize from fifty meters by how they stand, how they walk, and how they carry themselves.

When being hassled, the good memories go and the past injuries return. So, I think of being planted on my ass in Tennessee watching Sam get handcuffed.

Our Haworth, Vermont cop, here in the present, returns with our documents. This time, he stands in front of Sam's door. "You both have hundreds of POI entries in VCIC."

I silently think, yes, we both have been listed as "persons of interest" in the Vermont crime database. That is true.

The cop continues: "I couldn't find any outstanding warrants for either of you."

That's also true. Sam and I know that one becomes a person-of-interest for one of two reasons: first, for being a suspect. Second, for being a witness. The state's computer system doesn't have a category for being rescuer, incident commander, or firefighter. We're all lumped into the "witness/suspect" list for the police's computer system.

The Haworth cop says: "Someone reported a suspicious car at the construction sites and around the ski area."

Now the cop's story changes some. Do two ladies in an expensive Volvo seem like the sort who would be casing construction sites for theft? Probably not. Maybe this guy got a phone call from someone watching the construction sites through his security cameras.

Next time through, I should wave and smile for Ernie and his cameras. I'll wave with a full hand, all fingers upright and correct, by the way. Don't you think otherwise.

Sam remains silent and still. The spider with her web.

If she gets tickets for failure to stop, failure to use a turn signal indicator, and failure to stay right on a highway, she won't complain or negotiate with the cop. She will conclude the transaction with a tense, "Thank you, sir." One of her friends will extract the digital driving history data from the Volvo and she will capture and store the dashcam's audio and video data for the hearing that will be held in the county court.

If she does not get cited, then she has a couple of choices. This is an interaction that she wins, no matter what that cop does. He just doesn't know it yet. He started the fight. He's the only one fighting the fight. Now it is up to him. He gets to decide how to conclude the episode. Unlike two idiot college kids who are miles and miles from home—two idiot college kids with limited resources and limited skills—this poor cop is facing my Sam, my grown-up Sam. I can almost feel sorry for this guy.

The VCIC computer hits should provide this cop a clue. We are either bad guys with unfortunate luck with hundreds of police interactions. Or maybe, we are on the good guy's team.

The silence breaks with the cop saying: "I am going to let you go this time with a verbal warning." He hands Sam our documents. "Keep your speed down and obey the signs, understand?"

"Thank you, sir," Sam offers. She puts the documents in the cup holder then spins the window up with the buttons by her left hand.

She never once indicated she was a deputy or a veteran, so I asked why.

She responds, "He should treat me exactly like anyone else. I need no favors." I think she wanted the fight and the showdown in the county court. She would subpoena the cop's mobile phone records too, striving to ask: who called him the moments before we pulled out of The Branston Club's construction areas? Why would a small-town cop care about two people driving through a construction site in an expensive car? One would assume that this Volvo contained a potential investor or home buyer. Instead, we got pulled over.

We're not like everyone else, are we?

I ask, "Eberbach's identified us, hasn't he?"

"Probably," Sam replies. "But I think he doesn't know much about us yet."

"We're just two busybody ladies like on a British television mystery. Eberbach, he's the big man with the juice."

"That's the message he just delivered, isn't it? 'I am the man with the cops.'"

"Poor little Ernie."

"Poor Ernie," Sam adds.

A guy from Rhode Island buys a neglected and abandoned ski area. He develops a vision plus a marketing plan for the use of the land. This vision includes massive construction and jobs for the region. He invests significant money in the region, single handedly changing the unemployment statistics for the Trent Valley, a valley suffering a century's long slide into depression and economic recession.

Mr. Rhode Island, Ernie von Eberbach, has enough momentum and has invested enough to get photographed with the governor and to get a quarter of a million dollars in tax credits. He promises cash, and growth, and visibility, and opportunity for everyone associated with him.

People love Vermont. Pristine land, tree-lined mountain roads, hiking, scrummy local food at good restaurants with cows mooing outside the window. Crayola-colored autumns, people fly fishing for trout with their Orvis gear. People driving to Ben and Jerry's for ice cream on a summer's day. People carving snow on Burton snowboards. Bread and materials from King Arthur Flour. Pancakes and waffles bathed in Vermont maple syrup. Giant red barns made from wood standing on stone foundations.

This Vermont is a brand people buy and buy happily. Buying Vermont is an investment in goodness, our future, mother nature, and a carbon-neutral life. White woolly sheep with black-and-white cows grazing green pastures.

People from away do not see the challenges Vermonters face. For years, Trowbridge struggled to keep enough kids in the local school. With population declining and retirees moving in, kids are not queuing up for our primary school. Visitors do not see the falling-down houses and the abandoned properties. If they do see a barn with a swayed roof, they view it as charming and part of the landscape, not indicative of underlying economic and social issues.

Bring in money, skiing, a year-round resort promising real jobs and we can see why a selectboard may swoon. I understand why an economic development agency would praise their own actions.

Finally, Southern Vermont will get a little taste of the prosperity that other regions in the nation have enjoyed.

The selectboard has already promised lower local taxes. The magical thing about the one-percent local option tax on hotel rooms and restaurant bills is that out-of-towners pay those bills. We benefit, unless we too eat at local restaurants, then of course we pay the same tax.

Flatlanders won't tolerate the terrible mobile phone reception. That will get better, people say. Flatlanders will want faster internet. We'll benefit too, people say.

And where is the cost? And will the taxes really decrease?

Here's a bit of math the people at town meeting fail to do. The town can collect more taxes by lowering the property tax rate while simultaneously raising the assessed value of properties on the town's grant list. X times Y is Z. If you lower the value of X and increase the value of Y, then Z increases. Reducing the tax rate feels great. Then the listers, the old-timey term for tax assessors, increase the value of your property. Your tax rate is now less, and your property is worth more. You win. Your children win. You are worth more money. Your children's inheritance went up. And, due to the basic properties of math, your tax bill just increased. Don't fall for the headline announcing, "Great news, your tax rate just dropped." Don't go spending that money. It isn't there.

Towns' budgets rarely decrease; therefore, taxes must always adjust upwards.

# 6 | Two Vermonts

Every emotion tangles together in an uncontrolled me. I start picking fights the moment Sam enters into the kitchen on Sunday morning.

I scold Sam for stacking metal bowls on top of each other, expecting them to dry overnight. I have shown and proven to her that metal on metal just doesn't dry. I hand-dry the bowls with a towel then stack the bowls in their drawer. The bowls clang loudly as I slam them into a stack and slam the drawer shut.

I next find fault with the sticky counter that she didn't wash down the night before.

When we sat at breakfast, I manifest enough anger to drop my demerara sugar cube into my cranberry juice glass instead of my teacup. I then spill cranberry juice on the oak breakfast table when I pour a glass.

Sam continues not to respond, nor provoke me any further.

That passivity only pisses me off further: Who can just sit there?

I stomp upstairs. There, next to the door sits Sam's two-week bag. On the back of the closet door hangs her dress uniform. Stupidly, I kick the bag. It doesn't move.

I bury my face in a pillow, steaming at Sam and at the world.

When Sam steps into the room, I lay still. I swing a hand at her when she sits down on the bed next to me. A blind, ineffective swing that she easily catches in her hand. I keep my face firmly planted in the pillow. Sam places my hand next to my hip.

She lays. She places half of her body on mine, crushing one shoulder, half of my back, one arm and one hip. She gently pins me down to the bed, saying nothing. She wraps her right arm around my right shoulder, squeezing me.

We'd both been through this before. Leaving used to be easier.

Or maybe it wasn't, and I forget this slice of hell each time.

Today, I lost my temper. My Sam, Sarah Ann Musgrave, squeezes me. My anger melts into the sheets. As the anger recedes, the remaining emotions form a cocktail of sadness, loneliness, frustration, and now embarrassment. Embarrassment fills the gap vacated by anger.

She has me pinned to the bed. I struggle to move but when I push to roll towards her, she releases her grip.

"I'm sorry, Sarah," I mumble. My damp eyes confirm my message. "I do know you have to go; I just don't want you to go."

She says nothing.

"I like chasing bad guys with you and even being harassed by cops with you. It's all better with you than without you."

Sarah says nothing.

My face sinks into her chest. Tears leak. Sarah holds me tightly again.

I have three gray hairs in the calico-colored mop on my head. Therefore, I should be smart enough to work through her routine departures.

When she departed for her last big trip which promised a year-long tour to Afghanistan, I behaved better than this. She was still full-time active duty then. Unlike today, when she is quote part-time unquote. Maybe I did not actually behave better than this. I certainly tried to behave better than this. I did a better job of not being such a brat in front of others. That was an entirely different kind of departure, too. First, she was able to tell me she was going to Afghanistan. Second, she travelled with her unit which in turn was attached to a larger battalion. The battalion coalesced at a base, trained some, then made a grand show of their overseas departure. I spent a week next to a military base in a hotel room.

On that last day, we all stood in a large gymnasium for saying goodbye; families and soldiers. At the end of Act I, the departing soldiers moved to the back doors and loaded buses. For Act II, families were invited to various events and tours. I didn't go. The real Act II involved our soldiers being transported by buses to another gymnasium where the soldiers laid down their packs. They waited and waited and slept on the floor and waited. When a plane arrived, precisely one planeload of soldiers were transported to the military airport terminal for more waiting. Eventually, soldiers boarded the available plane. The pattern repeated itself until the battalion and all support staff had left the base. Sam described the boarding to me: uniformed air force personnel queued the soldiers. The soldiers put their knives, side arms, and rifles on the conveyor belt. They put their small day packs on the conveyor belt. The weapons and bags were scanned by X-ray as the soldiers stepped through a metal detector arch. After going through the arch, the knives returned to pockets and belts, the sidearm to holsters, and the rifles got slung back on shoulders. In case you question this, the FAA requires bags to be screened with X-ray prior to boarding and passengers to be scanned by metal detectors. The soldiers and airmen complied with that rule before gathering weapons for the ritual of boarding.

Today, Sam is going D.C. for a couple of weeks. Sam will meet with her academic cohort at the National Intelligence University, a school that calls itself NIU but is not Northern Illinois University. Although, like the real NIU, it does have a campus store with mouse pads, luggage tags, phone chargers, flashlights, black quilted potholders, and even oven mitts. I suppose the quilted potholders and oven mitts are for the loving spouse back home. Each item from the NIU campus store carries the NIU logo. For a school that requires top military security clearances from every student, it seems odd that one would use a bag tag that says: "I went to spook school." Nobody would wear, or should wear, a ballcap with the NIU logo. The logo has "NIU" in gold, adorned with their all-seeing eye staring out.

Sam's advancement to colonel requires that she complete a master's degree. Hers is called a Master of Science of Strategic Intelligence. Acceptance to the school and the program requires a TS/SCI clearance, a clearance she has held since her earliest days in the Army. NIU requires candidates be actively engaged as military officers, or senior government officials. Due to the classified nature of the school and the program, Sam can't even do the homework at home. She can't discuss the curricula.

She and I have rules we have always lived with—a lot of rules, and rules that seem passé. I know she must lie to me. She must lie to the U.S. Army. And she lies to others during the performance of her duties. She also knows she should not lie to me—she doesn't want to lie to me, I believe. On the other hand, I cannot lie to her. I totally suck at lying. I can't lie. Therefore, I go with yankee blunt. Screw you if you can't handle it. We've invented ways of communicating that are sufficiently truth adjacent to meet all standards and requirements.

Sometimes I wonder what goes on behind those closed doors, in the SCIF, or her work in the field.

But of course, I know, don't I? She gathers and interprets information the same way we do for our investigations. The government closes and locks the doors to safeguard the technology that they use, the data collected, and the assets around the globe. In my mind, it is all a giant "murder board" with photos and red yarn tracking people and events around the globe. I know that they don't call it a murder board and their satellite images with drone footage are more accurate than online maps. Their cameras are better than our cameras. The public mapping software does me just fine. At home together, we chase fraudsters, not terrorists.

Saying goodbye to my Sarah has not gotten easier with the years.

Sarah continues to hold me while I think about cooking smaller meals, doing my own dishes, eating alone at the table. I'll probably eat my meals with an audiobook playing next to my plate. And like I've done in the past, I eat more meals in front of the television. And no board games and no bed games. No play at all.

I do write more when she is gone. I get podcast episodes recorded and planned out. And I'll spend more time at 911 calls hanging out with the Trowbridge Rescue squad members: Chief Alex Flynn, Harry, Rob, Al, Regina, and the others. I'll go to community meetings and a hearing that would otherwise torture Sam.

Another downside of Sam going to work, anywhere on the globe, is that she can't communicate with her mobile phone. We lose the ability to send cute text messages and call randomly during the day.

The DC area is safe, safer than Iraq and Afghanistan, isn't it? I do not have to worry about her personal safety. But I do.

In two hours from now, Sam will drive down the driveway to the paved country road. She will take a left down the hill towards Massachusetts and the interstate. By suppertime, she will call me from her lodgings.

I roll over. Now to my back. She knows what to do next.

One hundred and twenty minutes later, I do not watch Sam drive down the driveway to the paved country road. I watched her get into her car. I, then, turn my back. Bad luck to watch her disappear behind the shoulder of the hill and disappear from sight. She will take the left down the hill towards Massachusetts, the interstate, and DC. My parting words, offered silently, were: "Have fun stormin' the castle."

Now, the house is empty.

Now, the house is silent.

Now, I am alone on a hilltop in a two-hundred-year-old house in Vermont, sitting on an ancient stone foundation that is forever musty and crawling with critters.

Meanwhile, Sam will attend classes, discussions, and do assignments with a cohort of similarly aged military officers. The selection for the master's degree at NIU, the school Sam and I call "Not Indiana University," means you're on track for promotion. Selection for lieutenant colonel and colonel require a degree like this. The government pays the bill, the travel, the time. In fact, the government owns the university. The government has paid for every bit of Sam's education after her initial semesters.

From the day Sam dropped out of college, which is where we met, she decided to step into a world that would simultaneously revere and desire her skills while threatening her with a discharge for being Sam. The U.S. Government has spent at least a half million dollars training Sam. They paid for her undergraduate degree, training required for her military occupational specialization. They trained her for her career branch within the army. She spent twenty-four weeks in Kansas at ILE, a course taken by captains. Add her medical bills following the Purple Hearts? Let's round the entire bill up to a million dollars. She is a million-dollar soldier; a million-dollar asset.

But we still choose not to socialize with officers in her units, in DC, or when she is around the Pentagon. If we went to dinner together with officers and their spouses, then someone might think that Sam "creates an unacceptable risk to the high standards of morale, good order and discipline, and unit cohesion that are the essence of military capability." All because I am sitting next to Sam at the dinner table.

So, we don't travel as a couple to any military functions. For the big send-offs to lengthy overseas deployments, we fade into the massive crowd of families hugging and kissing.

You may think that the immediate threats of discharge have subsided, but the impact to her advancement exists. Fucking "Don't Ask, Don't Tell." Without continued promotions, she'll get quietly dropped at the curb through the army's up-or-out process. Politicians running for offices still promote the return to policies and laws that discriminate against capable, experienced, dedicated American soldiers. I am on every bit of her paperwork: wills, living power of attorney, medical power of attorney, emergency point of contact, etc. You'll find our marriage license too, in a written ledger book in the Trowbridge town vault. Look at Sam's body, and you will find her wedding ring. When in uniform she ties it around her neck. That ring sits on top of a tattoo shadow of the same ring. Even if the ring disappears as the result of injury or death, my ring will be where we placed it. So instead of going to DC, enjoying dinners out, museums, and playing the role of wife, I remain in Vermont. I remain in Vermont to keep Sam and her career safe during these last promotions.

When I flew to the U.S. Army hospital in Landstuhl, Germany after Sam's leg was blown apart, the staff there treated me with all the courtesy and respect of a spouse. I had the paperwork, but they didn't ask for it and I didn't have to answer. I observed a goodly number of queer soldiers in the medical units while I was there. When stepping through the doors of that facility, I entered a part of the military where the only thing that mattered was a soldier's health and that of the family. No shits were given about the rest.

DC, the Pentagon…that's all a different sort of army. And that's where she's headed today, back into that world. Once in DC, she'll step into the shadowy parallel universe of the American intelligence community.

Me? I walk back into our empty kitchen and our quiet house with nothing to do. Instead of doing anything useful, or important, or necessary, I turn on the television waiting for Sam to call from the other side of her drive. I don't even want the fire tones to make me stir.

On Monday, she'd be in classes. On Monday, I'll get up and face the day, and spend the day in our office, alone.

When I wake from a nap, the sun is still above the horizon, to my regret. The fucking day lingers and fails to end with the needed darkness. The TV is still on. I text Sam: "We should budget time for both a fight and the makeup."

Within a minute, I read: "I always do. XXOO."

On Monday, I enter the office determined to be busy. Sam has cleaned it. Her work stuff is neatly put away. I look through the editions of the local newspapers. I undertake deeper reads into the national newspapers. Try my hand at researching Act 250, again. I do find an Act 250 hearing for The Branston Club scheduled for Wednesday. I find that the Trowbridge Community Club will meet on Tuesday. I have a fire meeting tonight.

Busy nights! Best way to get through Sam's trips.

I am ready for a fire call—maybe a nice little wildland fire. New England, in contrast to western states, prefers to catch fire in the spring after the snows melt. Winter leaves the woods dry—dry leaves on the floor, dry branches ready for a spark. By the time proper summer gets going, the forests tend to be a lot moister: leaves are green; ferns, grasses, berries, and bushes become lush. It would be nice stomping around the woods with my Indian Chief five-gallon nylon spray pump. Maybe a car accident—of course not one with real injuries.

For all the days when I avoid thinking or saying the "Q-word," I am willing to say it today. I don't want quiet. The perversity of the gods thrash every emergency room, every fire station, and every cop shop when a rookie's mouth utters the phrase: "Oh, it seems to be quiet here."

Given the gods tend towards perversity, saying the "Q-word" on purpose likely has no impact. We must live within their love of randomness.

Thinking about the randomness of the deities makes understanding Act 250 more difficult. Reading a few case histories and published decisions explains nearly nothing about the process, only shows me results from around the state of Vermont. Here is this woodshop, which got tagged as a factory, required to have their outside lights off by nine p.m. each evening and their machinery cannot make sound louder than ninety decibels in the evenings after six p.m., after one p.m. on Saturdays, and never on Sundays. As if still trying to reinforce the old-timey "blue laws." The owners appealed, stating that neighbors employ noisy chainsaws, lawn mowers, and motorcycles during those same quiet hours. All of those bits of equipment are louder than ninety decibels. The woodshop owners pleaded that the permit described rules more restrictive than most town zoning plans. The ruling stated that the town's plan did not address noise restrictions in areas zoned as rural residential. The owners identified that the restriction would increase the costs of operating their small shop by either having to soundproof the walls and air filtration system, or by limiting overtime opportunities. The permit further limited parking at the shop to five vehicles and subjected their air filtration system to periodic inspection.

My reading of Act 250 rulings over the decades shows significant variations in how the rules are interpreted and what restrictions get placed on business owners. Joe Woodshop Owner can't have more than five cars on his property for the business, but does that mean he can't have more than five cars in his driveway? No family parties? And why are Sundays different?

The abutters to a winery forced Act 250 rules to require that tours of the facility be done with horse-drawn wagons, a rule nobody else had witnessed. Act 250 thus said that no tractors can be used to pull a wagon filled with visitors through the vines. I struggled to reconcile that contradiction. In Vermont, farming is a by-right activity. Therefore, using a tractor to farm ought to be permitted by right. And here is a winery now subject to the rules of a manufacturer instead of a farm.

Something similar happened in Trowbridge shortly after I arrived.

A family from New York bought a large hillside parcel that, over the centuries, had provided farmland for sheep, then dairy cattle, then horses. By the time this family bought the property, the land had not been grazed well in a decade. The family stated out loud that they would be making a go of a dairy operation based on goats and sheep, primarily to make cheeses. After fencing and rebuilding several sheds, they let the critters graze. Instead of using the original milk parlor, they built new. They invested tons of money in the latest labor-saving milking technology—carousels that rotated the critters around centralized milking stations.

Then, out of sight from the paved road, they built a modern, clean, cheese factory. They did everything right with respect to food safety. Their operation did and will continue to pass various high standards for diary operations. Neighbors observed that milk trucks arrived at the farm late in the day, often full. A full truck sounds different than an empty truck. Full trucks drive differently. They shift through gears differently. The milk trucks left the property empty. This family started making cheese while raising goats and sheep.

They ran into two problems. First, some observed that the critters grazing the fields had not been in the family-way yet. There were no lambs and kids bouncing across the green hill. That indicated that the sheep and goats likely were not yielding milk for cheese. Second, the trucks of milk carried in more milk than the farm would produce with their current flocks.

Abutting neighbors, who also hailed from outside of Vermont, identified that this farm operated a cheese factory. These neighbors who celebrated the sylvan roads, the sway-backed barns, the country lifestyle decided that this farm was subject to Act 250. Why? Because more than fifty percent of their raw materials did not originate from the farm's own operation. The law makes provisions for a small farm that creates finished goods from their own yield. But if they purchase fifty-one percent of their raw materials from other farms, the state of

Vermont calls it a factory. The Act 250 costs stack up as the family, having spent all of their capital on the land and new buildings, now faced legal and regulatory challenges that were never in the budget. With Act 250, they must fund traffic studies, environmental impact studies related to water supplies, water runoff, wastewater management, soil erosion, and the list continues.

I understood little of this history because unless you are subject to Act 250 or decide to use it as a cudgel against your neighbors, you don't understand the law.

Within a few years, that beautiful new dairy fell abandoned, like so many other productive farms around the area.

This family honestly believed that moving to Vermont would improve their fortunes and allow them to expand an idea that they started on a few acres in rural New York. They thought: we've done proof of concept on these cheeses, let's buy a bigger farm in a farming state to sell more cheese. Here's a lovely farm store near the road selling cheeses and other dairy products. Here's a lovely farm tour of our modern milking shed. Here is our social media history telling you of our products and reverence for old-world craftsmanship. Here is our little cheese making area. Here is our cheese cave that we've dug into the side of an ancient hill. We're the von Trapps of cheese people. Come to Vermont for the cheese.

Actually, Vermont is known for great cheese.

Too bad. White woolly sheep and goats will not be grazing that hill any time soon. Just another abandoned New England pasture. Aspens will move in, then white birch. The expensive wire fencing shall rust away. A century from now, people will still find bits of wire fence tangled with stone and stick.

Act 250 news articles, stories, past permits, and reading of the law filled my Monday work hours. I skip the midday walk. I just don't want to walk alone. The lunch salad seems a shaggy affair with browning lettuce and mildly frozen cucumber.

I arrive at the fire meeting ten minutes before seven p.m. The unspoken agreement is that the guys socialize for a while before the meeting. Several of the guys gather at six thirty or even earlier. I am still learning the rules that these men learned from their earliest age, and I may still have them wrong.

First, no real greetings are needed. Enter, take a seat. Make some eye contact with guys who look over at you. Maybe nod, or just keep eye contact for a second. That's "hello." No handshaking, no hugging. No names.

Second, listen to the current conversation before starting one. Unless there is an urgency or a sidebar that was previously agreed to. If a discussion with someone was previously arranged, then you two may sit next to each other and whisper.

Third, conversational rules. No direct questions about health, activities, or family, unless something significant has happened that is known to most of the guys in the room. It is ok to ask about a recent mishap, expected baby, or upcoming major event. You ought to avoid chat that is too private or confidential. Safe topics: roads—road construction, road repair, road names; weather—too much moisture, too little moisture, state of hay crops, upcoming storms, recent storms; recent 911 calls—always a favorite, and relatively safe—engines, cars, trucks, and tractors. All of these are safe and popular topics. Funny stories of tourists, out-of-towners, lost people—likewise winners.

If discussing oneself or one's own family. You're always "fine." With the worst of all possible situations, you may answer with "it's getting better." Be proper in your yankee stoicism. You are fine and you better be fine with being fine even if you are not fine.

In most years, Trowbridge sheds itself of several fingers. To be fair, about five fingers in ten years is an average. A story about a building crushing your thumb is acceptable but the story is best if funny and you drive yourself to the hospital. A bit of a tag line such as, "I had my grandson shift the truck for me," does well. You may want to ask: "Why didn't the grandson drive?" but most know he's only eleven. Then the room anticipates the required punchline that must follow: "Oh, he can't see over the wheel yet." Or, "I got in trouble last time he drove the truck." Or, "He can't reach the clutch and steer very well." I observed that, during the year, no one who lost a digit calls for the ambulance or dials 911.

If one of the firefighters whacks their own foot with a splitting mall, these guys would offer to call a tow truck for the toe.

At seven p.m., Thomas Reed opens the meeting: "Ok, let's get started." He leans on the one real desk in the room. His lifelong friend, Jonas Allan, takes notes. Jonas is also a selectboard member—I mean "selectman." Chief Reed reads the financial report into the minutes. Accounting is still being done in handwriting on large green ledger sheets. Chief Reed reads a summary from a torn envelope. He itemizes the heating oil bill, contributions received, and cash in the bank. Within minutes, the discussion pivots to a recent call.

The men never reproach one another. The men are gentle. They are kind to one another. They gently ask if a better way may have been available. Yes, we probably should have kept someone near the truck to communicate with dispatch. Yes, maybe we should have setup the water supply at the stream instead of heading straight to the scene.

The conversation relating to meeting topics and emergency calls blends back into the pre-meeting socializing rhythm. Some men will talk quietly one-on-one or in a small group of three. By half-past seven, the business of the meeting draws to a close.

Al stands, saying: "I need to get home for supper. I make a motion we adjourn."

A quick "second" is heard then perfunctory "ayes" fills the room. Then some leave. Others only stand to change groups that they are talking with. I find myself next to Harry at this point. I would hug him, but this is not a hugging crowd and the time for hellos is long over. Conversations continue, men leave, groups reshuffle. The cycle continues until the last one leaving the fire station turns out the lights.

I shuffled around the room asking the others about Ernie von Eberbach. None of them had firsthand experiences. "Oh, I've heard of him. He doesn't pay his bills."

"Let's hope I never get stuck on one of his jobs."

One lonely day-and-night solved.

Lather, rinse, repeat, only this time with the female side of the town leader crew. On Tuesday evening, I attend the Community

Club meeting. Chief Reed's wife runs this group. These meetings are symmetrical. Like the fire meeting, the women arrive early.

Arriving early is a Trowbridge thing. If you invite people for an event at the house, people will arrive thirty, fifteen, and even ten minutes early. They've come to help. They've come early to make sure you don't think that they will be late. They've come early out of respect. Nothing is worse than being late or an overdone roast. This century-old practice predates the modern expression: FOMO—fear of missing out. The early people will set the table for you, fill water glasses, prepare the wine, and expect to help you host the event. Likely, they will stay late to fill the dishwasher and help clear the table with you or for you. "I hope you don't mind, I brought a pot of soup. I thought I'd warm it on your stove before supper." Then you'd best stand aside. Arriving early means a private word on a topic that may not otherwise come up.

Per local custom, I arrive early for the Community Club meeting at the Community Hall, a hundred and fifty-year-old building in the village. Topics for the current year's meetings include community suppers, fundraising events for the town's warrior honor roll, and building upkeep. And the Old Home Days gathering we are planning for next summer. These families reside at the civic core of Trowbridge. At the Community Club meeting, socializing includes talking about people, especially the elderly and those needing care. You can gender-swap the acceptable topics. Remove trucks, engines, and tractors for gender-normative, supposedly feminine topics, and the meetings would be similar. There is also a basic, unwritten understanding that the Community Club turns out for larger fires, bringing food and water to the firemen, as we are still called in Trowbridge. The term firefighter has not yet caught on. But of course, we still have selectmen and "men working" signs to identify where the town boys are working on the roads. Don't ask me why the town road crew are "town boys" during the day but "firemen" when at a scene or at a fire hall.

If Sarah were home, I would be less eager to plod off to community meetings. Soft spoken and kindly intended folks make a poor substitute for a night watching TV with my feet under a blanket shared with Sam. "Stop fidgeting." She called me that for a week back in college, "Fidget Brighid." Back then I thought I was just nervous about asking a woman out and going to dinner with Sarah. I kinda do fidget anyway.

 Sam's not home and off to meetings I go.

 I don't care a fig for Old Home Days and the monthly dinners. I do my bit and show for work bees as expected. I have my own agenda. The Community Club plans to update and rebuild the town's honor roll. It hasn't been updated since the Korean War. I care deeply about honoring our veterans and acknowledging their sacrifice. Seems an obvious mission for me, given my wife is missing one third of her calf and has a tiny scar on her chest where a medic reinflated her lung after an explosion.

 I expect to see Sarah Ann Musgrave listed on the honor roll for Trowbridge, a town where she and her family have been since nearly the founding of the nation. She's earned the spot.

 Wednesday, during business hours, I pack myself off to the Act 250 hearing in Haworth. Adversarial tensions exist in the room, palpable from the doorway. I listen, take notes, assess people, and recognize that these people fail to identify the core topics at hand. I am missing context. Like walking into a Trowbridge fire meeting, you just don't know that most of those men have family trees that touch. And even if their trees' branches don't connect at a cousin, uncle, or in-law to an in-law, these men of Trowbridge fire grew up together. Even as an incomer to Trowbridge, I know two and three generations of most of the men at the meetings. I am required to know the biographic data for those who died young and before my time here. I ought to know the rivalries and feuds. The context of a Trowbridge fire meeting involves nearly a century of families, a century of stories, a century of trucks, a century of memorable events. It took me years to see the threads that connect this community.

 At the Act 250 meeting, I acknowledge unknown history, unknown problems, unknown events, and yet unknown transgressions. This is not Trowbridge. I don't know the players and the background like they do a few miles south. Some players in this room represent

"The State." Some players represent the "Winchester Regional Commission." Some players represent "The Branston Club."

The Winchester Regional Commission argues that they are unable to review the master plan for the development at The Branston Club. The Regional Commission claims that the projects have been submitted in a piecemeal fashion. The Regional Commission observed that project applications often arrive after construction has started. This team, the Regional Commission, had recently submitted a letter to The State. At The State table sits the District Environmental Commission and the Natural Resources Board. On the left sit the representatives of The Branston Club. My guy, Ernie von Eberbach, sent his lawyer Frank Jager. Ernie is not present for this hearing.

I follow the action in the hearing using sporting terminology. I understand that this isn't a classic sporting event. On a soccer pitch, there are two sets of combatants and the referees. In this hearing, there are three combatants refereed by some sort of a judge. I almost understand what I am looking at. This doesn't look like a *Law and Order* episode to me. To make it worse, there is no program book that links players with their teams and their roles on the field.

As self-appointed score keeper, I give three points to the Regional Commission. They drive home the need for a master plan, as detailed in the recent letter. The Regional Commission states that the plan must identify all current and planned projects. That seems like the definition of a master plan. Goal. One point. The Regional Commission scores again while identifying that some projects started without permits. Goal. Two—nil. The third shot on goal comes when the Regional Commission identifies that The Branston Club constructed a corridor for power through a forest, a forested wetland, and a wetland buffer zone, in violation of state law. Goal. Three—nil.

Watching six-year-old children play soccer is more enjoyable. Silently yelling "gooooaaal" in my head prevented me from being bored out of my gourd.

The next point goes to The Branston Club. They show that activities and plans existed in the approved plan. It takes me a while to catch up with the state of play because in the short stack of documents I have, the Regional Commission is spot on. Then, in a legal twist, The Branston Club shows that they operate within the structure of a plan approved in the 1970s for the original Upton Mountain Development—the development that lay abandoned for decades. In buying that land and development, The Branston Club team argues, they bought the existing approvals. It isn't the Club's fault that a forty-year-old plan approved in the early days of Act 250 lacked the details and sophistication of its modern counterparts.

Sounds like a wimpy goal, like the ball slowly rolled in the net. The room looked around with a unified "huh, how did that happen?" And no, I did not pull the 1970s documents from the original property development plan at Upton Mountain, The Branston Club's former name. I had no idea that the 1970s version of these documents were still relevant.

Score: three to one.

Now the soccer analogy falls apart because instead of two teams and two nets, there are three. Sort of like the American game we call Chinese Checkers. In comes The State looking to score points.

The State team demonstrates that a dock and a beach that was not on the plan also got built too close to the emergency spillway for the snowmaking pond. Is that one point or two? I am awarding two points to The State. Now, the scoreboard reads: Regional Commission with three points. The Branston Club with two points. And The State has earned two points as well.

Then The State advances to tie with the lead. The State team shows that the wellhouse was built ninety percent larger than the approved plans. That landed hard in the back of the net. Goooaaaal!

Unlike the gentle manners of the firemen of Trowbridge, these guys swing hard with punches expecting to cause damage.

Thankfully, my fire pager pulls me from the room. My pager and radio bring the room to complete silence. Every single person there knows the sound and shuts up so I can hear the details of the call. Even the lawyer shuts up mid-sentence. That's a rural Vermonter for you. Even a loudmouth lawyer who will bark and argue through numerous bangs of a judge's gavel shuts his mouth when a fire and

EMS pager go off. It could be his house, his family, his cousin, or his neighbor. Everyone wants to know, and everyone wants us to get it right. The lawyer, still standing, watches me.

I lift my arm and wave, communicating: "I'm it" and "thank you for the quiet" and "see ya." Then off to my red pickup truck.

I am third to the scene.

Driving from Haworth to Trowbridge with my red-and-white emergency lights, I think about Sam's experience in Afghanistan. She talks about the tribal lands and tribal borders of Afghanistan. I am learning to substitute local family names for the various tribes. Incomers earn their own spot in tribal politics depending on where they come from.

Incomers rarely see this Vermont, unless they get snared in the Act 250 net by deciding to open a business.

This is not the Ben & Jerry's Vermont, the Cabot Cheese Vermont, the Currier and Ives Vermont. Most days, we are just trying to take care of business, earn a few dollars, and respond to the everyday crises of people here in our hills.

# 7 | Sam's Journal—Leftovers

Sarah knows I do this. Furthermore, she has given me permission. Even in a good marriage, a marriage filled with love, I feel shame when I open her journals.

We all know that Sarah, my Sam, is not a verbose and gregarious person. It doesn't mean that she is cold or distant. But like Sister Owl, she embodies stealth. That she loves me for me amazes and delights me. My nature is more corvid-like than raptor-like. I squawk and clatter like a raven or a blue jay. You know if I am pissed, happy, feeding, watching, or playing. You can look all day in a forest and never spot an owl. You can't step into our backyard without the blue jays and ravens offering commentary. That's me. Curious, noisy, emotive, and visible.

And there's Sam, so still she becomes invisible, folding light and sound around her like a physics thought experiment.

Therefore, I open her journals. And before you think her journaling resembles what I did as a youngster, it doesn't. Until college, I was more, "Dinner was pork chops. I hate my mother's overly dry pork chops." And "Stevie tried flirting with me today. I just don't get why he makes my friends' knees wobble and mine just don't. Something is wrong with me." The loopy-formed letters and little affected heart-dots disappeared from my writing within a month of them appearing. So did the red and pink ink. I told my diary I tried. I don't reread my diaries. They are too embarrassing to look at.

Sarah's journals…they serve as explainers of her to me. She does talk with me. And I do know most of the stories, at least a bit.

I regret that I focus on the times when she is going, gone, there, then returning. But that is the life of an American soldier right now: going, gone, there, returning. Repeat. Her home time seems like skinny minutes between ramping down from a deployment, recovering, then ramping up for the next show. She leaves her digital journals on an encrypted server of ours. She types in Times New Roman, single spaced, as if each entry were a classroom essay assignment.

I sit upright in our bed. Her pillow remains at strict attention, toes on the line, back erect. Sam's picture is on her side table. Whilst I love looking at her in her dress uniforms, this photo is a candid shot of her throwing leaves. Her arms are above her head like a "Y." Her smile radiates. And her right calf doesn't have a half kilo of flesh missing. This young Sam has no scars while she plays in white shorts and a goofy t-shirt.

I read my Sarah's words to myself…After that, a little cry. No doubt, I'll wake tomorrow laying diagonally across our shared, but empty, bed. My head will be on her pillow and my chilly feet will be on my side of the bed.

Sam wrote this entry in early January of 2006 during her second deployment to Iraq.

> My young brain hosted competing thoughts about war. At once, war seems a stupid affair, conducted by stupid people, doing stupid things, for stupid reasons. Within the instant, I understood that I would endeavor to make the process better, more effective, safer for everyone. Me, Sarah Ann Musgrave, will transform the United States Army.
> 
> Instead, we transformed each other.
> 
> I did not know, upon enlisting in 2001, that the army already coined the term "transformation" with new meaning, linking it with impenetrable jargon. Frankly, no one defined their concept of "transformation" to me as a young, enlisted soldier. I had to learn that the army is the army. The army is always the army. What did I know of division numbers, brigade formations, and inventories of military assets? Nothing. My first job on that first day involved placing my left foot on the yellow painted left foot then placing my right foot on yellow painted right foot. My second job required that I learn how to get yelled at by men yelling loudly. The entire army,

## 7 | SAM'S JOURNAL

*the history of the army, the body and soul of the army becomes embodied by the drill instructors who rule your hours from waking to sleep—then even into our sleep.*

*I joined an army that had just announced plans for transforming itself to meet the demands of the modern world. Within a year or two of their plans and announcements, the army found itself fighting in distant wars. In one war, U.S. soldiers rode donkeys across faraway mountains. Me thinks that the Army crystal ball misguided the boffins responsible for developing long range visions. Donkeys and combat warriors? Seems retrograde instead of transformational.*

*I ought not be too critical about the army's failed planning. Private Sarah Ann Musgrave, me, found herself deep in an organization discovering that the challenges of the future had already occurred. To a kid who rarely heard "Sarah Ann" from teachers, friends, family, and others, I suddenly heard it daily. From growing up in a community that let me be my own version of Sam, I enlisted in an army that defined me as a female soldier, living in female barracks, and in a female company. As a kid, when picking sides for games, I got picked early and for the winning team. Just me: Sam. For the first time, I got placed on the girls' team. While that ought not be transformational, I admit I failed to anticipate the plot twist of being put on the girls' team. Welcome to the United States Army.*

*The U.S. Army and I would be exploring these new challenges together.*

*In the decades prior to my enlistment, in the 1980s and 90s, our Army stood facing familiar enemies with paved road connecting the potential battlefields. Our mythology, captured in war movies, took place in cold, wet fields of Europe, dry, hilly terrain around the Mediterranean Sea, or the wet jungles of the Pacific Rim. With World War II and the related lingering Cold War finally over, the U.S. Army asked itself: "What's next?"*

During my first year of university, I asked the same question of myself: "What's next?" I looked across the globe thinking there is something different out there. Like spotting a shark fin near a Cape Cod beach, I did not ask, "Was that real?" It's a flash of gray in gray water. No real opportunity for second chances on that decision. I did not doubt myself. During the fall semester, suicide bombers attacked the U.S.S. Cole. I felt the ripple, then again asked: "What's next?" After the Cole bombing, I enrolled in Arabic classes for the spring 2001 semester. In March of 2001, I again heard and felt the echoing impact that resulted from the destruction of the Buddhas of Bamiyan in Afghanistan. After that latest bombing, I enlisted. During my three semesters at university, I found myself asking: "Who else is seeing this?" I asked: "What is going on out there?" University was the wrong place for me.

 I joined an army that had already decided to transform itself with or without me. In 2000, the Army appropriated the phrase "transformational" to mean: lighter, more survivable, more lethal, and a fully digitized force readying for the information age. I enlisted months prior to September 11, 2001. At nineteen years of age, I stepped off a bus, dropped my bag, put my feet on the yellow marks as instructed.

 In 2003, I flew into a theater of combat operations for the first time. The night before departure, I wrote The Letter. Every soldier writes this letter: either on paper or in their head. My letter was my letter. My letter discussed my fears of incapacity resulting from injury, my fears of failure, my fears of fear. I feared poverty resulting from injury. I feared the yet-unknown syndrome of this new war. I dreaded being discarded by society to limp or wheel between vet shelters and the street. We're asking soldiers to give—give their lives, give their youth, give up their families, give up nearly everything. The night before flying into Iraq, I could not fathom the other side of the contract equation. We'll return seeking jobs, opportunity, and health services through the VA. I envisioned three models of combat veterans: the lost men on the streets of Cambridge and Boston who wear reminders of their time in Vietnam, the old men who survived World War II, and the invisible set of individuals who lived normal civilian lives. I failed to see myself as a member of any of these three groups. Flying into a combat zone, I projected my thoughts into the unknown future.

These thoughts possess magic. You can have them exactly once. You'll never go into a combat zone for the first time, again. These thoughts can only be visited in memory. It is never your first time again. That's the magic. That's why capturing them, capturing the fears and hopes, is so important. You can never write the "Night before First Combat" letter again. After the first time entering a combat zone, you've already had the thoughts and you've already written this letter.

From that first time, you will always be able to finish this sentence: "The last time I did this…"

"The last time I did this, we lost a month's worth of combat pay because we left at five past midnight on the first day of the month."

"The last time I did this, we stopped in Shannon, Ireland to refuel and have a real beer."

"The last time I did this, I baked in the Kuwaiti heat for weeks before going into Iraq."

"The last time I flew in with a unit like this, I got medevacked to Germany with my left leg half blown off."

As a twenty-year-old three-stripe sergeant, I flew towards Iraq for the first time. In 2003, I did not really know why I was going to Iraq. I sat on an airplane with my rifle between my feet, barrel pointing forward. An orange plastic tag inserted in the barrel provided visual evidence that the weapon was unloaded. At that point, less than fifty percent of the U.S. Army had deployed into our two simultaneous wars. I'd spent weeks in gymnasiums doing paperwork and getting shots. I'd spent time shuffling through warehouses being issued equipment in a daze after having completed PLDC, the leadership development course for sergeants.

Leadership courses in the Army coincide with promotion into leadership roles. The young three-stripe sergeant learns that he or she is the backbone of the army; learns that he or she is a non-commissioned officer. For each significant promotion, there exists a course, a cadre, a class, and a graduation.

I learned asymmetrical warfare as a kid in Lincoln, Concord, and Lexington, Mass fighting against the imaginary and dreaded Red Coats, the British soldier of the day. We'd play games in the woods and in the fields. You could not catch us kids in those woods and on our trails. We disappeared into the landscape. This seven-year-old could wipe out a column of red-coated soldiers who marched in neat orderly lines. Those British soldiers and their Hessian mercenaries expected to fight on the plains of cold, wet Europe. The Red Coats were taught to control the high ground, move with purpose, and smash one massive force against another. One of my childhood friends, Daniel Tuttle, lived three houses down from me. His father worked at Harvard. Danny moved here from Oklahoma, one of the rare kids that was not born in a local hospital. Danny's family walked the Trail of Tears from North Carolina to Oklahoma. He opined about our mock battles and our approach to them. We learned and listened. We practiced the rhythm of shoot, run, load, hide, and attack again along the same road.

My mother hated the games we played in the woods that surrounded that mustard-colored house. So, I lied to her. The beginning of a long future of lying to my mother, and others.

Most don't get my humor—too dry, too cerebral. Furthermore, I just don't smile enough for people to think that I am funny. The UCMJ prohibits me from criticizing the civilian leadership of the army, but it can't prevent me from thinking that Secretary Rumsfeld's logic fails us all. I cannot call our leadership idiots. Yet, I can think it. I can try to tell a funny story that no one ever finds funny.

Eight decades ago, during World War II, the British government had captured nearly all of the German spies and their radio transmitters. We turned their spies against them. Under allied supervision, these German spies transmitted real information back to Germany, feeding mostly accurate information to their government. This Allied effort improve the efficacy and surprise of the D-Day invasion of Normandy in June of 1944.

Verification, validation, accuracy, and reliability all factor into intelligence reporting. General Patton commanded the First United States Army Group during 1944, a unit comprised of Hollywood special effects teams, inflatable tanks, and fake radio transmissions. Allied command presented information supported by aerial photography (now called geospatial intelligence), radio traffic (now called signals intelligence– SIGINT), and spies on the ground (human intelligence—HUMINT). If a command gets information that tells a consistent story from a variety of sources, command believes the story to be validated and accurate. If people who have reported accurately in the past provide supporting data, then the reliability score increases. This is our game. We either help verify information or find new data. We strive to provide information that proves accurate and reliable.

The Nazi leadership heard consistent stories of Patton's army staging for an invasion at Pas-de-Calais. Human intelligence corroborated the signals intelligence. The grainy black-and-white aerial photography supported those stories. And of course, according to the Germans, Patton would naturally be selected to lead the invasion force. The Germans believe he was the best leader that the Allies had. The impact of our successful and unified intelligence campaign resulted in an observable benefit in June of 1944.

When I first got read into my TS/SCI clearance in 2003 as that young sergeant, I was briefed on a project with a specific code word. I signed papers. The army provided me a list of nations I can never enter because I possessed this information. The de facto contract, they informed me, lasts a lifetime. I need the small colored square on my identity badge so that I can enter intelligence fusion centers. I'd been in the army for three years. I am now standing in a palace once belonging to Saddam Hussain hearing this information and signing these documents. I crossed a threshold.

Years later, watching a movie with B in our Vermont living room, I heard a phrase that alerted me like a dog whistle. I paused the movie: "That's something I was never supposed to mention to anyone, ever." B then opened a related Wikipedia page and read to me. She told me more about that specific project than I ever knew. Frankly, never once in my years working with intelligence did that original project and code name ever appear again in my daily work. It was a gateway project to the land of secrets that lay beyond. That codeword was my looking glass. I stepped through into an odd universe. Regardless, I had sworn to keep that secret secret––now detailed in Wikipedia.

In 2003, flying into Kuwait with my unloaded rifle between my feet, I imagined CNN footage and old movie footage as we flew across the Atlantic. I wrote the night-before letter silently, in my head. We stepped from the plane in the dark. A staff sergeant said aloud: "The last time I was here, it smelled exactly the same. Burning petroleum and heat." I breathed in the stink. We boarded waiting buses. A U.S. Air Force sergeant stood at the front of the bus giving a briefing she'd given hundreds of times. "You'll be transported through the city to an undisclosed location in the desert near the Iraqi border. You must keep window curtains drawn at all times during the trip." The older staff sergeant I sat next to put on a headset, then turned on his Apple iPod. He looked at me: "The trip is exactly as long as Pink Floyd's The Wall." I rephrased his statement: "The last time I did this, I listened to the whole Pink Floyd The Wall album."

At the undisclosed location, which was known well to several of these soldiers, the bus stopped at a row of massive white tents. A sergeant stepped on and yelled: "All enlisted and junior NCO males, off here."

The bus advanced. The NCO yelled: "Senior NCO, company grade officers, male."

I got off at the next stop following the call: "Female enlisted and junior NCOs." As a young sergeant, I was a junior NCO. The bus went around the camp. I watched it near the gate which is when the bus turned around. It drove back to our section. Three female majors and a female master sergeant stepped off the bus with their bags.

In the resulting confusion, we learned that insufficient provisions had been made for "field grade female and senior NCOs." This group of four women had ridden around the camp then back to the gate before making the observation that no one called for "female field grade and female senior NCOs." As if the army said, "You don't exist." These four women joined us outside of our designated tent. I had remained outside because every one of the sixty bunks in our sixty-man tent for female enlisted and junior NCOs was already occupied. There was no room for us. Now, we made thirteen women standing together outside of a full tent. We placed our small day packs and larger rucksacks at our feet.

A young blonde major trotted off seeking assistance.

And a male first sergeant came to our group yelling—before looking. "Get into your tent, grab a rack." The female master sergeant responded: "Sar'n't, there isn't any room. All cots are occupied." She quit the sentence there. Clearly, our group of female soldiers were not expected. We were the leftovers.

Within two days, there were ninety women in our sixty-man tent including six field grade officers and several E-9s, senior NCOs. The leftovers, the forgotten soldiers, got packed in together. Soldiers slept in a row head to toe down the center aisle.

On the third day, the nightly inspections stopped abruptly. Three nights of conflict between male NCOs supposedly in charge of the quartering of the young female soldiers faced off against the reality of being outranked by women living in the tent. Each evening at 2100 hours, four men came to the door yelling that men would be entering. Time for bed check and inspection. The sergeants expected the soldiers to rise and stand at the foot of their bed assuming the army's at-rest position. The field grade officers refused to budge for the first two nights, remaining on their cots watching DVDs, listening to music, and reading. Because you know who cannot force a major out of bed to stand at attention? A sergeant first class. The female master sergeants, E-9s, stood like recruits at the foot of their racks being inspected by NCOs with half their experience. The master sergeants had to support their fellow NCOs, but with eighteen or twenty years in the army, the senior NCOs resented the imposition. On the third night, the blonde major informed the entire tent that this was officer's country then ordered the males out of the tent. She stepped forward: "Get out!" With her finger pointing towards the door like a stage actor, she repeated herself, "Get out now, this is officer's country, and you have no right to inspect my quarters."

The major was not defending me, or any other woman in the tent, from the intrusion. She decided she needed a new place to call home. In army-speak, she communicated: If you want to inspect this tent of ninety young women each night at bedtime, then you will be required to find me quarters suitable for my rank.

Never once in 2003 did I think that I would return to that

camp in Kuwait. Of course, I was wrong.

I did not know that my chosen army career would run concurrent with two wars.

For years, the army and the people who planned the Army's transformation from its Cold War posture to the nimbler force that integrated technology onto the battlefield failed to anticipate the realities of the twenty-first century battlefield and the twenty-first century soldier. This is not your grand-dad's army with rows and rows of white men.

When I placed my two sneakers on those two yellow footprints at bootcamp, I understood and accepted my own commitment to transform as the army needed me to. I knew that I had joined an army which was committed to destroying me. Either on the battlefield as a casualty of endless wars; or socially/economically through a series of laws that discriminated against gays and lesbians. Put your sneakers on the yellow feet, then pull up a cloak of disguise for your entire career, for your entire life, for every aspect of your life.

I spoke the words of the Soldier's Creed. I honored and believed the words of the Soldier's Creed. It begins:

"I am an American Soldier.

I am a warrior and a member of a team.

I serve the people of the United States and live the Army Values.

I will always place the mission first…"

I then committed and continued to commit to being a guardian of freedom and the American way of life. Even while speaking these words over the years, irony rang through the sentiments. For decades, the United States Government systematically discriminated against people like me for being people like me.

Before leaving university, I agonized about this decision. I read history and laws. In 1953, Eisenhower signed Executive Order 10450. Decades of discrimination have existed and does still exist as the continuing result of the Lavender

Scare. Progress seemed slow. In 1975, the Civil Service Commission ended a ban on queer folks. In 1977, the State Department lifted their policy. Two decades later, in 1995, President Clinton signed Executive Order 12968 stating that the United States does not discriminate on the basis of race, color, religion, sex, national origin, disability, or sexual orientation in granting access to classified information. That meant that gays and lesbians could hold high-level security clearances. That was five years before I enlisted, still fresh in everyone's minds.

In that same year, Clinton's team invented the "Don't Ask, Don't Tell" compromise. Before making my decision, I acknowledged that the U.S. military tossed one thousand members out annually for being queer. In the five years between Clinton's executive order and when I enlisted, over five thousand service members were dismissed for being homosexual. During my first three years of service the trend continued; nearly thirty-five hundred people were kicked out of military service between 2000 and 2003. The Army discharged more people than any other force. "Don't Ask, Don't Tell" ruled with a firm grip from my first day through today.

The leadership who made decisions during the Don't Ask, Don't Tell era continue to make decisions about promotions, opportunities, and careers. Black soldiers, sailors, and airmen did not rise through the ranks quickly after the 1948 ruling that started to better integrate the troops. Hostility, violence, and closed doors existed for decades, and continues. Change comes slowly to the United States Army.

I knew stepping from that bus to bootcamp in 2001 that I was just as likely to be raped, beaten, or abused by my fellow soldier as I was to being outed by these soldiers. In 2003, of ninety women in my sixty-man tent, two women got sent home after reporting assault and one woman got sent home after testing positive for pregnancy. Pregnancy is a medical condition not permitted on the battlefield. In 2003, pregnancy no longer prompted the termination of a career. Once upon a time, a pregnant officer saw her career end.

Jetting around the globe for the U.S. Army, people now try to avoid making the assumption that Major Musgrave is male. Then there are those dreadful moments when the only safe place is with your team—your team of men. Suddenly the rules that require separate accommodations to provide for my safety endanger me. So instead of being embedded with soldiers you trust and respect, the army forces separation from your own crew. I got placed into quarters that were less safe, less secure, and less desirable. As the creed says: "I am a member of a team." Then the rest of the team secures a tent together. During that mission to northern Iraq, I was required to sleep alone in a sixty-man tent a bit too close to coalition troops who had a less progressive view of women in uniform than the U.S. Army. The old Soviet Army occasionally identified women in uniform as having been issued as "morale gear." Now, we have former Cold War adversaries as allies in our camps. That scared the shit out of me. The UCMJ cannot protect me from them. And if I hurt one of those soldiers, then the UCMJ will end my career and likely lock me up. Sometimes, you just have to say: fuck the rules and pick the less bad option. I left my empty tent too close to former Soviet soldiers and moved in with my male teammates.

Even through all of this, even after being blown up by an IED, even after having my leg damaged, even after all of the fears, I don't regret my decision in 2001 to leave school to join this army, my army. I still know that this army needs me; it needs me to be me.

It needs me to be me because I can ask a human being a question and get an answer that tells me something important. People tell me things, information that no satellite, no drone, no wiretap will ever yield. By the way, I value the lies humans tell me too. Yes, lies inform me in a way similar to *someone who tells the truth.*

*Psst, want the secret we've taught our adversaries?*

*Turn off your phone. Avoid being seen by the open sky where drones and satellites reign supreme. Oh, right, the Viet Cong tried to teach us that lesson in the 1960s in Southeast Asia. Another fact that is not a secret.*

*Stay off of the internet. Still not a secret.*

*If you do not cast a shadow and do not flip a binary digit in the electronic world, then you have rendered all of our gorgeous and expensive spy tech useless. Granted, living life within these constraints seems untenable and undesirable to those of us who enjoy life within the net. Yet globally we face populations of people opting out of the digital universe. The population of Amish in America continues to grow year after year.*

*Ok, the Amish likely won't start an armed insurrection in our country, but they represent a population globally that avoids the very technology that we believe makes life better. Other groups make the same decisions every day.*

*Just one meal and one night with B. That's what I need. I'll ping B tonight and tell B of my longing, my love and discover what I am missing back home.*

She calls me "B" instead of "Brie" or "Brighid." I don't mind. As long as she loves me and thinks of me even while journaling about the history of military intelligence. By using "B" instead of "Brighid," she's not saving ink or space. No, she is following the fucked-up rules. Somebody in the government draws a line between being queer and being queer. According to the rules, you can maybe possibly explore thoughts of being queer. You can have a queer thought as long as it is silent and unfulfilled. The army regulations state that you need to express yourself in your born gender and have sex with a partner who is of the opposite gender. The court martial comes when you become affectionate and loving with someone. Therefore, kissing a woman, as a female solder, is illegal, unless it is your mother, your sister, your

cousin, or your close friend. You just can't follow up the kiss with sex. The army decided that sex is the criminal act.
    Don't ask.

# 8 | Gooaaal!

"Brighid, I owe you 10K."

I read the text again. And again. Then I got a picture via text from Duke. The image had a check written for just over $700,000. So close to the amount owed that the difference is a rounding error.

I send, "Don't you dare pay me!"

I follow that up with, "I am a pissed off lioness with a thick mane. I am out to sink this guy. We'll square it up someday in the future. Pay your bills and don't worry about me."

I'll get paid. I'll accept some money from Duke, of course. And I've got other clients. And we do fine on Sam's income. For a part-time soldier, she gets more combat pay, specialty pay, and reimbursements than I ever imagined possible. Her income as a major ought to support a family, a home, and the rest of the 1950s vision of domesticity. When she travels for the army, they pay for everything. The household expenses go down and her income goes up when she heads overseas. We both need to recognize that this part-time reservist status is bullshit. She is a full-time professional soldier during two wars that may last her entire career. She really did enlist months before 9/11, like she had a telepathic connection with the bad guys, or a crystal ball. "Oh shit, something bad is going to happen." Then it did.

You know what I don't need? I do not need ten thousand dollars from a guy who hasn't seen any income in a twelve-month period. For fuck's sake, take the family to dinner, buy a new bike for the kid, and pay the debts. Please, Duke, put my bill on the bottom of the list.

Meanwhile, I want to see Ernie von Shithead do a perp walk. I picture him wearing a ball cap, sunglasses and a blue blazer draped over his handcuffed wrists. Know who can do that? Me. I can't do the official arresting, although that would be fun. "You have the right to remain silent…" I have three people at the FBI who gave me a cool coin the last time I was on the 23rd Floor of the Jacob K. Javits Federal Building in Manhattan.

My desires don't need justification. But if Ernie von Fuckface thinks he can buy off firefighters and locals with a promise of a new fire station and fancy ladder truck, then fine. Except, I know he's lying. How do I know he is lying? That's a dumb question. The old joke would tell you that we know he's lying because his mouth is open. I am not delivering a punchline. What I see and hear is that The Branston Club did not promise a new firehouse and new ladder truck. He supports the ambition. He promotes the need of it. He didn't promise it. He promised $5.5 million in new local taxes that will be paid annually.

Ooh, big number.

Nobody else has picked that apart yet. First, his gameboard spreads over two towns. Haworth is not getting all $5.5 million. That money will be split between Haworth and Carlton, Vermont. Therefore, we should cut that number in half. Where does that money come from? Property taxes and local option on meals and hotels. Therefore, the properties have to be built and sold before the towns can tax them at full value. Right now, these parcels are unfinished construction sites. Completing the entire project requires the Act 250 permit to be approved and issued. Then all of the permits get to cycle through local review and approval. I've been to an Act 250 hearing and read the history. That process is slow. That money will start trickling in years from now.

The first time a five-story condo building gets occupied, the fire department needs to be prepared with new plans and new apparatus. They can't buy more trucks or a modern big truck until they upgrade the existing fire station which was built south of that famous traffic light. That fire station sits in the primary floodplain of a river that enjoys flooding. That fire station sits on a triangle of land that keeps eroding into the river.

Haworth needs to spend millions today to support The Branston Club. And when is the sweet sip of real money coming?

My answer: Never. Sorry, Chief Wegman.

Let's make-believe that Ernie is honest and follows through on his promises. The Haworth fire chief will have to go to a town meeting proposing that the town issue a bond for a new fire station and new apparatus. That's not a thought that small town yankees have easily. You spend the money that you have. You don't spend money that you do not have. Basic rules in rural Vermont.

In order for the Town of Haworth to fully support The Branston Club, they will commit millions of taxpayer's dollars to expand public services on the promise of future income, just like Duke Hazen, the owner of Great Pines Construction.

Why did Ernie pay Duke's over-due bill?

I have found answers.

First, Duke already earned that money and honest folks pay their debts. You pay your debts and others pay their debts. It is like the golden rule for doing-unto-others.

Second, even a dishonest business guy knows that to string Duke along and get a second season out of him and his crew, he needs to pay last year's bill. Otherwise, there is no cash to buy this year's materials and pay wages.

Third, my friend, a Connecticut lawyer, wrote a demand letter. It had all of the things in it; a reference to Vermont Statutes, Title 9, Chapter 102, entitled "Construction Contracts." Ernie's lawyer, Frank Jager, wrote back identifying the clauses in the signed contract that require binding arbitration and prevent the dispute from entering a proper courtroom. We countered with chapter-and-verse from Vermont statues that detail some rights that construction companies have. Oh, and there was that one graph in the law about breach of contract that permits civil action in a courtroom. You can't hold the terms of a contract sacred if the contract is in full breach. If the contract is in breach, then this is an argument to be fought out in a civil courtroom between real lawyers and a real judge.

Fourth, Ernie knows that Sam and I are investigating him.

I get that a civilian driving a fire-engine red pickup truck with twinkly lights is not much of a threat. British mystery books and TV shows are filled with busybody women investigating local doings. It's a genre. Me, a skirt, a peasant blouse, herbs hanging in the window, chickens in a coop, sheep in the fields. Me, with my crazy hair queued back in a big barrette. Me, in a 200-year-old home. Me, married to another woman. In the time of my own ancestors, I would have been dunked in the local pond or tested for witchcraft with a heavy stone placed upon my chest. Apparently, if I lived, I was a witch. If I died, I was a simple, mortal woman.

I am not a witch, by the way. I do feel the earth in a way that my mother's family called earthfast.

And I don't belong on a British mystery either. Sam is a cop who has been trained by the United States Army and the Vermont Police Academy. I am a professional researcher who investigates corporations for malfeasance, misfeasance, and nonfeasance. Sometimes my clients pay me well and whistle a merry tune. They carry out an equitable merger. Then there are the other cases. Those cases feel like holding smoke and weighing snow with a warm hand. Mergers fall apart. If it is bad enough and criminal enough, the offending party finds themselves investigated by the FBI, the SEC, or another law enforcement body. You go to jail, pay fines, and do the guilty-guy thing. You've seen the dance. Proclaim the world is a sham and you've been victimized by a massive conspiracy. Then appeal the facts, appeal the ruling, appeal everything while the judgements stack up against you.

Duke isn't safe. His family isn't safe. His legacy project isn't safe. He got last year's bill paid today. By tomorrow the money will be gone. The loan accounts, credit card accounts, and other debts will get erased. His status will improve from owing a ton of money to not owing a ton of money. Tomorrow, his bank account will be just as empty as it was yesterday.

Tomorrow, he will pay off the debts and on Monday, he'll borrow again to buy materials and meet the first payroll of the spring season.

A win is a win.

I knuckle down to another day's work. I open the *Trent Valley Viewer*.

Oh, Brian, you clearly are not seeking a Pulitzer for investigative journalism for your frequent reporting on The Branston Club.

Someday, my friend, you will look back over your body of writing for the *Trent Valley Viewer* to discover what you missed each week. Three weeks ago, you reported on the RedOaks TV and Film festival coming to the valley. For eight years, this festival has been hosted on the west coast, bouncing between LA, Seattle, and Portland. Now, it is coming to the Trent Valley. You wrote, "The festival will focus on the independent work of television, web, or film. Vermont will give the perfect fall foliage backdrop to the Hollywood folks coming here."

I ask, why now? Or is the question: Who?

I sniff Ernie von Eberbach in this scheme. I smell a soupçon of his fragrance. No trace in the literature or in the public discussion, until this morning. Brian, your article just told me old Eberbach is giving in-kind donations of staff and food for events at The Branston Club. Bingo! Which further indicates that part of the event will be hosted at The Branston Club.

Now Brian, I am still failing to parse the facts about Carlton Legg, a local musician. Your writing is so bad, I can't figure out the facts.

You guys at *Trent Valley Viewer* heralded the man in the local press for concerts, events, and his recent album. He's closely related to the huge clan of Leggs in the town of Langford just to the west of Trowbridge. Ironically, the Legg family seems to frequently crossbreed with the Foote family. Carlton stands as a local hero strumming and singing at venues in the region, then is suddenly blacklisted at The Branston Club. Brian, the only quote you give me is Carlton Legg saying, "I don't want to tell stories out of school."

Come on, Brian, find your inner Woodward and Bernstein and ask the questions.

Since I smell Ernie's stink, I'll have to find a way to head to Haworth to talk with people. Why did a local artist from a respected tribe get blackballed from the largest potential entertainment venue in the region? Ok, maybe I am a bit like those British TV busybodies. Nobody is paying me to investigate Carlton Legg's blacklisting. It just isn't right. And if I catch Ernie in the act, the evidence will go in a white banker's box for the feds. I can do real sleuthing too.

What does Carlton Legg know about The Branston Club? Why is

a ski area publicly blacklisting an artist? It seems spiteful to ostracize a local guy with a guitar and a raspy voice. Ernie, you bought nearly every inn, restaurant, and public venue in the valley. Your actions mean that Carlton needs to find a job or travel further for paying gigs. And if he looked for a day job, the only employment is at your construction sites.

Furthermore, with the arrival of the RedOaks Festival, local hero Carlton Legg will be barred from participating. He's our local guy. That festival could be his chance. Now, he has learned that he can't sing that one song that gets him discovered by Hollywood.

Instead of addressing that disappointment, Legg gets quoted in the paper for saying, "I'm not a rat."

With the use of investigative calculus, I estimate the first derivative of "I'm not a rat" to be "I have information I will not share." I'll text Harry or Robby or Alex or Regina or Al. One of the squad members will know him.

Carlton Legg's family is camped in Langford. In the world of ironies, Trowbridge and Langford fuss at each other. The neighboring towns are so alike that no one can tell them apart, yet an angry fissure exists at the boundary of the towns' ancient clans. The Legg clan lives in Langford and Haworth. This tension sometimes flares at fire scenes.

"Oh, those assholes only called us over to roll up their hose."

We live in a grid of towns that fit like square tiles on a checkerboard. Yet, this fire department avoids calling on that fire department. Ambulance services war with rescue squads. People get in the habit of distrusting and disliking neighbors. What I have seen is that mutual aid agreements sometimes describe the awkward movement of chess pieces instead of logical arrows. One mutual aid agreement bounces up one over two, like a knight. In another, mutual aid flows diagonally like a bishop. These decisions result in slower mutual aid response times. The other result is that fire departments pick their friends and families as their mutual aid partners. They avoid the tribal feuds of long-ago.

A fellow says, "I'm not a rat" in the paper, then days later I arrive wanting his secrets. "Hey Carlton, I am Brighid from Trowbridge. I am on the fire department with your cousin…" I am not even sure if I am serving with his cousin, but no doubt there is some cousin-ness somewhere in the world of friends and acquaintances. I certainly have seen dozens of his tribe at fire scenes in the region. Yet, depending which appendage of the Legg/Foote clan Carlton stands, my association could be immediately helpful or not helpful. I have no idea. I'll ask the EMS squad on the best approach for Carlton.

How widely known are our interests and activities? I have become confident that Ernie von Eberbach knows that Sam and I are asking questions. Given our engagement with Haworth Police plus my time in the Haworth town clerk's office, and my attendance at meetings and hearings, he's got to know. Information flows through our rural communities so rapidly through the threads of a human network.

Does he care? I doubt it. A lot of people dismiss me easily and quickly. I am a woman of unknown age and dubious character. In the Vermont landscape, I resemble the modern version of the 1970s back-to-the-Earth hippy—in a red pickup truck.

I listen to the fire scanner tone out the Trent Valley ambulance from the regional base in Haworth. My ears pick up their two musical notes as easily as I hear the two musical notes associated with Langford Rescue. My attention shifts to the dispatcher sending the ambulance to Langford for a 59-year-old male with chest pain and difficulty breathing.

Brian Stuart, intrepid reporter, did give me a new lead by telling me that Carlton Legg was blacklisted. For that lead, I thank you, Brian.

I return to Brian's articles on the Act 250 hearing that I attended and ran from. Thankfully, someone dialed 911, causing me to leave.

Eberbach has a lengthy quote in the article. He said: "We understand that we may have gotten ahead of ourselves in some instances in the past, for which we have taken corrective actions."

Here is a guy that normally uses "I" as much as possible. Past quotes offer proof such as: "I am bringing famous people and billionaires to this forgotten valley." "I am building an amazing and massive timber-frame lodge that is amazing and special and unlike anything anyone has ever seen anywhere."

In this article, he gives a noncommittal non-apology and the language falls to the vague "we." The royal we. His language distances himself from these acts. Ok, got it. Let me guess, you are about to blame someone else, deflect attention to another, right?

In another quote in the article, Ernie said, "In other instances, the woman, in coordinating the permit review process for the State of Vermont, provided us with ever-changing targets. First, we are told that we do not need permits for every action because we're being reviewed by Act 250. Then I get vilified because we capitalize on opportunities while achieving benchmarks towards our shared goals. I am here to help this valley, bring employment, bring revenue to the businesses here, and provide opportunities for thousands. We've had non-material mods and minor changes to an approved project and we respectfully disagree that these violate our permit in any way. We operate within the framework of the Act 250 permit and this review process. Our project has the full support of the selectboard." Can I hear his tone of voice when he said, "woman." Maybe I am just making that bit up?

Eberbach went onto state that he would file simple applications "to resolve issues without additional delay, conflict, and cost."

I heard some of the infractions during the 250 hearing. Ernie's team did not get a lot of points in that three-way match with the Regional Commission and state agencies. The infractions were named in brief as if all there previously knew the facts. This article does the same by glossing over them: a bridge over a stream; golf driving range installed; a boat dock near a dam's spillway; a road near a spring pond; and a large parking lot that is missing from any plans; running power lines through a forested wetland.

Weeks of reading and meetings and one public hearing leaves me utterly confused by this Act 250 process. The law was written in the 1970s to regulate the environmental and adverse community impact by ski areas in Vermont. The law has been applied to farms, manufacturing businesses, residential development—and when being applied to this ski area in Southern Vermont, the applicant bought his permit approval as part of buying the land. He is building the most exclusive private club in Vermont using plans drawn up forty years ago. The regional commission, the State of Vermont, and Eberbach argue over a supposed master plan.

Eberbach states: You have the master plan.

The State counters: the plan did not describe this parking lot, nor this boat ramp, nor this utility corridor. The State of Vermont begins to think, hey, maybe we do not have the master plan.

Maybe with Eberbach's arrogance, he thinks a plan is a sketch, a starting point.

I put myself in Eberbach's mind. To him, Act 250 is just more anti-business regulation created by socialists and hippies. Ernie sees himself as a modern business leader. He's endeavored to bring local politicians on board with him. He'll think, "I have hired half of the valley for doing the construction work. If the state shuts me down, the region will revolt." He is arguing that his vague and old plan is good enough to get him to the finish line. I am too big and too important to fail or to be stopped.

Eberbach has also observed that the permits filed after the fact cost the same as those filed beforehand. Why bother filing on time? Nobody fines him. Let's admit that Vermont's fines rarely feel very punitive. The biggest fine for missing a construction permit is one hundred dollars per day. That's less than the daily leasing costs of an excavator. It is significantly cheaper to pay fines than to have equipment and crews idle on a good weather day.

The State of Vermont and Ernie von Eberbach play by two different sets of rules, and Brian, the local reporter at the *Trent Valley Viewer*, does not yet see it. Nor do any of the selectboards or commissions or state agencies.

The State of Vermont and our laws were established by conservative old yankees who expected people to operate within standard rules governed by fairness and morality. Any fine should make people feel shame. The publicity for infractions will harm a person's reputation. People want to be good and avoid bad. People will act to protect their honor, their reputation, and avoid public shaming, even over a one-hundred dollar fine.

Ernie von Fuckhead plays by his own rules. I don't think that morality factors into Eberbach's formulas. What does he care about good or bad? A hundred-dollar fine is just an expense of doing business. Regulations are evil. Regulations are anti-business. Regulations are to be ignored, squashed, or fought against. With millions on the line and a boom in employment, some members of the boards and commissions seem to be siding with him. He got a permit for a wellhouse. He built a wellhouse. So what if it was a bit larger than the one planned in the 1970s? Things change.

While I work, I listen to samples of Carlton Legg's music. I bought the guy's CD from his website. Why not? The guy got blackballed. And I bought an album. He'll be putting a CD in a jewel case and mailing it to me, one town east.

You know that moment when you say to yourself, *I have a very bad idea.* The heart rate ticks up. Cortisol enters the bloodstream. Under normal circumstances, I'd talk with Sam about this. She would work me towards a solution that was less stupid. We'd go for a walk in the woods and talk about it together. Sam helps me decide if an idea is bad or good.

Know who does not offer helpful communication when wrestling with ideas? Chickens. They have their own lives. I appreciate the birds. I care for the birds, and they give back to me, although their gifts come in hard brown shells. They don't listen to me and don't answer back when I attempt to have conversations with them. I count them. There are ten, now. That's the other problem with chickens: raptors, foxes, dogs, and the unknown things that cause them to lay dead on the wood shavings below their roosts.

# 9 | Morgan Harmon

On Wednesday afternoon, Sam walks into our office. In greeting, I ask, "Hey, how is my favorite human road cone?" She wears her ugly brown sheriff's uniform now covered with a high-vis vest. I should admit I have never liked the sheriff's department uniform. On the other hand, her formal army uniform did stir my insides nicely. When I see Sam in her army uniform, I feel pride. She still looks fantastic in it, but I know the cost of wearing it. I alone know the discomfort that her leg brings, and the hauntings brought on by the hole once poked into her chest, and the ghosts who visit. I've known and loved this woman from recruit to private to sergeant and major. The sheriff's uniform, on the other hand, doesn't flatter my Sam in any way. Furthermore, she wears it without much pride.

"Another day sitting on a bridge with blue lights flashing looking down at a river from the interstate." I stand offering a proper and warm greeting. Like Sam, I, too, have been stationary for days. Sam sat in the front seat of an older police cruiser while being paid to sit at a highway construction site. Me, I have sat at my desk since eight o'clock on Monday entirely focusing on a suite of tasks. I delayed peeing until I couldn't. I'd nibble at my desk instead of taking time in the kitchen for lunch. Sam likely paced the length of a police car to push away stiffness in her leg and her back. Police-style vests have less weight and less bulk than the military version she wears on deployments. Spending hours sitting with a duty belt laden with pistol, cuffs, taser, and ammo cinched around the middle, and a ballistic vest above, brings pain after a few hours. What she could endure as a private has become harder now after multiple combat tours and age. I envision her sitting still until she couldn't. She would get out of the cruiser, pace until that brought her discomfort, then sit again.

On Monday, I phoned around the region to find a law firm that could help us pursue Eberbach. Web-based maps illustrated nearly two dozen options in our corner of Vermont. The criteria include: civil litigation, class action, contract law, criminal law knowledge, and the willingness to take on a major employer in the region. The websites run by law firms described wide-ranging services: soups, trusts, estates, wills, real estate, civil, nuts, divorce, criminal, and more—soup to nuts. Those I called opted out after the introduction. Most sounded just busy. Some explained that they offer limited criminal services such as driving under the influence but not major fraud cases. Some stated that they had a conflict of interest given they already had dealings with Eberbach as a client. My list grew shorter and shorter as the personal injury, worker compensation, auto accident, and real estate firms fell away. One lawyer's website resulted in a message reading "Not Secure" followed by "Your connection is not private." So much for a mildly prestigious address on High Street; that idiot can't even keep his website compliant with modern standards. Nope!

I call a fellow without a website. He answers a mobile phone on the second ring.

"Oh, no problem," he said, "I am in the office." But I hear a blue jay and rustling leaves. I can hear the man breathing. "Today, Pisgah State Park is my office."

"Are you a lawyer? What do you practice?"

"I am a lawyer. Why don't you tell me what you need?"

"Sounds like I am interrupting."

"I've got a headset. Talk and I'll walk. We're good."

"Ok, I can call you later."

"We'll see how this goes."

"Fine." I went on to introduce myself to Morgan Harmon. From his tone, I accept him as a confederate. I start by telling him of our home and our trails before venturing into the stories related to Ernie von Eberbach and The Branston Club. I describe aggregating unpaid vendors into either one case, or several civil cases. Morgan keeps listening as he walks the New Hampshire hills. I arrive to my core question related to pushing a civil case into the criminal realm. Morgan encourages my talking, so I keep going.

"You got me up that hill." He pauses, then says: "Sure."

"Sure? Sure what?"

"Sure, I'm happy to take this on. I am mostly retired and moved here full time from New York. I am licensed in Vermont. I worked in Manhattan, clerked for a while, then as a prosecutor, then with a large firm."

"I saw that," I offer. While Morgan Harmon does not have a website, he does have a name that appears in various press clippings, scholarly articles, books, and social media websites. His last dustup involved denial of tenure at Columbia Law. In the article, he stated: no tenure, no teach.

"How did you find me?"

"I went to an online map, right clicked, then typed 'lawyers near me.' Your name came up, but no website. I poked around the internet for a bit." I skip the fact that he had landed on the bottom of my internet-based list. One finds things in the last place looked. The last place I looked was on top of a New Hampshire hill.

He comes to dinner on Tuesday. We eat lamb while talking late into the evening at our dining table. What starts as a strategic session evolves into a pleasant social evening filled with laughter. During the first hour, I focus intensely on the plan. Sam and Morgan strike an instant rapport. She touches his forearm and shoulder a few times while laughing. She is not always the stoic, leather-tough warrior. She is also an amazing host.

My plan is everything to me. First step involves me building a website and finding ways to get information out to the construction crews and unpaid vendors. We'll build a client list. Establish contracts with the clients while working towards a legal strategy that brings Eberbach and The Branston Club down. I bought the domain Branston dot club as an online rallying point. I think we can use Duke to help spread the word. Not that our names are not out there already. I attribute recent hostility to this growing conflict. Right or wrong, that anger focuses me. My strategic plan borrows from its ancestors, a backwoods version of mesothelioma, environmental cancer-cluster, and bad-drug lawsuits. The classic David versus Goliath struggle. I have my slingshot in hand ready to aim. I desperately want to impress Morgan with our services, our preparation, and our case.

The man sits at our table swapping ironic stories with Sam. Two bottles of wine disappear before I deliver an apple tart to the table. Sam opens a third bottle as I pass around dessert plates. I resent their laughing because we have work to do.

We three clear the table. We three fill the dishwasher while rinsing the wine glasses. Morgan gives us both full and proper hugs before pushing the mudroom door open.

He then grabs my upper arm, gently saying: "Listen, I'll swing by tomorrow while Sam sits on the highway. We'll work for a minute, then you can take me for a walk in your woods."

With that comment, I finally relax. Climbing the stairs, Sam informs me that I was a complete and total prat for having ever doubted myself. "He doesn't give a shit about your plan. He wanted to get know you." She also paddles my bottom gently while following me too closely up the stairs. With two steps to go, she pushes me. I tumble gracefully onto the carpet. She fake-falls on top of me. I squeal about being crushed and tease her for being clumsy.

You get it. Cut-to-black, as they do in the movie business.

Wine on a weeknight. Maybe we should do that more often?

Focusing on my plan, I build a website. I register the website with various search engines. Create dozens of useful links to state and legal resources. And I build a contact form that enrolls the visitor in an email process used for sales, newsletters, and related communication. I write the welcome email. I write several emails that the system will send automatically on the third, seventh, and fourteenth day after a person enrolls.

I design this website with articles and keywords to entice Vermont contractors who are being screwed by Ernie von Eberbach and The Branston Club. The interested visitor, fed by information provided by Duke, will enter their email address. That goes to a system that stores the email address along with their IP address, time, and date of contact. The visitor gets a welcome email. I get a list of people who visit. Their visit yields pretty good data. First, through the site's analytics, which can be vague. Second, I get the data the users enter onto forms. Most would be suspicious of a website, especially my neighbors. You should always be suspicious of a website offering help to recover money due. To assist in establishing trust, I leverage those who contact us to spread the word verbally and with paper flyers.

The website, which used a bit of internet magic, does not provide our actual name or address. I pay the extra money to obscure our firm's ownership of the site. That said, I expect that like Duke, people will arrive at the door instead of signing up on a random website. They will want to see that we are real and on their side.

Timing for my plan seemed critical. Sitting at the shoulder of the year, households brace for summer, families plan activities, and outdoor construction ramps up. Ernie von Eberbach's failure to pay vendors created nearly universal hardship for the families of each contractor involved. Last, Eberbach stands tall in this valley as a hero offering employment to all with needed skills. By next Christmas, he'll be the Grinch who stole presents and meals from children. My goal is to prevent any local family from losing their homes and maybe make sure that gifts do appear in stockings and under yule trees.

Morgan arrives in the morning for a brief work session in the office. He listens perfectly while I outline my efforts, my plan, and my timing. When I ask what he thinks, he answers: "The case will tell us where it needs to go."

I want a different type of answer, nearly any other answer or response. He stands, causing me to stand. Yielding, I say, "Want to explore our trails?"

"Please!"

We walk across the pasture towards the stone wall.

Morgan states, "You know I have no staff. I have no paralegals. I have no resources. The only office I have is a former bedroom that I converted. You will be it. You do know that, right?"

I guess I did not think that through.

"I'd like to make money, but not much. I am pretty immune to guys like Eberbach. My wife died too young. I walked away from Columbia because they didn't offer me tenure. And I will forever be an outsider in Vermont. Less than two percent of Vermonters are like me."

"So, you think that two percent of Vermonters are lawyers? Or did you mean two percent of Vermonters are widowers?" I know perfectly well that Morgan is referencing the lack of ethnic diversity in this state.

His smile shines in the crow's feet at the edge of each eye. "I'll admit that I thought Vermont would be cheaper than it is." Folks that move to Vermont are wealthy and white. That said, the state is benefiting from some immigration from overseas. Those folks are neither wealthy, nor white.

To that I respond, "The old saying here is that if you want to be a millionaire in Vermont, show up with two million in your pocket."

The joke fell flat.

"Are you willing to work as paralegal, researcher, and dog's body on the case?" he asks.

"Absolutely. Are you willing to coach me on approach and strategy? I just don't know the limits of the law and the interaction between state and federal law. Federal law seems to have stronger fraud statutes, but I did not find any cases from Vermont being pursued in federal court. Oh, and I don't have access to any of the legal databases."

"Certainly. And I have enough friends that can lend us a login for the databases. We can research case law. Ever done case law research?"

The two of us continue walking up Nidoba Hill. As we step from a mixed hardwood region dominated by beech trees into a hemlock forest, rocky outcrops appear on our left.

"Probably not the way a paralegal does it. I've never had that kind of access before. Could be useful. I pay for services that provide background checks and financial information, but these services fall short of the legal databases you are familiar with. Coincidently, the data I get is often owned by the same company, or companies, that host the legal databases."

"And you do understand that we both make more money if the Eberbach case stays within the domain of civil law?"

I have to think about that. I like seeing the bad guys getting hauled away in cuffs, the perp walk. If we slog it out in civil court, we will collect a portion of the amount owned. Eberbach will be obliged to pay court fees and lawyers' fees. But is that justice? Is paying bills, paying fees, paying fines, paying legal costs justice? Morgan and I walk in silence.

I say, "I guess justice is paying for birthday gifts and having good meals on the table. Justice is getting the families paid. Justice can be found in keeping the deed to the family home, right?"

"Only if you accept that, then it is right."

"It has to be good enough. I'll make sure that good enough is enough for me."

We come down the hill then turn on our Lakeshore Drive trail. We stop at the Douglas Tree, only because it is my habit, a habit I learnt from Sam. The forest had returned to deciduous mixed with the occasional white pine. Morgan offers me raisins from a bag he pulled from a thigh pocket.

We continue downhill towards the Pine-at-the-Fork. Taking the right at the fork follows an abandoned road, a sunken or hollow way through the wood passing a former farmstead with empty cellars. Carrying onto the left, we pass the pond for which we named the Lakeshore Drive trail. We return through the stone wall and pasture, just as we did when leaving. Stepping clear of the wood, two flickers rise from the field, taking to flight. I often reach for Sam at this point. Sam and I walk this last bit hand in hand looking at our house. Instead, I vector my body just slightly closer to Morgan, inadvertently bumping his shoulder.

"We've got leftover lamb and rice for lunch."

Morgen sits at our conference table while I continue to work.

At three in the afternoon, he stands at my shoulder and gives it a bit of a squeeze. "Don't get up. I am heading home."

"Oh. I lost track of time." He pats me between my shoulder blades twice then leaves the room. I hear the digital dog, as I call our driveway alarm, make a deedle sound as he leaves.

The next sound comes at three thirty with the digital dog announcing someone on the drive. I look, seeing Sam's car. She must be the only sheriff's deputy to drive a high-end Volvo to the station before picking up whatever piece-of-shit cruiser they have her drive to the bridge on the interstate highway.

Sam walks straight to my desk and gives me a greeting. "Morgan was here, huh?"

"Most of the day, yes. How did you know? Did you see him on the road?"

"No, he smells fantastic. I kinda love his soap or scent. I can smell it in here. Anyway, I'll go change. I'll see you next door, ok?"

"Ok." I don't look up to see her in her sheriff's brown uniform with road-cone colored safety vest. I keep reading and searching. I fight to pull myself away. It is time to check the websites at the end of the day. And there he is. Number eight on the list: Ernie von Eberbach signed up for my newsletters. He is also number ten on the list. As number ten, he used one of his supposedly obscure holding companies, Trent Lands, LLC, as his nom de guerre. I redirect both of his email addresses to a separate thread. Like a honeypot, I created a special series of emails that were mildly misspelled, had incorrect information, and were written poorly. From now, Ernie will get the honeypot emails on a regular schedule from my website. My aim is to convince him that we are complete idiots. I research the other email addresses. All appear legitimate and reasonably local. One is a lawyer in the area. Not knowing affiliations, I shunt this person to the same stream of honeypot nonsense that Eberbach will get. I update Morgan via email that we'd gotten Eberbach's attention.

On Thursday, our next walk-in client comes down the driveway. He carries the silly flyer I made.

"Is this you?" he asks me when I greet him in the drive.

"It is. Are you a contractor up at the hill?"

"I am."

"Have you been paid since August?"

"No." The conversation reflects elements of distrust.

"Would you like some assistance with that?"

"What can you do?"

"We can force him to pay."

"How?"

"In the courts, with Vermont law that was written to protect contractors like you from being shafted by guys like him."

"There is such a law? I've never heard of it."

"That's because nobody down here ever sues anyone over anything." Guys down here fight it out, feud it out, or freeze each other out. I wait.

"Do I know you? Who are you?"

I tell him that my mother was distantly related to the governor. I tell him that Sam's family has owned this property for over two hundred years and that she was raised here before joining the army. I tell him that Sam has done multiple combat tours, and was twice wounded, and earned the Bronze Star Medal.

"Can I invite you into our office?" Talking with this guy felt like trying to pet an unfamiliar dog. The dog wants the attention and tries to get close, but when seeing that he is close, he skitters back and gets slightly mean. "Or you can come back, your choice? There is no pressure."

"Are you a lawyer?"

"Nope, but there is one just beyond the door, in our office."

I wait with practiced Vermont silence. I can't change the physical dynamics. He faces me and the office. I face him and his truck. We look at each other like we are in a stand-off. I would have preferred to pivot so that I stood looking at the same view. I want to find a means of getting next to him instead of opposing him.

"Do you have another plan or another way of getting paid this year?" I ask.

"I've never sued anyone. No one I know has ever sued someone. Won't it just piss him off? He won't hire us for next year."

"He may not hire you for next year and maybe you can find someone who pays their bills. Do you really need Eberbach?"

"He's got us all trapped. If we stop working, he won't pay us and maybe he won't hire us to continue. All I really need is to hang on. He'll wants us back when the ground firms up."

"And for what, fifty cents on the dollar?" I shut up and wait again.

And wait another couple of heart beats: "Is that why you got into business? This guy is a crook."

He steps closer. "I am Ben Tozier."

"Ben, I am Brighid. Come on in."

"Ben, this is Morgan. He is the lawyer on the team." Ben does not offer his hand to Morgan either. I'll need to explain that behavior to Morgan later. How do I say that he didn't intend offense and wasn't being rude according to small-town Vermont rules? I fear Morgan feels offended by an adult man not offering to shake.

Morgan nods.

Ben asks: "What do I need to do?"

"Ben, you don't need to do anything," Morgan answers from his seated position. I hear the sting.

I jump in, "If you want help, then bring us your contracts and invoices and copies of any checks you've gotten. And we'll have you sign a standard engagement letter. You engage us; we're bound by client confidentiality rules and all of that. We can take it from there."

"I brought all of that with me in my truck."

"Do you want to get it?"

He steps back out. Silently, I say, "Fifty-fifty." Either Ben Tozier will return, or he won't. It is a binary proposition at this point.

Morgan burns me with a look. I lift one finger, communicating: wait one sec, wait, shush, and all of the above. I also raise my eyebrows followed by a shoulder shrug. How else do I say—Hey professor, welcome to Vermont, it ain't you, it's them?

Ben returns. The contracts seemed identical to those we've seen from others. I accept them.

"I'll scan these and return them tomorrow, is that ok? And I have a client engagement letter ready. Come to my desk."

I sit with Ben behind me. I pull up a blank client letter. I asked for name, address, company name while filling in blanks. I print it. With little ceremony and no hesitation, he signs it. I sign it. I scan it. I hand him a printed copy.

"I'll drop the documents at your house tomorrow. Is that the address you gave me, your house?"

"Yes. My wife is there."

"Ok."

I walk him back to the driveway and his truck, thanking him.

In the office, I sit opposite Morgan Harmon, a lawyer raised in Westchester County, New York, educated at Ivy League schools, who practiced law in Manhattan. I sit there explaining that he should not expect handshakes, hugs, much physical contact, or much warm conversation from the folks he meets in Trowbridge. It isn't your accent. It isn't your skin color. It isn't your education. It isn't that I am married to a woman. That's a man, referring to Ben Tozier, who wouldn't hug his own mother except maybe on her birthday. What do you expect? The folks who colonized this region fled both plagues and civil war in England. And for four hundred years, Vermonters keep distant from everyone. Increasing space and decreasing contact became a plague-based survival strategy.

The fire department tones ring from my hip and from the scanner that plays quietly near my desk. "Trailer at end of road, thirty-year-old male, possible overdose."

I turn to Morgan, saying: "I'll either be one hour or four." I meant, either I will revive him with Narcan, or stand by a dead body awaiting the state police and their detectives. I drive quickly over the dirt roads. I keep my siren wailing the entire time. The rule of threes from Alex. We humans get three minutes without oxygen, three days without water, three weeks without food. Violations result in death. Narcotics suppress breathing before the breathing fully stops. Death comes in minutes.

I rush into the trailer. I feel the body. I roll the body then look carefully. I test the jaw. I wiggle the little finger, then using the stethoscope I carry in the thigh pocket of my turnout pants, I listen to an empty chest. I slow down. The emergency is over. I use my phone's stopwatch to listen for a full minute with my eyes closed, peaking only occasionally at the phone. I move the stethoscope twice around the chest, listening again. The lack of sounds, the stiffing muscles, the cooling body provide me definitive proof of death.

I look to the young man standing there. He is wearing a dirty ball cap. I shake my head then say the familiar words: "I am very sorry, he has died. There is nothing we can do. Can you step outside with me?"

We retreat from the trailer. I make a quick radio call: "Trowbridge Command confirms untimely. Please return the ambulance with my thanks and notify VSP." I have yet to call the hospital and take the rest of the steps required by our protocol. Instead, I look at the phone for the time, then take a few discrete photos of the place, the trucks, and the living man next to me. I walk with him to a pile of tires. I invite him to sit, then I squat in front of him. I examine his eyes, feel his wrists for pulse and skin temperature. I ask for his name and ask for any ID. He retrieves his wallet which remains tethered to his belt buckle with a brightly chromed chain. He hands me his driver's license. I photograph it, front and back. I put the driver's license in my pocket, telling the young man to stay put. State law provides me no authority to arrest or detain anyone at an emergency scene. Yet, I also know I can't let this guy go before the state police arrive. This became a crime scene the moment I observed a dead human on a sofa in a dingy mobile home. I return inside to find a few bits of evidence: pills, needles, an ID, etc. I retrieve the dead guy's wallet from the back pocket of the jeans that he was still wearing. I also give a lift to his shirt, giving the body a more thorough examination. Maybe I assume drug overdose too quickly while missing a mortal wound. Instead, I find a neat tattoo on the fellow's upper chest that reads: O+.

I step away from the trailer, making my official phone calls to the hospital then to the state police dispatcher. To each organization, I give similar information albeit to very different audiences. To the doc, I discuss my diagnosis of death. She looks up the patient's history, asks relevant medical and social questions. With the state police, I provide them with the name and date of birth of the dead guy. I follow up with the name and DOB of the witness. This time, I have to answer more questions about me and the scene, the safety of the scene, and the environment. I make the suggestion that the associate medical examiner and detectives get dispatched. I am informed, as I often am, that only troopers can make that request. Rules. He'll be just as dead when the trooper arrives. Time here is time not at home.

I return to my truck. I confirm that I set the dashcam to record. I set my phone to record audio, then I sit with a clipboard doing paperwork. I record the time and date of each action. I record my assessments. No matter how slowly I work, I will still have to wait in silence for the trooper. I find a VA card in my victim's wallet. I text Morgan with an update. I text Sam that I was stuck at a scene with an "untimely." My text informs her that a twenty-nine-year-old veteran died in a ratty trailer in the hills of Vermont—unkempt and uncared for; this death is untimely.

Sam texts back: "I heard."

With my thumbs, I text: "Sitting here with a woodchuck who'd rather run than wait."

I also text Harry and Alex: "You out there? Tac 4 if close, happy to have you here."

After thirty minutes of waiting, my witness asks: "What are we waiting for?"

"The state police."

No reply.

Ten minutes later, he rises. At first, he paces once then twice. Then he wanders towards his own truck.

"Do you mind returning to where you were seated?"

I hold his license in my pocket. He knows that. I had already reported him to the state police. He knows that too. I have a photo of him, and he probably knows that as well. I cannot chase him, and I cannot leave the scene. He likely knows that too. If he runs, the state police will be looking for him. My woodchuck returns to the tire perch, having decided to wait quietly with me.

I wish to tell the police to speed up. I always wish to tell them to speed up. Supposedly, a crime scene with one dead body is not urgent enough to warrant blue lights and siren from those guys. Does my woodchuck have a knife on that belt or under his shirt? Does he have a gun? I presume he has a gun in his truck. Furthermore, I presume that I could find a gun in the dead guy's truck. And I know that there is a gun in my truck. Three trucks, three guns. But here in this ratty dooryard of stacked tires and a rusted gas can, My witness cannot reach a gun faster than me.

Maybe.

One winter, I responded to an orchard for the report of a dead body. I had trouble finding the body because the recent dusting of snowfall obscured my not-a-patient. I did the minimum to assess the body. While stepping through the field, my foot fell into a wet muddy hole which pulled my shoe off. I thought the ground was a bit more frozen than it was. I sat there alone on a hilltop orchard knowing that the dead human had been shot, and shot at reasonably close range. I sat in my truck waiting for the state police, imagining the shooter just out of sight in the woods. I only knew I was safe because I returned home safely. As Sam told me early on: when the enemy is in range, so are you.

Those words return to me sitting near this trailer. Three trucks, three guns. The other phrase that stuck to my idle brain was six-point-five meters (or twenty-one feet). When holding a gun on someone who is closer than six-point-five meters, they have the advantage. The normal human brain just cannot react fast enough to pull the trigger. I hope that I can move faster than my witness. His eyes are a bit too pinpoint and his pulse a bit too slow to be a serious threat. He too had his brain fried by narcotics today. He lives. His friend dies. Sad day for him.

Me, I don't want to be in a brawl, or have any trouble. I just want him to sit calmly.

I breathe easier when a trooper enters the driveway.

I stand. "Hey, do you mind talking with the witness before we go inside?" I sure hope that she understands my one-ton hint. Dead bodies can wait. Together, we step to my guy sitting on the tires. Within a few quick words, Victoria says to the human woodchuck slash witness slash friend: "Listen, my car is warm, how about I let you sit in there."

We walk him to her cruiser. He sits willingly. He sits in the backseat of a police cruiser. This seat serves as a detention cell from which he cannot escape. I hand the drivers licenses for both men to the cop, Victoria. "Thank you. Thank you, thank you."

"No problem."

"That was a long and quiet wait. He made me a little nervous."

"Should we go in?"

"You can. Glove up, though. There is too much in there. Kinda scary. I found a few needles. It is dark inside too. I'll hold the door and a light, how's that?"

She does her thing, taking photos and documenting the scene more completely than I did.

When she is done and I hand duplicate paperwork over, I ask: "Any chance I can go?"

"Noooo, you know the rules."

"How come I always have to wait for the detectives on scene? Can't they just come by the house for tea and a chat after they are done?"

"Oh, so you want to leave me alone with your woodchuck guy, huh?"

"You're a cop. That's your job."

We stand with our back to the cruiser, chatting and teasing each other a bit. Victoria asks about Sam. Victoria is clearly delaying her return to interview with the witness who is still whacked out on narcotics.

"He has outstanding warrants, you know."

"No, but I guessed. He'd have bolted if given a minute."

Victoria adds, "All drugs related: possession, intent, and then a failure to show. Think there is a driving under the influence too."

"He's under the influence now." I am normally too guarded on scene to say this aloud. "I would like to get home before dinner. Is that going to be possible?"

She responds by saying: "Richie is on his way. Maybe he can transport your friend there. We'll see. I should interview him." Victoria gives me a complete non-answer.

"I'll be in my truck." After sitting, I radio dispatch: "Trowbridge Command reports state police on scene. Command transferred to VSP. Units remaining on scene."

When I get home, I walk into a warm kitchen, a kiss from my wife, and a hug from Morgan. I drop my gear on my chair, then wash very thoroughly in the kitchen sink with hot water. I wash my face, my neck, and my hands to my armpits. Then dry with a tea towel that I toss towards the mudroom and the laundry.

We three sit for an informal meal of roasted butternut squash in the kitchen.

# 10 | Pepper Spray

As I drive towards the village center, I hear Alex Flynn on the radio.

"Pull over, hop in."

I park at the firehouse, grab my go-bag.

Alex pushes the truck up the hill towards the former village of Trowbridge Centre. The post road travelled this way for centuries. At the top of the hill, the land opens. To the north of the village green stands an old church building. The paint peels. To the south, you can see the cellar hole and chimney of the former inn. There are no actual homes in this village anymore. The post office disappeared before World War II. Instead, there is a hodge podge of store-bought mailboxes supported in an irregular lattice work of construction lumber. Mailboxes and no homes? The modern postal service first shuttered their post office. Then they curtailed their willingness to deliver mail to driveways and homes. The compromise results in mailboxes where homes aren't and homes where mailboxes aren't. Let's admit that this doesn't work in the days of ecommerce deliveries.

He pulls left hard then shuts down the emergency lights.

"Dispatch, 14RC1 staging away. 14RC1 establishing Trowbridge Command."

"Trowbridge Command established."

Alex, as rescue chief, turns on the police radio. I don't have this frequency programmed into any of my equipment. I never listen to the Vermont State Police. I am surprised to hear Haworth Police on the frequency. We hear several cops transmitting messages in a blend of plain language and code.

We sit at a T intersection where an ancient bridge crosses an older stream. We're low in the terrain as if sitting in a salad bowl.

"Did I ever tell you how I got my first medal?"

"No."

The night is dark. The lights are off. The truck runs. The radios squawk.

"Aaron, my first ambulance partner, and I are napping in Cambridge off of Mass Ave out past Porter Square, a region we used to call, 'Area 3.' I am probably reading some mystery novel written by a friend of my father and Aaron is likely napping.

"Just like this, we found ourselves in the middle of a police response. He says, 'Let's go. There's a division of police heading for us.' I kick the ambulance into gear and roll down Mass Ave. He points right, which is east.

"'Faster!'

"He reaches over and turns on our emergency lights. Then some dumb cop tries to wave us down. We feed him a bunch of bullshit and fly east towards Harvard Square and the river. We got well away from there before our dispatcher started yelling for us. Aaron makes up a location another mile east. With that, the office sent another rig to the scene."

I ask, "What was the scene?"

"A bank robbery. Aaron and I ran like rabbits from bank robbers. It was all over the news and the station that day. They held up a bank in Harvard Square. Somewhere after Cambridge Common, the dye pack exploded. People were telling stories of a man driving a Plymouth up Mass Ave with his blue face sticking out of the driver's side window while his partner wiped blue dye from the inside of the windshield. They crashed into a fence behind the old Sears building. There's a parking lot there with a Dunks."

"I can picture it."

"We had two fucking idiots working there. One was the big boss's nephew. The other was shaped like Danny DeVito. If you can picture Abbott and Costello, they were like that except the tall one was fat too. They were the heroes. Adam, the shorter one of the pair, kept telling his story of how he cleaned the blue dye off of the robbers so the cops could cuff them. Their ambulance was on all of the news stations."

"So how did you get a medal? Oh, look, blue lights." Given that we have no leaves on the trees, bright light travels through the bare sticks that make up our wintertime forest. The blue dances high in the treetops. The intensity fades, then they disappear. I think he headed too far east.

"Aaron gave it to me. It was a stupid plastic chicken. It was yellow and he did a thing with a safety pin and some satin ribbon. Given his background with the army, he made a show of it."

Alex had spoken of Aaron before. He holds a special place in Alex's heart and history, a Vietnam era combat medic who himself got shot out of helicopters then decided a decade later to become an EMT then a nurse. In a way, Aaron is a grandfather to me. He was Alex's teacher. Alex is my teacher. I occasionally speak his words and use his techniques.

"You guys had some fun back in the day, didn't you?"

"We did. I miss him still. Or rather, I should say, I miss him more now that we've built this squad. I want to talk with him."

"I'd like to talk with him, too," I add.

The blue lights return to the forest around us again as a cop car speeds by. The chatter on the police radio is nearly nonstop.

"Vermont State Police, this is Trowbridge Command."

"Trowbridge Command, clear the frequency. We have an emergency."

Alex returns the mic to the cradle.

"Maybe I should turn the emergency lights on. They'll find us faster."

"Who will find us faster, the cop or the gunman?" I ask.

"Fair point. That is why the lights are off."

Our roof lights are off. The headlights are off. The dome lights are off. The only glow in the truck comes from the short stack of radios and the random lights for the dashboard. Speed zero.

"How about the next time we see blue lights, we turn ours on."

And that is what we do. We see blue lights dance through the forest. Alex turns on the red-and-white roof lights and the headlights.

"Dispatch, Trowbridge Command."

"Trowbridge Command."

"Dispatch, can you inform the police that they are in the right area, but a bit south of the scene. They are about a half mile off."

"Stand by, Trowbridge."

"Trowbridge, message relayed. They are asking that you turn on your emergency lights."

"Understood. We'll have our lights on."

That's our problem with an active shooter here. You can't sit through a Saturday or Sunday in September without hearing rifle and shotgun reports from everywhere around you. People sight their guns before hunting season. We don't get called to those active shooters. Owning and firing a gun in Trowbridge is legal. Firing a gun one hundred times is also legal. Walking the roads with a gun is legal. When a hunter shoots another hunter, we call it a hunting accident. This is the first time, we've ever been toned to an "active shooter."

Alex, a paramedic, and me, an advanced EMT, had arrived on scene in his truck with no plan. Alex wrote plans for all of these scenarios. The active shooter plan reads something like, "Stage away from the scene until called in by the cops. Do not approach the scene until directed."

Therefore, we sit in a bowl carved high in our hills. The quote active shooter unquote is in front of us on a one-track dirt road that dead-ends a mile or two further on. And buzzing through the forgotten village square are cops from two, even three, departments. We, the medical team, find ourselves between the cops and the active shooter.

I question Sam's need, desire, ability to go towards gunfire. That's just crazy.

"How did you and Sarah meet?"

"In college," I answer.

"We've got hours. First the cops have to find us. Then the cops have to do the cop thing. Then we do our medic thing." Alex looks at the clock on the dashboard. "I'll bet it is midnight before you lay down again. Is Sam in town?"

"No, she is in a class in DC."

"Oh. What sort of class?"

I know the topic is conversational and I either know something or can guess something about Alex's professional background—fluency in Russian, French, Spanish, and Arabic combined with years of government service.

"Sam's heading for lieutenant colonel. So, she's working on her masters."

"Nice. Cool. Colonel Musgrave. That will be nice to see."

"Yes." Although, in daylight, my face might hint at the confused emotions I have about the promotion. Up or out. With each up, we commit more time to the army.

"Come on, tell me."

"About her school? You know I can't."

"No, Brie, how you two met."

This time there are blue lights coming from several sources. They are above us and lighting the tops of trees. Our red lights fill the bottom of the bowl. We're simply out of sight. One of the problems with roads here is recognizing what a road is. Cops, firefighters, and EMTs should be able to tell the difference. The confusion comes with a mixture of factors. First, the signs that mark roads go missing. They fall. They get stolen. They get covered over by sapling trees reaching skyward. Road signs cost money. Second, street signs may not be where you expect them to be. They get offset due to stone walls, three-hundred-year-old trees, or clusters of mailboxes. Third, a town road can look just like someone's driveway. This road may lead to a single house or a barn. This road may be a private lane with a road sign. Fourth, if you didn't download the regional map to your phone's memory before coming up in the hills, your GPS map is shit. There is no mobile phone signal, so the map will not refresh. Fifth, first responders occasionally develop myopia. They look through the windshield trying to stay on the road, avoid deer, and dark road signs therefore invisibly whiz by.

"I stepped over her front bike wheel."

Alex asks, "What?"

"Ok, so in high school I was a bit odd." Thinking that maybe I am still a bit odd. "I wore bibbed overalls that I had embroidered with a caterpillar and butterfly. Embarrassing, huh?"

"No, sweetie, I can see it."

"I had long hair, but it didn't look like the other girls'. I wore loose peasant blouses and full skirts."

"You still do."

"I do! I know I do. I sewed some of my own clothes. I did a bit of knitting. Cool kids shopped in the cool stores and did brand names. There I was, freaky little Brighid, except I was a little tall and a little awkward. I went to school dances and did the things. But something was just off. I kinda knew that I was broken."

"You are not broken." Alex touches my thigh in reassurance. "I think you are pretty spectacular. If you were a bit older and a little more single…"

"You were a teenager. And you survived."

"Did I? I ran away at least twice, and I had the world's greatest parents. Brie, at that age, I doubted that the world was very ready for me."

"You ran away?"

"The first time involved me scrambling out of Boston to the Appalachian Trail. The second time involved me disappearing behind a wall of secrecy after I graduated. I didn't see my parents for a goodly while after that."

"That's not really running away, is it?" I ask.

"Depends. Anyway, here you are, the goofy girl with ugly clothes in high school. Did you have a retainer or head gear too? I know her. Every high school had that girl," he says.

"Almost. Alex, this is embarrassing, I would put a white t-shirt on over my bra before I put a white shirt on. I didn't want people to see my bra or even me. I was all so fucking odd. I look back and I had the same body that the super popular girls had, but I wore baggy pants and loose skirts. They had beautiful round breasts. I was embarrassed for noticing them. I felt something when I looked at these girls with their high pony tails and delicate eye makeup."

"You hid?"

"Never thought of it that way. Something was wrong with me."

"Stop it."

"Listen, Alex, it is how I felt. It was high school, what do you expect? I didn't like the boys coming on to me. That confused me. That was the goal of doing anything. Girls were supposed to get noticed by the cool boys and get their attention. Then I am supposed to shun their attention playfully. I didn't understand the game at all. I focused on school. I played soccer and tried a little basketball. That all felt normal.

"I had one girl on my soccer team with short hair and, y'know, didn't give a shit about what others said about her. She wore a leather jacket and jeans. That wasn't me either. College wasn't any easier. I was a freshman. Lovely rural campus, old brick buildings. I was a couple of hours from home, and nobody knows me. I see this woman on campus. She is like a magnet for me. She wore a tweed jacket with suede patches on the elbow. She often pushed her sleeves up, which I had never seen anyone do with a sports coat. Her hair was dark, trimmed neatly. It wasn't boy-short, but it also wasn't…I dunno. I saw her across campus."

"Did you do a little stalking?"

"No, of course not. I followed her around on campus a bit. I trailed her to her dorm. I learned her class schedule. And I learned that people on campus called her Sam. One day, I was near her dorm, and she was climbing on her bicycle. She was still looking down before getting her feet right and I placed my left leg over the front wheel with both of my hands on her handlebars."

"Bold."

"Bold is right. I'd never done anything like that. The most embarrassing bit is that I didn't have a plan. I stood there looking at this woman, as close as I have ever been to a woman. I say, 'Hey, I am Brighid.' Then I froze. I didn't know what to do next. Literally the worst pickup ever. What the fuck did I know about picking up women?"

"What did she do?"

"She smiled at me. She said, 'My name is Sam.' I stopped talking. That was it. I did not know what to do next. I froze."

"You were standing over a bicycle wheel. Were you in your bibs?"

"No, a long, flowing skirt. I didn't say this was planned or bright or anything. It seemed all really stupid that second. I did the stinky-sweat thing, turned red, got embarrassed."

"And…" Alex prompts me further.

"'Do you want to have dinner with me?' I said it. I managed to say that. It could not have gotten any worse for me. I had a bike tire in my nether region. My face was about a foot from hers. I was looking into her hazel eyes. It was the first thing that came to my mind. She said, 'Yes.'"

I continue, "I just wanted her to notice me, now I've gone and asked her to dinner. I had no plan. None. But she bailed me out. 'How about six p.m.? Meet me here and I'll find a place.' It felt natural and easy when she spoke. I couldn't even think through my own version of that. It was just babble in my brain.

"Alex, I've got to tell you, I was a mess. I missed my last class of the day. I basically emptied my closet. I tried on clothes, then I decided to change my underwear. I couldn't wear dreary cotton panties and a boring white bra. I picked a blue dress. I wore sexy underwear. I think it was the very first time I put on underwear hoping that someone else would be taking them off. Is that bizarro? Flat, black ballet shoes on my feet. Nobody could see my calves. I was a little concerned that my yankee legs were so very white. Then I had a stupid moment about a handbag. I am not a handbag person, y'know. I dumped my school backpack and found a date purse my mother bought for me once. I shoved my keys and IDs inside, some cash and walked out the door."

"I can see you. You must have been gorgeous. And by the way, kid, you still are. I think you are stunning. Sam is so very lucky."

"I've got some gray in my hair."

"You've got gray in your hair and we are sitting a half-mile from some stupid active-shooter scene waiting for the cops to find us." And it was then that two cops buzzed by. They were doing close to sixty miles per hour on a road designed for thirty miles per hour. Alex turns off our emergency lights and our headlights. We return to the dark.

We want the cops to find us, but not the shooter. I feared that the flashing lights and stationary truck would serve as a beacon for the guy at the other end of this mess.

"And..." Alex prompts. As if it doesn't matter much that the cops flew past at Mach 1.

"I still remember the waiter's name. Her name was Patty. The host seated us. We got a minute with the menu and Patty came over. She did the normal routine, welcoming us and introducing herself. I was all fidget-Brighid at that point. My cheeks were likely blazing red. I got moisture in the wrong places. But I did manage to get some eyeliner on and my hair was neatly tamed with a stylish hairband. This woman looked at me, then asked, 'Is this your first date?'"

"No, really?" Alex asks.

"Yes. I was fucking mortified. Let's admit I misunderstood the question. I had been on dates. I went to a movie or three with various guys. I had gone to high school dances. This was my first real date and we're just supposed to be two anonymous women at a table together in Western Massachusetts adjacent to a lovely historic college campus. You know my face. If I think it, I show it. God, I fuckin' blew it. Then Patty said, 'Let me get you each a glass of wine.'

"My nervous dunderheaded self, I was about to speak, correcting her and Sam kicked me, hard-ish on the shin. I was barely nineteen years old. I needed to tell her that she couldn't serve me a glass of wine. But Sarah shut me up."

"And?" Alex asks.

"And what? We ordered dinner. We ate. Patty gave us a slice of pie each. She hugged me after the meal."

"And?"

"And...nothing. It was our first date, that was the story you asked for."

"You're leaving me dangling here. Somewhere in your story were black panties, a black bra, and a blue dress. I was a bit of a hound in my younger days."

"I can see that." I offer a sporting flirt back, noticing that I have not yet answered Alex's question.

Silence.

Alex looks at me across the dark cab of the truck. We can see the cacographic noise of blue and white lights scribbling through the dark forest.

"Sam," then I feel my cheeks warm, "was magical. I couldn't have asked for anyone better. I had a skip in my step walking back to my dorm the next morning. I did have to pick my underwear up from her floor. Now you know. Happy?"

"Very happy."

"I answered your questions, Alex. What about you?"

"Brie, I am Popeye. *I yam what I yam.*"

We sit in the dark truck for hours. At eleven thirty, a Vermont State Police cruiser approaches us. We both get out.

"Hey, Richie," I greet the trooper.

"Hey, Brie, Alex. Thanks for coming out."

"Bit of a fluster-cluck, isn't it."

"You don't know the half of it," he says to us.

"We saw the Keystone Cops routine. Your team was lost in space."

"And now the decision is to call in SWAT."

"It is nearing midnight," I observe.

"That's the problem. Their shifts already ended. The time estimate for getting the tactical team down here is a minimum of four hours. But with the darkness, we've decided to rally at six a.m."

"Ahh…" Dumb comment. The questions bubble inside.

"Can you guys come back at six a.m.?"

"Fine. Can we bring you anything? Are you staying all night?"

"Me, I probably will be. The Haworth cops are preparing to leave. Since I live three miles from here, I'll likely get stuck on the overnight watch."

"Alone?"

"I guess so."

"One cop alone in a cruiser on an empty dirt road hidden in the hills of a forgotten town at an active shooter scene. By the way, how active was the shooter? We never heard a gunshot."

"There seems to be some debate about that. Sounds like he fired a single round in the basement of the family home."

"It is the son, right?"

"Yup."

"If you need us, have dispatch wake us up. We can come out with food or water. Luck."

"I can call my girlfriend, too."

"Alright, my friend. I guess we'll see you in six hours."

I wake at five. I turn on all of the lights, waiting for Alex to arrive at five thirty.

As we vector down the road towards the village, Alex radios dispatch.

"Dispatch, 14RC1."

"14RC1."

"As discussed on the phone, please open the call and show that we are en route."

"14RC1, en route."

We park in the same spot. This time, we have a heavy tactical vehicle parked nearby. I cannot not imagine a two- or three-hour drive sitting in the back of that steel can. What a dreadful experience. We missed the morning action where the entire tactical team shot the house full of tear gas. They shot through windows. They invented new windows by missing windows and hitting walls. They shot through doors and door windows.

Our patient has been doused in pepper spray.

Alex and I spend time using sterile saline and gauze pads to get the worst of the shit off of his face. Then I make a mistake.

The Trent Valley ambulance had arrived. Alex and I walk the patient to the rig. The young man is handcuffed. During the handover, I take my medical gloves off. Fine. I am done with the call. Then I wonder, does this guy have any knives or weapons on him. I have this vision of the tactical team blasting him with gas, tackling him in a big pig pile. They slap the cuffs on him then walk him up the road. I think, let's make sure before we put him in the back of an ambulance for a forty-five-minute drive to the hospital.

"Hold on," I say. "Let's check for weapons." Before touching the young man, I ask-ish for permission, "Do you mind?"

## 10 | PEPPER SPRAY

Then, without waiting, I do a very quick job, working from his ankles up.

All that would have been fine had my gloves still been on.

Idiot me, I wiped my nose with my now-bare hand.

Sam's told me about tear gas and her training. I can confirm that tear gas is painful and immediately generates buckets of snot and tears.

# 11 | The Douglas Tree

I decide to take a walk with my absent Sam.

"Where should we go?" I ask the woman locked in a distant classroom. "Lakeshore Drive?"

"Sure," she doesn't respond.

I walk east across the field towards a trailhead, alone with Sam in my thoughts and my heart. My boots squish on the saturated ground and greening grasses. Hints of daffodils that The Aunts planted at the distant stone wall appear. I approach the gap in the wall. Yellow illuminates the forest's gate, the fresh pops of green yield to blacks and grays of winter's distant shadow.

"How is it that the spring forest smells entirely differently than the autumn?" Neither of us answers the question.

The incessant peepers begging for attention fall silent when I approach vernal ponds, along the path. The Aunts had long ago planted colorful delights within the forest, pushing the garden far beyond the dooryard. Forty minutes of walking took me up a rise, past a pond and over a bridge, then a gradual loop back towards the house. Sam and I mark and maintain these trails. We mark the trails with plastic survey tape or a stick, unlike The Aunts. The Aunts carefully painted tin-can lids with red before nailing them to the trees. I still see some of these rusty disks high up on the maturing trees. Sam pointed them out to me during my first year in the house.

She'd told me of the days when these rusty can-lids stood at shoulder height. The Aunts reached no higher than they could swing a hammer. In the passing decades, the trees lifted the red metal disks up and up. The metal rusted. In some cases, tree bark encased the steel, leaving a mounted blemish on the trail side of a tree: the scar of a branch that never existed. With these rusty trail markers, Sam ages herself. Sam finds her own roots in these hills. She has marked places on these hills with names only we know: Pine Fork, Douglas Tree, Cellar Tree, Grandfather, and Porcupine Ridge.

The Douglas Tree fell during one of the years Sam spent in combat. I was here with her when she finally found the spot where this tree once grew. She had looked for weeks and months during walks, insisting she had the right hill, the right view, the right spot, yet no tree existed. This tree once had twin ninety-degree turns that formed a seat. The first ninety-degree turn went from vertical to horizonal forming seat at knee level, according to Sarah. The second ninety-degree turn returned to the tree to vertical. Over decades, the level of the seat travelled skyward as the tree grew. I never sat on that seat. But Sam did, when she was young. The Aunts did. And so did Uncle Douglas.

When Sam found the stump buried beneath the leaf mold, she discovered that the Douglas Tree had been cut down low to the ground. The tree log entirely disappeared from the hill.

The disappearance of that beloved tree casts a void in Sam's soul the size of this unresolved mystery. Even today, she will stand on that hill seeking evidence of a long-gone tree. The stump since covered with soil has disappeared from the earth. Sam can stand at that missing tree with precision.

There is an obvious story behind the missing tree. The human that cut that tree trimmed the stump uncomfortably low, lower than any logger would have. A single tree stolen, poached from these woods by a careful, even courteous person. No damage, no tell-tale ruts, no basal scarring on nearby trees. Someone stole Sam's Douglas Tree. The tree stood whilst The Aunts lived. Then the tree disappeared during the years that Sam was on active duty rolling in and out of the war zones. I think that the Douglas Tree was stolen by a local artisan and used in a sculptural presentation. That's my explanation of the mystery.

The tree is gone, the canopy above long ago filled in, and the evidence of the stump appears as ordinary as any other bump in the forest floor. The gap holds a lifetime of stories. That missing tree on an ordinary knoll in a Vermont forest remains the Douglas Tree in her mind—and now my mind, too.

Uncle Douglas, who apparently was an uncle to Sam's aunts, died before The Aunts did. Long dead was he, before I started visiting this property, yet I hear his stories and feel his spirit in this knoll. Striding down the hillside, the earth becomes spongier as I approach the stone wall and the fields surrounding the house.

I study the pond's edge, gauging the volume of jelly eggs in the green water. Soon, those eggs will host millions and thousands of black dots jiggling with promise. I watch the eggs jiggle in the cold spring water, recognizing that I have not yet put my own eyeballs on Ernie von Doodle-head. I've seen dozens of photos. This is a world one needs to explore, even when you have photos. No photo call tell you that frog eggs vibrate.

Sam's journals from Iraq and Afghanistan described her desire to walk these hills barefoot with cold spring water squirting between her toes. She described these story-book streams to me from memories she carried. The soil here teems with life, unlike the ground in the perpetual battlefields where she has been spending her time. Over there, she described the ground as hard as concrete unless it was boot-sucking mud. She, like all soldiers, wore boots laced tight and tall. Above the boots, soldiers bloused trousers to protect the American feet and American legs from thousands of little critters and bugs. Regrettably, the tightly laced boots and bloused trousers did not protect Sam's leg from a bullet, shrapnel, or flaming metal powders. On this spring day, my imaginary Sam walked barefoot from the pond to our house next to me with her shoes tied around her neck and her hand holding mine.

During the walk, had Sam actually been with me, she would have discouraged me from writing this letter. I hear her voice. She never gives me a firm "no." Never the phrase: "Don't do it." Instead, she questions me on the benefits and risks of my actions, guiding me to evaluate my decision within the broader context of our work and our life.

You don't really need to ask what could go wrong with a plan, not if that person is a volunteer firefighter/EMT. Just listen to the fire dispatch service any hour of the day. Something is always going wrong for someone in the region. As I think, an ambulance and fire department get toned to the home of a five-year-old with trouble breathing in Bellows Falls, Vermont.

Sitting at my desk in our office, I write a letter to the members of the Haworth Selectboard and the town clerk. In my letter, I asked for financial disclosures of investments related to any businesses in the region, specifically any membership or investment in The Branston Club. This could go very badly.

I study the letter on my computer monitor while also looking over our southern fields. Doubt and regret flow through me. If the townspeople asked for financial disclosures from local politicians, no one would run. Rich people play poor here. Poor people are poor here. Folks with modest incomes struggle every day. If candidates for the selectboard filed financial disclosures, it would further divide these towns. Selectboard candidates rarely disclose their affiliation with political parties. Furthermore, few Vermont towns have conflict-of-interest policies. Those few policies ask that board members recuse themselves from decisions under specific conditions.

Ok, Sam, I get it. Writing a letter or filling out a Freedom of Information Act request form pushes the entire question of financial responsibility and financial conflicts of interest into the public space. It will tell them, the bad guys, more about us than we will learn about them. I waste time looking for the Vermont version of form. No such form exists, and no agency exists as a clearinghouse for the management of requests in the state, at least not at this minute. What does an FOIA yield according to Vermont laws? The answer can be found in the two relevant statutes: the Vermont Open Meeting Law and the Vermont Public Records Law. The Open Meeting Law mandates meetings of public bodies be public with a few obvious exceptions. The public records law states that public records include all documents, no matter the physical form, that are "produced or acquired in the course of public agency business." This law further ensures that anyone can request public records and a statement of purpose is not required. The Vermont Public Records Law places no restrictions on the use of public records. Request denials must be issued within two days of receiving the records request as cited in the *Vermont Statute*, Title 1, Chapter 5.315.

I rewrite my letter, turning it into an FOIA request. My letter now starts:

"Under the Vermont Public Records Law, §315, et seq., I request an opportunity to inspect or obtain copies of public record related to conflicts of interest between Haworth Selectboard members and The Branston Club...."

I see the gap. No public record exists between the members of the Haworth Selectboard and The Branston Club, a private membership organization. My blush of early excitement fades, even with the dread of doing something obviously stupid. The Town of Haworth can comply with the law and yet provide me with no new information and no documents. "Here you go, Brighid...." There is nothing. There are no documents to request. If selectboard members do not make financial disclosures to the town or an election committee, then the data are not available through an FOIA request. My FOIA letter would alert the selectboard members and Eberbach of my investigative intent.

I delete the text. I delete the file from my computer. The letter is gone.

I ask myself, how do I prove communication between selectboard members, or any public official in Vermont, and this organization? Let me revise that question: how do I do it legally? I can prove that these people communicate. Trent Valley is a mountainside region in a small state. Communication between neighbors, between business owners, between two people does not prove anything. How, then, do I demonstrate a financial link between The Branston Club and elected officials? Even if I am successful, what law has been broken? Can't a Vermonter buy a membership in a Vermont ski hill? Some folks live in Vermont because of the skiing, the mountains, the golf, and all that outdoor Vermont-y stuff.

No laws are broken if a selectboard member buys a membership at The Branston Club. If a matter comes to the board for a ruling, then maybe the board member ought to decide to recuse himself, or herself, from the matter. That recusal leaves the board with two votes instead of three. In communities this small, the boards continually address matters that include familial, cordial, professional, or financial relationships. We just trust people to behave well and avoid shame.

If Jeff Rowley, chair of the Haworth Selectboard, bought a membership in The Branston Club for his family's enjoyment, then who cares? It is not against the law. From one perspective, he voted with his pocketbook by buying from a local business. He skis. Shouldn't it be ok for him to ski at the local hill, too? Why take his money to a faraway hill and a restaurant in another town? Better to support the locals. Taking his money elsewhere might be viewed as a disloyal act.

Sam's voice enters my head. "Remember, when the enemy is in range, then so are you."

Sleuthing seems more difficult when it is as simple as driving to the next town.

Looking at my murder board, I examine the column labelled "victims." It lists homeowners, members, investors, construction contractors, and other vendors.

Fraud and land deals stretch back through America's history. What are the options? Option one is that Eberbach sells land, homes, and condos at highly inflated prices then runs away with the cash. Can Eberbach sell more resources than he possesses? Unlike old Florida swamp land, Vermont has real land with real houses and real roads. Option two involves exploring if this land grab is part of a Ponzi scheme. Maybe this is a pyramid scheme that will reveal itself shortly. Option three involves victims not yet visible on my murder board. Does Eberbach have an investment scheme running in parallel with the memberships? What else does the land on the north side of a mountain in Vermont offer investors? Eberbach, the pitchman, describes the Vermont dream, the Vermont colors, the Vermont opportunity, and the Vermont mystique. He sells images pulled from a richly colored wall calendar. He sells Bing Crosby and Danny Kaye singing about snow and white Christmases from an old white barn.

I listen to a series of tones for Haworth and Langford both. Fire departments, rescue trucks, and ambulances for a motor vehicle crash on the state highway involving a tractor trailer and two cars. Dispatch must be pulling Langford in because the road will be closed, restricting Haworth's access.

Returning to my thoughts, I wonder about option four. What if Ernie von Eberbach is not a crook? What if Ernie operates a legitimate business, wending his way through complex laws while facing the normal business challenges of financing and pressures that every developer faces?

What if he is innocent?

I put a card on my murder board with a question mark drawn with a dark marker over the word "innocent."

My brain works back around to additional victims. I explore if there are hidden sources of money. The phrase "EB-5" flashes through my head like lightning. The United States hosts a visa program that encourages foreign investment with the gentle reward of a Green Card, a lawful permanent residency. Could Eberbach be selling the Vermont vision to foreign investors with the promise of a Green Card?

Now I have something to ask for in an FOIA request. With mental fires stoked, I read about the EB-5 visa program and start triangulating where the process starts or ends or has a nexus so that I can fetch the data.

Sometimes, I am dense and don't see it. I am working from our office overlooking the small valley that conceals Trowbridge from the world. I am researching and gathering data from people around me. I don't have to rely on FOIA letters and the internet to find data. I can go get it. I navigate my phone to the Haworth town website to discover the date and time of the next selectboard meeting.

I can go and ask questions.

## 12 | Selectboard Meeting

I arrive late, on purpose. I possess limited capacity for sitting in a room while selectboard members mumble to each other. I don't care about the road report and whatever procurement is on the docket. I sign the clipboard, take a chair.

I wait for the "hearing of visitors" section.

Even our local reporter, Brian, is packing his stuff and about to turn off his audio recorder.

The selectboard chair, Jeff Rowley, looks around the room for visitors.

He says, "Let the record show we don't have any visitors."

"Sir," I raise my hand. "Can I be heard?"

"Oh, who are you?"

"My name is Brighid Doran from Trowbridge."

"I guess I thought you were a reporter or something. You don't live in Haworth?"

"No. Trowbridge," I add again.

"Do you have business before the Town of Haworth?"

"Not really. I came to the public meeting to ask you a question. This is a public meeting, isn't it?"

"Of course it is. It is the Haworth Selectboard meeting." Listen, buddy, we both know the law here.

"Well, sir." Boy, I hate saying "sir." It comes so easily to my Sam. "You are my state representative, and you also sit on the governing board for the Town of Haworth. I'd like to know if you possess a membership with The Branston Club."

"Do you shop at the IGA? Do you ever stop at Green Mountain Greens? Do you buy coffee at the No Schist truck? And I hope that you do. We're here to support our community."

"Isn't this a little different? The regional commission and the state and the local selectboards are all engaged with discussions about permits. Even the governor has been brought in with tax credits. I may be asking a tough question. Maybe I should ask a different but related question? Does the Haworth Selectboard or even the state legislature have a conflict-of-interest policy?"

I sit. Invisible hornets buzz.

"Those are interesting questions. Does Trowbridge? I hope that you ask your board the same thing."

"Sir, our selectboard isn't ruling on the largest possible employer in the region. Our selectboard isn't involved with the largest land development deal in Vermont. This isn't a one-town topic." I leave out the bit where I reinforce that Jeff Rowley is also my representative to the state government.

At least Brian of the *Trent Valley Viewer* still had his audio recorder going.

I walk out unsatisfied and without a firm answer. Major Musgrave's voice echoes silently, "Don't shit in your own foxhole." She'll be back on the weekend.

In our office, I turn on computers and monitors, appreciating the waking spring. I had been hearing phoebes for a week or two, now. The families in the region are sugaring. Know how I know? Because every town around has been toned to a barn fire or garage fire in the recent two weeks. Visitors to the region see plumes of steam rise from the cupolas of these buildings then call 911 as soon as they get a signal on their mobile phone. Then they all say, "I saw a barn on fire." The dispatchers ask where. The driver says, "I was in Trowbridge on a paved road." Or, "I think I was in Haworth."

Chief Thomas often uses his radio to tell us to "hold in quarters" while he investigates.

We choreograph an awkward comedy of multiple civilian firefighters who drive around the woods with red-and-white twinkle lights looking for a nonexistent barn fire. Two trucks pass each other, each from different towns, everyone looking for a burning barn. Nearly everyone knows the calls are bullshit. You make maple syrup by boiling maple sap. That process makes steam and a lot of it. The ratio is about forty to one. Almost 98% of the liquid gets converted to steam. One gallon of golden maple syrup for forty gallons of liquid boiled.

Vermont sugar shacks in March belch steam.

Visitors from outside the region see the steam and yell fire.

The snow melts, the land softens, and the roads devolve to mud. Even the robins skip that shit.

In my work investigating mergers and acquisitions, I have a different set of parameters. First, the company doing the buying is paying me. I don't really investigate them. I do peak, once in a while, when they pique my interest. Don't bite the hand with the food. The target company, knowing it is being purchased and wanting the cash, discloses everything. Their CPAs dust off the books. The bank accounts look healthy. The target provides what they called a "full and complete disclosure." I verify that data and dig for the undisclosed. I don't even need a badge or a warrant. I say, "Give me this, please," and they provide it. If they don't, the next topic at the negotiating table will seem dour. I have leverage.

I've got no leverage with the State of Vermont, the Winchester Regional Commission, or the towns of Haworth and Carlton. I don't even rise to the de minimis standard of "interested party." I don't own abutting property. I am not a member or stockholder. I am not a taxpayer in the town. I ain't nothing.

Maybe I am not a gumshoe. I am not sneaky or stealthy or subtle. I don't really have the knack of pulling a Columbo, "Err, um, just one more thing, Mister Rowley, and I am sorry for askin', but there is just one fact that still seems out of place." Zing!

Our company, which I call the "Sam and Brighid Show," is actually called Nidoba Research, LTD. We named it for the hill on the property, an old Algonquin word. The firm pays for subscriptions to all of the corporate and criminal investigation sites that are commercially available. It is all for sale. There is no need to hack into anything if you have the right accounts and credentials. Please don't think that we use the resources at Sam's fingertips. That is illegal. For years, I have assumed that all data are digital and findable, until I encountered

Ireland during family research. Through genealogy, I discovered that some of that information is handwritten in parish church records. These serve as a digital dead end. Vermont's records are often on paper, in vaults, and not yet digitized. Also, Vermont requires little data on its citizenry. I know I am wrong, but in some ways, the Vermont government operates like an honor box at a local farm. The fashion of collecting every bit of data on every person, property, pet, and farm animal is not yet here. Sure, folks are expected to register their dogs with town governments and show proof of rabies vaccines. Not cats, not sheep, not chickens, not cattle. No paperwork is required for a cottage business except maybe for a reseller's certificate. You can skip that if you never collect sales tax or you barter.

I create a digital profile of Jeff Rowley, my state representative. He's white, like 98% of Vermont. He attended a prestigious boarding school in Massachusetts, the sort of school that modeled itself on British public schools. Upon graduating from Holden Caulfield Preparatory, or whatever, he then attended a well-known Ivy League school in New England. Ok, that doesn't narrow the list much. How about I tell you it is a well-known Ivy League school in New Hampshire. He easily found a golden path to Wall Street and, from there, got hired by a federal oversight agency.

Ironic, no? He worked as a financial regulator on behalf of the federal government. Now that he is responsible for state and local oversight of corporate development of public lands, he forgets the fundamental rules of conflicts and segregation of duties.

Do I shop at the local IGA in Haworth? I do.

Do I buy locally when I can? I do.

Jeff Hawley, as local good guy, volunteers for the town government as selectman, volunteers on the local economic development agency Discover Trent Valley, and serves as a state legislator. The good-guy label comes from his participation with the Lions Club and his other volunteer work. Does he view his role in local government as overseeing and enforcing regulations? Maybe not. My guess is that he makes money though the investment firm that he runs out of his home. I found it registered on the Secretary of State's website but there was no social media on the entity.

"Jeff?"

"No, this is his wife."

"Can I talk with Jeff?"

"He's out right now. Can I ask what this is about?"

"My name is Brighid Doran from Trowbridge. He is my legislator. Can I leave a message for him to call me?"

Fifty-fifty.

When the phone rings after my lunch break, I sense some surprise in my own bones.

"Brighid, this is Jeff Rowley."

"Thanks for calling. I didn't mean to ambush you the other night. That wasn't very fair of me." Not only did I ambush him, I did it when a reporter ran a tape.

"The question came out of the blue."

"I looked into your background. Impressive. I see you still run an investment firm, but that came after years of working for a financial oversight agency. I didn't mean to hit so hard. I figured you were a guy of the world. You did Wall Street for a couple of decades. Then you did oversight on those same firms."

Turning to a defensive stance, he starts, "The town has owned that mountain for decades. I thought I was helping a new business out. I need to admit that your question really troubled me."

I remain silent.

"You know the numbers here. Declining population, aging population, young people leaving the area for better paying jobs."

"Those are difficult numbers. Were you looking for a way to help your neighbors?"

"I was. I am. We had abandoned commercial buildings on the town books. The town owned an abandoned ski area. We're not collecting taxes on these lands. And these lands are being used, now, to keep people employed."

"Those are difficult problems to solve, aren't they?" I probe.

"They are and when someone comes along with a plan that involves fresh streams of revenue and investment in the region, it feels like an answer to the question."

"Especially when it promises year-round employment. It is a nice get for a region. Do you think The Branston Club is acting honorably?"

"It takes every business time to get started and launch. He's having to buy the land and pay for the development which includes labor and materials. That is a big lift. I think that they will get there."

"Interesting. Meanwhile, you are on the regional economic development board, what is it called, Discover Trent Valley?"

"I am."

"I don't really understand the nature of those public-private entities. Are they involved with regulatory oversight and compliance?"

"No, not really. More like a matchmaker bringing opportunities, people, and money together."

"Let me ask a follow up...is the state legislature involved with oversight and compliance?"

"No." But that isn't his entire answer. His voice trails a bit as if questioning himself.

"The state legislator passes the laws that others must enforce. Therefore, regulatory oversight is done within the executive branch. Do you agree?"

"I guess so." Oh, I am pushing his brain to think new thoughts.

"You can see the nature of my questions. As a member of the town's selectboard, you are voting on permits, and town budgets, and allocation of town resources, and other topics. Is the selectboard a regulatory agency? Or does it have regulatory responsibilities?"

"No, like the legislature, it is a governing body," he says.

I pause. I say, "Ummm," to indicate a difference of opinion. "Like you, Jeff, I grew up in a small New England town. I carried the mic around town meeting, and sold brownies until I could vote. Mrs. Lenster taught me that the attendees of a town meeting serve as the legislative body and that the selectboard operates as the executive body. The selectboard is the legal authority that issue warrants, collects fines, and enforces municipal codes. Was Mrs. Lenster wrong?"

I hear him thinking. He knows the selectboard's duties. Towns

## 12 | SELECTBOARD MEETING

fine for late permits and charge for water and sewer access. I know the answer. The selectboard is the municipal executive branch and my teacher, Mrs. Lenster, was right. She had to be right: her husband was the captain of the town's militia. He wore knee breeches, a tailed coat, and carried a Brown Bess musket when he came to visit our classrooms. The same uniform he wore when doing parades.

I also know that by statute, the town is an interested party in the Act 250 process. On one hand, the town issues its own permits for construction and development. Then it has the added responsibility as a participant in the state's own Act 250 process, which is clearly a regulatory effort.

What thoughts are going through his head? I've got no crystal ball, and I can't read minds. If I could, then I would not read Sam's journal while she is traveling.

"I represent a client who isn't being paid promptly by The Branston Club."

"Are you a lawyer?"

"No, I am a researcher. I help with due diligence during mergers and acquisitions," using the shorthand he would be familiar with. "A neighbor, a friend, ask me for a bit of help when his bills went unpaid last year."

"How much?"

"I dunno. I mean, I dunno if I am at liberty to share that. It is a pretty basic contract dispute, but as I look into this guy, I find more and more troubling history and financial practices that don't smell right."

"Who is it?"

"Again…confidentiality, I think, huh? Local guy, local family, local bank, kids in the local schools. Ticks all the boxes. I don't mean to come across as judgmental. I am reading everything I can and attending the hearings."

"Oh, that's where I saw you. Were you at the Act 250 hearing?"

"I was. This land development stuff is very new to me. The law seems to be about negative impact on the neighbors and community: road use, resource use, clean water, clean air, and something about local aesthetics that seems to be hard to nail down. It does not appear that the town, state, or regional commission has performed any financial investigation into this guy. Shouldn't we be asking if he can pay for it and how it is paid for?"

"You're asking good questions, Brighid."

"In my work, I perform legal and financial investigations on firms."

"Oh, I know. I was an M-and-A guy for decades. I know exactly what you do."

"Nice, then you understand. I come in with my financial crime brain looking at these relationships and I see competing interests and an effort to honor the intent of Act 250, but something is missing."

"What's that?" Jeff asks me.

"The money side of the equation. We seem to be involved in encouraging economic development on one hand, while regulating soil, water, air, roads, and public resources. I keep trying to find the financial disclosures and financial plan."

"I don't think those exist."

"As in not part of the law? Or part of the law and never submitted."

"I don't think it is part of the law."

"Jeff, don't you think that is odd as a former member of a financial regulatory agency, at least according to your own website and some social media sites."

"Public moneys are not involved."

"Aren't they?"

"No. The town isn't providing money to the project. We're not investing."

"Aren't you? Even indirectly? I read about a new fire station and new ladder truck. I read about sewer pipes. I read about hiring inspectors. More roads mean more plowing, which means larger staff, which means more trucks. The towns of Haworth and Carlton both have to increase their spending to accommodate the demands of this project. Isn't that true?"

"Right, but it will come out of the taxes we collect and from the

## 12 | SELECTBOARD MEETING

sale of the abandoned properties."

"Only if Ernie von Eberbach completes the project by selling memberships and selling properties. If he doesn't, your town is out millions. In a few years, the properties will all return to the town government after tax foreclosure. The town will still own those abandoned lands except now with incomplete construction projects and concrete cellar holes. It could actually cost the town more money to remove the abandoned building than the town made in the initial sale. Let me pivot for a sec. What do you know about EB-5 visas? Is that topic on the table?"

"I don't even know what an EB-5 visa is."

"A foreign investor can buy a Green Card with a sizable enough investment into an authorized project."

"Never heard of it."

"Ok. Well, Jeff, I have taken enough of your time."

"You are welcome. You left me with a lot to think about. But I never gave you an answer to the question you first asked."

"What's that?"

"You asked if I owned a membership to The Branston Club."

"I already know the answer, Jeff. You told me when you asked me if I shop at the IGA. I don't know if you paid full market value or accepted it as a gift. But given I have watched the price of membership soar year after year, I am assured that the early memberships were hugely discounted as compared to the expected future value. Not only do you have a membership, but the paper value of that membership has soared."

"I never admitted to it."

"And I am not a lawyer, and I am not a reporter. I am just a researcher trying to protect a client. That is between you and your gods."

I transfer the audio recording file to our office file server and write notes.

Corruption is a big city problem.

Financial corruption starts and ends on Wall Street.

Those are easy assumptions to make after settling into tiny-town

Vermont. Selectboard guy who tripped on having twinned motivations that twisted together can call it community support. What is Ernie von Eberbach thinking? Why is he doing what he is doing?

Morgan listens to the interview with Jeff Rowley a few times. I watch him smile now and again as he takes notes on yellow legal pads.

Morgan thinks, works, and acts with deliberate care. In another generation, he might have used a pipe. Cleaning the pipe, loading the bowl with precision. Gentle rhythmic taps. That's the speed. He communicates, "I am having a think," reaching inside his jacket pocket for the pipe and pouch of tobacco. Those days are gone. Instead, the very modern Morgan reaches inside his leather case for his pen. It is gorgeous with a dark red wood inlayed with gold filigree. He closes his eyes, then unscrews the cap with utter patience and calmness. His pen makes a delightful sound when working itself on the paper, like the sound of a spade going through spring soils. He writes a phrase, then recaps the pen. He holds it vertically over the paper as if discovering its affinity for gravity.

He looks at me.

"What make you ask about EB-5 visas?"

"There is a thing behind a thing. And maybe a thing behind that."

He unscrews his cap and writes another phrase. His ink is blue. His handwriting evolved with that pen or one like it in his hands. The result is a distinct open script that is rounded. The line flows. The writing reflects none of the cramped rushing that I put into my letters.

"And you got there?"

"I didn't get all the way. What do have we for options? We've got Bernie Madoff and all the flavors of a pyramid scheme. We've got the Florida land deal whereby a speculator generates interest in ecologically important swamp that he needs to sell off. He creates beaches from mangroves, drills a rail line down the state and sells an art-deco-flavored dreamscape in the subtropics with perfect weather. The con, the long con. You've got basic theft. The fraudster dips his beak in every transaction coming and going. Programmers syphon money within rounding errors. Credit card readers skim personal financial data with every swipe. Money launderers fit in this category. You've even got the black box scam, like my guys doing FEMA fraud in Florida. Money goes in, paperwork comes out and jobs get done. But inside the black box, someone or some family built a engine that grinds up a community and steals everything they can."

He writes, "Black Box" in blue ink, then draws a six-sided cube with his fountain pen. This sits below a 3D rendering of a pyramid. For my siphon vision he draws as a pipe with a valve on it. It drips into a 3D bucket.

With no discretion, I look at his notes. I shan't say that they had been drawn unconsciously given they did represent the words I used. I snag a plain white piece of printer paper and my boring store-bought black pen. I draw a dot, a line, two lines, a three-sided triangle, a four-sided square. One, two, three, four. Morgan watches me.

"It's number two that I am not seeing fully. Look what you did. You took my descriptions and made them a doodle. Fraudsters tap into a line siphoning off what they want. The line, maybe with a bit of a "Y" in it. Three-sided is your classic pyramid scheme. And my black-box fraud became a cube or four-sided square. One, two, three, four. Two is missing."

I point at my drawing with two parallel lines. "What is that?"

Morgan unscrews his fountain pen. He draws and shades a cube with the skill of someone who practices rendering straight lines. He then draws an old-style iron pipe parallel with the bottom of his cube.

He sees what I am saying.

"I drew two parallel lines. You put a line under a cube. You could put the line under a pyramid. That's what I have been trying to see in my mind's eye. You did it by accident."

"Sorry, Brie, I was drawing what you described."

"Fine, give me the credit. I love your pen by the way. What is that thing we are not seeing? How many jokes exist about land speculators selling the Brooklyn Bridge or ten acres in old Florida? I asked myself: why invest real money and buy real land and make real news for a short-term con? It doesn't make sense. We are watching a long con unfold. We have no financial regulatory agency in Vermont. The six state troopers we have spend their days chasing drugs, speeders, and driving from one scene to another because they are grossly understaffed and underpaid. Our fraud laws are stuck in the early twentieth century—fines for painting horses and wearing the badge of a Civil War army veteran. This is a catch-and-release state. Even drunks rarely get locked up for long. 'Here's your citation to appear.' When you cross the state line, it seems to read: 'Welcome to Vermont. Next rest area is in a hundred miles.'

"Every state has some economic development funds and tax credit. Either bringing in businesses, building homes, or filming a movie."

"Right, so why now and why Vermont?"

"I think you answered the Why Vermont question."

"Sort of. Act 250 is a quagmire. It is a bizarro popularity contest. If you get your neighbors on board and work your way through the environmental stuff, you might get through the process in a few years, and it might cost you less than $100K. It is like walking into a blackberry bramble."

"Ouch. Ernie probably thought he could manipulate that. You said he bought all abutting lands."

"Within reason, yes. He is sure trying."

"That's his Act 250 mitigation strategy."

"Not working well enough. They need someone who can just do basic paperwork to keep their records cleaner. It's like those idiots who get stopped for speeding when hauling drugs up I-91."

"You could help him with that," Morgan says to me. "Why this visa, the EB-5?"

"First, I can't get through barriers around the program. That makes me suspicious. Second, it is a visa program that promotes foreign investment in the United States. If you invest sufficient money into an approved for-profit, commercial project, then you and your family can be given a visa by the U.S. Government. That visa is the first step towards a U.S. passport. What if the goal is to get visas or even sell visas? You need an approved for-profit commercial project that has significant community benefits that the local and state government are behind. The sort of project that attracts tax incentives and the like. The Branston Club meets those criteria."

"It does," he adds.

"Run The Branston Club scheme, whatever that is. Build your twenty-million-dollar timber-frame lodge made with steel I-beams. Sell condos and townhomes in a multi-tiered structure addressing the budget of people who are almost wealthy or actually wealthy. Get a few high-flyer billionaires in the game. There are always a few assholes who are willing to sell their family name to be stamped on a bogus project. Roll into a community desperate for investment and employment, such as rural New England where workers have reputations for integrity and old-world craftsmanship.

"Get the attention of Vermont's governor, two senators and our one congressional representative. Show them the value of the project and get federal, state, and local recognition for the work."

"And you can get an EB-5 project approved," he finishes my thought for me.

"And you can get an EB-5 project approved," I repeat. "Then name your price for the investment needed to get a visa. Guess who doesn't care much about the difference between 500K and a million or even two million. Some oligarch, oil prince, or cartel financier wanting to legitimize his life."

"The cost of admission."

"That's it. A two-million-dollar fee for a legit U.S. visa that leads quickly to citizenship and a blue American passport."

"That's not an investment to them, it is?" he asks.

"No, they don't expect a penny in return. They paid for a service, a visa."

He points to his paper with the rendered cube hovering over a pipeline. "Ernie von Eberbach gets funding from the offshore sales of visas, but only after the project gets started well enough to be considered above board."

"Morgan, even Act 250 plays into their hands. Oh, just too much government oversight. They cry too much regulation on a businessman trying to restore a ski resort to its former glory."

"Yes, it does. The money slips through the pipeline, but the quote real project," he taps at the cube, "gets stalled over boat docks, wellhouses, and powerline corridors."

"That's it. 'We're the victims here,' Ernie can yell. This was all approved. We have the plan, we have the approvals, now Act 250 is barking and nipping at our heels. It is slowing us down. It is diverting funds."

Morgan taps his finger on the drawings: a pipe, a pyramid, a cube and a cube with a pipe under it. Speaking slowly, he says, "It doesn't matter if the front-facing fraud is a pyramid scheme or as you call it a black-box scheme."

"Morgan, it could even be fully legit and above board. The money is flowing through an invisible pipeline."

He asks, "How did you do with the EB-5 research."

"Zilch. Nada, nothing. EB-5 is a null dataset. There is zero transparency on process. I can't even find the agency to submit an FOIA request for a list of authorized projects. The Vermont state government says that it is all federal. The federal government agencies state that the projects are not in their domain."

# 13 | Angela

I watch a white car come down the driveway. She parks away from the door while leaving the drive open, a practiced behavior for a rural person. She took a minute freeing herself from the car. She closes the door heavily, again providing a warning that someone is in our dooryard. She approaches the house slowly. I turn on the electric kettle before walking to the door and my guest.

"Hey," I say, firmly enough to provide guidance as to which door to use. This two-hundred-year-old house has too many doors and some of them haven't opened in a century.

"Hey," she says.

"Come on in." I wave the guest to the office door.

We stand at the entrance while she looks down at a small collection of boots, clogs, and shoes. I offer: "No, just come in." I wear leather moccasins, always ready to jump into my fire/EMS uniform and boots.

"I am Brighid." I offer my hand in an American style.

"Angela LaFontaine."

"I put the kettle on when I heard you in the drive. Coffee or tea? My coffee is terrible but I make good tea."

"Tea is fine, thank you. This is beautiful."

Angela appreciates our view. Our giant windows embrace the southern exposure. Hemlock-covered Nidboa Mountain to the west, the blue-misted valley hiding Trowbridge village below us, with a sense that Massachusetts remains just out of sight, or maybe in sight but just below the last Vermont bump.

"Sugar? Cream? What would you like?"

"A little sugar is nice. Jeez, what a view. This is your office?"

"Yes, it is."

"How do you get anything done in here?"

"Sometimes we don't."

"And no kids." Angela asks softly, swallowing awkwardly at the end.

I put her tea down next to the money chair—the chair with the best view.

"LaFontaine, that's an old family name from around here."

"It is. Still a few around. It is my husband's name."

I wait.

"He's a contractor and been working up at the hill. He hasn't been paid since August, mid-August."

"He works for Eberbach then?"

"Yes."

"Is he still working?"

"Yes, and he is still trying to pay his crew. Now he's laid the guys off for the season. He and his nephew go up every day trying to finish what they started. I tell him to walk away."

"And he won't."

"No, he won't. I heard you helped some of the others up there."

"Sort of, but there isn't much we can do."

"That's not what I heard. Maybe you can tell me what can we do?"

"A few things. First, he can and should stop working until he gets paid."

"He says he can't. He's got a contract and deadlines. If he fails to meet the deadlines, then he'll never get paid."

"That's not actually true. He due for the work he's done and his materials."

"Lem says otherwise. He's got a wicked bill coming due at the yard," probably meaning the lumber yard.

"Angela, contract law requires fairness or consideration for both parties. If Eberbach doesn't pay, then the contract is in breach. Game over. If you bring me the contracts, I'd be happy to look at them." I pause, "I need to say that I am not a lawyer."

"Last year Lem worked until the snow came. He didn't get paid for several months. He ended up taking small jobs around the valley to cover the bills. Bathrooms and handyman fix-it stuff. None of that pays like building a house. We made it. Then in the late winter, Lem lined up a couple of bigger jobs. Eberbach still owed him tens of thousands of dollars. Eberbach called Lem. Lems says Eberbach went into a big explanation about how the money is flowing again and he desperately needs Lem back. Lem says: 'Not without payment for last year,' then hangs up the phone.

"Eberbach called a couple of more times. Lem sent him to voicemail.

"Eberbach texted: 'I sent you 15K', which was less than half of what was owed. Lem answered the next call. They did the dance again. Lem told him that he had a couple of jobs lines up. Eberbach agreed to higher wages and bigger contracts for the summer."

I ask: "And the other jobs, did he ever start them?"

"No, as soon as the weather allowed, he was back outside. Eberbach promised payment on the past due amounts. He told me, we'll get paid plus interest. Last year, Eberbach paid the May bill quickly. The June money came by July. The July bill got paid in August. The August invoice never got paid. No money for September and October."

"How are you making it?"

"We're not. I am going to the food pantry once a week. I put in for SNAP. I've never been on food stamps in my life. I've got to feed the kids. Thank God that they get meals at the school during the day."

"I hear ya."

"I am late on the town tax bill too. I went down with a few hundred bucks in wrinkled twenties and some of my egg money. I promised to get more to the town clerk. I stepped into the office on the last day of the month. I delayed just as long as I could."

"That's horrible."

"I am trying to keep it from the kids, but I can barely afford gas for the car. They take the bus everyday now. I only go out if I have too. We've never been rich, but we always had what we needed, and that's all I ask for."

"I'll help, but you know as well as I do that Eberbach is a crook."

Her look expresses more than any words could. She'd clearly never said it as plainly. I just told her that she is being robbed monthly. Eberbach has stolen money from her kids' mouths. I wait and sip my tea.

I turn my attention to the view. The old pastures, now hayfields, still looking winter-dingy. I watch dark-eyed juncos, wrens, and sparrows alight on the weed stocks, causing the tops to wiggle. Occasionally a bird clings to a stock that bends too far. The bird releases before falling over. The stock springs vertical again. The bending-and-springing action reminds me of Robert Frost. And Robert Frost reminds me of autumn and winter, of splitting firewood, and the thousands of little jobs that have to be done on a traditional New England property. Frost's Vermont home stands an easy drive from here. His words mingle with these views and this weather. A bent birch takes me to a tattered paperback book of poetry from high school. Its pages are deeply dog-eared and torn. The paper has gone yellow. Pencil markings on the inside faded from decades of use.

The memories of the old poetry book bring my thoughts to a copy of the U.S. Constitution that Sam carries with her on missions. Her copy is parchment colored and includes the Declaration of Independence. It came with a membership to Colonial Williamsburg. We got this document that same year she enlisted as a private. That trip was to be our last trip together. Sam and I ran down to Virginia immediately after exams. She was breaking things off with me before she went to bootcamp. MEPS was our deadline, the end of Sam-and-Brighid. MEPS, the military's entrance processing station, was the threshold where our early relationship had to end. Don't Ask, Don't Tell means not having a girlfriend waiting at the post gate. Sam then decided to postpone the break-up until after going to Virginia. She has carried that slim volume with her on six continents. That booklet now includes one Hawthorne poem that I printed in five-point font and stuck in there for her. She doesn't really need to carry Frost with her. She just had to close her eyes then return here to this house, come home to our hills. Frost comes with these visions.

Angela asks, "What can you do?"

"Initially, I can look at the contracts and help there. I can advise

## 13 | ANGELA

on legal recourse. And we can add your family's case to our ongoing efforts. And I can have my friend Morgan write a formal demand letter. There is one helpful Vermont law."

"That's something, I suppose."

"Maybe it isn't a lot right now. People around here fail to see this guy as a crook. He's still got politicians and civic leaders buddying up to him."

"Can we go to the police?"

"Funny thing about police. They focus on criminal law. Financial crimes blend civil and criminal statutes. The local cop doesn't get involved with that sort of stuff. And financial crimes land in several jurisdictions. No matter what we say to the Vermont State Police right now, they would hear us describing a contract dispute—tort law. There are very few law enforcement agencies that focus on civil law."

"How do you know this?"

"First, we were joined by a lawyer recently. His name is Morgan Harmon. Second, Sam is a part-time deputy for the Winchester County Sheriff's office. Therefore, she has gone through the same training as VSP. Third, she served as a military police soldier in her early years with the U.S. Army."

"She? Sam?"

"Sam is Major Sarah Ann Musgrave, U.S. Army Reserves."

"And you? Are you a private investigator?"

"Not really. We provide research services which has an odd overlap with investigations, primarily corporate stuff."

"You and Sam?"

"It's me and Sam. The army has funny rules yet."

"How did you get involved with Eberbach then?"

I answer vaguely, "A family, like yours, came to us last fall asking for help."

She asks, "Did they pay you?"

"Surprisingly, The Branston Club paid the bill in full. Right now, I circle around Ernie von Eberbach like a red-tailed hawk." I avoid answering the question of our firm getting paid.

"We can't pay you."

"I know. I am not asking for anything. Neighbor helping neighbor. We can't do much, but we can give you peace of mind and a plan."

"Ok," Angela asks. "Has Sam served overseas?"

"Yes, been about everywhere."

"Iraq?"

"Yes, one one-year tour, several shorter tours ranging from weeks to ninety days."

"My brother went over."

"Oh, when?"

"In 2005 or 2006."

"She was there about that time. How is he now?"

"He committed suicide two years ago."

I leave that statement unanswered.

Soldiers and suicides: when is someone going to notice and care?

"I am very sorry for your loss and the loss to your family. Her units have also lost several soldiers to suicides."

I ask, in an effort to move the topic to safe terrain: "Angela, are you related to the family that owned the small gas station in Langford?"

"That's my husband's cousin."

"And there is a family of LaFontaine living in an old farmhouse along the state highway. And didn't a LaFontaine run the café for a year or two in Langford? Somebody in that family married a woman from the Metzger family out of Mass."

"That's me. I grew up seven miles south of here, next to the Buttrick family farm."

"Oh, that's a gorgeous farm."

"He's a cousin of mine. Is Sam from here?"

"Pretty much. This is Sam's family house. Her family built this house in early 1800s. I think they owned the land for a couple of decades prior to that." I ask Angela: "Are you ok? Can I get you more tea or anything?"

"I'm ok." Angela doesn't move.

I reach my hand to her shoulder. "Bring those documents by

## 13 | ANGELA

anytime you'd like. I am always here unless I am not." I hold out a real paper business card. "Our mobile numbers are printed on there. Please call or text whenever you need." She picks up the cup and refills it with tea.

"Sugar?" I ask.

"Yes, a bit, please."

Two cups of warm tea and Vermont silence. I watch a broad winged hawk ply his trade along the forest's edge. He came out below the treetops, flying effortlessly, weaving between trees. He works with the stealth of an owl. A surprisingly large bird who flies freely and fast between branches.

"Pretty amazing, right?" I add.

"I should get home. The kids come off the bus soon."

"How many?"

"Two."

"Both at Trowbridge Primary?"

"Yes."

"Can I get your phone number?" Angela rattles off a local landline number. I don't ask for a mobile number, assuming that she had dumped that service months ago.

With that, Angela stands with her cup. She carries it to the small sink in the office. She turns on the water.

"That's kind of you, but I'll do that. Go meet your kids. I've got you now."

I learned that line from Alex Flynn. People breathe when they hear it. They unclench a tiny fraction. "I've got you" means "you are safe." It means, "We'll take care of the rest." It means, "Go do what you need to do, it is ok." It means, "It is ok to let go." And they do. They let go. Alex told me more than once that you sometimes need to give someone permission to feel better. Sometimes you must tell a patient to brace up and fight for their life. Then, occasionally, give a patient permission to relax into the coming darkness.

I think that our team of Sam, Morgan, and I can help Angela.

Ernie von Fuckface will get tired of my demand letters. Who knew that the legislature cared? In 1992, somebody somewhere got screwed enough that the legislature passed a small body of laws within Title 9, Chapter 102. I love this bit:

> "If arbitration or litigation is commenced to recover payment due under the terms of this chapter and it is determined that an owner, contractor, or subcontractor has failed to comply with the payment terms of this chapter, the arbitrator or court shall award, in addition to all other damages due and as a penalty, an amount equal to one percent per month of all sums as to which payment has wrongfully been withheld ..."

Sounds like blah-blah-blah. Instead, focus on the one percent per month. Annualize that to twelve percent per year. Ernie, if you keep not paying your bills, the costs increase every month.

I walk Angela outside. I look at a car she can't afford to fill with fuel because of Ernie von Eberbach. She'll leave here, getting home in time to meet the schoolbus. Tonight, she'll feed them food from the food pantry because of Ernie von Shithead. Fucking shithead.

The next morning, after I see the bus travel down the hill, I call Angela. "Hey, do you mind if I swing by to get those contracts?"

"Great, see you shortly."

I scan the contracts and documents as PDFs onto our server. I dig through the mudroom to find a case of canned food for emergencies. In my years here, we've never touched those cans. I back my truck up to the barn door. I pull a whole bag of chicken feed from a slightly-mouse-proof storage box. I also grab a bale of wood shavings. I put it all into the bed of my truck.

At Angela's home, I deliver the contract documents, canned goods, bedding for her hens, and chicken feed to Angela before the yellow bus climbs the hill at the end of the school day.

"Angela," I say, standing next to my now emptied truck, "if you know of other families or businesses that are engaged with The Branston Club, let them know that Sam and I are here to help. Spread the word a bit. Let's see what we can do to make this better for everyone."

## 13 | ANGELA

Obviously, not better for Ernie von Crooked-ass.

These contracts flow with the same complexity that I saw in Duke's contracts. I step through lists of required and optional clauses. This contract had been built block by block by a crew of practiced lawyers. These lawyers demonstrate skill in the realm of the construction trades. The language is dense. The documents are long with external, but included, documents. No tradesperson would honestly expect to understand or even comply with these documents. The contract references separate book-sized attachments that in turn describe the minimal standards for each of the building trades and materials deployed. I take a blue highlighter from my desk. I draw an "A" across every clause that places a burden or requirement on the construction team, specifically Lem's small team of Vermonters. I also tag the Force majeure clauses with an "A."

I find the penalty sections, circling them in yellow. I circle the fees sections. I label them with a blue "B."

Like dissecting an owl pellet or butchering a chicken, my skilled hands rapidly parse a whole to discernible pieces, here a leg bone, here a breastbone, etc. And in this pile goes the offal.

The blue sections battle against the yellow highlighted sections, with blue identifying requirements placed on the contractor and yellow identifying the burden on The Branston Club. This serves me as a scoring system for the fairness captured within documents.

Contracts, at least in the American system, are based on English common law. These contracts require consideration. Consideration means fairness. "Consideration" is a legal term for equality. B buys services from A. The Branston Club "B" buys goods and services from Lem, "A." I evaluate the rights, interests, responsibility, benefits, and losses described within the contract. If "B" demands adherence to a schedule of "A," then consideration is due. If "B" demands specific quality in materials of "A," then "B" must make consideration for those demands, usually a premium price for the materials. Missing from the contract are the terms of payments, schedule for penalties for late payments, and the recourse for failure to pay in a timely fashion. When consideration reaches parity, then "A" equals "B." The contract may be viewed as fair if the blue highlights equal the yellow highlights. Isn't this the very icon of justice, a blind person holding a set of scales? "A" and "B" keep the balance level.

This shitty contract explicitly details the stages of remediation for inferior quality of work or materials. The cost of remediation rests entirely on A's shoulders and wallet. Lem pays for any bad shit that happens.

If Lem misses a key deliverable date, he gets paid less. If his crew makes a mistake, the cost of repair must be borne by Lem.

But what if "B" misses a deadline? What if ol' "B" misses a payment? The contract makes no mention of any recourse. The team who wrote this contract avoided terms that would cause "B" any pain, cost, or discomfort. Absent from these hundreds of pages is a table detailing the fees, percentages, and fines that Eberbach must pay for a missed deadline.

If Lem missed a deadline, it costs thousands of dollars. If Eberbach misses a deadline, it costs nothing. If Lem fails to finish a project, Eberbach pursues legal action and attaches to the bond he required of Lem. If Eberbach fails to pay an invoice, Lem is shit-out-of-luck. The parties argue it out in a confidential arbitration. Eberbach's contract describes binding arbitration which again puts Lem at a disadvantage. Binding arbitration cannot be appealed. Without courts and subpoenas, Lem has limited ability to perform discovery or demand documents from Eberbach.

Apparently, Vermont's history includes real estate developers who have abused the construction trades in the past. The legislature passed a law that reads:

> *The owner shall pay the contractor strictly in accordance with the terms of the construction contract.*
>
> *In the event that the construction contract does not contain a term governing the terms of payment, the contractor shall be entitled to invoice the owner for progress payments at the end of the billing period. The contractor shall be entitled to submit a final invoice for payment in full upon*

## 13 | ANGELA

*completion of the agreed-upon work.*

*Except as otherwise agreed, payment of interim and final invoices shall be due from the owner 20 days after end of billing period or 20 days after delivery of invoice, whichever is later.*

*Except as otherwise agreed, if any progress or final payment to a contractor is delayed beyond the due date established in subsection (c) of this section, the owner shall pay the contractor interest, beginning on the 21$^{ST}$ day, blah-blah-blah.*

I groove on this language. These rights are described within Vermont Statutes.

Here's why consideration matters. If the contract fails tests for consideration, then the contract may be invalidated as a whole document. Furthermore, if Eberbach's massive contract does not include a section on the owner's payment obligation, then the process reverts to the state law, rendering the value of this stack of paper useless. The state law says that Ernie must pay the bills within twenty days. The law continues, stating that if the owner, in this case Eberbach, fails to accept work within thirty days, payment is due to the contractor, Lem. If there is a delay in payment, then the delay costs the owner interest, penalties, and attorney fees. Vermont state law imposes a degree of parity that an unfair contract may skip over.

Restated, Eberbach's prior year's due amounts ought to be penalized at one percent per month. The current year's invoices are each due within twenty days of invoicing.

I like this construction law for three reasons. First, it is modern. Second, it addresses a real problem. Third, it seems to have a few teeth. Most of Vermont fraud laws are stupid.

Did you know that it is fraudulent to paint or disguise a horse? Not helpful, but still in Vermont's law books.

In Vermont, we have a fraud statute that informs us all that it is illegal to transfer chattel without notice of lien. What the heck is chattel? Isn't that an old term for wives, livestock, and even enslaved human beings?

It is a fraud here to misrepresent livestock.

Here's a big one. This fraud law is still on the books in Vermont. We have a law that defines fraud as wearing a badge associated with the Grand Army of the Republic or the Ladies of the Grand Army of the Republic, unless of course you are a member. That war ended for the first time in 1865. If you wear a badge associated with the Grand Army of the Republic, you may face a fine of fifty dollars and imprisonment for up to thirty days. Given every single soldier who fought for the United States during the American Civil War is dead, we might think of scraping the law from the books. Cool badge, now available at auctions. It has an eagle holding crossed cannons in his talons. Draped from the cannon is an American flag with thirteen stars. Hanging from the flag is a five-pointed metal star. Wear it today in Vermont, and you'll be subject to a modest fine and a bit of shame for violating the law. While the law's intent is good, it has been superseded by a federal law regarding "stolen valor." After a century of war that included the Spanish-American War, Mexico War, World War I, World War II, Korea War, Vietnam War, the Cold War, Grenada Invasion, a bunch of incursions into central America, Gulf War 1, Iraq, Afghanistan, and in what seems to be an endless cycle of belligerence, the federal government passed a law that makes falsely representing military service or military valor a crime.

I struggle to find a crime in the Vermont law books that Ernie von Jackass has violated, one year deep into his con. He hasn't painted a pony while wearing a badge from 1865. Even submitting incomplete paperwork or paperwork with errors to the Act 250 agencies is not really a crime.

Here is an odd distinction: if he stole five-thousand-dollars' worth of goods and cash from a Vermont home, the Vermont State Police will arrest him. Steal hundreds of thousands of dollars with crooked business practices, he's good to go. Not a crime here. Families may lose their life savings, live on food stamps, and see their home go for auction after tax foreclosure. Freedom, baby. We just call that capitalism.

## 13 | ANGELA

Steal money from a Vermont family leaving the children hungry and the family relying on federal and state food programs, and the victim must sue in a civil court. The victim must hire and pay for lawyers. They must pay for the discovery of evidence. They must be prepared to pay court costs. Poor folks can't afford civil court. And why? Because American rules of justice stand inverted. The LaFontaine family is wrong until they prove themselves right. The victim, with few resources and no money, holds the burden to demonstrate that they have been wronged, that the wrong is due to the other party, and that the wrong violates a Vermont law. The victim stands as prosecutor and must present evidence against the crook. That takes skills, money, and time.

The state plays the role of the judge. The state holds the rule book. The state, as judge, cannot advocate for the aggrieved victim.

I am not a blah-blah-blah, chapter-and-verse type of person. Too many years with Sam. I am happy for the fight. Let's go.

Admitting that, what if I am "the it." What if I am the backstop for the local contractors and vendors with this guy?

Let's admit that The Branston Club isn't painting horses and selling chattel—and hey, Vermont, let's get some newer rules on the books.

I am stuck finding any Vermont laws that Ernie is breaking or has broken.

What are the options open to our team?

I am not a lawyer. But Morgan is. I am not a PI, but Sam is a professional spook and part-time cop.

Option one, our team does the minimum. We draft a few demand letters. I stay focused on the better paying corporate clients. No muss, no fuss. Help neighbors, and live life. This assumes that our demand letters keep working. Our success rate is one hundred percent. One out, one paid.

Option two, we can accept each client as a distinct case.

Option three, we aggregate the cases for a possible class-action or multi-party case. We use our resources to fight in the courtroom until resolved, then we get paid on the back end as part of the contingency fees and settlement package.

Option four, we find, define, or discover the threshold for criminal activity. We build a criminal case and push the evidence to law enforcement agencies who do the rest, like I did with the Florida case.

Here is the most important question. Does Ernie von Shithead possess the intent to fault on multiple contracts simultaneously? Is that behavior criminal? When does this behavior become racketeering? When does it become a criminal conspiracy?

If we aim for a criminal investigation, how do we get the attention of the Vermont Attorney General?

The Vermont Attorney General supervises criminal prosecutions and consults with state's attorneys. The attorney general prepares for all prosecutions of civil and criminal causes in which the state is a party. In Vermont law, there are thirteen words that could be our leverage. The attorney general shall prepare for all criminal and civil causes "when, in his or her judgment, the interests of the State so require."

Vague, huh? Keeping hardworking families off of food stamps, that should be an interest, no? What about preventing construction companies from filing for bankruptcy? Is that interesting enough? What about families losing their homes to tax sales and bank foreclosure because The Branston Club refused to pay their invoices? Is that cause for interest?

If the attorney general determines that the state's interests include protecting Vermonters from crooks like Ernie von Eberbach, then the AG can act.

With this tiny bit of knowledge, I can't find any cases where the Vermont AG took on financial crimes like the Southern District of New York famously does. The Southern District of New York had made a reputation for going after fraudsters, market manipulators, mobsters, and white-collar financial criminals. Here in Vermont, we hang a big welcome sign at the border. Come on over, we have no real fraud laws, we have no experience investigating fraud as a crime, we have no resources to pursue you. Welcome.

We appear to lack the budget, the investigators, and the statutory

## 13 | ANGELA

foundation to pursue Eberbach and his kind.

Then the fire/EMS pager goes off. My attention turns immediately to the scanner: "Trowbridge Fire respond in Langford to establish a landing zone." With a quick look at an online map and satellite photo, I confirm my destination. Like Batman to the Batcave, I slide into my response gear with EMT uniform trousers, turnout pants, and my uniform sweatshirt. In my truck, with lights flashing, I head north and west towards the hayfield described by dispatch. They dispatched the air ambulance at the same time, giving me at least forty-five minutes to establish the landing zone.

While driving, I take a mental tour of the checklist for establishing a helicopter landing zone. I think that I'll need road access for the ground ambulance to get to the LZ. The ground ambulance has lower clearance and less tolerance than the helicopter, and my truck. The path needs to be pretty gentle.

I stop on the highway adjoining the hayfield. I use my mobile phone to look at the satellite image again. I see two access points for the field. One is directly off the highway and in front of me. The other looks like a disused path for grazing animals and ATVs. Easing forward, I take the right turn onto the field. This roadside ditch is not a significant obstacle and is serviced by a culvert. The ambulance will be fine crossing that. Success number one. Access to the field is accomplished.

Next, I look for overhead power lines that run parallel to the highway. I estimate that the right-of-way is about twenty meters from the road and goes through this hayfield. With my LZ incident action plan and drawing on my lap, I confirm distances. With an LZ of seventy-five feet per side, I need the LZ center to be no closer than one hundred and fifty feet. Converted to yards or meters or paces… that's fifty yards or fifty very large paces.

I drive my truck to a point representing my best guess for fifty yards. Before getting out, I make the call to dispatch announcing the establishment of "Langford LZ Command." From the back seat of my truck, I grab one collapsible road cone. I walk to the power line, then carefully, with exaggeratedly long strides, I pace and count to fifty, vectoring back to my truck. I've got ample space on this huge field, so I add a margin of ten more paces. I say to myself, "The north edge of the LZ is sixty yards from the power line that runs east-west parallel to the state highway." I will repeat this phrase when briefing the pilot via the radio. A second tick mark on my checklist of successes. The LZ has been marked with cones and is sized in accordance with instructions.

I lay reflective orange cones at the four corners. Using heavy-ish stones carried from the field's edge, I weigh down faraway cones. The cones lay on their side with the stones in the broad base. The cones rest on their side with the tips pointing towards the center of my square. I use my firefighting irons to weigh down the two near cones. My Halligan tool sits inside the cone to my north, my fire axe to my south. I reposition my truck in accordance with the drawing. I point it towards the center, at the same angle as the cones. If I could see myself and the LZ from the air, I'd see that I replicate the drawing on my paper accurately. The ground is level-ish for Vermont and firm. The wind, I observe, is light and variable. Getting clever, I tear a bit of yellow crime scene tape, then tie that to my radio antenna—a windsock that will aid me in gauging the wind's speed and direction.

I wait.

I watch Harry park his truck a goodly distance down the highway. He leaves his emergency lights on. He slips into a reflective vest, puts on his fire helmet, then walks slowly down the road.

I again want to hug Harry. When he arrives, I tap him on the upper arm, feeling his canvas barn coat. The barn coat smells like barn, hay, wet dog, and sheep. That tap constitutes my version of a Vermont embrace.

We climb into my truck without a word.

Langford LZ established. Now we wait.

With the more powerful truck radio, we hear the tactical frequencies and the activity at the scene. We tune my portable radio to the landing zone tactical frequency. Harry tunes his handheld radio to the dispatch frequency. In this manner, using three radios, we monitor all active frequencies simultaneously. We watch two additional ambulances approach from the east. Here we sit, well away from the action, in an empty field.

Harry, never much of a reader, reviews the drawing, then scans the terrain in front of us.

He asks: "Distance to power?"

"One hundred sixty yards at a minimum."

"I agree."

He asks: "Size of square?"

"Seventy-five paces."

"Yup."

He then asks: "What do you get when you give Viagra to a politician?"

"I have no idea, Harry, what?"

"A taller politician."

That's my friend Harry.

Spying the limp crime scene tape tied to my antenna, he says, "Nice windsock."

"Cheap, but effective."

Silence settles again.

After a while, I bring up Ernie von Eberbach. I ask about Carlton Legg. And of course, Harry knows Carlton. They've plied their trade at various farmer's markets, county fairs, state fairs, and festivals in New England.

"Can you introduce me?"

Then he tells me that Carlton keeps distance from his family. They don't get the music scene and his efforts there.

Eventually, I blurt, "I just don't get how every Vermonter goes through the week without a hug or a handshake."

With a smile and twinkle, he adds, "I'll take a hug from you any time." I stroke his brown canvas coat again, returning to silence. We watch our field and the skies above. We listen to the chatter on various radio frequencies. We sit there in the field prepared to help an unknown patient get to a trauma center that would otherwise take 90 minutes of hard travel over paved highways.

We then hear the excited calls on the dispatch frequency. "Trent

Valley Rescue One departing scene en route to establish the LZ." Three minutes later, we hear the call that the ambulance has departed the scene, also now headed to the LZ.

The sirens of the approaching trucks disrupt our calm and peace. I step from my pickup, put my yellow fire helmet on my head, and grab my portable radio and Harry's portable radio, allowing me to monitor the LZ tactical frequency and the dispatch channels at the same time.

The red rescue truck swings hard from the highway to the field, then accelerates aggressively through the field with his siren still going. The driver pulls within feet of me and of my pickup. The driver leans through the window and screams:

"Get that fucking truck out of my way, bitch."

The passenger hops down. He storms towards me, also yelling: "You fucking dyke, you fucked up this entire LZ, for fuck's sake."

The passenger, a firefighter, yells over his shoulder: "The LZ markers must be fifty yards. Who the fuck trained you?" That firefighter leans over, picking up my collapsible cone and holding fast to my Halligan tool. "What the fuck is this? We need a real cone."

Harry eases himself from my pickup and walks to the driver. "She did everything right." He holds up the checklist and the drawing. "It is exactly as they trained us. And this is their form." The driver pulls on the air horn waving the other asshole back to the rescue truck.

Harry continues, "You can replace our cones and send us away, or you can let us stay. But at this minute, she is Langford LZ Command."

"Fuck that, she can go home. She's not even from Langford."

Hearing that, and hurt beyond all pain, I walk to my two nearest cones. I pick them up, pick up my Halligan and my axe.

I hear the helicopter's first attempt on the tactical frequency. I ignore it. I am no longer LZ Command.

With two cones in my truck and my irons tossed on the back seat, I hear the second call from the helicopter. In a soft voice, I say, "Harry, want a lift?"

He hops in. Then together we hear the helicopter's third call to

## 13 | ANGELA

LZ Command.

In a split second, we hear dispatch call on the primary frequency: "Langford, the helicopter is attempting to reach you on tac three."

"Fuck 'em." I have tears flowing freely down my face.

As we approach Harry's truck, I say, "You know, I have never been called a dyke in my entire life."

He leans across the center console of my truck. He embraces me. I collapse into a proper cry with my torso twisted awkwardly across the bench seat. Harry holds me as we remained parked at the side of the two-lane Vermont state highway.

# 14 | Friday Night

Harry follows me home. He follows me into my driveway. He follows me into my kitchen.

I kick my boots off. I drop trou, reaching for the same skirt I had on before the call. I pull off my uniform workshirt and find a button down to put on. Harry just doesn't care. The components of my uniform lie in crumpled piles on the floor. The idea of picking them up to hang and air them out disgusts me. The thought of going on another 911 call infuriates me; fuck legs, arms, bodies, active shooters, and hours directing traffic in all weather. Then my own peers treat me like dog shit.

I read my text message.

"Home in 2hrs. Harry called."

I look at Harry. He knows that I know that he called my wife to discuss the behavior of the Langford firefighters. I want to be furious at him. Instead, I collapse into his arms with an unbuttoned shirt. I found it altogether too easy to cry into his armpit. He gives me a hug, love, and warmth, and I slather his uniform workshirt with tears and snot. Probably less gross than the fluids that come out of a ewe's backend when she delivers. Definitely less gross than blood to the elbows after holding a bleeding head at a car wreck.

Just another badge earned while trying to make life just a tiny bit better for others.

He sits me on my own sofa, then plops down next to me.

Twenty minutes later, I give him permission to go home.

"I am fine."

"Me too." He doesn't leave.

Thirty minutes later, the digital dog deetles. The digital dog informs me that someone broke a hidden laser beam on the driveway. I stir. I rise. I fold the blanket that Harry put over me. I finally button the shirt and tuck it in. I rinse my face in the kitchen sink.

Harry is in the mudroom with his barn coat on.

Sam comes in looking only at me. Then pivots and embraces Harry. Her hands go up and around his neck. She kisses him on the beard and whispers something into his ear. Harry exits with haste.

Sam touches my face. She strokes my puffy eyes. Then she kisses me with a mature love, the love born on a college campus that has survived wars, deployments, promotions, and challenges where the army has rules on their books that require prosecution of Sam due to this same love.

In my ear, she says, "I am the only one allowed to call you a dyke."

Fuckin' words, man. I don't answer.

Two hours later, I offer a plate of scrambled eggs. Her hair is already dry. Mine is dripping down my bathrobe.

"How was class?" I ask Sam.

"What class?" She responds.

"Right."

"How was DC?" I ask.

"The same."

"Any new injuries?"

"Not even a papercut."

"My favorite kind of deployment."

I deliberately turn off my scanners, radios, and hip pager for the weekend.

We never return to the office either.

# 15 | Sleuthing

I skipped the preteen and teenage thoughts of marriage and family. Back then ideas swirled, solutions didn't. My mother called lesbians "angry women." She disdained lesbians. I should not admit to wanting the white dress wedding, but I did. I don't want to admit to wanting a loving, family-style home, but I did. When I rattle around this house, the old confusions return. This house raised generations upon generations of Sam's family. Her family tree might slope diagonally. I feel the emptiness when Sarah deploys. We have a dining room that seats eighteen. Oh, and we can dress the table with matching dishes for just about that number. There are bags of silver wrapped neatly in blue fabric. The silver is unnecessarily embossed with the letter M adorned with curls and scrolls.

Now, we are three.

I actually need to shop and plan for three. Why not?

I feel and breathe Morgan even when he isn't in our home. He is more cayenne and pungent garlic. I am more caramelized onions and roasted garlic. He is tweed and worsted wool. I am linen and coarse wool.

If he doesn't come through the door before breakfast, I miss him. I explore the alternatives. One, he's already here and maybe asleep in his own room in our house. Two, he's about to walk through the door. Or three, none of the above.

Weeks ago, he was a random human being. Now I explore the idea of worrying if I don't know where he is. He plugged into our lives.

"Hiking. Thinking." That text dialed the concern-o-meter to zero.

"Sam, I think today is the day we put our eyeballs on Ernie von Asshole."

"Why not? You honestly haven't done that already?"

## 15 | SLEUTHING

"Honestly? You ask me 'honestly.' I can't even fib to you without you busting on me. No, I have never gone out and scoped out our guy."

"You've gone this long." Now I think she is teasing me.

"And today is the day we break the streak."

"I'm game. Well, I am always game."

"Yes, you are. And sometimes a bit gamey?"

Given we are alone in the house, a bit of silliness follows. Certainly, we get full silly in front of Morgan. Shall we admit there are things we don't do, say, maybe, in the kitchen?

I text Morgan. "Gumshoeing."

In my truck, Sam asks, "What do you expect?" She is wearing hunting clothing. I grab an old army camo coat to complete the ruse. She has a shotgun. My truck—red, with emergency lights, a firefighter's license tag, and Vermont plates—is at home anywhere on our dusty roads. In case you are wondering, we have a spring tom turkey hunt that spans the month of May but only until noon. Be vewy vewy quiet, we're hunting turkeys.

"I expect to see him on the phone, pacing."

"And what will you learn from that?"

"I dunno. I just want to see Ernie von Asshole in action. Is he a finger in the air guy? Is he wearing wireless ear pods or sitting at a desk? In one version he holds the phone in his hand while pointing and gestating with the other hand."

"Ok. That's it, just watch?"

"Some video, I suppose. Can we capture audio?" I know the answer to that question. I carry the plastic pelican case that we use to transport our directional microphone, and cameras.

"He is a predator. So, I guess I'd see that."

His house is a modern adaptation of a classic alpine cottage. The angles make our effort difficult. His house opens to a valley view. The trees have been pruned back and the ground slopes away from the house. We pick a spot that is roughly at the same elevation as the living room floor. Sam builds a ground-level perch fifty meters from the window. Stacking one flat stone on another flat stone, forming a backrest from a tall maple, she sits. Hunting gloves, a balaclava covering from nose to chin, and a floppy boonie cap crowing the top, she watches the silent, yet animated, protestations of Ernie von Eberbach.

Around us, we hear the clicking and rustling of squirrels, both gray and red. A little red critter gives riotous alarm. Everyone in the woods knows of our presence now, except for Ernie. He paces and talks. He must be loud; his mouth opens wide with each word, each phrase. Sam carefully lifts binoculars to confirm that two white ear buds. He speaks with his arms and hands and fingers.

We see no one else in the room. We cannot see the back of the room. Eberbach makes it easy for us. He uses his big window as his stage. With the arm flapping, he's no classical music conductor but a toss up between a very bad stage actor or a very loud preacher denouncing the sins of the world in a Baptist tent revival. Let's both admit, I've never been in, or even near, a Baptist tent revival. I feel like I am the sort of human being that they would need to save or stone. Fifty-fifty.

Sam shoots video through a telephoto lens.

At ten o'clock, she stands to walk the perimeter of the house. Her plan is to complete a 360-degree lap around his place.

She rises.

Ernie disappears from the window.

I shift positions and scramble for higher terrain. I find him lying flat on the sofa. He has a blanket covering his feet, shins, and knees. His head rests on his hands. He is calm. He is stationary.

I attributed shark-like behavior to this guy. Move or die. Dead eyes searching for prey.

Instead, I see a guy nearly asleep on a weekday morning. He owes millions to families in this valley and he looks like a lazy teenaged boy. I think his eyes are open, but he's not deeply committed to keeping them that way.

I spy a picture of a man at home, safe, comfortable. I see a human being with few worries, content to be a happy bum.

Sam returns.

## 15 | SLEUTHING

"He's got a driveway alarm and a couple of cameras. I marked the locations. He's got the TV on. It looks like an older World War II movie."

"Seriously, a movie?"

"Yeah, why?"

"Look at him. He is laying on the sofa watching it."

"He's almost asleep."

"I took a few pictures from that side of the house."

"Did you get a picture of the movie? I am super curious."

"I think so."

"Let's head home. I don't need to watch this man-child sleep in front of a movie on a Wednesday morning."

In my truck, we loop through the ski area and housing development areas. We see rows of foundations and messy gravel driveways. Sam snaps photos as I explore the cul-de-sacs and looping roads.

The twenty-million-dollar lodge resembles a child's neglected project. Work has restarted, but the balance between industry and neglect is out of whack. Winter weather and wind has frayed the edges of the blue tarps. Perimeter fencing has holes, and three panels lay flat on the ground, and as I noted to Duke, the timber-frame structure resembles red steel I-beams—at best, this is a hybrid steel-and-timber frame. I guess a dishonest person could call it a timber frame. Another tick in the lie column.

The site looks shabby, even abandoned. Given the lack of payments this spring and Duke's proximity to bankruptcy, I sympathize with Duke's attitude towards this site. I look at a pair of blue worksite toilets that seem to have not been washed since last summer.

Our photos chronicle a frustrating and sad story. And yet, Ernie von Eberbach insists that the famous, the wealthy, the important are here now, arriving soon, buying memberships today. "We've sold three hundred memberships, and we'll sell another fifteen hundred this year." In Eberbach's mind, he's already built an eighty-thousand square foot lodge with a movie theater, high-end dining, video editing suites, and spas.

Reality consists of shredded blue tarps fluttering in the breeze.

Reality looks like rusty steel I-beams and dingy gray timber. And a guy asleep on his sofa watching Clint Eastwood.

Sam says, "It's dozens of properties. I think he is buying everything that abuts anything he owns or can get his hands on. It's all registered with different owners, LLCs, and such. If it touches the airport, he buys it. If it's on the roads coming towards the ski hill, he buys it…

I answer, "I see what you see."

"What is the end game then? He's camped in the middle of this whole deal. His name is on everything. Sure, he's put a layer of LLCs in there, but that's weak protection."

"We'll need to figure out the victims and identify where he is pulling money from."

She asks me, "He is a fraudster, right?" I've been convinced since the first meeting with Duke. Sam's been in school and doing her army thing and a few days with the sheriff's department. She's not constantly in my head. It is a fair question.

"He is a lying fraudster who is actively defrauding hundreds of people, right now. It's all fraud. Yes, I think he is a fraud."

She is asking a different question than the question I answered. Sam, Morgan, and I agree about the fraud. I think Sam is asking me if Ernie is the fraudster. Something about him has caused her to explore that question.

In the office, I transfer the photos and audio to our servers. I put Sam's picture of the living room and Ernie's TV up on the big monitor. Richard Burton, Clint Eastwood, and a castle. The internet triangulated the information to precisely one movie, "Where Eagles Dare."

Morgan returns to our home and kitchen with a goodly pile of asparagus. With a couple of egg yolks, butter, horseradish, Worcestershire sauce, and lemon, I whipped up a hollandaise.

After dinner, I lie with my head on Sam's lap and my own feet under a blanket. Morgan sits in the neighboring chair with his legs up and we start watching Ernie's movie pick while we sit in our living room.

## 15 | SLEUTHING

The following morning, I see the banner headline in the Trent Valley Viewer announced the goodness and quality of The Branston Club's objectives. Ernie is quoted saying, "I am doing good for people and the community. We should come together to help save the region from economic failure."

I guess he wonders why people are resisting his beneficence. Pay your bills and don't push locals into requiring subsidies to feed their families.

# 16 | People are People

Duke texts, "Home? I need help."

"Ok. Here!"

I tell Morgan, who is sitting at his desk, "Hey, Duke has an issue and he is heading this way."

Absolutely, we both want to know what issue. Texting is tough. Texting while driving is bad. And cell coverage is horrible. We wait.

We hear the digital dog announcing the arrival.

We meet him standing in the office door. I see it before Morgan. His left hand is wrapped in a dirty blue towel sealed with silver duct tape.

I point and shout, "Kitchen."

I scoot ahead after saying, "Morgan, can you escort him to the kitchen sink?"

I meet them both at my sink. I stoke the fire in the kitchen with another two logs. I extend my hanging kettle into the warmer flame. I shuffle bottles and jars, placing one in a warming niche in the two-hundred-year-old kitchen fireplace. I pour liquid into a big Mason jar and create a mise-en-place type workspace for myself.

"My turn." I elbow my way to the sink, wash my hands aggressively with hot water and soap. I dry thoroughly. I glove up. starting with my favorite purple nitrile gloves.

I work and talk at the same time. I use my EMT voice which is like a primary school teacher's voice. I use short words to describe my actions. I narrate quietly.

"Duke, I am going to unwrap this." I start by peeling the duct tape away. "I assume this is worse than I expect, right?"

He grimaces.

"And you know that by law, statute, protocol, and courtesy, I must tell you to call 911 and that you must go the emergency room after I get this stabilized."

He nods, but looks away as I open the blue towel. The blood has soaked in. Pulling it from the wound undoes clots and opens the tissue.

"My friend, how come you didn't call 911 from the worksite? You've got worker's comp for this."

"Not me."

"It's the law, isn't it?" I try for that teacher-voice, non-judgy tone.

"It is except for owners. I excluded myself last year when…" He stops talking as I fully remove the towel. I throw it onto the slate apron for the fireplace. Gross. There is truck or equipment grease on the blue towel as well as common workspace grit.

Morgan isn't looking good either. I wiggle my finger at the lawyer indicating that it is time for him to get out of my way, or at least put his ass in a chair before he gets worse.

I roll the Mason jar around, then empty the contents down the drain. I fill the jar with about a liter of very warm water from the hanging kettle in the fireplace. I lay out two sterile syringes. Do another quick inventory.

"Hey, Morgan, can you bring Duke a stool so he can sit or rest on it?"

I strip my purple gloves, then don a pair of sterile surgical gloves. Yeah, don't ask. EMTs don't need sterile glove on ambulances or at emergency scenes. Nothing is sterile in the field, so why bother. You just don't want your patient's cooties on your skin. I am sterile. I sterilize my Mason jar with one-hundred percent, or two-hundred proof, raw grain alcohol. I pull sterile warm water into the syringe.

"I am going to start to flush this. You'll feel the warmth and discomfort." Sure, discomfort. He knows I am lying. I know I am lying. I start flushing the wound. Gently at first to get him used to the water and the temperature. Then I start using the syringe like it is a firehose. I use the pressure and the water to lift up debris and wash it away. I wash away yucky blood clots, filth, bits of jobsite, and whatever other shit the boy's put into the wound. Pull the plunger, fill the syringe, push the plunger, directing the stream of water into new regions of the full-thickness cut. The blood starts up again, but more at a trickle, an ooze.

As I work and prattle, I ask the questions.

"Duke, are you allergic to any medications?"

"Are you allergic to any foods or environmental stuff?"

"Duke, what medications do you take every day? What meds did you take today?" As I work, I step through the normal questionnaire for a patient's medical history and risk factors.

Then, like a curious scientist, or a geeky girl dissecting an owl pellet, I open the wound with my fingers. I examine every bit of it. I search in the nooks and crannies. I rinse away blood as I search for foreign objects, boogers of hydraulic grease, tree stumps, dead cats, old beetles, or some evidence of what caused the cut or what the boys did at the original scene of the accident.

"Looks clean," I tell the man who has long ago stopped looking and stopped listening to me. I patter on with my nice-teacher voice.

"Let's start treating this." Here I face a decision. I have two options for my next task. I can hit him with a medicine that will help with pain and swelling, except it is a tincture in alcohol. That will sting like hell. Or I can use a more diluted version that is in water and won't sting. The tincture is better. I don't think Duke could take me spraying ten milliliters of an alcohol-based drug into his wound.

"Morgan?"

"Yeah?"

"Can you come and hand me a jar?"

I point with my sterile glove. "Hold it." I pull the fluid into my syringe.

"Ok, Duke. This is liquid aspirin. It will help with swelling and give some pain relief. Its technical name is salicylate. Ok with you?" I can feel a wave of relief pulse through his tense body. I'll accept that as consent. I lean against his shoulder again, then fill the wound with my liquid aspirin.

"Remember, I am telling you to go to the emergency room and get this seen by a professional, right?"

He nods.

I dose his hand one more time with the aspirin juice, which looks rather like brown tea water.

"Thanks, Morgan." He returns the jar to the warming niche. "Now for the golden fluid next to it."

He holds that jar for me and I pull it up into my syringe. "I am all set. Thanks for the assist." He is happy to leave the sink, the bloody towel, and the fireplace area and return to the breakfast table where he can watch from a distance.

"Duke, I am just delaying a bit for the liquid aspirin to work. Then I will do another medicine. This one is a triple antibiotic and antimicrobial. This is called aqueous apiarian."

I don't count. I just wait. I'd like to get to two or even four minutes.

I then ease the golden liquid into his wound. I start at the bottom, making a layer against every bit of flesh, fat, and skin. I finish at the top of the cut. Brown aspirin juice and golden antibiotic juice drip down the hand. I wipe it clean with a sterile four-by-four gauze.

Again, I study the wound. I tap it dry with my sterile gauze.

With my sterile gloves, I open the small bottle of cyanoacrylate glue. Starting at the bottom of the canyon, I lay in a small line. I pinch the tissue closed. I lay down another line of glue and pinch that closed. I work my way up through the depth of the cut, glueing and closing as I go. I eventually get one neat and straight line. Thankfully, the ends and middle align nicely. I did not create an ugly fold or bubble or buckle in his skin. This should create a scar that will be neat, straight, white, and barely visible in a few years.

I open another sterile dressing. I put my aspirin juice and antibiotic on it. I place it on the closed wound. I then pull my gloves off, dropping them in the sink. I wrap his hand with elastic gauze.

"Remember what I said. I cannot treat this wound. I sent you to the ER and told you to get proper care by licensed medical people. Right?"

"Right. I heard you," Duke answers compliantly.

"I'll give you a few extra-large nitrile gloves. If you get around dirty shit, put a medical glove on this. Keep it clean. You already put enough crap in there to give yourself lock jaw and maybe even give birth to an alien, who knows. Clean, dry, and change the dressing every day. In fact, morning and night. Change the dressing after work, please."

He looks at his hand. He wiggles his fingers. He makes a fist.

"Jeez, man." He looks at the work in awe.

"No! You drove right by a clinic to get to my kitchen and there are three hospitals within forty-five minutes of here. You were never here and I never did anything." I am already cleaning my crap.

He stands. He looks at his hand one more time, then wraps it around my shoulders and back. He pulls me in for a huge hug.

We all know I kinda like hugs. I let it happen and put my face on his chest. It is kinda like he is crying for doing something that men would call *emotional*. That's alright.

He lets me go.

Then he kisses me on the cheek like he is my mother or a relative I never see. Alright, that's a first in Vermont. I rub his shoulder reassuringly, "You'll be alright. The cut is full thickness. It was filthy, but I think it will heal fine in three to ten days. Seriously man, if you see redness, swelling, or feel a new kind of pain in the next days, go to a real doctor. Deal?"

"Deal. And thank you."

I walk him and his tall boots through the mudroom and out to the porch. I wave him down the drive and watch him head north back towards the job site.

In the kitchen, I clean my work area in a minute. I toss the nasty plastic medical waste into the trash can. I take my aspirin juice from the warming niche. I put the lid back on the other stuff.

"Morgan, tea?"

"Sure!"

I mean, I already have the water hot. I make a small pot of chamomile.

I sit at the breakfast table with my clean hands around a steaming mug of afternoon tea. Morgan is staring at me oddly.

"Ok, Brie, let me get this straight. A wounded man walks into your kitchen. You tell him to go to the ER and that you can't treat him."

"True. I am not licensed except during 911 calls and on ambulances and such."

"You then treat him with water from a cauldron hanging over a mature fire. You use willow bark tea and honey to treat a wound that you sealed with super glue."

"Cauldron? No, that is a kettle. Tea? That is a basic tincture of the active ingredient in aspirin. What do you think I am? I am a trained medical practitioner."

He grunts, "Um, um," deep in his throat. It sounds like disapproval or disbelief.

"Aqueous apiarian, that is bullshit, my friend. You made that up. I know enough Latin to know you said bee juice."

"Ok. It is honey. It works and has worked for millennia."

I am still not a witch, no matter what Morgan thinks or saw.

Anyway, we're talking about fraud. If I treated that client in my kitchen, you might just think I practiced medicine without a license, which is a form of fraud. That I can't do, ever. Therefore, I didn't do it.

Back to fraud and people who commit fraud. I think fraud is actually pretty boring. It takes fancy cinematic efforts and a cool soundtrack to make them interesting. For example, *The Sting* is a great movie. *The Thomas Crown Affair* is a great movie, twice over.

People are interesting. Here is a guy that with a plan to harvest cash from a mountain top in Vermont. He'll spend a few years Hoovering up every dollar he can. My job, our job, is to find a way to recognize the behavior and stop him. He has hired nearly every construction crew in Southern Vermont and Western Mass to work at his site. He has hired almost every lawyer in the region. He is feeding the political machinery of the state.

# 17 | A Diagonal Family

"Brighid."

I answer after seeing Duke's name on my phone. "Hey, Duke. How is the hand?"

"I am putting you on speaker phone with Brenda."

"Hey, Brenda."

"Listen, we're calling because we just got our invoice returned," Duke adds.

Brenda's voice sounds like she is fighting tears and anger. "I am so sorry. They found mistakes and rejected it."

"That's horrible, and you guys needed that payment."

All of the crews need their payments. Duke and Brenda were the first of our clients in this fight.

"Tell you what, bundle everything up and come over. We'll get it sorted. New team sport."

Duke answers, "We'll be right over."

They enter our office with brown boxes, one with a narrow-smiley-penis-like logo on it. Duke places it on the table.

Morgan flips through it first, looking for the letter.

Brenda is explaining that she did everything right. Her tone, her fear, her circular talk sounds just like the victims of car accidents sound. She starts the story again of how she generates the invoice each month. She tells the room of her spreadsheets and filing, about how she organizes the invoices from the subcontractors and suppliers. "I don't know how I made a mistake." With that cue, she starts the story again.

I know this behavior, have seen it before.

"Brenda, we've got you. Let's go make some tea." In the office, we use a proper electric kettle, one you cannot confuse with a cast iron kettle, or even a cauldron hanging in a huge fireplace.

"How is Duke's hand? Is it healing well?"
"What?"
"Duke's hand. Tell me how it is?"
Then I ask about kids.
Then I ask about getting my hair cut.
Then I ask about sugar and cream.
Then I suggest that she bring down a box of Swedish ginger thins from the cupboard.
Then I suggest she arrange them on a plate.
Then I ask about her kids. Her animals.

My goal is to get her mind free of the circular racetrack that it is looping around on.

We all hear Morgan say, "For granite's sake, this is off by less than one percent."

He has his finger on one line. "Two digits reversed, a six and a nine."

Sam speaks up. "I've got an offer. How about we do your invoices? We do last month's and all future months?"

"We can't afford that," Duke protests. But he looks at his wife, still upset by the packet that arrived in the mail hours ago.

"Duke, you can barely afford otherwise. Look, you've got the best lawyer in Southern Vermont standing there." Sam points with an open palm as she was taught to do by the army. "And here, you've got the best researcher and analyst I have ever met."

"Yeah," I add.

"Each month, as soon as you bring your invoice materials here."

I interrupt, "Actually bring some mid-month then after the end of the month."

"Ok, do what she says. Bring your invoice materials. We'll jazz them up. We'll treat every invoice as if we are preparing for a court case."

"And you'll charge us?" Duke asks, nicely.

"Yes, but it will be minimal. We can probably crank out invoices faster than you. We'll have Morgan do the lawyer thing. Brie will do the evidence and scanning thing. I'll serve them as if they are court papers and I'll play the role of the mean deputy."

Duke mulls it over, staring at the table. When he looks at his wife, he immediately says, "Ok!" He shakes Sam's hand in agreement.

That's it.

With a sub-one-percent error, Ernie's delaying tactic will cause him more headaches and more bullshit and expose him to greater losses.

After we see Brenda and Duke off, I write an email and update our website. To the existing clients, I offer invoicing services as part of our client relationship. It is just another legal document we'll use to pave our way to the Winchester County Courthouse. On the website, I describe the service with a marketing twist.

The Branston Club side knew what they were doing. Legal or not, they stepped into a gray area. They returned the invoice to the Haworth Post Office on the twentieth day after the invoice was received. They asked for a hand-punched cancellation and postmark. This avoids any delay that may result in the travel from Southern Vermont to White River Junction where all mail in the region gets postmarked. It took five days for the invoice to travel from Haworth to Trowbridge, two towns that connect at an intersection of four town lines. It took five days to travel the eight miles.

Like the too-big wellhouse, like the powerline corridor cut through a forest and marsh, like the boathouse, this maneuver was another demonstration of ill will. Another demonstration of deliberate delaying tactics.

That's it. I modify the engagement letter template. I update documents for Duke, Angela, and our other clients. Technically, I ask permission. Sort of, I guess, maybe. I likely indicate it is a new service. My phrasing reads like: "To expedite invoicing and track compliance, we are offering to create invoices on your behalf," blah-blah-blah. Frankly, the cost of us doing this will be cheaper than their various attempts. These guys all bang nails and build stuff.

Morgan informs us that he is out to take a walk. And we know he means to leave us alone. Morgan may leverage the law the way loggers here wield a chainsaw and my friend Harry can clip the fleece from a sheep. To Morgan, the law is a sharp tool in the hands of an expert. But unlike a chainsaw and clippers for wool, Morgan does his work silently.

He returns to the office. "Wanna join me? It is lovely out."

So much for silent explorations of Vermont and federal statutes while exploring our forest.

I look at Sam. She at me. In a flash, we're both up. We lock our computers out of habit.

I dress my feet in socks and boots and pull on my too-heavy barn coat. I'll regret this warm coat after we start going up a hill.

And "Morgan at our side" is a euphemistic exaggeration. We found him in our office and at our table. We invited him in. Then, he stepped into our lives. And don't go all throuple on me. In case it isn't clear to you yet, it is me and Sam. Has been since day one. Through hell and joy, it is she and me. But hearts are bigger than we can ever explore. Like the universe, hearts are infinite and expanding, if you let them be so. Like it is said at any large family dining table, "There is always room for one more."

With that thought in my head and Sarah's hand in my hand, I recognize that for so many families in Trent Valley, the "room for one more" may not be the case. They have been robbed of their savings. They are being robbed of their credit. They are being robbed of their spirit. In a community where neighbors rise from warm beds to respond, unpaid, to an emergency at a neighbor's house, generosity feels stale.

Sarah and I have plenty. We have plenty plenty of times over. The gardens yield more than we can eat. For years, I am able to put up a winter's worth of potatoes. Each fall, we all send a few animals to the abattoir. I trade lamb for venison. I trade lamb for beef and pork. I get ten eggs per day ten months of the year. We have no mortgage to speak off, given the house was built in 1810 or whatever.

And our clients pay our bills.

And Sam's employer, the United States Army, pays her electronically without fail.

Morgan asked after Uncle Douglas and the Douglas Tree. Sam

and I stop at the same knoll each time we walk that trail. We each had mentioned the Douglas Tree to him. Which means that three human beings stand on top of a forested bump talking about a tree that hasn't been seen in years. The Great Missing Tree Caper, an unrecorded and unreported crime. That absent tree stands for something. It carries its own spirit and the spirit of those who knew it. Thus, the spirit of Uncle Douglas reached into another human being. Uncle Douglas, meet Morgan. Morgan, Uncle Douglas.

"Uncle Douglas would climb that hill then sit on this tree. He would sit, light a cigarette, puff silently for a few minutes, then unwrap a Hershey chocolate bar. I remember his red face with his heart beating visibly through his gobbler's neck. As he got older, and I never knew him to be young, his huffing and puffing had a wheeze hint to it."

"How old were you?" Morgan asks.

"Jeez. Young. Five, six, seven, something like that."

"Uncle Douglas was your uncle?" Morgan asks.

"No, he was my aunt's uncle," Sam says.

"And your aunt was your father's sister?" Exploring again.

"Nope. The Aunts, there were two, were my mother's aunts. One of them was anyway."

I did once ask Sam which of The Aunts was her aunt and she said, "Both." That ended my curiosity. Different day, different century, different laws.

"Uncle Douglas, then, is your great granduncle." Morgan asks.

"Yes, I guess so and The Aunts were my great aunts."

"This was Uncle Douglas's place?"

"Legally, it was. He had inherited it. Douglas Musgrave. His niece moved in to care for the place when she was young. He preferred Broadway and, from stories, I hear that later he travelled with shows and sailed, or steamed, to Haiti, Cuba, and the Canal Zone during the cold winters. His steamer trucks are still in the house. I played with them as a kid. I sort of thought of him as an old-style vaudeville performer. He played the piano and sang a bit. Frankly, knowing my family, I'd guess he was an old queen who outlived his career, his friends, and his community."

"And this tree was his tree. You said he sat on it."

"This was a magical tree. It looked like the letter 'L,' sort of. It grew straight out of the ground, then turned left." Sarah uses her hands to describe the trunk turning ninety degrees. It was about as wide as Uncle Douglas's amply endowed backside. Then the tree made another ninety degree turn straight towards the canopy. The tree made a seat. The tree was a seat. He sit here flicking cigarette ash into the leaf litter."

"What happened to the tree?" Morgan asks.

"Mystery. I came home from a deployment and it was gone. Completely and totally gone. Not a twig or scar. Gone," Sam offers.

"My guess," I add, "is that some fine arts crafts person borrowed it for some amazing furniture or sculpture."

"I can see that. But they stole Uncle Douglas and his tree," Morgan says.

"But did they? We three are standing here talking about both. There is something here. I can feel the invisible roots under my feet," I suggest cautiously. You've got to be careful talking about the spirit of the forest, the roots of a long-gone tree when you hang a kettle, or cauldron, in your kitchen hearth. It is one thing to be called a "dyke," another to be married to someone as amazing as Sam. But maybe I ought to dial back this tree-spirit-reverence thing. I am not a witch.

As we return to the trail, Sarah Ann Musgrave returns to her diagonally shaped family tree. Uncle Douglas, an unmarried man who travelled with and likely loved fellow theater people, left the property to The Aunts. The Aunts skipped Sam's mother, giving the property to Sam decades before they died. Sam has owned this property since she was thirteen years old. The Aunts cared for Sam during summers, winter holidays, and scooped her from whatever shitty hell Sam's mother would occasionally place her in. They paid for the first two years of university. They paid for her sports, after-school activities, and bought her the toys, clothing, and stuff she needed.

"For over a century, this property and my own family tree has taken on the look of a mountain brook cascading and tumbling down the slope of a hill."

"I have seen Uncle Douglas's passport and trunk. Kinda fun to play with and think about even as an adult," I say to Morgan. "Maybe we can show you someday."

My family tree is chaotic and has a wreath hidden in it. Two sets of second cousins married each other. It doesn't draw well with family tree software. Two brothers married two sisters. The sisters and the brothers were second cousins to each other. The truth is the truth. Let's just say it was colonial times and the options were more limited. And you already know about my family's tendency to name everything "Londonderry" whether it is or isn't actually Londonderry.

We pass by a familiar cellar hole and Pine-in-the-Fork.

"Sarah's family tree has one little surprise in it."

"Does it?" Morgan asks.

"Yup," I tease.

"Her family story is that they got off the boat in Nova Scotia and emigrated down here, all those years ago. My research showed me that her Musgrave ancestor absolutely stepped off 'the boat' in Nova Scotia as lore informs us."

"But?" Morgan encourages me forward.

"It was his ship. That ship, that ship that landed in Nova Scotia sailed all the way from Manhattan Island. They left Manhattan in November of 1783."

"And why that date? Am I supposed to know that date?"

"That is the month and year the British army left New York City after surrendering. The Revolutionary War had just ended. Her Musgrave ancestors were English royalists."

"Ship captain, ship owner."

"And the son of English gentry. Bartholomew Musgrave."

Morgan helps the story along. "Someone moved down here, married into a family where everyone fought on the American side, and instead of being a ship owner, gentry-gentleman, our hero is a poor immigrant who stepped of a ship and married onto this property."

Sam does not actually like being teased about great granddad Bart Musgrave, the United Empire Loyalist. It does mean that she has relatives who fought against each other during the war that spanned from 1775 to 1783 and the Treaty of Paris and Treaty of Versailles. To her, the parchment-colored copy of the Declaration of Independence and the Constitution that she has carried into war zones are living, breathing documents that have touched her family since the earliest drafts.

I am proud of her family. I am proud of my goofy family stamping Londonderry on the map whenever they could. I acknowledge the complexity and conflict that our colonial ancestors experienced and inflicted on others. It can be both.

In the office, I am plowing through invoice data for our clients, generating invoices and compiling the evidence needed for future lawsuits. Morgan is drafting documents on his laptop with his gorgeous fountain pen next to the left side of his keyboard. The major is on the phone with Command Sergeant Major Prince, mumbling discretely about battalion business. Morgan and I are carefully not listening to the details.

And we hear it. The loud tractor-trailer-type horn. Someone coming down the hill lays on his horn and lets it rip, giving us the full doppler effect of a sound coming and then going.

If I am outside with the hens, the woolies, or gardening, I do hear friends such as Alex, Regina, Al, and others give a polite toot-toot as they go to the village or climb the hill from the village. That is friendly behavior for neighbors. Some asshole decided to let us know he found us.

# 18 | Lieutenant Colonel

I pack.
I unpack then start packing again.
"Should I wear the dinner clothes in the car or dress after we check in?" Sam doesn't answer. She carries three outfits to the car on hangers. She returns to the bedroom for her overnight bag.
I am still not packed.
She says, in a near whisper, "It is only one night."
I wanted Sam in her dress uniform so that I could wear something fancy-ish. I mean. Come on. I have never been invited to such an event. I sat in a few bleachers during the early phase of her career. I applauded along with everyone else when she graduated from bootcamp. Unlike the other slick-sleeved graduates, my Sarah had already earned her first promotion by being the fittest, fastest, smartest, and likely toughest boot in the show.
Sarah informed me frequently that Colonel Jackson had stated that the ceremony would be performed in standard duty uniform.
We leave the driveway in Sam's Volvo, making the left turn down the hill towards Massachusetts then towards the base for her normal drill weekend. And I have never been to her new base. I am her stage-door Johnny ready to meet her at a post's outer perimeter just beyond the sight of MPs.
Our weekends plans start with dinner hosted by the Jacksons at a restaurant. In the morning, after a night at an off-base hotel, we will return for her promotion ceremony. The colonel suggested that I pin Sam's rank on her in front of the entire unit. I observe that Sam had put her wedding ring on her finger instead of discreetly wearing it around her neck. Normally, I too wear our ring around my neck. Her reasons differ from mine. With the EMT and rescue work, I fear losing the ring and/or losing my finger. Trowbridge, Vermont loses

18 | LIEUTENANT COLONEL

too many fingers each year. For Sam, it sidesteps the obvious question about her spouse at home, the presumed husband with a quiet day job. I followed Sam's lead and put my ring on my own finger.

I select a blue dress for dinner with Colonel and Missus Jackson. It is nearly the same color and shape of the dress I wore on my first date with Sam back in university. I listen to Sam mutter "Darius" and "Ann" under her breath.

For years, Colonel Jackson has been her big boss. She referred to him as "sir", "colonel", "the colonel" and "the boss". She never uses his first name except for odd administrative tasks. With this promotion, she will be permitted and expected to treat him more equally. One rank will separate the battalion commander from his executive officer, Lieutenant Colonel Sarah Ann Musgrave, the battalion's new deputy commander.

At the restaurant, the colonel will be dressed in civilian clothing with his wife. Sarah is already wearing 1940-style high-waisted trousers that may well have been sported by Marlene Dietrich or Katharine Hepburn. She looks elegant and stylish. During dinner, it will be Darius, Brighid, Ann, and Sam. I get to meet her boss and his wife—for the first time.

Sam drives east down Route 2 towards the base. Me, Fidget Brighid, fidgets irrepressibly. It has been years and years and years of service. I went to the medical center at Landstuhl after her leg injury. In those hallways, I was just another soldier's family member embracing hope and fighting tears. Tonight, we will sit at a dining table with her superior officer. We are each wearing our wedding rings. No one has to "ask," and we don't have to "tell" him anything.

At the hotel, I change into the blue dress I selected. In a nod to our first date, I skip the normal granny-panties I wear on the farm for something a bit more…more.

At the restaurant, the colonel introduces himself and his wife to me. Darius shakes my hand. Ann offers each of us an international kiss on both cheeks—la bise. Seated and settled, I hear Ann call her husband "D."

Within minutes, Sam is calling me Brie, the same comfortable name she uses for me at home.

The wait staff comes for our dessert order. Ann is first to speak up. I follow. Darius uses the moment to explain the ceremony to me. He reviews the choreography, explaining how I will come to the front and center of the assembly to exchange Sam's Velcro rank patch, removing the golden oak-leaf cluster of a major and attaching the black oak-leaf cluster of a lieutenant colonel. Darius explains the tradition of punching the new rank on. He told me that some will tap Sarah on the collar bone. Some will land a proper hit. Some will punch her in the shoulder, the traditional location of enlisted ranks. With the new-style uniforms, rank gets worn on a square Velcro patch on the breastbone, dead center of the chest.

After dinner, the colonel offers me a polite hug, but only after Ann grabs me for a full-hearted embrace.

In the morning, Sam skips physical training, roll call, and early evolutions. Instead, she and I wait at the hotel until nine o'clock. At nine thirty, we hang around the headquarters building. She introduces me to command staff and the command sergeant major, CSM Prince. At ten minutes to ten, we walk into the drill hall where a podium has been set up. The podium is braced by the colors, U.S. flag, Army flag, and unit flag. At a table by the wall rests a store-bought sheet cake with a flag and a lieutenant colonel's oak-leaf cluster in the center.

At precisely ten o'clock, CSM Prince calls the thirty people in the room to attention. Then the staff personnel officer, the S1, reads aloud:

"Attention to orders:

The President of the United States, acting upon the recommendation of the Secretary of the Army, has placed special trust and confidence in the patriotism, integrity, and ability of Major Sarah Ann Musgrave. In view of these special qualities and her demonstration to serve in the higher grade, Major Musgrave is promoted to lieutenant colonel of the United States Army by order of the Secretary of the Army."

At that moment, I turn from the assembly to face the colonel.

He faces me. Without looking at notes, he administers the oath to my Sarah:

"I, Sarah Ann Musgrave, having been appointed a lieutenant colonel in the United Stated Army, do solemnly swear that I will support and defend the Constitution of the United States of America against all enemies, foreign and domestic; that I will bear true faith and allegiance to the same. That I take the obligation freely; without any mental reservation or purpose of evasion; and that I will well and faithfully discharge the duties of the office upon which I am about to enter, so help me God."

I step into the center from the right side, standing before my Sam. I remove one gold oak-leaf cluster. I put the black oak-leaf cluster in its place. Then to be a bit "in" on the game, I tap her gently with a loose fist over her new rank and bra strap. I did it. Everyone saw me do it. It was silly and proprietary of me, given I am the only one allowed to do it. You just can't punch or tap a female battalion XO between her breasts on the bra strap. Not allowed, not anymore.

I move toward the crowd. I feel Sam grab my wrist. She places me to her left. Together, we turn to face the members of headquarters company. Darius then says:

"Effectively immediately, Colonel Musgrave will be my executive officer and second-in-command. Thank you."

"At ease."

Without a word, all the soldiers in the room form a line. Sam positions me next to her in our receiving line. Each soldier passes by, starting with the colonel. As each soldier approaches us, they address us formally. Those holding rank of major and below, including all enlisted personnel, snap a proper salute before shaking my hand and Sam's hand. One young first lieutenant and one female staff sergeant give me a sympathetic shoulder tap as well, as if I had been promoted, too. Bizarrely, I heard several soldiers address me as Missus Musgrave, a name I had never before felt authorized to use, due to the army's legacy.

Soldiers proceed through the receiving line then return to the informal muster. As the last soldier finishes, the CSM steps forward to present Sam with a sword.

Sam speaks to the assembly.

"I thank you all for the trust you have offered me since I joined this unit. I shall endeavor to support you with the same generosity and dedication."

"Ma'am, I have a question."

I am pretty good with rank. Three chevrons up, two down and a black diamond. The insignia identifies him as a company first sergeant.

"Yes, top?" Sam answers.

"Sorry, colonel, the other 'ma'am'. Missus Musgrave?"

"Yes, top?" I parrot Sam but with more informality.

"How long have you been together?"

Sam interrupts, "According to the army, we met recently."

I finish for her, "We met as students at university. I was a first-year, she was a sophomore. So I have know Sam as a student, civilian, recruit, private, private first class, specialist, and sergeant. Then she was promoted to staff sergeant during her Green to Gold Program. Then two lieutenant ranks and on now to lieutenant colonel. But you never asked, and we never told. Listen, Top and the rest of you, you don't need to ma'am me." Shit, it took me years to get barely comfortable saying "sir." Hearing "ma'am" at my age is disturbing.

"Sorry Missus Musgrave. Rules is rules. It is either Missus Musgrave or ma'am. I ain't gettin' took to the woodshed by the CSM. Ma'am." He smiles at the edge of laughing.

Top and the CSM push me to stand next to Sam as she prepares to cut her cake. Then, to my own surprise, I place my hand on Sam's as she makes the ceremonial first cut of the cake. There is genuine applause for us.

Then it is Ann's turn. She is the battalion commander's wife. I am now the battalion XO's wife. Together, we are a new team. As a welcome gesture, she hands me a knife. Together, the wives of the unit's commanders cut squares of chocolate cake, placing them on small paper places. The soldiers, in yet another neat line, each take a piece of cake and move back to the scrum.

# 18 | LIEUTENANT COLONEL

Within forty-five minutes, the ceremony ends. Two young sergeants get detailed with the cleanup.

Sam walks with me to the parking lot. "Can you return at four to pick me up? We can run home then." I kiss her.

We kiss.

We kiss on the base, with her in uniform after being promoted and appointed as battalion executive officer. Her soldiers welcomed me. They welcomed us both.

On Sunday, the lieutenant colonel rises early from our bed at home. She drives the two hours back to base. She spends the day moving into the XO's office. She explains to me that her duties instantly shifted from the heady jobs of analyzing data, writing reports, collaborating, and leading sophisticated teams had fallen away with her promotion to XO. As a senior staff officer in a battalion, her duties have now become administrative. This promotion puts her on track to be selected as battalion commander when Darius gets promoted or retires. If she is later selected as battalion commander, I will exchange the oak-leaf cluster for the eagle of a colonel, a "full bird." For the next years, the colonel Darius, the command sergeant major Prince, and Sam will serve as den parents, leaders, caregivers, disciplinarians, coaches, teachers, and part-time ministers for a military intelligence battalion spread across several bases in several states. The best part of the job will involve building teams and promoting young soldiers. The worst will involve death notifications and disciplinary hearings.

Thus begins a new mission for her and for us. I begin to wonder if the battalion XO's wife now has special duties. No doubt I will learn them, in time.

Which causes me to think of the difficult parts of her new military venture. At the end, or after a mission, she always feels loss as the cycle closes. At the outset of a mission, she must learn the people on her new team. If lucky, the pretty boy is Ugly John and the tall one is Little John. After weeks, she tells me that you can't really imagine being without the team. You train, you argue, and you fuss and figure each other out. You learn skills, strengths, weaknesses, and abilities as the soldiers train and plan together. The soldiers sleep together, travel together, you touch each other while doing medical training or physical training. After the mission, someone gets promoted or transferred, or someone gets hurt. The team disappears and you find yourself alone, again. That's the end of the cycle. Mission end often comes with a sense of loss and isolation. That's what she's told me.

Around and around the mission cycle clock ticks, just like a calendar marking time in Sam's career. For the next years, her new team includes the battalion's personnel officer, the security officer, the operations officer, the plans officer, the signal officer, and the finance officer—also known as the S1, S2, S3, S4, S5, S6, and S8. Darius, the Colonel, and she also have the four company commanders to work with. Her team is twelve to fourteen people who then lead and care for a battalion of 653 soldiers. Under standard allotment, each soldier has a sweetheart, one or two parents, then zero or more children. She, the CSM, and the colonel are responsible for one thousand, maybe two thousand souls in or associated with the battalion. Success boils down to completing missions without injury or death. This military intelligence battalion needs to accomplish these goals while facing two wars and global instability.

Sam's job is to be the approachable one, the XO.

"Colonel, ma'am, can I have a word?" She will hear that phrase five times during every drill weekend and call-up. She stands as proxy between the colonel and the soldiers. The commanding officer will send his proxy into situations where he wants unofficial influence or contact. The soldiers will come to my Sam with issues and problems as a gateway and proxy to the commander.

Leaving the house, she says, "I will hear, 'gotta mo?' one hundred times today."

"Hon, I've got one question. Can I get an army ID, like a dependent card?"

"I'll log into DEERS and get started." We kiss.

Know what an army ID means to me? First, I can go on bases and deal with less paperwork. Second, I can shop at the post exchange. Third, I can walk into the medical center in Landstuhl, Germany as the wife of a combat soldier injured in the line of duty. The last time it happened, I got stuck at the gate working through Sam's chain of command so that her roommate and legal power-of-attorney could go sit by her bed. Fuckin' rules.

Her duties started the minute she walked into her new office on that Sunday morning.

"Sam, do you mind looking into this?" Darius hands her a drunk driving citation for a staff sergeant. Within a month, she predicts, she will have to know the name and disposition of every Nana, Noni, or Abuela who gets sick, the status of every young soldier who missed drill. She will determine if certain bad behavior is criminal or not. Is missing a day classified as an unauthorized absence, or something bigger such as AWOL or desertion? Is grandmother actually sick? Or is this a pattern in a soldier's life? In each case, she says, she and her staff will reach out, then quietly investigate.

Sunday evening, Sam tells me that she took CSM Prince off-post for lunch to ask for his help and guidance. He's been at a similar job. She admits that he is likely better at the duty than she will ever be. The CSM is a soldier's soldier. He wears many of the same ribbons, and devices that she wears. He too has served multiple combat tours. He too has been injured in the line. He too has earned recognition for merit, valor, and heroism.

She returns home that first Sunday looking exhausted. She will be the first called for soldiers in crisis. Sunday night, she and I spend time in front of the TV redoing the rank on all of her uniforms, including her one formal dress uniform that she often carries in the car. As of this day, she will have to go meet families with the sort of news no family wants to ever hear about their soldier. She will repeat words I say too often, "I am very sorry but…" She must inform families that a soldier has been killed, injured, or is being disciplined. She already feels the burden of that duty. It is the cost of rank.

Monday comes. I find my Sam in our office sitting in the plush leather chair with the fire crackling. I think she is asleep. The quality of the light tells me that we are approaching eight o'clock in the morning. I let her snooze.

Before eleven a.m., Sam and I both process new clients at our desks. We fill in the client engagement letters, collecting and scanning piles of paper contracts, invoices, and proofs of payment.

I text Morgan about the new clients. He texts from the Appalachian Trail saying he'd be down soon. While the tacky murder board has been whisked to the dusty parts of the barn, I rebuilt parts of it electronically with a private and secure website. I create a client tally sheet that I display on the big monitor. Six clients, excluding Duke, have unpaid bills that together approach one million dollars in value.

Some contractors built a row of attached townhomes for The Branston Club. Others built detached homes on Ernie's properties. Some homes were huge, McMansion-type messes with four- and five-bay garages and six bedrooms. Each club member gets a place in accordance to their wealth. The more money you spend, the bigger your place and the more prestigious the condo. The Branston Club expects to be a weekend place for families to gather, for parties, for couples and groups of couples to go skiing or out on snowmachine trails. The contractors build homes and condos in a variety of sizes and price ranges, all while being screwed by Eberbach. Each of these business owners pay interest to cover daily expenses. Like Duke and Angela, birthday presents, food, fuel, and electric bills get put on credit cards while Ernie von Cheap-ass delays and delays paying invoices.

The lives of contractors and their families are being churned into a turbid pool of debt, doubt, fear, and anger. These families once treated themselves to nice dinners out on special occasions. That became steak dinners at home. As debts grew and fear of never being paid increased, the steak became ground beef at home. Then beef disappeared, being substituted for turkey and chicken. Even Friday evening beers with the crews got wrecked due to finances. Where the crews once travelled to local bars to sip a Friday beer, they now open a can of cheap beer from an old cooler kept in the back of a pickup truck. Gone are the days of tipping bar and wait staff and supporting local business.

At three p.m. another contractor drives down the drive in a van with logos, phone number, and web address on the sides. We get him to sign on as a client as well.

At five p.m., I text Morgan: "You ok?"

At five-oh-five p.m., I get a text from Duke. "Paid 1 invoice."

Thus, therefore, I make the assumption: nobody else has been paid. Nobody has been paid for any invoice this year.

I think of Angela feeding her kids fresh eggs and government cheese and swiping her SNAP card at the local grocery stores, stretching dimes to dollars. I think of the despair shared by the contractors and their families as they strip their lives bare to pay their own staff and keep paying for materials. Instead of new shoes and new jeans, the money goes to buying plywood, nails, and lumber to build homes for unknown and faraway rich people who may never decide that "they belong here."

# 19 | You Don't Belong Here

Truck horns and pistol fire on the road tells us: "We do not belong here." We are no longer welcome in our home. That's what the harassment feels like to the three of us. You are not one of us. You need to find a new place.

"Go away."

How is it that our team is the enemy to locals when in fact a guy from Rhode Island sitting high in his modern alpine chateau yelling on the phone, watching old movies, and not paying his bills is the real bad guy?

I have an answer and it is not because our lawyer graduated from elite schools and walked away from a prestigious university over a tenure fight. And it is not due to the varying degrees of melanocytes found in our team's skin. We have a handful of clients who are borrowing from empty futures to pay bills with local vendors. These clients are paying wages for all of the workers on the hill. We have a hearty group of families taking it on the chin—or getting kicked in the ass—so that they can pay everyone else and keep the projects going forward.

We, as advocates, are being cast as the bad guys and enemies to the progress of hardworking laborers and retail shop clerks who rely on The Branston Club's money. At least they *think* it is Ernie von Fraudster's money.

We are the bad guys. The local workers are the good guys and The Branston Club is the goldgiver. Ernie's generous hand is the source of all goodness and light.

Read the *Trent Valley Viewer*, you'll see the truth! Here is Ernie shaking the governor's hand. Here is Ernie standing with our DC representation. Here is the selectboard chair applauding Ernie's investments. Here is Alec Ballou, the owner of several businesses and chair of the regional economic agency, notifying Ernie that the state has deemed this project valuable enough to get significant tax credits. Here is the Haworth Fire Chief expecting a modern firehouse and a ladder truck that can reach to the roof of the modern condos that Ernie is building.

There's the truth. Right?

The truth is that we are upstarts, incomers, flatlanders, who, with our socialist ideals, are here to disrupt the largest and most modern economic engine here in our hills. Our team is hitting Ernie with the same type of negative waves that environmental regulations have imposed on his project.

Meanwhile, over Angela's ongoing objections, I am driving to her and Lem's house. I asked for invoicing documents but she knows that I am also bringing chicken feed to her family. Ready for rural chicken math? A bag of pellets costs the same as five dozen eggs. That is sixty eggs. A bag of pellets and sixty eggs cost roughly the same. With me? With eight to ten chickens in your run, you get a month's worth of eggs from that bag. At ten eggs per day and an average month of thirty days, one bag of chicken feed generates three-hundred eggs. That's the math. Ten times thirty is three-hundred. Three-hundred eggs is five times greater than the sixty eggs that it costs to buy the bag of feed.

On the first day of a month, you invest in sixty eggs. At the end of the month, you've harvested three-hundred eggs at a profit of two-hundred-and-forty eggs. Chicken math.

Angela still doesn't want charity from the team that is trying to rescue her husband and family from financial ruin. The last time I picked up her invoicing documents and dropped off chicken feed and bedding, her car was gone. She objected and accepted my chicken feed. I lied to Angela. I told her I was knocking these costs off of her future bill. Maybe I will?

I pull into her driveway. Emptiness and stillness. There are no children's toys in the yard. There are no hens in the run.

"Hello?" I yell. "Angela?"

I rattle the door which is mildly locked. I could mule-kick it as trained at the fire academy, but I have a guess. I wiggle to the state highway and turn north on the paved two-lane road. I look down onto the sprawling farm that once served hundreds of dairy cattle. Confident that Angela sold her car, whatever. The car, the house… likely both repossessed or foreclosed on. I debate driving down her parents' driveway. There is a line between caring and being a busybody. I don't know where it is. Is driving down the family drive asking after her the sort of care I should offer? Or do I respect her silence?

I drive on.

I am a woman whose family created several of the old towns of New England, most of which do seem to be called Londonderry. And Sam's family fought on both sides of the American Revolution. She is currently serving as the executive officer and second-in-command for a military intelligence battalion with the United States Army. The threshold for acceptance in our town and our region should be as simple as this: adult human plus heartbeat. Maybe you are the sort that believes in all of that America First stuff, then the minimum qualification is a U.S. passport, Green Card, or visa.

Calling me a dyke in anger hurt my feelings and made me cry. So, fuck you.

Telling me to get out of my house and that I don't belong in these hills, that pisses me off. So, fuck you. And your dog, asshole.

Back in the office with a small pot of Earl Gray tea and a pyramid of demerara sugar cubes, I navigate to Spies-Я-Us dot com, which isn't actually Spies-Я-Us dot com. It is a super cool audio/video store in Manhattan that closes early on Fridays and remains shuttered on Saturdays. They've got all the same stuff but without the creepy fake-spy nonsense. I don't really want to know I am shopping at the same place as pedophiles and lavatory-looky-loos.

You know what I bought! Like a six-year-old in a candy store with money and no parental supervision, I stuff my digital cart. If I like an item, I double my order: pile of game cameras that use mobile phone SIM cards. I make sure that they have both infrared and sound. I buy locator tags, the sort you use on luggage and handbags. The sort of thing you should never stick on a straying spouse or the spouse's car.

I buy upgrades for the home Wi-Fi to get a full-coverage mesh network and order Wi-Fi cameras. Imagine Sarah entering the armory before a battle. Guns, bullets, grenades, more guns and more grenades, and a vest. That's me. Except, I need surveillance gear. Button cameras, lav mics, small audio-recording devices. If it helps with surveillance, I buy it.

You don't have to tell me that I live with a professional spy. I should talk with her, plan with her, get product reviews, do all of that good collaboration and communication stuff.

Don't pet a porcupine.

My credit card thought I was torturing it. The credit card company pinged and called and emailed. And I thought that maybe the owners of that Manhattan store would call the lady who made their days' revenue possible. I need to admit that we already have hard plastic cases with a few similar tools. And I spent the type of money that could have bought Angela a working used car.

You pissed me the fuck off.

On a Friday morning, I beat the store's Sabbath clock by completing my order before close of business..

To Sam, I confess.

To Morgan, I explain.

I circle back to the old fantasies of bad guys wearing handcuffs and being escorted by law enforcement officers wearing blue nylon jackets. Don't get confused about the term fantasy. That's not us. When it comes to the bedroom, Sam and I are as normal and boring as… well, I don't really know. I can't say puritans or pilgrims. They would have stoned us or burned us or ostracized us. I don't really know the scope of what Christians do behind closed doors. Just know that feet, handcuffs, and weird-ass leather shit isn't us. What goes on behind the bathroom door and the bedroom door is the precise definition of private—as long as we agree that the minimum standard involves adults and consenting, the rest is private.

I do fantasize about justice and fairness. Are you ok with that? I am.

One week later, at three-thirty in the morning, Sam and I dress. I put on an old-style uniform of hers, the old woodland pattern. This one has the shadows of sergeant chevrons and name tapes over the pockets. She also dresses in camo and includes a balaclava to obscure her face. I hate three-thirty a.m. 911 calls. They mess the entire day up. I am dead-tired before supper time. My big red pickup with emergency lights, radio antenna, and firefighter/EMS tags is the best street camouflage. Nobody bothers with a local firefighter. Dusty license plates are local license plates.

We've got tactical maps printed on paper and folded.
We've got tactical red LED lights.
We've got a tactical plan.
We park. We make one slow 360 circuit of Ernie's home.

I smile, having fun playing soldier. Sam is a soldier. I am wearing an old uniform that she wore early in her career when she was an MP. I am an actor playing a role. Sam is the real thing.

We mount two cameras in trees. One peeks into Ernie's living room from the east, the other from the west. We place one on another tree to capture traffic on the drive. I stick a tracker tag on his car. Then another in case the first one is discovered. I put a Wi-Fi monitoring device that will send us traffic. It can be programmed remotely if I want something more than the email that travels on Port 25. I may decide to pick up the web addresses he visits. Modern web browsers and websites actually encrypt the traffic as it travels from the phone, tablet, or computer to the hosting site. No more easy harvesting of personal data with Wi-Fi—as long as people keep their systems patched and updated, that is.

While it is still dark, we sneak our camouflaged selves to The Branston Club's office. Wham-bam, we wrap that up. We roll into our driveway as the sun starts rising, which is the time of the day when our road sees the heaviest traffic. I mount a few Wi-Fi cameras pointing away from the house and need to sneak two out to the road. One will read license plates going south and one will capture vehicles and their license plates going north.

That is what "fuck you" feels like in a digital age. My internal dialogue involves me looping through the same narrow band of thought: I don't belong here? I am the bad guy? I'll show you who the bad guy is! I think you know that while Sam is deeply loving and caring, she doesn't chatter. She is entirely silent in the woods and mostly invisible, even to me unless I stick to her side.

After a shower, I drop my hair from the tight bun. I dress in my normal house clothing: long skirt, linen blouse, and bare feet that flash nakedly across the floor when I walk. I should tell you that I have generated a few looks at bus stations and train stations over the years from women wearing long dresses and kerchiefs on their heads. I smile, saying silently, no, not one of you, sorry. And if they did know me, they'd beat me with sticks.

Sam and I walk into the office together.

"Morgan, Morgan," my rather stupid morning pun. *Morgan* means morning in Dutch, see. My humor can be as bad as Harry and his farmer/dad jokes. Harry honestly wears a t-shirt that reads: "Outstanding in his field." Of course, it has a farmer in a straw hat with a hayfork in his right hand. Harry does makes me laugh. I have a kind of love for him that I haven't known in my life. He could be my uncle or first cousin. I want to see him, and I want to spend time with him, even if we sit directing traffic in a blizzard.

Know who else feels shit on?

Morgan.

Morgan smiles at the two of us. A hot shower—we did share in case you keep wondering what goes on behind that door—fresh clothes, and a quick egg. We are both bright eyed and shiny faced. Given my rather Irish tones, I may still be carrying a bit of a warm glow on both cheeks. Oh well, let him wonder.

He commandeers the big monitor.

"Ready?"

"Nope," I answer. "Need tea. Give me one." I lift the basket of loose leaves into the compost bin.

"Ready."

He has animated his presentation. A curtain folds back from the standard lawsuit form.

I stand from the seated position and walk forward.

We all study the lawsuit written on behalf of Lem, Angela, and their dying construction company.

"Next!" He advances the slide. The next image is identical save for the names of the plaintiff.

"Hold on a sec," I say. Morgan returns the prior slide. I continue, "Guys, I think Angela abandoned the family home and moved back to her parents old dairy farm." I feel bad for Morgan. I am stepping on his good news and good work with a downer. "I am only guessing, but I'll bet that their property is being foreclosed. I knew she was behind on tax payments. She probably couldn't cover the mortgage anymore."

I see the disappointment roll through Morgan. "That's very hard."

"It is. It is hard on her, her family. It is also hard on the towns. Abandoned properties and foreclosures hurt town finances and increases other problems."

"Yeah, I can see that. Well, I'll buzz through these slides."

Each slide is a new lawsuit.

"Next!"

"Next."

"And next."

Four lawsuits for four of our five oldest clients.

I wander back to my seat as Morgan explains.

"Duke didn't yet qualify. He got paid for last year, the others did not. Duke got paid once this year. And that foolishness they did with returning the invoice due to errors is legally ambiguous enough that I decided not to press the issue."

"Where are we at?" Sam asks.

"On these four, just north of a million. For all clients, including Duke, that number is starting to look like five million. And item number last. Brie, here is an outline for a press release. Time to get some press on our side."

"Absolutely."

"If I write it, I'll sound like an Ivy League lawyer."

"Maybe because you are an Ivy League lawyer."

"Fair point, but you'll add all of that Brighid-ness to the press release."

## 19 | YOU DON'T BELONG HERE

"Absolutely."

I email the press release to the *Trent Valley Viewer* general press release address and I include Brian Stuart, intrepid reporter. Most of The Branston Club's press releases get published with little editing and no fact checking. My press release had statements such as, "The Branston Club owes approximately five million to local construction companies," and "the owners of local construction companies are using personal credit and family savings to fund payroll and materials at The Branston Club."

We are not the bad guys. Ernie von Loser and his gang of thieves at The Branston Club are the real bad guys.

I send the press release north to the Vermont television stations. Confusingly, all Vermont TV stations are three hours north and we are well outside their viewing region. But occasionally, they do cover the other Vermont. I also got the information to the premier non-profit news organization based in Montpelier. They claim a readership of about six hundred thousand people. Coincidently, Vermont has about six hundred thousand people.

With my efforts at exposing the criminality behind this fraud, I hope that the idiots honking at the end of our drive will stop honking at the end of our drive.

While waiting for Morgan to finish his paperwork, I log into the surveillance equipment. I check each camera. I bookmark their web links and save the username and passwords that we set up. I see Ernie on the phone pacing in front of his big window. I inventory the cars and their license plates from The Branston Club's office. I check the location of Ernie's car and its associated location tag. This effort serves to calibrate the location tag, because I can see his car on a video camera which corresponds with the location data I am getting from the tracking device.

Sam comes behind me. She unclips my barrettes, then, with fingers, combs my still damp hair and scratches my scalp. Her thumbs massage the muscles at the base of my skull. I close my eyes. I drop my head in compliance. I don't purr. First, Morgan's in the room. Second, I am still a porcupine. Possibly, with her hands on my neck,

I could, maybe, be a porcupine that purrs sometimes?

Morgan prints the lawsuit documents and prepares the delivery receipts for Sam. She is dressed in a blue flannel shirt and clean jeans, cinched comfortably with a belt. On the belt she wears her five-pointed sheriff's badge and a small 9mm pistol. Her trip will scribble an oval on the map. Up to Route 1, through that dreaded traffic light to The Branston Club.

"You've been served. Sign here."

Then to the county court in the shire town so small, even the sheriff moved out. Then she'll continue east, come down the Connecticut River before cutting back into the hills. The trip, with associated paperwork, should take about three hours.

I want to go, but she's made this trip several times as Deputy Musgrave. Just after the first of the month, she delivers the invoices for all of our clients.

"You've been served. Sign here."

Right, invoices are not technically served the way a subpoena or lawsuit is served, but we used the same rigor because, what we call invoices today will be later be discovery documents tomorrow.

Morgan gives Sam a hug, then politely returns to his desk and avoids watching us. I walk my Sarah to the door, then to her car. Fade to black, scene cut.

Sam returns after lunch with receipts for all the lawsuits. They have been served and filed with the court. Notice of the lawsuits has been posted to the Vermont news media.

"Hey, Carlton, thanks for calling me back. As my message said, I am Brighid Doran. I am working with a team actively suing The Branston Club and Ernie von Eberbach. I read a quote of yours a few months ago in the *Trent Valley Viewer*. The quote indicated that you may have information about Ernie and the club."

"Who are you?"

"I live over in Trowbridge. I am an EMT and on the fire company here. I bought one of your music after I read the article about you."

"I remember mailing that."

"I think you know my friend Harry, the shearer and sheep guy."

## 19 | YOU DON'T BELONG HERE

"I do. We did a lot of festivals together."

"Yeah, he said that he knew you. We're very good friends. Anyway, we represent the construction contractors up at the hill. Some have gone over a year without payment. I thought maybe you'd have a little information for us."

"I dunno. Those guys can be pretty scary. I need to not say anything."

"Ok, so don't say anything. I am ok with that. Maybe you can drop a hint, something that might point us in the right direction."

"You saw that they blacklisted me from everything in the region including the TV and movie festival that is coming."

"I did. That was horrible of them. You must be pretty pissed off."

"I am but, y'know, karma."

"Carlton, think of me and the team here as karma's helpers."

"He isn't what he says he is."

"That's your clue. 'He isn't what he says he is.'"

"Yes." He clicks off.

To the room, I repeat Carlton's cryptic words. "Ernie, according to Carlton Legg, isn't who he says he is."

Sam says, "Don't you just love informants? They are like the witches in the Scottish Play. Those words can mean anything while always being correct."

I post my Ernie profile on the big monitor for us all to see. Photos of the man in Burlington and Montpelier glad-handing politicians and civic leaders. The benefit of a distinctive name and a highly visible project. The various social media sites have him originating in Rhode Island. None of the databases show a criminal record or pending lawsuits. From his own narrative, he made his fortune greening up the trash hauling business.

What Ernie is, is boring.

I watch the video of when he was informed of the lawsuits. At least that is my assumption as I watch this silent film. It is silent because we decided not to break Vermont laws and perform surveillance inside his house. The law is broken when we attempt to capture audio recordings from the living room or bedroom.

I assume, based on body language and timing that someone called him. "Hey, boss, you're being sued by contractors over payment." Ernie listened, then returned to a basketball game on the TV.

That's not normal, is it?

I play that video for our team and jump to the live feeds. I expect him to be waving hands in the air, conducting an invisible orchestra and fuming with anger. I expect him to be yelling at staff and lawyers. I expect him to be on the phone with bankers for bridge loans and working to find cash.

If I got hit with a pile of lawsuits, I'd be on the phone with lawyers.

No, there is Ernie von Couch laying on his sofa with a green-and-black blanket over his hips, legs, and feet.

"Trowbridge Fire and Rescue, respond for an eight-year-old boy, pale, semi-conscious, difficulty breathing."

I don't even change; I sprint to my truck.

# 20 | Then There Were Nine

I get my new ID card in the mail. Across the top it reads, "U.S. Department of Defense/Uniformed Services." The various boxes read like this. Relationship: Spouse. Sponsor Pay Grade: O5. Sponsor Rank: LTC, meaning lieutenant colonel. And there is my name: Brighid Doran Musgrave, below my picture.

I exist.

You know what I mean. I didn't exist to the army for most of her career. If I existed, then she didn't have a career, therefore I didn't exist. Now I do. I am a real spouse. "I am real." Isn't that what the puppet said?

I sit at Morgan's desk with my new ID card, showing it to him. Does the impact make sense to him? It must.

"When I went to Germany for her leg injury, I had a beast of a time. I got called by the family support group for the unit. But nobody had made arrangements in Landstuhl for me to walk through the gate."

"What did you do?" Morgan asks.

"I had all of Sarah's paperwork. Her will. Her power of attorney for financial and legal affairs. I had her medical power of attorney. I had her advanced directives. Paperwork of that sort doesn't get you through a U.S. Army gate in Germany. I had to call the family support group leaders, who, then, had to call the FSG liaison NCO, who called a headquarters officer who runs the division when the entire division is overseas. I was on Sarah's records as her person. He called the gate and then I spent a goodly amount of time at the gate with the documents, my passport, and my driver's license. Maybe a half day stuck at the gate with Sarah undergoing a second surgery. I am out of my mind with worry and the gate guards focus on global terrorism and access to a U.S. base in central Europe. We had competing objectives."

"But you got in."

"I did. Now with this, I wave it and drive on, thank you, have a nice day."

"With that card, you are a member of that club."

"Yes, I am." It feels so good. I can't control what happens to Sam during her deployments, but I am now fully entitled to be a part of it.

"Hey, Morgan, going to be around for supper or heading to your place tonight? I've got to dash to a community club meeting."

"Yeah, I'll be here. I'll whip something up if that is ok with you?"

"Of course." I haven't had lonely night hot dog fried rice in months. Morgan has a bedroom and leaves items here. He is catlike with just enough communication that prevents me from getting all maternal and worried. He tends to stick around for meals more when Sarah is gone. Oddly, he tends to sleep away from the house when she is gone. But with the honking and gunshots, he's become nearly permanent in the house. Sarah lent him a shotgun for the bedroom. That's a scary sound, the sound of a shotgun chambering a round.

Morgan is a friend. I've got Chief Alex and Harry, of course. I've got Al, Regina, and Robby in and out of the house. Our little EMS squad is a fearsome lot.

Still carrying the warmth of my new ID card, I join the community club pre-meeting chatter. I take my seat, quietly nodding to the other ladies in the room. We buzz through the prior meeting minutes, the financial report, and with ongoing business, I ask about the town's honor roll. Carol Reed, the fire chief's wife, lets me know that an Eagle Scout candidate came forward to build it on behalf of the club. The club will pay for materials and the Eagle Scout kid will donate his labor.

"Will Sam be on the board? And can we review the design?"

"We'll see."

I have my new ID card. I pinned Sarah's new rank. There's no "we'll see" in my book.

"What is the problem?"

"We're looking into it. Let's move onto Old Home Days."

I get steamrolled. Acceptance only goes so far. I haven't a clue as to what is going on. I am an honored and qualified member of the fire company. I've got the training and cards for nearly everything we need from directing traffic to interior firefighting. I am an Advanced EMT and captain of the rescue squad. My credentials and commitment cannot be questioned, or at least should not be questioned. Yet here I am, being squeezed out of a project that is so, so very dear to my heart and soul. Sam's family were here since the git-go. Sam was raised here and has owned the house since her Aunts gave it to her when she turned thirteen. Two Purple Hearts, one of which removed almost a third of her calf, the other involved a collapsed lung and a hole in her chest.

Maybe I'd feel better about this had we not dealt with honks, harassment, and noisy gunfire. I am out. As in, they don't want me in, thus, therefore, hitherto, I am out.

I am out.

At home, Sarah is supportive and loving and understanding and kind and gentle and everything.

Somewhere deep inside her brain echoes the phrase, "I told you so."

In the office, Morgan informs us that the lawsuits have entered the first phase: the battle of the motions. The first motion informs us that The Branston Club is effecting a change of council.

Francis L Jager, Ernie's long-time advocate, suddenly discovered that he and his office face a conflict of interest. He can either represent the town governments as he has done his entire career and as his father did before him. Or he can represent The Branston Club. If the Town of Haworth demonstrates the need to exercise oversight on the largest residential and commercial development project in the region, then he can't be the lawyer sitting at both tables. He's got to choose. He can generate his common and routine income from the towns. Or he can accept a taste of every real estate transaction that Ernie executes. As attorney of record, he'd get to bill for the title search, the purchase and sale, and all of the closing activities.

Coin flip? Fifty-fifty? Does it matter which side Frank Jager takes?

The first motion from the Winchester County Court is a request to change council. Frank Jager has decided to step away from The Branston Club and retain his legacy practice. As Morgan reads the boilerplate text, we hear a gunshot. When living around guns, you learn their sounds. Rifles crack. Shotguns boom. Pistols sound different based on caliber. We heard the crack of a small caliber rifle coming from near the road.

Sam stands. Morgan freezes in his chair. I can't decide what do to. I am fairly confident it was a 22-caliber, which couldn't penetrate a wall. I remain seated, then I click to the cameras we have pointing at the road. I spin the time backwards. I find images of a pickup truck. From the film, I can see the driver point a bolt-action rifle out the window towards our chicken coop and fire a single shot. The camera angles permit me to catch him from the front and the rear. I get a full face image. I can see the make and model of this truck. I have his license plates.

"He's moved on up the hill. He's gone." I say loudly to the room.

Morgan starts to rise.

Sam grips her pistol while opening the door.

"Single shooter, blue Ford pickup. I have license plate and a full-facial on the guy. It is good enough for an ID."

I store the images and data in a folder on our server. Morgan is recording contemporaneous notes into a digital audio recorder. Sam has stepped from the door. I rapidly follow her. Then I vector towards the coop while Sam scopes out the terrain.

My hens are profoundly stressed. The kind of stress you see after the foxes get too close or a hawk swoops in. This time, I have a dead chicken. A beautiful Rhode Island Red hen dead on the ground with a hole through her chest. I use my phone to take photos of the evidence. I also place my finger at the bullet hole and take another picture. I needed proof that a bullet went in and through my hen. One of my ten birds.

I pick up my hen by her feet, leave the enclosure and walk to the porch. I lay the bird down, step inside and get a sharp kitchen knife. I let her bleed out, then remove the offal. I don't have the heart, patience, or energy to pluck this bird. I reflect the skin back and remove her skin, feathers, and all. It is easier than boiling water and all that. The healthy robust hen that I rose from a pup now looks to be half of her original size. With feathers and skin gone, I see the damage that the bullet did to her chest. Confirming textbook lessons, the exit wound is about three times the size of the entrance wound.

I breathe through a stew of emotions. I am simultaneously pissed, scared, pissed, angry, disappointed, and fucking pissed. I feel a tear on my cheek. I don't cry over dead humans and the gods know I have seen enough of those. And my birds die, all things die. My layers give and give. Then when they are done after a few years, they die quietly in their enclosure. I offer words of thanks and bury my old hens deep under the compost pile. See, I don't consider that a waste. They die of some disease or chicken old age. Someone killed this chicken with malice. Someone killed this chicken to hurt me, to hurt us. Someone killed this chicken to send a message of meanness and hatred. Foxes aren't mean. Foxes are foxes. Chickens are chickens. Blue Ford guy manifests meanness and violence.

Ethically and morally, I know I must dress this bird out. I cared for her, clipped her flight feathers, checked her feet for infections. I carried buckets of water through blizzards and in the dark to keep her alive. Monthly, I buy feed at the farmer's coop and haul each back on my shoulder to her coop. And now I must accept her death as a fact of farming. I look at the torn and ruined flesh on her chest with anger. I would prefer to bury her under the compost pile. I don't want to touch this wound and look again upon this act.

Her skin and feathers rest in a plastic bucket. The offal is on top. I cut off her feet and remove her neck. I then cut away the bullet wound and related damage. That goes into the bucket. I carry the remaining bits of the hen to the sink. I then wash the carcass. I cut off bits of good-enough meat for a stir fry. The rest of the bones and flesh get put into a pot with onions, carrots, celery, and three bay leaves.

The deal about gunfire in our Vermont hills is that it is normally benign. Folks sight rifles during the late summer. On weekends, you can hear people blasting at paper targets with pistols. Once in a while, you'll see people doing trap or skeet in their yards. From September through the fall, people hunt. Nearly any time of the year, a farmer or landowner will crack off a shot to discourage an unwanted four-legged visitor. Blue Ford guy violated all of the rules. He used his gun with malice. In doing so, he violated a number of laws.

In the office, I hear Sam, "Morgan? Do you want to look at what I am sending to the sheriff?"

"Sure." He stands, walking to Sam's desk.

He reads through her email and confirms the attachments. I lean in, too. With dry military writing, she described the events with zero emotion, zero judgement, and zero reference to laws. Just the facts.

"Good?" she asks.

"Good," Morgan answers.

"Me too." 'Cuz, why not?

Normal returns, as it does. It does for me after every 911 call. It does for Sam after every deployment. We are trained crisis-response professionals. It doesn't have to be any different when it is at home or afoot.

Morgan drafts further discovery motions and responds to motions set forth by The Branston Club. No, we are not changing venues. Victims, crime, and parties are all in the same location. No, we are not changing judges. No, The Branston Club is not entitled to take more time to pay invoices from our clients. Lawyer Morgan can't just write, "No, stop being stupid, you asshole." He has to make it sound like an Ivy League lawyer wrote it. Why? Because he is an Ivy League lawyer.

And a motion that said, "Dear judge, every week of delay costs my clients tens of thousands of dollars, given the plaintiff has unilaterally decided to stop paying invoices in violation of the law."

Me, I do my thing getting the documents, evidence, photos, and videos together for Morgan and Sam. Basically, both are telling me what to do. Vermont law states that you cannot discharge a weapon within five hundred yards of a house; you cannot fire a weapon from the road right-of-way or across a road; you cannot aim a weapon at people except in self-defense; you cannot drive with a loaded rifle or shotgun.

"Trowbridge Fire and Rescue, respond to a one-car accident…"

Morgan and Sam both watch me listen to the radio report. As soon as dispatch finishes, I do the Superman change into my EMS and fire gear. You'd think that responding with emergency lights and a siren is chaotic. I find it calming. There are no mean people and murdered birds. I drive with total focus and plan my arrival. Control the scene, check for environmental hazards, check the condition and stability of the car, triage patients, plan extrication and transportation. I ease into my high-vis vest after parking several meters back from the scene. I have a single small sedan with its nose parked up on the hollow-way embankment. An old, and forgotten, speed limit sign is nodding over the hood. This poor sign hasn't been seen in decades. It has an older style font and is well rusted. The sign seems to bow to the car with its square head and rod-skinny body.

I appreciate the irony too. Here is a car that failed to hold traction on a curve in the road, likely because it was speeding, and then it smashes into a speed limit sign. Here's the sign bowing down saying, "You should have listened."

The car is totaled. The door is open. The driver is gone.

"Dispatch 14RC5."

"14RC5."

"14RC5 establishing Trowbridge Command. You can have the ambulance hold in quarters. We have no patient. The vehicle is abandoned. The vehicle is on all fours, no fluids leaking. Can you confirm that VSP is en route?"

"Trowbridge Command established. Holding ambulance in quarters and notifying VSP."

I photograph the car, the plates, and as Al arrives, I am opening the passenger door.

"Hey A-1, do a little traffic action on that side. There's nothing to do here."

I retrieve the car registration, photograph it, then return it. It is a name I recognize and a family name known well around these hills. In fact, Alex and I spent hours sitting a kilometer away from his house during our town's only "active shooter" incident. As per the VSP, this kid pulled the trigger on a 38 caliber revolver once, then crawled through his bedroom window and went to sleep for the night while the cops circled the forest trying to find the scene. Then the next morning, the Vermont SWAT team smothered the house and the guy in pepper spray.

Regina arrives. Alex pulls in.

"Alex, want command?"

"Not really. What's going on?"

"Remember the kid and pepper spray…that night we sat in the dark in your truck. Well, this is him. He seems to have walked away. Robby says that he is living in a small trailer about a mile down the road."

"What do you think?" Alex asks.

"Me? I might think about sending Robby down the road to put his eyeballs on our patient. But he can't be too badly hurt. He walked away. There is no blood trail. I guess the only thing I worry about is a head injury. A subdural hema-tomato would kill him overnight or tomorrow," I say to Alex. If you are not hip to the goofy word play used by EMTs, we sometimes call hematomas "hema-tomatoes" because, well, why not? With my accent, it comes out as hema-tomatah.

"Sound good." Alex is a great teacher.

"Do it?"

"Is that what you would do if I weren't here?"

"Yes."

I walk to Robby. "Hey, my friend, can I ask you to jump down the road and put your eyes on our patient? Stay out of site until others can join you and we go in with a larger force. Remember, this is the young man that got tangled up in that 'active shooter' thing."

"Yeah, I know him," Robby answers.

"Be safe. If you confirm that he is there, let me know on the radio."

"You got it."

He's a hunter. He has shown me signs in our woods that were new to me. If there is evidence of our guy walking back, Robby will spot them. I watch Robby walk to his truck then drive off.

Ten minutes later, he uses the radio to confirm that he is on-site, that our patient is likely inside, and that he, our patient, did walk home.

"Dispatch, Trowbridge Command."

"Trowbridge."

"State police on scene."

"VSP on scene."

Richie spies me and Alex together.

"Got a runner?" he asks.

"We do. We have him under surveillance. He walked home," I answer.

"Do you know him?" Richie asks.

"I do and you do. Remember that morning I tried huffing pepper spray and you called in SWAT? This is him."

"He is a troubled kid," Richie says.

"Frankly, Richie, I think the young man is probably fine, it is his father who is fucked up. But maybe too much damage has been done." I unlock my phone. I show Richie the photos including the vehicle registration card.

Richie looks at Alex. He wears eagles on the collar of his EMS uniform. I have a pair of metal railroad tracks, my little captain's bars. Ok, they were Sam's captain's bars. We didn't have a fancy promotion ceremony. I got elected by the squad. Then the next time I showed at a scene, I had captain's bars pinned through my denim workshirt collar.

"Alex, you got this scene?" Richie asks.

"Absolutely."

"I'll call for a wrecker. Any other evidence I should worry about in there?" he asks.

"Messy, but no evidence of the sort you might be asking about." Providing the deposition-quality answer.

"Come with me," he says to me.

He climbs into his cruiser. I return to my truck. I drive past the scene. Richie pulls in behind me.

I turn right into the drive. When I park, Richie parks next to me.

Kindly, he didn't block me in. Robby joins us.

The young man meets us at the door.

Richie introduces himself and then we introduce ourselves as if we've never seen him before. Even Robby, who watched this kid grow up.

Trooper Richie sees what we all see.

"Have you been drinking today?"

"Yes, sir, I have been."

"Did you have anything to drink after you walked home?"

"No, sir."

Oh, shit, kid. The trooper lobbed a soft slow pitch for you, I want to yell. I can't. I can't tell him that Richie is offering him a way out of the drunk driving charge.

"Are you sure? You didn't walk in the house and pour a glass of something?"

"No, sir. I came in and laid down."

Most people do not talk themselves into a drunk-driving arrest. Frankly, most cops don't give drivers a way out.

"Let me examine you. Is that ok?" I ask.

He nods.

"Let's have you sit on the sofa." Robby applies the BP cuff and pulse ox. I do the Alex-handshake. This informs me that my patient has a pulse, a good pulse pressure, and his skin is just plain normal.

"Headache?"

"No."

"Any chance you hit your head?"

"I don't think so. I was wearing my seatbelt." Great, so he remembers to say that but fails to admit to having a drink at home after the accident. Had he taken even one sip at home, the breathalyzer would be rendered useless, and a good lawyer would tangle up even the blood alcohol level test done after a blood draw. The cops do an estimation of drunkenness based on level and time. All that goes badly if you drink booze, or more booze, after going crunch. Most drunk drivers don't get to walk home after going crunch, then lay on the sofa for ninety minutes or two hours. Actually, we have no idea what time he crashed into the hidden speed limit sign.

I test his pupillary response and avoid accidentally triggering a nystagmus test which Trooper Richie might observe and treat as evidence.

"Listen," I say in very soft tones, "I know you are under twenty-one, so you don't want to admit to drinking to the trooper. I get it. But which charge is worse? Underage drinking at home or drunk driving at twenty? Maybe you did have a few sips of that vodka or a beer when you came home."

I try.

Richie and Robby are deliberately not listening to me. Which means they heard everything, but are positioned to deny it.

"Do you know me? I am not very popular with your father's church, if you know what I am saying. My wife and I live up the hill in the big gray place. Please feel free to stop in and get to know us. I don't know you and I don't know the hardships you've grown up with. I have heard some about your family's beliefs and such."

I just don't want to call a closeted kid "gay," even if it were true. But he has spent twenty years hearing that people like him, and that Sam and I are evil. We deserve no rights. We are not permitted to marry, love, be loved, raise children, or use a bathroom in public buildings. Maybe with a few thin words and an open hand, I can let him know that life can be joyful. Sam was raised by her Aunts. My mother, while a little old-school and a bit unkind with words, just repeats, "I don't understand." Which is mild compared to hatred.

"He tried to send me to conversion camp when I was sixteen."

"Painful," I offer in support.

"Richie is sympathetic. I know he looks like a big burly mean cop. He lives right down the road. He is part of our community. If you are willing to ask for help, arms will open for you, his included. If you don't ask for help, none of this will end well."

I see accidental death or suicide for this young man before he is twenty-five. Frankly, I believe that the incident with the revolver was not about harming others, but harming himself.

"Tell me you have a headache and that you banged your head.

I'll get the ambulance over here and you can go to the ER for a while instead of a jail cell. And please trust Richie. He's one of the good guys. Understood?"

"I do."

"Ok, my name is Brighid Doran. I live in the big gray house on top of the hill overlooking the village. If you need me, follow the pitchforks and torches. It is a lovely home, a warm home. A home with an open door and lots of good people. Got it?"

He nods.

"Dispatch, 14RC1. Please send the ambulance for twenty-year-old male with head pain after a car accident." I give the address.

I step outside with Richie, leaving Robby with our patient.

"I know you heard everything. Take care of him, will ya?"

Trooper Richie grabs my upper arm with tenderness. "I will and I am glad you called the ambulance. Send him to Winchester Memorial and I'll get back to the accident to gather evidence."

"You got it."

# 21 | Arrested

"He's on the move," I announce to the office. "Heading south." I display the map on the big monitor. "He already crossed Route 1 and heading towards the Mass line."

"Is that unusual?" asks Morgan.

"Very. He normally moves between his home, the office, the local stores and once in a while he drives east to the bigger grocery stores."

Sam is looking up, too.

"I want to follow him," I say.

"What are you going to learn?"

"Something new. He is doing something new."

"Ok. I am game," Sam says, while standing.

"You guys go. I am happy at my desk. Your lives are just too exciting for a gray-bearded widower."

I rib him, "Bullshit, sir."

"I'll drive. You vector me." We climb into the truck. I drive due south. From what I saw on the map, Ernie von Dingleberry will shortly leave the populated mountain valleys that have mobile tower masts and head into the dead zone for cell service. My plan is to get into Massachusetts before him, then swing west on Route 2 and intercept.

In the army, this would be a normal configuration, according to Sam. The driver, me, behind the wheel. The truck commander, or TC, works with the comms equipment and blue-force tracker, a moving map system that shows real-time locations for members of the "blue" force, those individual and units on your own team. I cross the line with a bright white greeting from a sign that welcomes me. The top is shaped like an open book.

When we get to Route 2, so does our target. I go west. Ernie turns west too.

# STOLEN MOUNTAIN

I am behind him and between us is a Massachusetts State Police barracks. Which, due to physics, means that there are more cops in the inner ring and nearby. Think about your basic picture of an atom. See what I mean. In Trowbridge, we are well beyond the outer ring for Vermont State Police, therefore you never randomly come across them as they go to and from their station for meetings and shift change. I lock my speed with cruise control.

We listen to music, and I climb the hill towards Florida, Massachusetts. Up the switchbacks, pass the bronze Elk, then climb down the mountain. I am gaining slightly. He turns into the town of North Adams and gets stalled by numerous traffic lights. I get within a block of him, and he drives towards a self-storage business. He lets himself in through the gate. We hover outside.

We see him coming towards us in a light-blue Toyota Tercel with yellow New York State plates on it. Sam snaps a quick pic of his face and car. As he turns south, she grabs another photo of his car plus plates. And there Ernie goes incognito. We follow him back east towards the other college towns of Amherst and Northampton.

When he parks in a public lot, we park nearby.

When he walks towards the shopping district, I follow. Sam sneaks to his car, planting another tracker. When he enters a brightly lit café, we follow.

We stand directly behind him in line, waiting for the maître d'.

Sam grabs my hand. "Come here often?" she asks the guy in front of us.

"Oh, sure, often. I love this place. You guys on a date?"

"Yes. It is date night for us. You know if you don't book them, then they never happen."

"So true," Ernie says.

Sam asks "What do you recommend?"

"I dunno, what are you up for? Everything is fresh and local."

"That's what I read in the review." It is rare for me to see army Sam playing at undercover work. She continues, "My name is Sarah, and this is my friend Bea." She offers her hand.

"I am Robert Rutherford, nice to meet you."

## 21 | ARRESTED

How does this make any sense? We track his every movement. We watch him on the phone. His lawyers are engaged in a game of annoy-the-judge and just-one-more-motion. Delay, delay, delay. We know a lot about him.

And here we are standing behind him in line at a café having a chat. He is completely clueless that we are the hounds chasing him and The Branston Club into the courts.

"What brought you out this evening? It looks like you are traveling solo."

"Solo. Me and a book. I have tickets for a play later. I love the theater, do you?"

"Oh, I know I should," I answer. "I am more partial to live music."

He gets escorted to his seat. We wait for a bit, then disappear from the restaurant. On the drive home, we update Morgan. The update includes: our guy has a second car with New York tags; our guy doesn't know us; our guy uses Robert Rutherford as an alias when not at home.

Morgan greets us with salmon fillet that he touched with maple syrup and dill. He made a deliciously messy pile of potato salad. Sam can cook. She's no dummy. But her expectations hover low after years of army dining facilities and field rations. Morgan and I share a passion for simple food made with tenderness and care. We chuckle and tell our stories. We make fun of the apparently ignorant Ernie von Clueless. We watch a bottle of a cold, dry Riesling drain itself into our bellies then our tired brains.

Weekday breakfast is catch-as-catch-can. The eggs are free and warm on the counter. Cheese and yogurt in the fridge. I gave up buying orange juice, opting for the more local and more sustainable cranberry juice. Imagine my ancestors having OJ every morning.

We gather and migrate independently through our morning routines. As a team, living in a hilltop fort, we forgo a morning briefing. What changed since I last saw Morgan? Or Sam? Nothing. I check the critters, harvest eggs through the morning with the carelessness of long-held routines.

Morgan announces another motion from The Branston Club.

"A motion to squash financial discovery about memberships," he offers. Each motion requires a response where Morgan writes "screw you" in properly conjugated legalese.

I click to look at the driveway camera after hearing the deedle-deedle of the digital dog. I expect one of our clients: Duke, Angela, Lem, or any of the newer contractors. I might expect Harry to stop by "on his way" somewhere.

But no, it is Sam's employer.

"Hey, Sam, the sheriff's department is here."

"Really?"

She fusses at her desk while seated. I too remain seated.

I watch the two cops step from their cruiser and vector towards the porch and mudroom door.

I stand and head towards the office door.

"Guys, we're in the office over here." I am very friendly. As the old saying goes, some of my best friends are cops. Those who aren't cops are EMTs and firefighters. Same side, right, I hold the door open for two stern-faced guys.

They look only at Sam.

"Sarah Ann Musgrave, you are under arrest. Stand up."

Sam stands.

"Turn around."

She turns.

They body slam her into the wall. Both men do it like two football players taking down the quarterback.

"Stop resisting."

They slam her again. I hear the distinct metal clicking of handcuffs.

They grab her elbows and spin her.

Morgan, now standing, says, "What are the charges?"

"Shut the fuck up and sit down before I arrest you too."

"I am Sarah's lawyer. She has the right to know what she is being arrested for."

"Sit! I fuckin' told you to sit. If you do not sit immediately, I will arrest you for interfering with lawful operations."

## 21 | ARRESTED

Sam gestures with her head.

Morgan sits and while, seated, he says, "You are required to tell her the charges."

"Not in this case, asshole. This is an arrest with special circumstances. Furthermore, because she is a sheriff's deputy, we must handle this arrest differently. So shut up."

They pull her from the office. They slam her against the porch post which is made of ancient chestnut and has been aging and standing strong for over 200 years. "Stop resisting, you are only making this worse for yourself," the taller cop yells again.

They hit her head against the metal rim of the cruiser door. They turn their cruiser around and chew up my lawn with one rear tire.

Morgan, after watching Sam's departure, goes into the house. I return to the office and clean up. I lock workstations and return critical documents to our safe. I lock that.

As I leave the office, Morgan is stood on the porch wearing a bespoke dark blue suit with immaculate shoes.

"Oh, I'll go change too." I run upstairs and leap into my blue suit, the one made for me in London with the slightly Victorian flair. I step into city shoes.

We stand at the sheriff's reception area. This room is small. It has no chairs. It has one door made of metal and it is locked. The welcome counter is navel-high with very thick glass. You speak to the officer on the other side with a metal talk-box like you'd see in a prison movie, or a real prison. There is no receptionist. There is no officer.

Morgan rings the electronic bell.

He smiles up at the camera, showing his perfectly straight white teeth wrapped by a professional smile.

He rings again.

I call the sheriff's department from my mobile phone.

"Sheriff's department. How can I help?"

"We're at your front door in reception."

"You'll have to wait." Click.

We wait.

For the most part, Vermont is a catch-and-release state. Even murderers can get served with a ticket-to-appear citation if the murder seems to be a one-off situation.

We wait.

A deputy comes and gets us. We get placed in a conference room.

We wait. I monitor the cameras at home with my laptop and mobile phone. I monitor Ernie and The Branston Club.

The deputy brings us Sam.

They push Sam into a chair with her hands cuffed behind her.

A deputy stands at the door. Morgan rises. "I am her attorney. This is an attorney-client meeting. Step out and turn off all recording and monitoring equipment."

"As we said, these are *special circumstances*."

"There is no such thing. Not in federal law and not in Vermont law."

We four stare as the clock ticks.

The deputy steps out, shutting the door.

Sam puts both hands on the table after fussing at her shirt. She advances her hands to me. She glances at them, sending me a message with her eyes. I palm the gift and discreetly put it in my pocket. She then slips me another device.

She then raises her free hands to flip the camera the bird. She mouths either "fuck you" or "vacuum." I can't tell which. And neither can they.

By the time they barge in, Sam's hands are cuffed behind her back again. We three are seated exactly as we should be. Morgan's colorful fountain pen writes notes on his yellow lined paper. We look at the deputies in mock surprise. Guess whose mobile phone camera was running and recorded that. Sure, it also caught Sam's hands free. Unless they can see through walls, Sam's hands are bound by metal handcuffs and she is sitting at the table with her lawyer in a confidential session. If they had not seen the stunt, then they would not have entered the room ready to fight.

Boy, they put her down hard on the conference room table. One puts both hands on her head then slams it into the oak table. The other removes the chair from under her backside.

Shockers. She was cuffed.

"You done?" Morgan asks calmly.

They are in a bind. If they admit that they saw her uncuffed, then they were spying on a privileged conference via their camera. If they don't admit that, then they can't justify giving her another concussion and placing her in a stress position.

Two-fister lifts his hands. Sam stands slowly. She smiles at the two, "I'll see you later."

I place the chair back next to the table.

"What are the charges?"

Sam answers, "The core charge is stolen valor. Everything branches after that. Felony perjury. Resisting arrest. Obstruction of justice. The more I play, with them the more charges I get."

"Stolen valor is a criminal offense?"

"Not really. It is a misdemeanor. But that unpins the perjury charge. They are saying that I lied on the police academy application and on the sheriff's department application. My thinking is that they need the police academy application to hold up. The sheriff's department is not a government agency, so they can't really expect to defend their application form with a felony rap."

"You ok?" I ask.

"These boys are clowns who watched three episodes of *24*."

"Did they interrogate you?" Morgan asks.

"Oh, they were so tough," she winks and nods to the camera.

"Let's have them finish the interview. No doubt you asked for a lawyer."

"I had two phrases I repeated. 'Lawyer, please' and 'no comment'. At one point I started signing them. That was a trick I learned in a classroom once.

Morgan rises, opens the door. As expected, the two deputies are standing at the crack of the door. Morgan sees it too. "Deputies. Are you standing at the door of a privileged meeting? I think that you have been listening." Words said for the benefit of my recording. Because recordings are evidence.

"Why doesn't one of you run and fetch the boss? The other one can come in."

The sheriff enters the room. He seats himself at the head of the table.

"Is that a camera?" He points to my mobile phone.

"It is my mobile phone and it has a camera."

"Show me that it is off." I lift the phone.

Morgan says, "I am sorry, Sheriff. If this is an interview, then we require that it be recorded. You have at least one camera running. So either you produce a real digital recorder with multiple tracks that permits us to walk away with an identical recording, or we will exercise our right to record this interview. Your decision, sir."

The sheriff looks at my phone.

"Let's review the charges," Morgan prompts.

"Miss Musgrave has been arrested for stolen valor. And because she lied on several government application forms, the charges include felony perjury for lying on those forms. We are in discussions with the state's attorney to add on financial fraud charges, too. Miss Musgrave financially benefited from her deception. Unfortunately, Miss Musgrave resisted arrest and hindered our effort for jurisprudence. She assaulted a deputy. That is a tough charge. She'll be held over until a dangerousness hearing and the judge can determine her bail."

"Do you have questions for my client?" Morgan asks.

"I do."

"Go ahead."

He starts with, "Did you lie on your police academy application?"

"No comment." Sam says with a smile.

"Did you lie on your application for this agency?"

"No comment."

"Listen, counselor, she needs to answer my questions. She needs to help herself out. I am the only one that can turn this around. Tell her to cooperate."

"Sheriff, here is my business card. It has my email and mobile phone number on it. My office is located in Trowbridge and is commingled with Brighid Doran Musgrave's business. You can reach me at any time at the same address where you had your deputies arrest

## 21 | ARRESTED

Sarah. As for Sarah and her cooperation, you're looking at your investigation from the wrong side. You are required to prepare and present the evidence needed to arrest and detain my client. You are required to prepare the evidence for any and all future criminal court filings. She is within her rights to offer 'no comment' to every one of your questions. In fact, I would suggest that she add the phrase, 'under advice from my lawyer, I make no comment to this question or any question.'"

"She needs to answer for her lies and her bullshit. The State of Vermont has invested a lot of money in her training. She is a certified police officer. This is about the integrity of our agency and all police officers in Vermont. Miss Musgrave, did you lie on your police academy application?"

"Under advice from my lawyer, I make no comment to this question or any question."

"Did you lie on your application for this agency?"

"Under advice from my lawyer, I make no comment to this question or any question."

"Sheriff," Morgan interrupts his failed attempts to get answers from my Sarah. "What prompted this?"

"We were contacted by the fire chief in Trowbridge with the information that Miss Musgrave has never served in the army."

"Did you verify that information?"

"Yes, I did."

"Very well, then. Continue."

I tap Morgan. I show him my laptop. There are two sheriff deputy vehicles entering our driveway.

"Sheriff," Morgan says in an authoritative voice, "do you have a search warrant for my office?"

"No."

"Sheriff," he turns my laptop screen, "there are two sheriff cars in our driveway. That building is my office. I am a lawyer. I am actively defending this suspect. Furthermore, I am involved in a multi-million-dollar lawsuit that is taking place within your very court building. Do you have a search warrant to enter that property?"

"Yes. We do. A judge signed off on it."

"Did you tell the judge that you were going to search a lawyer's office?"

"No."

"Then please call your officers back. If they search my office, they will be in breach of several laws. And you will have lied or mislead the very judge you depend on for a lot of your work and credibility. Do you understand?"

The deputies are approaching the kitchen door with a battering ram.

"That is my house. I live there. I work at that kitchen table."

The sheriff makes a call from his portable radio while stepping out of the conference room.

The two deputies return to their car. They back fully onto our lawn then accelerate again, cutting the lawn and tossing dirt into the air like idiot teenage boys.

A deputy comes into the conference room. "You, you're going to the cells for the night. You two, leave."

My Sarah winks at me.

I wanted Sarah's name on the town's honor roll that lists everyone who has served in wars. There are neat columns for the Revolutionary War, the Civil War, the Spanish-American War, World War I and II, and Korea.

But how can you completely fuck up verifying that Lieutenant Colonel Sarah Ann Musgrave, U.S. Army Reserves, presently serves in the U.S. Army?

The answer comes from Harry, at our kitchen table. He got it from our own medic Regina who runs a local intel network of her own.

"Regina says that Carol called some people who called people at the Vermont National Guard. They said that they didn't have any Musgraves on the rolls and hadn't seen the name on any Green Mountain Boy roster in several decades. Then she called the VA." He meant the chief's wife and chair of the Trowbridge Community Club. "She called the VA?"

"Yup. She called about the patient status for Sarah Musgrave."

"No doubt the VA said something bland like, patient data aren't public and no."

"When you want to hear no, then you'll hear it. But Regina said that Carol called a nurse who called another nurse who works at the VA. They did a patient search and there are no patients with the last name Musgrave."

"Oh, ok."

Let's admit that Harry was at our kitchen table even before we got home. You want to know how he got in? He turned the knob. Which the deputies could have done too. But they opted for the big iron door key that smashes locks instead.

"Darius, this is Brighid Musgrave." I love using that name. "I've got an ironic story about your new XO."

By the time Morgan and I are doing our dishes, my email alerts me to a breaking story from the *Trent Valley Viewer*, "Local deputy arrested for lying about military record." It describes the deputy as one, female, and two, living in Trowbridge, Vermont. The breaking news alert included the mugshot they took of my Sarah.

United States Army versus Winchester County Sheriff's Department. Not really a contest, is it?

## 22 | Dinner Guests

People have said to me that they feel a wave of physical relief when they hear sirens coming to help them. The patients say, "Oh, thank god," or, "You found me." You slowly work at getting them out of the mess. In that first second, they are victims with all of what that word means: trapped, helpless, powerless, stuck, hurt, and still getting hurt. A calm interview, reassuring words describing the plan, and warm and authoritative touches convert the victim to a medical patient. When we are done with them, we have them (normally) wrapped neatly and warmly on a stretcher in the back of an ambulance that will carry them to definitive care. After the fact, patients have told me that after seeing the face of a rescuer, their first thought is "I'll live."

In the United States, this rescue and relief is often marked with a doo-do-di-do of a mouth trumpet marking the advance of the horse-mounted calvary of America's middle years. A hundred and something years later, people still say, "The calvary is coming," when referring to any sort of rescue effort.

At 2030, Colonel Darius Jackson and Command Sergeant Major Prince stand at our mudroom door, which gives me with that same sense of relief, washing over me like a gentle Mediterranean wave. The colonel stands with twin eagles pinned perfectly to his dress uniform. Six rows of ribbons mark the legacy of our endless wars. For the CSM, rows of hash marks and service strips. Any veteran would know how long the CSM has served and how many years he has spent overseas. The marks start at his wrists and travel nearly to his elbows. Presidential unit citation, Silver Star Medal, Bronze Star Medal with a "V," Purple Hearts, campaign ribbons and the Combat Infantryman Badge with a musket resting on a field of blue, embraced by a wreath of laurel.

I guide them into the office.

## 22 | DINNER GUESTS

I have tea water at the ready and Morgan makes French press coffee.

Morgan is dressed in his own version of Class A, a bespoke suit with the crispiest of lines and the sharpest of blues, whites, and reds.

Jeez, the shoes on all the men gleam.

"Colonel, Sar'n't Major, this is our friend, colleague, and lawyer Morgan Harmon. Morgan, Darius Jackson and CSM Prince."

Each presents handshakes, proceeding formally.

Darius does not appraise the office, our land, or me, frankly. He looks at the wall monitor. All business.

"Gentlemen, shall we sit?"

I begin by playing the first video. The sound Sam makes resembles crinkling paper. She mounts the stupid silly idiotic why-did-you-buy-it buttonhole camera into her flannel shirt. "Brie, I love you. Don't worry. These fuckers know nothing about me and my training. Whatever they do will be nothing compared to SERE and other training. As they say, I've been imprisoned and tortured by far worse. My wallet plus my CAC is in my desk." She holds her wallet up, opens it, and thumbs the military common access card or CAC. "My pistol is in the drawer too. Call Darius." Her hand flashes a tiny key and a flat bar of metal that is about the size of a hair pin. She shows me that she had the tiny tools needed to pick handcuffs.

The recording then proceeds through every painful second of her arrest and her supposed resistance. We don't see the quote resistance unquote because her button camera is flat against the wall.

"I have footage from another angle," I offer, pausing the video and showing the scene from a discreet security camera mounted high in the opposite corner. Her resistance, that of a ragdoll, show us how two adult police officers lifted Sam while slamming her into a wall.

"I'll continue, but I nipped out the boring bits. I have the entire stream unedited for use in a courtroom and forensic analysis."

The Colonel and CSM show no emotion, evaluating the footage with the polished skill of career professionals.

During the interrogation, Sarah skillfully pointed the camera at the faces of her interrogators. She captured their name plates. And in her repeated "No comment," she provided the first and last name of each deputy. In fact, if they had listened closely, they may have noted that their prisoner provided articulate voice commentary on their actions. "Don't raise your hand to me. I am already a prisoner."

"You don't need to go behind me."

From this side of the buttonhole camera, one might just think that Sam was the director in her own movie.

"Hey, Sheriff." I hear the smile in Sam's voice. "Forgive me for not standing. I am shackled at the ankles and waist and locked to the chair." More director's commentary for the courtroom.

"I just came in to say that some of the boys are heading to your house with a search warrant. We'll collect our uniforms while we're there. We'll collect anything else we need as evidence, too."

"You got a judge to sign off on that?"

"Of course."

"I am certain that Brighid will treat them with respect."

"No. She and your supposed lawyer are in the lobby cooling their heels."

"He is a real lawyer, got degrees and licenses and fancy suits—all the lawyer stuff. He's probably pretty good too. Don't worry. No doubt, you are following the law and playing by the rules. He'll find no evidence of wrongdoing. And if you did cross the line, you'll trash the recording, right?"

She is no ragdoll. No hapless victim. She is, in her own way, in charge.

The tape ends when she slides it and her separate audio recorder to me in the conference room.

I hand the tablet to the Colonel.

"The password is 1-2-3-4. And this," handing over a thumb drive, "is the raw footage for all cameras and audio recording. I'll keep Sam's wallet, but here is her CAC and Vermont driver's license."

"Thank you, Brighid." He taps me on the shoulder. "We'll take care of this."

"We've got you. You are on the 'us' team now," the CSM says.

"I wish I were going, and I wish I could see this," I say. I turn to hug Morgan. I pull him in tight, squeezing him like a pillow, except with his hiking and exercise, he is as fit as the two soldiers.

I envision the irony of our local deputies deciding to stop this car. These three do not look like the stock photos of Vermonters. Police around here sometimes stop a not-a-Vermonter for being not a Vermonter. Too bad the probability of that interaction is very low. Some deputies do engage in that behavior, but they will likely stop chasing this car when they see the blue and white U.S. Government license plates. As a fleet vehicle, it also has red, white, and blue emergency lights.

I listen to the digital dog deedle as the three leave the property.

I open the *Trent Valley Viewer's* website. The article did not change significantly during the night. The word "alleged" did not appear in the lead. It did appear twice in the first paragraph, then got dropped entirely through the article. It describes a local deputy committing fraud by lying to the State of Vermont on official paperwork. Allegedly? The article states that Sarah benefited long term from the fraud by earning high-paying wages while employed as a deputy sheriff. The sheriff identifies the importance of acting swiftly and definitively to protect the vulnerable population of Vermont from (alleged) predatory fraud perpetuated by any individual.

"Harry, did you see it?"

"Regina sent it. Yeah. Damn. How do you feel?"

"I feel everything. Well, no, I am not feeling shame. I am feeling pride. The CSM just said I was part of the team, his team."

"And you are part of our team."

"Some big portion of me is pissed off at Trowbridge."

"That's easy to do."

"Remember when we tried to get married?"

"I do. It was when we first met. I was the only justice of the peace who did not go to that church and carried a more humanist view of love and life."

"I was so hurt and shocked that a town clerk in Vermont could deny a marriage to me and Sam."

Technically, the town clerk didn't deny the marriage, she simply refused to perform her duty, saying it conflicted with her faith, her teachings, and her pastor's views.

"She accepted the form when I turned it in."

"Yes, she did."

"And our marriage registration sat in that office on paper for years. The army never found it, although I doubt they ever looked. I wonder if she ever registered it with the state?"

"That was a lovely day. I was so honored that you asked me to be your officiant."

"I am just happy to count you as my friend, now. What if we did get married by the town clerk?"

"We'd have still been friends."

I call Alex next.

"Hey."

"Hey, yourself. Tough day?"

"No, but yesterday was. Just about now, the Winchester County Sheriff's office is being invaded by the United States Army with Morgan in tow."

"Impressive."

"You think women are funny about their shoes. You should have seen these men today. Six immaculate shoes with perfect black polish. And the watches?! As part of their warrior stance, each man wore a huge and heavy watch that cost the same as a car. The colonel had his military academy ring."

"What are you doing now?"

"Pacing, I guess. I should plan supper for later. I'll have a houseful."

"Want company?"

"I dunno. Harry offered, too. I couldn't be any more fidgety. I bet I am terrible company. Anyway, I think I'll run to Hampshire Hill Farm for a pile of steaks. I'll get some wine and booze while I am out."

I change into EMS trousers and my workshirt. I clip my radio to my waist. I check my hens then jump into my truck. Maybe a 911 call will come in. Now would be a good time.

I drive northeast up over the hill to a neighboring farm. I select five Scottish Highland steaks from the freezer. I leave a handwritten check and a note of thanks. I gather a big pile of asparagus. Then, I head to the package store. I get three bottles of a red Italian wine and one good bottle of single malt. At a commercial farm stand, I buy a few russet potatoes and a handful of mushrooms.

I don't often wear my EMS uniform just out and about. If a call is over, I put on a vest or pull off the workshirt so that I look less uniformed. Today, I need the armor.

At home, I salt the steaks and listen to the driveway alarm deedle.

Alex enters my kitchen. I offer a hug and give a kiss to both cheeks.

"Lemonade? Iced tea?"

"Tea, I guess."

I kick up the fire. We sit. Alex is wearing EMS trousers and looks ready for action.

Regina lets herself in. She pours herself a glass and sits on the sofa next to Alex.

Harry would not find himself left out. He arrives twenty minutes later.

Robby texted, "I'd be there but I am working. I am there in spirit." I didn't know I had invited him. I approve of some conspiracies, I suppose.

Al comes in. He is wearing working jeans, a canvas shirt, and as usual, has a pistol on his right hip.

The thing about a group like ours is that we have spent nights and days working together. We've worked wildfires, house fires, car fires, car accidents, folks falling from roofs, from trees, from trees with chainsaws. We have seen domestic violence, rape, child abuse. We've treated wound from weapons, four-wheelers, snowmobiles, and construction equipment. We have witnessed people lose fingers, legs, and lives.

"Remember when…"

We laugh at the gore. We squeeze our eyes through the tough bits. We touch each other's arms and thighs while we grab crackers, cheese, apple slices, and pour wine, lemonade, iced tea. Nobody is leaving until someone in Trowbridge dials 911 or Sam walks through the kitchen door.

"Remember…" A new memory of an old adventure visits the squad.

Al puts another log in the living room fire and puts three logs in the kitchen hearth.

"Those are amazing looking steaks."

"Hands off! Not for you." He did put his nose nearly to the meat.

Regina hits the only target that matters to me. "We need to create a real and true honor roll for those who have served from Trowbridge."

The squad clearly supports the effort, given the amount of noise they made.

"To that end, I drew this." She passes around copies of a computer-rendered drawing. The memorial is three layers of slab stone. The rear one is granite and blue-ish in color. The top edge is cut to resemble distant hills. The in-between layer looks like our local schist with its gray-green color. Its top edge resembles mountains in the middle ground. The front layer is marble with a top shaped like hills. These hills are lower and closer. On the marble, Regina represented the regions for the columns of veterans who served in our wars.

"I love it," I say.

"We just need a place to put it."

"We need to pay for it."

"And someone needs to make it."

"Money."

The feedback captures our enthusiasm.

"This is no Eagle Scout project."

Regina says, "You know Harry's name won't be on the Trowbridge Honor Roll either?"

Did I say that Regina runs a local intel network? She just learns things by listening to the air.

Harry says, "I heard."

"Why is that?"

"I didn't go to school here and my parents weren't from Trowbridge."

"But you've lived here all of your life."

"Not quite. Not yet anyway, I should have a few years to go."

"You know what I mean."

I study Regina's drawing. In tiny six-point letters, I read both Sarah's name and Harry's name. I don't know who sees, but I have tears swelling in my eyes. I look down at the drawing with greater intensity. I feel myself get wrapped up. I rest my head on Alex's shoulder.

The driveway alarm deedles.

The room goes silent. Each of us shift, preparing to stand.

I get up and walk to the door. I walk with slow, deliberate grace. But I do want to run; run like a little girl.

We hug. We kiss. I babble. She holds my face. Behind me is my squad. Behind her is her commanding officer and senior-most NCO in her battalion. Behind them is our new friend Morgan Harmon. The scrum moves backwards to the living room. Hands are shaking; names are being passed around.

"Al, can you help?" I whisper, because if I ask for help the entire room will put out two hands and follow. I lead him to the basement. I pick four bottles of wine from the shelves.

From the hutch in the formal dining room, I lift down a dozen wine glasses and place them on the coffee table in the living room.

Regina is in my kitchen cutting crudité, prepping more cheese, fruit, and a sour cream dip. The story of the day gets told. Darius tells his version first. His tunic is off. He is in stocking feet and the top buttons on his jersey are undone. Morgan tells his own version.

I had already told myself the story—whether it is true or not, it is what I want to be true. I could envision it just as easily as you. Three gorgeous men dressed to the nines in their finest, each wearing watches that could not be paid for by any of the deputies or sheriff. The colonel lays out Sam's military ID. He shows the deputy her official U.S. Army portrait, the one taken after her promotion to LTC and battalion XO. He shows the sheriff the written citation for her Bronze Star Medal with the V-device, an award given for valor on the battlefield.

Here's the sheriff babbling away saying, "I checked with the national guard and the VA. Anyway, isn't she a lesbian? Did you guys discharge some twenty thousand service members for being gay?"

Sorry, Sheriff, you are wrong.

Then I picture Morgan stepping forward to the desk with the tablet showing the deputies abusing a prisoner in their custody. Then he shows the slanderous news alert in the *Trent Valley Viewer*, the one that followed the press release about the sheriff's department terminating a deputy for lying. No doubt he proves all future claims of defamation of character while standing at the sheriff's desk. I picture the sheriff's defeated look. All resistance gone. All aggression gone. All confidence gone. The pale, white face of a man in need of blood, oxygen, and a great lawyer.

Then the four of them, in their black government SUV, drive to the offices of the *Trent Valley Viewer*. Within an hour of their visit, *Trent Valley Viewer* sends out a news alert saying, "Oh shit, did we fuck up," or something of that ilk.

Know that scene with Kevin Costner telling and retelling the story of him killing a charging bison and saving the life of a young man? We are sitting with the fireplace roaring and a mixture of human beings in various states of discarded uniform bits. The color of the room evokes earth tones: the oranges of the fire, red from hearth bricks, oak, and chestnut wood that panels parts of the walls. Each person in this room is a warrior. These people, these friends, stand up then run towards danger and conflict, an act so many don't understand. Then we tell our stories to the only audience that can stand to hear them: ourselves. Al, Regina, and Harry each demand encore performances of the various punchlines and highlights from the Colonel, from the CSM, and from Morgan.

I slip into the kitchen and start sautéing onions and mushrooms. I also make a quick hollandaise with the blender and hot butter. I rotate the grate over the fire in the kitchen hearth and listen to the ribald chatter.

In the living room, I point to Al, Regina, Harry, and Alex, "Ok, you, you, you, and you. Out. Someone has to stay sober enough to respond to calls. Anyway, I didn't buy enough celebratory steaks for everyone." Honestly, I don't think my crew was very sober. I hope

## 22 | DINNER GUESTS

that the rusty speed limit signs and baby trees along the road don't get harmed by my friends. Let's admit that there is no deputy sheriff in the town of Trowbridge this evening.

"You three…" I point to the CSM, Darius, and Morgan. "Upstairs and change. I put hospital scrubs and toiletries in two guest rooms for you two." I point at the Colonel and CSM. "Morgan can show you." They are about to object. Morgan puts his hand on their shoulders and backs, pushing them.

"When you come down, we'll eat in the dining room."

I give a mock grimace with wrinkled eyebrows and nose. I curl my lip like a dog snarling at her pups in warning and pointed them upstairs. With their backs turned, I grab my wife by her wrists. We kiss like teenagers hiding in the dark corner of a school dance. I touch most of her from her head down. I make like a fevered sexual animal, when in fact, I probe her body with my medical fingers exploring for damage and bruises.

"You, upstairs. Shower before I see you again." Yeah, sorry, I grab her ass and a bit lower than would be appropriate anywhere—except one's own kitchen, when totally alone—so maybe more inner thigh then gluteus maximus.

The CSM comes down first.

I touch his shoulder, then like Alex did with me, I fold him in close to my heart.

"Thank you," I mutter very close to his ear. I hope that he can't hear tears.

He hugs me back. You can figure out what I am thanking him for. It feels like the sort of thanks for everything. The big everything. Thank you for the air I breathe and the food I eat.

I offer a glass of twenty-year-old red wine that I decanted from a bottle Al carried up from the basement. I hear Morgan's feet on the stair.

"Sar'n't Major Prince, how do you like your steak?"
"Bleeding, ma'am."
"Morgan? Medium?"
"You know it."

I walk to the stairs. "Colonel, how do you like your steak?"

"Medium."

I lay five steaks on the grate in my hearth. My guests, my friends, are standing around the kitchen talking and supervising me. The CSM keeps the hollandaise stirred and mildly warm. The Colonel jazzes up a salad with items found in the fridge. Sam hands him a metal tube of anchovy paste and garden-grown garlic, encouraging something like a Caesar salad.

The colonel makes a toast at the table, "To the next sheriff."

"No, no, sir." But poor Sarah is out-voted as we all raise our glasses to her. "The sheriff," we all say.

"I appreciate the sheriff," Morgan says. "He is the only one we are suing who may have the money to pay. A lawyer needs to bill someone for his time."

"That's it, isn't it? We are about to win a settlement, aren't we?"

"Two," Morgan answers. "The sheriff and the newspaper, both."

Darius asks, "You don't think the ski hill thing is going to pan out."

"I do not. Someone, or a group of someones, came to Southern Vermont and harvested a lot of cash from a lot of people. They used the economic situation, lack of laws, lack of oversight, and hope as fertilizer for their scheme. They Hoovered up nickels and dimes and dollars from anyone who came close."

"You'll win though?" the CSM asks.

"We'll win the fight. I don't expect much else. It is like trying to put smoke in a box. None of what I do is as exciting as what you all do. You included, Brighid. I am just a lawyer. A win for me is a judge ruling in my favor and a well-crafted motion."

The CSM adds, "The Colonel and I may have placed that sheriff back in his chair. But you are the one to fear. We can only look mean. You can take his house, his life's savings, and his pension."

"True."

Wanna know who will never get grief for spending gobs of money on spy toys? This woman, me. That's who. The buttonhole camera paid for the entire purchase. I should not shop when that pissed off.

I spent stupid money. My little spy toys tell us a story that we could never have seen otherwise. Imagine the testimony of the deputies with the search warrant. They would have lied. "No, we did not carry a battering ram. We knocked on the door and announced ourselves." Bullshit, boys. The door was unlocked, and you didn't even try the knob. Oh, right, and you were about to search a lawyer's office which presents its own mess of legal troubles.

Video recordings are hard to refute. My Sam with short, dark hair, dark eyes, sinewy arms, and muscular legs is nobody's ragdoll or punching bag. Sam and I have sat on that sofa watching movies, while she points at this scene or that scene saying: bullshit. She does not refute that the United States Government taught her how to resist interrogation by locking her in jail cells and torturing her. She has shown me scenes in movies that represent the endless chasing and invisible herding that goes on during the search and evasion courses she attended. The Army paid for Sam to attend classes such as advancing against indirect fire; advancing against direct fire; lock picking 101, and electronic surveillance. Why not? If you are going to teach soldiers about handcuffs and plastic flex cuffs, you also need to teach them how to escape from those same devices.

We are very, very, very quiet that night behind our closed door.

## 23 | Cui Bono

In the office, I advocate for releasing the sheriff department's bad behavior videos on social networking platforms. Morgan keeps asking, "Why?" With each question, I explore new answers. He doesn't like the idea that I want to shame them. Doesn't help, he says.

"Cui bono?"

Does it help Sarah's career? No, likely hurts it. A military intelligence officer should not be easily found on social media. And further, without a nuanced understanding of her actions, she looks weak and victimized.

Does it help our lawsuit? No.

Does it feel good? Sure.

He guides me through my thoughts, keeping me on the straight-and-narrow path.

Cui bono is what a Roman investigator might have said instead of "follow the money." Finally, after two hearings, The Branston Club has told the judge that all financial documents will be presented. This will be their fourth attempt to deliver all financial documents. The definition of "all" seems fluid within The Branston Club's efforts. The judge reviewed Morgan's brief that showed the interconnectivity woven in among the various LLCs. This LLC owned this property, and that LLC owned that property. This LLC sold memberships. This LLC sold condos and homesites. In one stroke, Morgan showed facts that we found deep in the invoice data. While X LLC owned X property, Y LLC paid for the construction at X property. He was able to prove that money bled and oozed between the LLCs.

If the money flowed between the LLCs and they shared common leadership and they were registered at the same address and they were connected by the same Act 250 permit, then the organizations coordinated as if one company. That was the judge's ruling. One is one.

## 23 | CUI BONO

Tap, tap went the gavel, except I wasn't there to see that.

Until this point, The Branston Club argued that they only had to produce the financial statements for the properties related to the contractors engaged in the lawsuits. The judge countered by consolidating the cases from all of our plaintiffs. In doing so, she also consolidated the LLCs. Like Jenga, the dependency of X on Y became visible. Remove enough blocks and the tower will topple. If you stack your LLCs on each other, then the judge stated that you intended to operate as a single, unified entity. Therefore, The Branston Club with dozens of LLCs is just one company.

Sam and I make four trips with my full-sized pickup truck to retrieve banker's boxes of evidence. Some of the boxes include the invoices that I had prepared and submitted to The Branston Club.

I, we all, spend days feeding two high-capacity scanners.

Scan, read, summarize, inventory with an evidence control number, and move on. The documents fall into clear buckets. This bucket is bullshit trash, thank you Branston Club. This bucket is documents that we produced, and you handed back. This bucket is about stuff beyond our scope such as permitting and environmental compliance. This bucket is about contractors, contracts, and payments. This bucket is about revenue from real estate sales. This bucket is revenue from membership sales. This last bucket is the WTF bucket.

Unlike a classically trained scientist, I have my biases, my favorite targets, my own needs to serve. I want to find specific bits of proof in these boxes. Not very scientific of me to wade in with a known objective and prejudged requirements. I want actual crimes that we can bring to the attorney general of Vermont. Fraud seems underprotected under state law. What counts? The classic Ponzi scheme, money laundering, or some type of deliberate deception. Selling the same plot of land twice would count as a crime. I keep thinking that maybe the memberships sales are a pyramid scheme where the early buyers get the right to sell memberships to others where the sales at a lower tier feed revenue into each tier above them.

Maybe there is a big box of nothing going on. Every person, every action, has been choreographed to make a buzz. We're getting the permits. We're building buildings. We're rehabilitating a ski hill. We have real customers. Invest now to make a killing. Buy now before your dream lot is sold. Know that you belong here. You have earned a place on this mountain. Come for the views, stay for the whiskey and cigars. Come be among your own people. Buy a membership or lose opportunities to expand your own influence and network. With us, you are a winner. You need a condo in Vermont. You need a townhome with ski-in/ski-out privileges. You need a home on a mountain side with a five-car garage for your cars, snowmobiles, jet skis, and the real toys of a wealthy family. The Branston Club is your gateway to influence and wealth. Cue Scott Joplin on the piano and open the front door to the basement boiler room.

I am also searching for evidence of the parallel scheme. Are they selling EB-5 visas guised as investments in an economic revival project? If so, I should find the federal paperwork that approves this project and, hopefully, a list of EB-5 investors. Full financial disclosure for all LLCs should yield a detailed list of investors. Given they are investing, the records ought to include names, addresses, nation of origin, and amount of the investment. Something has to be handed to the federal government. No evidence, no visa. No visa, no U.S. citizenship. That scheme needs a documented flow that has tangled results.

Morgan explained that we are in the bury-the-opposition phase. If I buckle under the weight of these documents and I ask Morgan to file for an extension, then they win the point. If I scan, read, file, and repeat until I have digested every fucking box on the floor, then we win the point and we move to the next phase of the lawsuit.

Morgan helps too. So does Sam. Scanning and adding the digital inventory stamp and inventorying the documents is a tedious but manual skill. The office is silent, the papers rustle. Sarah, Morgan, and I mutter under our breath.

It is just work.

It may be a lot of work, but work. When you start repairing a stone wall in a pasture, the first stone is soon forgotten. Lift, place, check for level, brace with smaller stones, repeat. Quit when exhaustion overwhelms.

## 23 | CUI BONO

I leave 911 scenes quickly, not lingering to help direct traffic or shoot the shit with the squad. Out, do the thing, back to the office for more scanning and reading.

We eat simple meals. Walk short paths. Even Harry calls less frequently, which is fair because I am calling less frequently too. I skip community club meetings or maybe I have quit and just not made it official. I skip fire meetings, well, because the fire chief and chair of the community club share a bed.

When I need a break from reading, I review video footage and check on Ernie and the location tags.

"Trowbridge Fire and Rescue, respond to a one-car accident. Vehicle off the road into a tree."

I arrive first. The accident is on the paved road up the hill from us at a farm that someone tried to convert to a sheep and goat dairy. I do the routine actions: parking, vest on, survey for hazards. The truck is familiar, but then I do know most cars in our little town.

As my heart rate accelerates, I slow my walk. I do know this truck. This scene is wrong.

I open the driver's door and take a carotid pulse for a full minute. I remove the stethoscope from my pocket and listen to the chest for a full minute. I back up, shut the door. With my hand on the roof of the small truck, I say, "May you find peace." I close my eyes, offering my blessings to Lem. Poor Angela and their children.

"Dispatch, Trowbridge Command."

"Trowbridge."

"Please cancel the ambulance with our thanks. We need minimal crew at the scene. No apparatus required." I avoid all mention of untimely. Too many people listen to the fire and EMS frequencies on scanners. A word whispered on the radio at this scene will echo on phone and social media posts instantly. I can't do that to Lem's family.

I call dispatch on the phone, describing the situation and sensitivity.

I call the Vermont State Police dispatcher, a thing I rarely do. I describe the scene, setting, and indicate my suspicions of foul play.

That foul play may be suicide, or it may be The Branston Club exacting more revenge. I don't say "suicide" and I don't say "homicide" on the recorded line. The troopers who know me will understand the unstated message.

I pull my truck forward parking, parallel to Lem's truck. I wish to obscure any sight lines. I lay an emergency blanket over the rear of his truck, obscuring the make, model, color, and license plate. I do the same on the front.

I position Robby and Regina to finish making a privacy screen of the scene.

I photograph the inside of the car, carefully leaving Lem out of the photos. On the passenger seat is a bottle of cheap booze still dripping onto the vinyl. Next to the bottle is a small revolver, and an empty container of prescription medications. I zoom in to confirm that the script has been written by our local guy, the one we call Doctor Can't-tell-death, Doctor Cantell, MD. Lem had a plan A, plan B, and a plan C.

We've protected Lem's privacy. We've kept everything off the radio frequency. There is nothing to do except wait for the troopers. Frankly, I hope that it is a friend such as Richie or Victoria who joins us on scene. Thinking ahead of the horrible day to come, I acknowledge that I must attend to the death notification to Angela. We should do that as soon as…certainly before detectives and a flatbed towtruck comes along. We're racing time before rumors start.

Once troopers arrive, there is that horrible discussion about extricating Lem's body. Do we do that in the field? Or the VSP in their facilities two hours north of here? Please, please don't ask us to do it. Please transport the truck on a flatbed draped with tarps. They can't ask unpaid volunteers to take that duty on.

With the solemnity and reverence you see at the Tomb of the Unknown, we three stand our posts. One north for traffic. One south for traffic. Me in the middle just not knowing what to do except treat this as yet-another-scene. We do not lie to the cars who drift past the scene, nor do we tell them anything. Those few who do pass have to know. We're a rural fire and rescue team, we sprawl out on the roads, we make a show of lights and traffic control. Each rescuer goes straight to the scene in their own car, then you get a goodly number of big red firetrucks parked at the verge of the road. We create our own traffic jam with our response. We normally chat with neighbors, get yelled at by out-of-towners. On this day, we have the scene trapped tightly between our three trucks and the windows of the Lem's truck are covered with cheap, red, wool blankets we'd normally use for a patient.

Richie and Victoria come over the hill with their blue lights on. I feel that wave of relief. I relax. The rest of the duty is difficult, but in three minutes, I will not be in charge. While Captain Brighid Doran Musgrave remains in command of the scene, I cannot think about Lem, Angela, and the kids. Job one is protect his dignity. Job two is to protect the family from nasty rumors. Job three is to be a professional when I, or we, give the notification to a woman who can't pay the bills or feed her kids—a woman who sacrificed her car and mobile phone to cover a few bills.

I don't do this as well as Alex. I don't have Sam's training. I am me. I bounce. I fidget. I cry at singing competitions and unlike other Vermonters, I like hugs from friends. My face tells the truth, always, even if I want it to lie with me. No, my face blushes, my eyes well, and I have one million micro expressions that any human over the age of seven can read.

"Trowbridge Command, VSP on scene. Command transferred."

Richie passes the scene, then parks at an angle blocking the lane. Victoria does the same on the north side.

"What's going on?" Richie asks me as soon as Victoria is in earshot.

I tell them what I know. I show them photos of the interior with the booze, pills, and pistol. I do not tell them, and their recording devices, what I think. I don't need to, given that they are already thinking the same thoughts.

"The scene is yours. We'll do whatever you need, but…In fact, what we do need to do nearly immediately is notify his wife, Angela. I feel the longer we are here, the sooner she'll get bad information from a well-intentioned passerby."

"Do you know her?"

"Yes, they are clients. They've been to our house often." I look at Victoria. Call that sexism. Richie has his strengths, but I'd just rather go to Angela's house with Victoria. Unfair, huh? Frankly, it is a shitty job. When a cop and an EMT knock on the door in uniform with grim looks, people barely hear the words that we speak.

I climb into the front seat of Victoria's cruiser. We say nothing. This is not the easy silence of two Vermonters standing at the edge of a road with a slow/stop paddle. We are mission focused. We both stare out the front. I mutter, "Right here," "right here, down into that farmyard," and "park by the white house." In silent agreement, we both click off our radios.

I look at Victoria. "15-10?"

"15-11, I guess." This is a code within a code for the VSP. The answer to 15-10 is always 15-11 unless you are under duress, then it is anything else. The answer to 15-11 is 15-10 unless you are not ok.

We approach the door. Victoria in her tawny-colored uniform and me, in my EMS uniform workshirt. Victoria knocks.

Angela opens the door. She sees the cop, then looks into my face. Angela bursts into tears.

## 24 | Fraud, Not Fraud

Victoria pulls her VSP cruiser down our drive. I recognize her license plate number which is the same as her badge number which is the same as her radio call sign.

I greet her at the office door.

"I really came by to meet the colonel, I guess."

Sam stands. She hops on her gamey leg. Too much time sitting.

Victoria snaps to attention. "Colonel," and salutes my wife. Sarah answers the salute and offers her hand. "If you are Victoria, then I have heard a lot about you. Brie talks of you after calls and such. I am so glad to meet you."

My Sarah will be a great commanding officer.

"Ma'am, I just want to offer you my support and respect. What they did to you was wrong in the wrongest sort of way." This is what Victoria did not say when we drove from the scene to Angela's house. She didn't say it because we were on a call and because…because, sometimes, all you can do is finish a mission.

"Thank you, trooper. Please have a seat." Sam directs Victoria to our conference table. "Victoria, this is our friend and colleague, Morgan Harmon."

"The lawyer?"

"Yes, ma'am. I am a lawyer." Morgan is wearing a lightweight sports t-shirt and athletic hiking tights. Morgan sits at the table too.

"Tea?" I offer, because that's what I offer. All three decline.

"I enlisted. Army," Victoria says.

"How long did you serve?" Sam asks.

"About four years." Some emotion or memory passes across Victoria's face. "I backpacked for a few months, then joined the troopers." Sam does not probe.

"Brie says you are a great cop."

"I do. You are my favorite," I pile on.

"I don't mean to interrupt your day. I just wanted you to know that you have support and friends out there, colonel."

"Thank you."

Meeting over. Victoria and I walk to the door with Sam on our heels. We watch her turn the cruiser around, then we wave her down the drive.

Our first deposition arrives at the office precisely on time. At five minutes to one, the driveway alarm tells us that Alec Ballou is about to park.

We three migrate our lunch dishes toward the sink. The driveway alarm deedles again, likely the lawyer in a separate car. Today, Morgan is dressed like a country lawyer with a lived-in button-down white shirt, clean jeans, and a fleece vest. With hints of gray in his beard and crow's feet smiling at the edge of his eyes, he resembles a wonderful and warm college professor. The sort of man about whom college students would whisper about.

Both lawyers have digital audio recorders running. The video recorder is running on a tripod at the end of the table.

Morgan starts with introductory questions about background and context.

"Yes, I am the executive director of Discover Trent Valley. And I also serve as the executive director of Winchester Regional Development Credit Corporation."

Morgan confirms Alec's prior ownership of target properties including the Postilion House and two others.

"Yes, my father and I owned those. The land has been in the family a long time."

"And you sold them to Ernie von Eberbach?"

"We did."

"What was the sale price?"

"We sold them each separately."

"Fine, then for the purpose of the record, please list the properties and the sale value."

Alec does. I think Alec knows the next series of questions will be difficult. I see him emotionally brace himself.

"Can you please tell me the value of those same properties as shown on the town's grand list?"

"Not offhand."

"Do you need to review your notes? Please take your time."

And Alec and his lawyer do take time as they they root through papers.

"I guess I don't have that value at hand. Can we get back to you on it?"

"Brighid, do you have the Haworth grand list for the year these properties were sold?"

"I do," I answer.

"Do you mind presenting a copy?"

I slide a copy to Alec's lawyer. The properties are highlighted. He looks at the document and slides it to Alec.

"Mister Ballou, do you accept this document represents the town's tax assessment values for the properties that we are discussing?"

"Well, I'd need to verify with our own records. It seems official."

"It is and it is notarized by the town clerk. Can you tell me the total value of all three properties?"

"Not without a calculator. Do you want me to add it up?"

"Brighid?"

"I've done the math." I slide another document forward.

"Does that value represent the total tax value of the three properties you sold?"

"Yes, seems so. I mean, I can't be sure without doing the math myself, but it looks right."

Morgan lays out several pieces of paper. He flips the first one over. "Here is the sale price for the Postilion House. Right?" He then flips the second paper over. "And here is the tax-assessed value for that same property." He flips the third piece of paper over. "This is the difference between the tax value and the sale value." He flips a fourth sheet of paper over. "Here is your insurance coverage for that property. Is this value closer to the sale price or the tax assessment?"

Alec studies them as if the answer requires actual work.

"The insurance value is about equal to the tax value."

"When did you have the place assessed for insurance purposes?"

"I have no idea."

"We do." That's my cue. I slide dated insurance policy forms and an assessor's evaluation of the property.

"Did you insure the property for full replacement value?"

"I did."

"Is the Postilion House a 200-year-old inn built of brick, wood, and stone? Does it have a square footage of 15,000 feet with guest rooms, a commercial kitchen, and staff quarters in the basement and attic?"

There is no answer.

Morgan continues, "I assume some of the wood is old-growth chestnut and oak. And you could rebuild that property from scratch and make a working inn, BnB, with a full commercial kitchen for the amount you had it insured at?"

Again, no answer.

"Did you every worry fire or some other disaster that would cause you to lose a two-hundred-year-old historic inn? Did you expect that your insurance company would rebuild the inn to its current size and stature? You've been paying premiums for decades."

Morgan pauses for an answer.

"Please answer, Mister Ballou. Did you insure the inn for the replacement value of the inn? Or not?"

"Inflation. The costs go up every year."

"Ok. Inflation. Brie?"

I love this. I slide over a graph showing lines representing the assessed value and inflation index. The blue line and the green line walk the same shaped path up the page.

"From this graph, it appears that your assessed value and your premiums kept pace with inflation."

"The value of the property went up."

"The value went up when The Branston Club got interested. Is that what you are saying?"

"No, the value went up when The Branston Club announced

their project and expected to bring high-value clients and members to the region. The Branston Club was buying all sorts of commercial properties in the area."

"And you, the owner of the largest historic inn here, thought the value just soared. I can sell this and make a killing? That's just capitalism at work, right?"

"Right. I can sell a property for the value someone is willing to pay for it."

"Absolutely, Mister Ballou. Two people want the same thing, and the value of that thing increases. So did you have other parties interested?"

"I'd have to check my records."

"You are saying that you are having difficulty remembering if someone made an offer to buy your multi-million-dollar inn that your family has owned for two centuries? That offer may have slipped your mind? Ok, I'll let that go. Mister von Eberbach expressed interest and you sold it to him. And the value? The bank assessed it for nearly double the value that the insurance assessor gave it the year prior. And nearly double the value that the town's tax assessors gave it."

"Yes. The value went up. The bank did their own assessment."

"Well done." Morgan pauses. "Mister Ballou, we did not request your financial documents. This is a deposition about a lawsuit pending between construction contractors and The Branston Club. We never issued you a subpoena, did we?"

"No, sir, you did not."

"Brie?"

I slide the next document over to the lawyer. He reads it. He slides it in front of his client. They do the hand-whisper thing.

"Mister Harmon, do you mind if I confer with my client?"

"Please, go right ahead. Feel free to step out to the driveway. At fourteen twenty-two, we are pausing recording for a conference." Sam turns off our camera and our team's digital recorder. She points to their recorder, which is still running.

"I am thinking about supper, guys. Sam, any ideas? B?" Morgan asks.

"We can rustle something up. I may have enough young basil for a pesto." I mean, who cares what we are saying? We are just filling their recording with office and domestic nonsense.

Alec and his lawyer settle back into their seats.

"Fourteen thirty-five, recording has started again. Mister Ballou and his council have rejoined the deposition. Mister Ballou, we were discussing the financial logistics of the sale of the Postilion House, an inn, a property you recently sold to The Branston Club. We have established through tax records and insurance policies that you believed that your company would be able to rebuild the inn for the insurer's assessed value. And then we showed you the value of the sale price. This document that Brighid prepared shows us all the delta between the prior assessed value and the sales price. Correct?"

"Correct."

"Brighid?"

I present a document that includes financial ledgers about memberships.

"According to the records, you bought a membership to the ski hill." Morgan points to that transaction. "I'll return to the current value of that membership in a minute. But please look at this. What is this? Did you invest in The Branston Club?" Morgan's thumb is on a rather large number.

"This number is roughly the delta between the insurance value and the sale value. Is it possible that you took proceeds from the property sale then used that cash to invest in the real estate development scheme in conjunction with The Branston Club?"

"No comment."

"That came quickly. I'll let that go. This is a deposition, and you are under oath. I expect that your lawyer has informed you of your rights and that I can compel your answers. Let's return to the first questions I asked. Are you still the executive director of the Winchester Development Credit Corporation?"

"I am. I've said that."

"Please tell me about this organization."

"It is a public-private corporation."

"And does it work within a state agency?"

"No."

"Let me rephrase. Do you coordinate with any state agency on a regular basis?"

"Yes. We work closely with the Vermont economic development agency."

"And that is a state agency within the state government?"

"Yes."

"Does that agency have an office in Winchester County?"

"No."

"What about Ruland or Windsor County?'

"No."

"Please explain how this state agency conducts its outreach and supports economic development through the state. You've just said that they do not have staff or offices located around the state. How does an entrepreneur access these services?"

"Through the regional economic development groups."

"Is the Winchester Development Credit Corporation one of these groups?"

"Yes."

"Is it fair to say that some might see this role as being sanctioned and supported by the state government?"

"I don't know. You'd have to ask others, I suppose."

"Is there any other conduit in Winchester County or this region for a business owner to gain access to the services of the state's economic development team?"

"No."

"Very good."

"How is the Winchester Development Credit Corporation different from the Discover Trent Valley group?"

"Discover Trent Valley is a nonprofit organization that promotes investment, tourism, and local businesses."

"Sounds similar to the other group."

"Very different. We do more marketing."

"Is it funded by the state or federal government?"

"No."

"Have you ever received grants from the state or federal government?"

"Yes. Of course."

"Have any of those grants been used to support salaries or operational activities of Discover Trent Valley?"

"Yes."

"I am going to restate your responses. Please clarify for me if you need to. Discover Trent Valley is a nonprofit organization that has received operational funding from either the State of Vermont or the United States Federal Government or both."

"I guess that sounds about right."

"Mister Ballou, did you buy a membership in The Branston Club?"

Alec's lawyer objected with some nonsense about "asked and answered."

"Yes, I did. I already told you that."

"Did you make a substantive investment into The Branston Club above and beyond your membership?"

There you go. When I saw this in the records, I drew it out for Morgan. Remember I told you that deep in my own family tree I have a pair of siblings who married another pair of siblings and that both sets of siblings were second cousins to each other? I described this phenomenon as a "wreath" in my family tree. It is a tight little circle. It looks odd. The financial transactions between The Branston Club and Alec Ballou had a similar wreath. Money moved left, then right, then left, then right.

My interpretation is that Alec or Ernie or both worked with the bank to generate an inflated value. Or maybe they just manipulated the bank's assessor. The Branston Club got a loan that was worth twice the assessed and replacement value of the old inn. This means that the collateral on the loan may be significantly less than the cash borrowed. Then a sizable portion of that money got returned to the buyer as investment cash. This could be bank fraud. Very gray area there. Morgan told me that residential and commercial properties sometimes ear-mark expenses and make sure that the subsequent bank loan covers repairs, such as a new roof or replace old substandard electric wiring. The banks may or may not know. The bank fraud charges are up to the bank to discover and prosecute.

We have a quasi-government official using his private proceeds to invest in a real estate scheme that is not honoring its debts and is apparently not following state laws related to environmental regulations.

Alec looks at Morgan and me, not answering.

"Mister Ballou, as the executive director of two nonprofit entities that receive operational funding from the government, did you make a personal investment in a real estate scheme that is being given special privileges by the same agencies you represent?"

"No comment." The lawyer whispers behind his hand.

"Are you now, or have you ever been, a shareholder, or like equivalency, in any corporation or LLC related to The Branston Club?"

"No comment."

"Mister Ballou, did you, in your roles as a state liaison for economic development, advocate for and facilitate tax incentives for The Branston Club?"

"No comment."

"We have newspaper articles and firsthand accounts of you announcing millions of dollars in tax incentives issued by the state. The paper published photos of you with Mister von Eberbach and the governor of Vermont. The caption identifies this was a press event coinciding with the state's tax credits. Did you aid in the facilitation of these tax credits?"

The lawyer speaks up. "Mister Harmon, I think this interview is stepping outside the brief. I am advising my client not to answer any further questions. We can take this up with the judge."

"I understand. For the purposes of the recordings, we are terminating this deposition." He reads the time. Sam turns off the devices.

Alec and his lawyer packs up and leave without a word.

When I discovered this financial wreath, I asked, "Is this fraud? Or not?"

"I don't know. It looks like money laundering. It could be bank fraud. It could even be racketeering, all depending on the court and the prosecutor."

Why was Alec Ballou our first deposition? The answer has a lot to do with trying to capture smoke with a box. Bjorn Frederickson is a real person. He runs a small business that includes being the registered agent for businesses. He offers a staffed desk, a mailing address, and he is real. For those credentials, he invoices clients annually for being their official address in Vermont. There is no record of him in The Branston Club's financials except for the several thousand dollars they pay him annually for his services as the registered agent for their pile of LLCs. Bjorn, the Viking, never bought a membership in the club. He never invested. His name was never recorded as an officer or managing member of any LLC.

Therefore, we don't really need to depose him.

Ernie disappears the day the first subpoenas are approved by the court. Ernie has disregarded all court orders to date. We gave Ernie the first deposition appointment. We knew he wasn't going to show, but we got ready anyway. We knew he wasn't showing because car number one is parked in a storage lot in North Adams, Massachusetts. His other car is at an address in Cornwall-on-Hudson. And that car gets out and about, stopping at gas stations, grocery stores, antique markets, drug stores, and displays the normal activities of a guy living in Cornwall-on-Hudson.

Morgan communicated via email with the judge. She wrote back. He asked for bench warrants in the names of both Ernie von Eberbach and Robert Rutherford. He provides addresses in both New York and Vermont. Ernie's name had been listed as the managing member on every LLC registered by The Branston Club.

I was able to identify the local bookkeeper. We decide not to wring her through a deposition. This lady worked in the office, paying invoices and balancing books. From the records we collected, she worked for three months without any compensation. Finally, she too walked out of the office, leaving the doors unlocked and the lights out.

The Branston Club's stall-stall-stall tactics end. The delays are over. The motions phase of the lawsuit goes silent. We enter the deposition phase with nearly no one to depose.

Regardless, we configure the office for depositions with cameras at the ready, water pitchers and glasses staged on the long oak table. With the office configured for depositions, we three stand, leaving the room for the afternoon.

"Let's go for a walk."

Sam leaves her shoes on the porch, opting to let the early summer soil squish up through her toes, a sensation she writes about in her journals. A memory that sustains her while walking the concrete-hard soils of southwestern Asia and northern Africa.

Standing by long-gone Douglas Tree, we don't revisit family memories. We giggle about the prospect of putting the sheriff through a deposition. That is going to be fun. Not the soulless, draining effort that The Branston Club has proven itself to be. After the sheriff, we will depose the deputies. They will not be able to lie. They can squirm. They can feel uncomfortable. They may not overtly admit to felonies during their depositions due to the fifth amendment to the U.S. Constitution. The line goes like this, "… nor shall be compelled in any criminal case to be a witness against himself."

We won't get the sheriff and his deputies saying, "we abused and assaulted a prisoner," because we cannot compel them to admit to felonies. We can't force admissions to false arrest or false imprisonment. The depositions are for show. We'll run the video tape in our office. Morgan will ask questions while the law enforcement officers sit in chairs under oath. Morgan will ask another question. I'll show a video on the big monitor. He'll ask a follow-up. And in each case, the guy in the chair will say, "Upon advice of council, I cannot provide an answer to that question as allowed by the Fifth Amendment to the Constitution."

We'll read our lines from our script.

They will read their lines from their script.

We'll dance our dance whilst every party knows the outcome.

The only thing I can do to make it worse for the sheriff is prove a connection or communication between him and The Branston Club. And I have tried. Without phone records, email records, and surveillance on the sheriff, I will never get the proof that shows coordination between the sheriff's department and The Branston Club. We will never know if the accusations, harassment, arrest, and defamation campaign were triggered by The Branston Club in retaliation for our investigation, our support of unpaid contractors, and our subsequent lawsuit.

I wish to believe it. Does that count? Why else would the sheriff care? My Sarah is the least ambitious and most absent member of his force. When she does get a shift, he has her escorting windmill blades over the mountains or sitting on a state highway undergoing repairs. In her role as sheriff's deputy, she is the least-cop cop on the force. I do more cop stuff as an EMT. Could be that the sheriff got pissed off at her long and frequent absences. I admit to getting a bit pissed, but that's my right. I have that right. Her part-time employer does not have that right.

I acknowledge that I have not found collusion or coordination. I have a super strong hunch. Does it matter much? No. The sheriff and his deputies did what they did. And what they did was enough to terminate careers, prompt criminal investigations, and win financial settlements in court.

The deposition and these facts represent a sad day for Vermont law enforcement. Hopefully, there is a good deputy in the ranks who can stand as acting sheriff until a new election is held.

# 25 | Remember Us?

 Sarah and I leave the drive at six a.m. in her Volvo. She is dressed in her "I'm an off-duty cop from Vermont" outfit: clean jeans, flannel shirt, pistol, and a five-pointed badge on her belt along with a set of handcuffs. She has a lightweight barn shirt over that. I am sitting next to her, wearing my EMS trousers and a button-down white shirt. We leave Vermont driving southwest diagonally across Massachusetts and shave the corner of Connecticut. We cross into New York.

 I peek at the moving map and the locator we have on Ernie's car. It is still stationary as we pull into the village of Cornwall-on-Hudson at seven-thirty in the morning. I hang my Trowbridge EMS badge around my neck before I get out of the car. He won't read the little words that say, "Trowbridge EMS, 14RC5." I carry the bench warrant.

 Sarah knocks on the door. And again. And a third time, even louder.

 Ernie answers the door. He is wearing pajamas, a terrycloth bathrobe, and his hair is tousled, having only just woken from bed.

 "Sir, I am serving you a bench warrant from the Vermont District Court of Winchester County." I present the bench warrant with an outstretched arm. Sam holds her shirt back, letting the golden five-pointed star shine through.

 "Yes, alright. Come in."

 We follow him through the foyer and the living room. "Come to the kitchen. I need coffee."

 He turns, looking at us.

 "Have we met before?"

 "Yes," I answer, "we stood behind you in Northampton, Mass when you waited to be seated at a restaurant."

 "Right, I do remember. Sarah and B, is that right?"

"Yes, my name is Brighid Doran and this is my wife, Sarah Ann Musgrave. People often call her Sam." Oh, damn, I should have used Musgrave too. I like using it. Maybe I should get it on my Vermont driver's license too.

He shakes our hands.

"How did you find me?"

"We put trackers on your cars months ago."

"Not bad. Let me see the warrant."

I place the document in his hands. In my head, I say, "You've been served."

"And you remembered the name I used there."

"We did. And we correlated it to the owner of this property. And it appears that Robert Rutherford is a real person, unlike Ernie von Whatever."

"That wasn't really me, you know."

Sam interrupts, "Let's save that for the deposition."

"So, you are arresting me?"

I answer. "No, not really. You get a choice." How many times have I offered similar choices to good people who did something criminal? "You can follow us back to Vermont willingly for your deposition and we can squash the bench warrant. You'll drive your own car up and be home for supper. Or, we can go a different direction which involves local police and lots of paperwork. The result for us is the same. You pick."

"I'll get dressed."

Before getting into our cars, we exchange mobile phone numbers. Ernie, or is it Robert, makes a quick stop at a fast-food restaurant for coffee and a breakfast sandwich. He drives northeast with the two of us on his tail. When we got to Route 2 in Mass, I call him, suggesting that he follow us to our office. He follows like a lamb behind its mother.

He parks nicely and follows us into the office.

I direct him to the bathroom and offer tea because…that is what I do.

Morgan comes into the office with a tray of sandwiches and a

## 25 | REMEMBER US?

salad in a bowl.

"Maybe we need some lunch before we get started. Robert? My name is Morgan. I am the attorney who will depose you today."

"Nice to meet you, sir."

"Here, sit, have a sandwich."

Conversation is awkward. We each tell Ernie/Robert bits of our own stories to fill the time. With the meal completed and dishes at the office sink, Morgan says, "Why don't we get started? You ok with that, Mister Rutherford?"

"Yeah, sure."

"Sam, Brighid, let's get started." Sam initiates the audio and video recordings.

"My name is Morgan Harmon. I am an attorney representing construction firms hired by The Branston Club. We are presently suing The Branston Club. With me is Brighid Doran Musgrave, our principal researcher."

"Hey, my name is Brighid." I offer to the tape recording.

"And on the AV equipment is Sarah Ann Musgrave, a member of our team."

"Mister Rutherford, thank you for coming. You can call me Sam," Sam says for the tape.

Morgan takes over again. "Mister Rutherford, the bathroom is just there. We've got water and tea on the table for your comfort. If you need a break, please let us know. I notice that you did not bring an attorney with you. You have the right to counsel. Do you wish to continue without your lawyer present?"

"I'm good. Let's get this over with."

"Remember, if at any time you need a break or feel you need the advice of a lawyer, we will pause the deposition. Fair enough?"

He nods.

"Maybe for the audio recording, you should answer audibly."

"Yes. Understood."

"Is your legal name Robert Rutherford?"

"Yes."

"Can you give me your legal address?"

He does.

"During the last years, have you used any aliases?"

"Yes. I was hired to play the role of a guy named Ernest von Eberbach, a man from Rhode Island with Dutch heritage."

"You are saying that you used Ernest von Eberbach as an alias."

"Yes."

"Did you work for The Branston Club, a ski area located in Haworth, Vermont?"

"I did, in the capacity of playing a role named Ernie von Eberbach."

"Records show that you were the managing member and principal officer of numerous limited liability companies that were linked to The Branston Club. Is this true?"

"Yes. Ernie held those positions."

"In your own words, can you describe how your employment with The Branston Club started?"

"Sure. I was doing community theater. Towns north of the city hire me to direct or be a vocal coach for performances. I've been on the stage since I was a teenager. These two guys interviewed me. At first it was for an off-off-off-Broadway production. Then after two meetings, they handed me a non-disclosure agreement. I was going to play a part in a reality TV show. It was supposed to be like 'Undercover Boss' crossed with 'Big Brother.' We'd set up situations for the real contestants and see how they did. The plan was we would create drama and tension for the contestants. The rub was that the contestants didn't really know what the game was. Think *Survivor* but on a Vermont mountainside. My job was to play the boss. It was all supposed to be fake and for TV."

When hiring an actor, tell him it is a role that will make him money and famous. Maybe you just have to offer regular, steady, paying work. Few turn down biweekly checks.

"You signed legal documents using the name of Ernest von Eberbach."

"All part of the reality TV show, or so I thought."

"It does put your name on these documents."

"Not my name, but the name of my character. I was being paid for this role."

"What can you tell us about the people you worked for?"

"Not a lot. They had an office in Haworth. They hired a local lady as a bookkeeper. They kept hiring local girls as receptionists. The prettier the better, they said. I had to interview them all. For the most part, I did what they told me to do. I went to the office to sign documents or checks, then I went home. I went and shook hands with politicians, then went home."

"What about your employer?"

"Employers. They were always changing. They wore suits which looked a little out of place in rural Vermont. Some had mildly European accents. Some sound like they'd been raised in Brooklyn. I really don't know who they were. And I doubt that any name they gave me was real."

"Do you have any photographs of the others?"

"No, they were incredibly shy."

"I thought you described this as a reality TV set."

"It was. They had cameras up everywhere. I could see them. There little red lights everywhere around the office and various worksites."

"Were they operational?"

"I supposed, probably."

"Do you know where that footage is now?"

"No. I mean, I walked away when I realized that this was all fake. I mean, Jesus, my name is on every document. I needed to get away."

"Did you ever see the footage?"

"No, never once. Let's just say I did not get curious. The longer this went on, the more questions I had."

"When you ran, or as you said, 'got away,' you didn't get too far. You drove to your own home about ninety minutes from there."

"I didn't get paid for three months. The first two years were great. I paid debts, paid down my mortgage. Then the checks stopped flowing."

In my head, I said, *we know*.

Morgan did a spirited and professional job interviewing the

actor, Robert Rutherford. It is like squeezing a rock and expecting it to bleed. Robert Rutherford is a bottom-tier actor who teaches acting at summer camps, does summer theater, and community theater in the wealthy counties north of New York City. He has five television credits to his name and knows every line of *A Streetcar Named Desire*. He can sing every song in *Brigadoon*, *Oklahoma*, and *Pirates of Penzance*, but can't calculate a restaurant tip without a phone.

Robert Rutherford, a guy I spent months calling Ernie von Shithead, is just another victim.

Morgan asks the important legal questions. Did he not pay the contractors with the intent to defraud the workers or the home buyers? Did they sell the same membership multiple times? Did they sell the same plot of land to several people?

The money is gone.

Families are destitute. One man committed suicide. Two of our other families are consulting with Morgan about filing for bankruptcy protection. This is the local side of the fraud equation.

There are hundreds of other victims. There are those that bought memberships in a ski area that will never open. There are those that bought homes, homesites, condos, and townhomes that will never be finished. There are suppliers and lumber yards that will never have bills paid.

The State of Vermont is left with a pond with an out-of-spec wellhouse and a power and utility corridor cut through vulnerable forest swamp lands, lands that have expressed protection. The Branston Club flaunted environmental regulations in the drive to keep construction looking good.

Here is Ernie, a character with thin blonde hair, the rounded and red face of a man who grew out of his boyhood good looks. He played a role without ever asking the important questions.

"Morgan, did Robert Rutherford commit fraud?"

"We can try. There is nothing there. Frankly, he lacked intent. Also I doubt he had the resources to invent this scheme. Clearly, the guy has no money anyway."

# 26 | Blue Lights

I just don't expect blue lights in my rear view, if only for my arrogance. My red truck looks like most volunteer firefighter/EMT trucks. I see the Vermont State Police cruiser when he turns onto Route 1 at our one traffic light in the region. He tucks in behind my bumper. I engage my cruise control. With annoying pedantry, I adjust my speed to be precisely two over the posted limit. And there he sits. He, or she, sits so close I cannot get his plate number.

I used my blinker, signaling my intended right.

He does the same.

I turn right.

He does the same.

He turns on his emergency lights.

I pull over.

He pulls over directly behind me.

I should be sweating and questioning my every decision. Nobody likes being pulled over by the cops. It is expensive for some, deadly for others. Let's acknowledge that Sarah and I are off-limits to the sheriff's department. From a financial perspective, we sort of own that agency. I ought to know most state troopers in the region. It is possible I broke the law, but I can't believe that the trooper has anything on me.

I lower the window. I place my hands at ten-and-two on the steering wheel with my license, insurance card, and registration pinched neatly between knuckles on my left hand. I face forward. I can't see the cop. He is too tall for the windows and mirrors.

"Oh, good, it is you. I worried I might have picked the wrong truck."

"Richie, you can't just pull people over, man."

"I know. My bosses keep telling me that."

I relax. My shoulders drop. I return my documents and I flip on the hidden red-and-white strobes that I had mounted.

He says, "I thought you'd recognize me. I mean, the plate number is the same as my badge number."

"And, your front plate up my rear bumper, how could I see it?"

"Well, you were doing the limit, like no local ever."

"Two over, by the way, enough to earn a ticket but not enough to make it worth anyone's while. If you'd dropped back, I might have recognized you." I smiled. "Hey, let me get out."

We move to the verge of the road, standing looking towards the rising hill. Richie stands in his tawny-colored uniform shirt stressed slightly by the Kevlar vest. I don my high-vis vest, as per the law, to stand on the edge of the road.

"I've got a few questions."

"Y'know, Richie, you can't just pull over law-abiding citizens without, what's it called…ahh, probable cause. Isn't that it?"

"You crossed the yellow line."

"I did not."

"Right, well, honestly, I do have a real question for you."

"You can call."

"I can never find your number."

"I put it on every note I've ever written you." At the potential crime scenes in town, I inventory the names and dates of birth of each firefighter and EMT present.

"And those go into the evidence logs. I never see them again."

"No wonder you never send me birthday cards or call. You just ignore the documents I give you. Gimme your phone," I order the tall cop facing me.

He unlocks it, then hands it over.

I key in "Brighid Doran Musgrave" and my mobile phone number, my email address, and my home address. In our area, where you live and your address can yield different results. Our house has three addresses and is in two different municipalities and has two separate postal codes. Blame the various address-assigning entities. They just don't agree with each other.

I also key in my birth date of July 14th, just so that his phone will

## 26 | BLUE LIGHTS

annoy him each July, forever.

"First, I should tell you that dispatch got a call from a lady in Trowbridge earlier this week."

"Yeah?"

"She wanted us to investigate vandalism next to the school in the field there."

"What happened?"

"What she said made no sense, so I had to go look. She claimed that people dug up the school grounds and were destroying things. When I got there, I could see nothing except for the town's war memorial."

"What did it look like?"

"It had three layers of stone, granite, the green flat stones we have here, and what looks like marble."

"I supposed that names were etched in neat columns below the names of the various wars?"

"Yes. I have a picture. Need to see it?"

"Sure. I have no idea what you are talking about. Hasn't that been there for years?"

I look at his phone, trying to obscure the fact that my cheeks flushed red slightly with the lie.

I ask, "Is this a mystery? The town has a war memorial on town property."

He says, "According to this lady, the town has two memorials now." He lifts the intonation of his statement forming something like a question, he dare not fully express.

"Interesting. That's awkward."

"I did see some evidence of recent dirt work and dribbles of fresh concrete."

"Better call the detectives in. Sounds like that's above the pay grade for a senior trooper."

"That's what I said."

"Good."

"I doubt that this has anything to do with a recent settlement with, oh, say, the sheriff's department or the local newspaper?"

"I doubt it. I might add that when I compared the town's two memorials one seemed to have Sarah's name on it and the other did not."

"Hmm, odd?" I wonder if I should evoke the fifth. Screw it! We both know I am lying.

"Good enough. I'll put a pin in this investigation."

"Ok, so, next?"

"The fire." He stops.

We both pause to let the needed breath, reaction, and grief return to our hearts. Conversational whiplash.

"Fuck."

"Yeah."

We lost a young man who was the same age of many of the firefighters. His family is well known to everyone in the region. All there felt the same sadness, the same grief, the same dread. Richie and I have both tried to help him over the years. I witnessed Richie talk the kid down from a drunk driving arrest to an open container and underaged drinking charge. Alex Flynn and I spent hours waiting for resolution to a complicated crisis at his parents' house. We sat in the dark watching the blue lights of cop cars buzz about our forest trying to find us.

We both study the mountain to our east. We each avoid eye contact.

I observe that the trooper's uniform shirt has the same color as late autumn grasses that stand tall in fields where livestock once grazed. My focus returns to the highway, the two parked vehicles, the flashing lights, and the difficult conversation at hand.

—THE END—

www.ingramcontent.com/pod-product-compliance
Lightning Source LLC
Jackson TN
JSHW022307011225
95148JS00003B/281